Father's Day

FATHER'S DAY

A NOVEL

by

Alan Trustman

A BIRCH LANE PRESS BOOK
Published by Carol Publishing Group

A Birch Lane Press Book
Published by Carol Publishing Group
Birch Lane Press is a registered trademark of Carol Communications, Inc.

Editorial Offices: 600 Madison Avenue, New York, N.Y. 10022
Sales & Distribution Offices: 120 Enterprise Avenue, Secaucus, N.J. 07094

In Canada: Canadian Manda Group, P.O. Box 920, Station U, Toronto, Ontario M8Z 5P9

Queries regarding rights and permissions should be addressed to Carol Publishing
Group, 600 Madison Avenue, New York, N.Y. 10022

Carol Publishing Group books are available at special discounts for bulk purchases, for
sales promotions, fund raising, or educational purposes. Special editions can be created to
specifications. For details, contact: Special Sales Department, Carol Publishing Group,
120 Enterprise Avenue, Secaucus, N.J. 07094

Manufactured in the United States of America
10 9 8 7 6 5 4 3 2 1

Library of Congress Cataloging-in-Publication Data

Trustman, Alan.
     Father's Day : a novel / by Alan Trustman.
          p.   cm.
     "A Birch Lane Press book."
     ISBN 1-55972-126-X
     I. Title.
     813'.54—dc20   92-15116
                                              CIP

To Michelle

Father's Day

BOOK I

Chapter 1

IT STARTED WITH DIEGO.

He left Bolivia for good in the summer. Che was a childhood memory. The price of tin was still falling. The grass was greener in the Jamaican hills and the Peruvians grew better cocaine. The collapse of the Marxist mythology had undercut what might have been and the tumbling of the Wall had shredded the Curtain, but there were still opportunities for a willing boy with ambition. He went to Managua, Havana, East Berlin and then Paris for the first of the incidents. He wanted to prove himself before he presented himself.

He did.

With two robbed banks, one torched small department store, one bombed restaurant, one dead woman, one crippled child and two dead policemen. He returned with satisfaction to East Berlin with 1,600,000 French francs in cash and a small reputation in his chosen field. No group wished credit for any of his crimes.

1

He had a near-fatal accident and was carted by ambulance to the hospital. It attracted attention. There was talk. The new government considered arresting him but decided to ask him to move along as soon as he left the hospital. For Diego had come to the attention of a person who appreciated what Diego might have been in the old days and what he might possibly still be if the right hands guided and nurtured him. The game had changed and had no name, and the Nazis who had become Stasis were now faceless old men, but the power remained where it had been. All of it. With them.

They sent him to the north Lebanon terrorist training camps operated by East German instructors whose government no longer acknowledged or paid them. The Syrian army supervised the camps. Financial support came from others: Arabs; East Europeans; Germans. No one could control the personnel who would fade without warning into the desert night in response to various calls to arms, but those who would pay might use them.

Diego thrived there from the first moment.

Chapter 2

I WAS IN Gstaad when he started. I was skiing there with Hugo. My son and I both loved the place. The town was tiny, the main street quaint. The Rösti were crisp and the slopes hardpacked. We would have had a better time in Aspen, of course, but Hugo's mother wouldn't let him travel that far and Europe was where I was trading.

Hugo was my only child. His mother was French and brilliant. She and I had been married exactly 111 days, long enough for the boy's conception.

We were both twenty-one when I met her in Paris on vacation. She had rich black hair, long non-French legs and a perfect complexion, and she was sitting at the Dôme with three female friends, drinking something bubbly and crimson. They were looking at my non-hip Brooks Brothers suit. I decided she must be English and opened with the clumsy line, "Could you please tell me what you are drinking?"

They conferred, giggling, and she said, "What you mean is you'd like to take me to bed?"

"Frankly, no," I said, "I'd rather not wait that long. What about the men's room?"

A glint in her eye and she rose. There was scattered applause from the tables adjacent. Nervously, I followed her into the W.C. An Arab exited as we went in.

Inside, she turned and smiled at me. "No," she said.

"Good," I said. "Sex I can always get. I'm in France for the romance." Something in her eyes softened. She took my face in her hands and kissed both cheeks, then my lips. Lightly. I was entranced. I entrance easily. Postadolescent seeker of romance finds poetry in the men's room of a French restaurant. "I think we should wait here five minutes," I said.

She said, "Ten. We don't want to ruin my reputation."

When we emerged, all the cafe patrons stood and applauded. We left to the sound of cheers, she with a slight abashed wave to her friends. It was not until the following morning that I asked her what her name was or about her reputation.

"Brilliant," she said, and it was true, she was, and that was a third of our problem. She had been admitted to the École Nationale d'Administration, graduate school for the bureaucratic and executive crème de la crème, and regardless of what they like to say, the E.N.A. does not take that many women; no Frenchman turns down the E.N.A. and certainly not a woman, not one with ambition. Her ambition was another third of our problem. It was a side of her I had not noticed when I was the focus of that ambition.

My romantic naïveté was the other third of our problem.

I had seen it by the time we got married, but I was desperately in love and so was she, I think, and love conquers everything when you are young, or at least so numerous idiots have written.

Her local mayor married us at the end of the month in the presence of one of my old school friends and her brother and sister and parents. We tried France. The Harvard Business School had admitted me for that fall; I wrote them and requested delayed admission after a period of work experience. It would be good for me, I told them. I think I believed what I was saying. I got a job in Paris with an American bank. They assigned me to correspondence with the stateside branch. I knew in a week that I had put myself on an endless road to nowhere paved with nothing. I quit. We cross the ocean.

We visited Old Lyme to see about job opportunities for her in the States and to meet my mother and father. They loved her and put a cheerful face on the problem of her religion. They desperately wanted grandchildren. Véronique was good to them. She almost liked them. They helped place her as assistant buyer of French luxury goods for a retail chain based locally but the store promptly sent her traveling and she found the work boring. She brushed her cheek with the back of her hand and blew air up past the tip of her nose, Parisian sign language for "boring." She rolled her eyes: very boring. Soon the sex and the Problem were all we had. Could romance overcome adverse career logistics? Perhaps for some, but not for us. We believed in confrontation.

Unfortunately, we found no solution. We decided to part and remain good friends. We were discussing an annulment when we discovered that she was pregnant. The pregnancy carried the marriage for another three weeks. Then she told me over orange juice that she was going to have the child even if we decided on divorce. She paused.

I said, "You mean you want one."

She hesitated. Then she nodded.

I swallowed. "Okay."

Then we cried and said good-bye in the traditional way. I have never had orange juice again. Oh, well, maybe I had learned something.

Had she?

She did brilliantly at the École Nationale d'Administration, became an inspector general of finance, then a vice president of a major industrial concern that escaped nationalization—thanks in part to her. Notwithstanding the flourishing career, she was also an excellent parent, and equivalently brilliant was her second marriage—to the Papal-titled head of a family industrial conglomerate (Rome handed out altogether too many titles, some jealous people said; hereditary aristocratic titles were more significant).

She and I spoke on the telephone twice a year, usually about Hugo's travel plans, and much of the time she seemed to remember who I was. We had only one major further argument, that over the choice of the boy's name. Victor Hugo was her favorite author, but Hugo didn't fit with Collins.

"Why not?" she asked.

"Don't be stupid," I said.

"Oh? Stupid is not a word frequently applied to me."

"Please," I pleaded. "Victor? Please? Vic is at least a possibility. No?" I found myself adopting her French inflection.

It did not work. She told me I couldn't govern from the grave, and what made me think he would bear my name for long? Be grateful for the visitation.

I was. I had my son, twice a year, every year, a week in the wintertime, either at Christmas or in the spring, and for two weeks of summer vacation. I sent him postcards from all over the world and presents on his birthday and special occasions. I funded trusts with my private Swiss bank to provide for his education and to provide him with gifts of capital at ages twenty-five, thirty and thirty-five, all unknown to him, or to his mother or her husband, and he sent me long letters every two weeks written in French on blue transparent stationery in his spidery child's handwriting.

When he was four, I had started him skiing, holding him on the slopes between my legs, the two of us having a wonderful time falling. That had been good for one season, until we discovered that his stepfather had qualified for the French national team and had a chalet on the outskirts of Val d'Isère. The kid had adored the discovery. I, of course, hadn't. The following December, I had pushed for the Caribbean and had been told politely that he didn't much like to swim and preferred, please, a ski vacation? We had skied together the following March and every December or March thereafter.

Hugo passed me on the slope for the first time at the ripe old age of seven. The following summer, his mother and the Marquis had their own children, twin girls, and Hugo cut our summer vacation short to rush home and see them.

We resumed the next Christmas at Aspen, and in subsequent years tried Snowbird, Sun Valley, Kitzbuhl, St. Moritz and now Gstaad. Of all those resorts, Hugo preferred Gstaad the best. He insisted we should return there every year. "Because it is so easy for you, Papa."

He was thirteen. I leased an apartment.

I bought him a new set of K-2's, which he said he wanted because they were American, but I insisted on Salomon bindings. I knew there were good American bindings, but they were too new and I didn't trust them. All I needed was to send him home with a broken leg and his mother and I would have big problems.

We ran Eggli on our last afternoon, whoosh-whoosh-whoosh, top to bottom, me first, Hugo following at a caretaking distance. We had fondue on the mountain, and then, on our first easy run of the afternoon, we were making big wide slow turns on the lower slopes and—wham!—a young German in red nylon ran over my skis and I lost it and cartwheeled into the trees.

"Papa!" Hugo was shouting.

I shook myself, full of heavy snow, but nothing seemed to be hurting. I waved an okay, and he blasted off down the mountain.

I was back on the *piste*, donning my skis again, when I looked down and saw German red nylon far below. He had paused by two girls and they were talking. Off to their right, there was a little one barreling toward them at top speed in the egg position. Hugo? Oh, my God! It was. No, kid, not such a big one—

Hugo crashed into the German boy with his hip and sent him flying in a monster all-four-bindings spill! Hugo paused, shouting. The girls who had been standing with the German were shouting.

I kicked the snow from my boot, stomped into my binding, snatched my poles from the snow and headed downhill. I could hear Hugo's high-pitched voice screaming imprecations. I caught *salaud*, *imbécile* and *ordure*, and heard the proud *mon papa!* at least twice as the German boy lumbered up the hill toward him.

Hugo had managed to shed his skis and hit the German boy with a headlong dive. The two of them rolled down the hill again, punching wildly in the grand European tradition, mostly pushing and roundhouse cuffing, until the heavier German boy sat on top of mine. The girls continued shouting.

"Hugo!" I stood on the slope above them.

They paused. The German boy looked up at me, confused, his nose bleeding.

I chose my shouted words with care. "Hugo, you leave that boy alone! You come up here! You apologize to him!"

Hugo insisted on fondue again that evening, our last, with a bottle of the tart white Swiss wine for me. He smiled while I remonstrated with him.

"In the first place," I said, "it was dumb, and not deliberate. That German did not know what he was doing."

"*Oui, Papa.*"

"Don't you 'Oui, Papa' me. In the second place, it was my fight, not yours. In the third place, he was a lot older than you and you must learn to show respect for your elders. And finally, he was bigger than you. Don't pick fights unless you can win them." I paused.

He was grinning. I could hear the unsaid "*Oui, Papa.*"

"French boys don't know how to fight. If you want to fight, I will teach you how to fight. Look, you punch from the shoulder. You jab, straight. Look." I showed him.

His head bobbed sideways and he laughed at me.

"The French don't even like to fight," I said.

"But am I not half-*Americain*?"

"You were going to get your faced pushed in. That boy was sitting on top of you, and if I hadn't come along just then—"

"But I knew you would," he said, "that is why I hit him. If you hadn't come along when I figured that you would, my timing would have been mistaken." His eyes were blue and innocent and mocking.

I drove him to Geneva and put him on the plane the next morning, Sunday. As we went up the stairs to Departure, he gave me my birthday presents, three matching sets of Orlon net gaiters and ski caps, and told me how sorry he was that he had to return to school and would therefore be unable to be there tomorrow to celebrate the happy occasion.

Chapter 3

IT WAS MY thirty-fifth birthday. A good time for contemplation.

When we were young, they taught us the traditional things: work hard, do well at school and learn to be good with people so you can get a good job and off daddy's dole. Work even harder, do well at the job and learn to be better with people so they like you and promote you. Be patient, take it slowly, in little bits. Earn it and enjoy it. The nice apartment, the bachelor days. Then the house rental, the car, the wife, the kid. The first house purchase. The feeling of responsibility. The life insurance, the second kid. The Boy Scouts, the Little League, the first small community service, the taste of street-level politics. The summer house, the second car, the third kid. The country club, the pension plan. And then at last the summit: the charity that makes you feel really big, the semisuicidal hobby, the red sportscar, the mistress.

But our world wasn't like that. We were the victims of Reaganomics. We were deprived of the fun of struggling. Washington borrowed a trillion dollars from the Japanese and poured it into the economy. Everyone with smarts made money, everyone who worked made money and the stupid and lazy went to Wall Street and made more money than anyone else. It was the era of mergers-and-acquisitions, leveraged buyouts and paper peddling. They called it investment banking.

Conspicuous consumption is the opiate of the deprived adolescent. A few of us were talented but most were plain arrogant: We were overcompensated, greedy, immature and lacking in values. We were still in our twenties and more wealthy than the dreams of our parents. We gave textured new meanings to the words "ass-hole" and "rich."

And so, at thirty-five I was no longer either young or upwardly mobile. There was no more up for me to go. I was rich. I had all the money I would ever need. I had never done anything crooked. I had never even been tempted. I was even spared the corporate bullshit. They had taught me the trade of a loner and they had left me alone to do my thing. I loved what I was doing every day of my life.

I traded currency and precious metals.

It was the greatest game in history and I could play it with the best of them.

It had that exquisite eternal tension I loved, with the markets now open around the clock. Imagine waking up at three A.M. with five times your net worth on the line, and the markets panicky against you, foreign markets run by sharks, with no government regulation. Should you cut your losses and slink away, or hang in there with your balls on the table until the Zurich opening? It was, of course, gambling, and I could have lost my ass without warning any day, but everything in life is a gamble. Right?

Maybe less of a gamble for someone. Recently I had felt some-thing strange going on. There seemed to be someone with access to enormous funds, a big new player in this biggest of games, with knowledge of what the central banks would do, who had an ex-traordinary sense of timing. The wire services would report weak U.S. balance-of-payment numbers, the dollar would promptly weaken, as it should, but after a drop of a minimal 20 pips, someone would buy billions of dollars with Deutschemarks just as the New York markets closed, and the dollar would end up, not down, for the day. The next morning, the Bundesbank would make a surprise cut in German interest rates and the dollar would soar in value. Could the unknown buyer have known in advance? It happened twice and it worried me. That sort of thing could destroy the game.

The little trader is helpless. I was somewhat better off. I had sources. I asked my bank. What did they think? Had they picked up any rumors of the existence of such a person? They considered the question fanciful but, of course, one never knew. Perhaps they would make some inquiries, if I wished. They were perfectly positioned to do so, located as they were in the critical Geneva and Zurich corner of the small world of international banking.

I was thinking of those conversations the morning of my birthday. I had coffee and placed my bets for the day. Limit-orders to be filled if the market moved.

I was shaving and watching the morning news on the tiny bathroom black-and-white TV. The news was, of course, in German. It was about Paris. Something had happened. There were smashed storefronts, wrecked cars in the street, people screaming and bleeding, ambulances, bodies on stretchers and a close-up of a kid. The kid looked like Hugo. I cut myself. I put a toilet paper swatch on the cut.

What had happened?

I found myself staring stupidly at the flickering screen. A soap commercial. Business news.

Was Hugo dead? Or badly hurt? I switched to the French channel. Soft news. A book. Disease in Africa. The Ba'ath Socialists and the Shi'ites. The Croats and the Serbs. I felt dizzy, helpless, panic.

I reached for the telephone on the bathroom wall, Swiss shaving cream, blood, toilet paper patch and all, and called my bank in Geneva. There is one thing about trading. You need focus and discipline. I liquidated every position I held.

I finished shaving. I washed my face. I put another toilet paper swatch on the cut with fingers that trembled. I looked at myself in the mirror. I could do anything I wanted and I wanted—what?

I wanted my kid! I needed to be with him. To hold him, hug him, reassure him. To be in turn reassured by him. Something they had said—hospital?—gave me hope that he was not dead. "No!" I slammed my hand on the counter, stunned at the feeling of torment.

Here it came: Some sort of explosion. A woman was dead—and a couple of police—and Hugo. He was badly hurt.

I found myself struggling on the plane. Why had I not spent more time with my kid?

The Swissair hostess looked at me. "Sir?"

"I can't talk about it." I heard the tears in my voice.

"Are you all right, sir? Can I get you something?" she said.

"It's my son. An explosion."

"I'm sorry, sir," she said.

"Why would anyone want to hurt him?"

Chapter 4

Bonnie and Clyde was Diego's favorite movie. It had made robbing banks seem easy. Diego expected nothing to be easy and prepared his solos carefully. The factories in the arrondissement by and large paid their employees on Thursdays. They would cash their checks at lunchtime. The cash to meet the payroll demand would arrive from the main branch early.

The bank, despite its depressing function as bank, was cheerful and rather pretty. It had a gray concrete and glass façade and occupied three adjacent store properties in the middle of the block, ten meters from the Metro kiosk from which Diego emerged at 11:30 A.M. He wore faded blue-and-white-striped coveralls and a dirty Tyrian-purple, peak-and-bill cloth baker's cap. In each hand he carried a huge coarse canvas sack tied with a drawstring. He entered the bank and patiently waited in line. He reached the teller window at 11:33 A.M.

Diego smiled and hefted the canvas bags through the window to the teller, Jeanne-Marie, a large lady with a faint mustache and goggle eyes behind spectacles. As he did so, he withdrew from one of the bags a small, locked aluminum briefcase and from the other, a stockless Uzi. There were screams.

"Silence!" Diego shouted, and spoke to the guards: "Drop your weapons and back away from me. *Vite, vite.* Quickly."

Each of them shrugged and did. They were both in their sixties.

Diego fastened the aluminum briefcase with a padlock and chain to the post beside the teller cage and said to Jeanne-Marie calmly, "It will explode if you touch it or I press this." He flashed a small transmitter in the palm of his left hand. His right hand still held the Uzi.

"I will press it if you do not fill both bags with cash, all of the cash you have on the floor, or if anyone is stupid or I hear an alarm or the siren from a gendarme car, or if you fail to fill both bags in a minute and a half, or I am not satisfied with what I get, or if anyone follows me out the door in the first minute after I leave. When I leave, you count slowly to thirty, and then, I suggest you all leave. All of you. Quickly! You and you! Help her! Quickly!"

The other two tellers, Marc and Phillipe, were young men in their twenties, Diego's age. Neither was adventurous. They jumped to assist and they did, effectively, except that Marc dropped the bag while Phillipe was holding it.

"Idiot!" screamed Diego. "If you drop it again, I will drop your life on the floor with it." Diego grinned his nervous grin at the TV monitor and checked his watch. "Time!" he said to Jeanne-Marie.

"But, Monsieur, there is more—"

"Give me the more."

She shoveled currency into the bags and handed one through the window. Diego took it, pulled the string. Jeanne-Marie boosted the other bag through the window. Diego took it, pulled the string. He grinned at the two elderly guards and said, "You two, count with me. Start counting. One, two, three. Keep counting!" They did. "Nobody leaves until thirty, right?" Diego went on, "But everyone leaves at thirty!"

He was gone.

Obediently they counted, the cadence continuing slow, and then picking up in volume and speed.

Outside, Diego entered the kiosk and moved down the stairs, slowly counting to himself. At thirty, he was paying at the booth. He could hear the faint screams and shouts from above. He sauntered through the turnstile, holding the bags, and silently counting up to ten, when he pressed the transmitter in the palm of his hand.

The explosion was muffled and seemed far away but he knew the damage the Czech explosive would do, the charge sized and shaped in accordance with the lessons he had purchased for 1,000

Deutschemarks from the Dresden ex-Stasi. There would be no unshattered glass in the block and the bank would no longer be pretty.

Diego exited from the Metro one stop away. His dirty red rented Renault hatchback with the tinted and deliberately smeared window in the rear was the third car down from the corner parked in the adjacent alley. He carefully opened the hatch, dropped in the two stuffed canvas bags, exchanged his baker's cap for a Tyrian-purple beret, took the two empty bags from the trunk, checked to be sure of the aluminum briefcase bomb in one, switched the Uzi into the other, locked the hatchback and strolled away.

The second bank straddled the corner a block away, with temporary entrances on both the rue and the avenue. There was a pharmacy on the corner itself which the bank had not been able to occupy yet, despite its purchase of the building. M. LeClerc, the pharmacist proprietor, had refused offers of payment beyond reason and was determinedly operating for two more years until his lease was up. The pharmacy's stock was inadequate, its floors unclean, its lighting and fixtures in disrepair. He wore the same T-shirt and baggy butcher overalls every day, kept a caricature Gauloise dripping from his lower lip and broke the arrondissement record week after week for personal cigarette consumption. The pharmacy was unappealing and he was, too. The bank itself was ugly enough without him.

One bank pretty, one bank ugly. Diego enjoyed the sound of the words. He realized that he was happy. Today he would dominate the news. It was the first time in his entire life he had ever felt important. In the distance, half a mile away, he could hear the police sirens.

The Metro kiosk was on the corner diagonally across the street. That was a weakness in the plan. He would dodge through traffic if he had to, but there was always a possibility of someone running out of the bank and shouting something to a driver of one of the cars and the driver then trying to run Diego down. Was that paranoid? It was his business to worry about things.

Diego smiled to himself and hefted the bags through the bank door. The time was 11:50 A.M. This bank was a bit more crowded. There appeared to be more money behind the counter. Higher denomination bills. He reached the teller at 11:58 A.M. It was nearly *High Noon*. His other favorite movie.

Diego smiled and hefted the canvas bags through the window to the teller, a tiny Moroccan lady in a print dress, her name Mme. Barzin. As he did so, he withdrew from the bags the aluminum briefcase and the stockless Uzi. There were no screams this time. Dead silence.

The guards were young and wore colorful uniforms. Diego spoke quietly, "Drop your weapons and back away from me. Now, please. Quickly."

They did.

Diego fastened the aluminum briefcase with a padlock and chain to the post beside the teller cage and said to Mme. Barzin calmly, "It will explode if you touch it or I press this." He flashed the transmitter as before. He gave her the same warning and instructions. He turned to the tellers beside her. "You and you! Help her! Quickly! *Vite!*"

The tellers beside her were laconic Frenchmen, respectively late thirties, early fifties. They had seen it all. "No," said the older one.

Diego's Uzi chattered twice and the older man crumpled, wailing, his thigh punctured twice. The women tellers beyond him were squealing. "You three! Come help her!" Diego commanded.

All three of them did.

Diego grinned his nervous grin at this TV monitor and checked his watch. "Time!" he said to Mme. Barzin.

She shoveled the last of the currency into the bags and handed one through the window. Diego took it, pulled the string. She boosted the other bag through the window. Diego took it, pulled the string. He grinned at the two guards and said, "You two, count with me. Start counting. One, two, three. Keep counting! Everybody!" Everyone did. "Nobody leaves until thirty, right?" Diego went on, "but everyone leaves at thirty!"

And he was gone.

Obediently they counted, the cadence continuing slow and then picking up in volume and speed.

Outside, the traffic was impossible. Nimbly, Diego stepped into the street. Brakes screeched. Horns blew. Fists shook, middle fingers pointed to the sky, imprecations were shouted. At thirty, he was still not quite across the street. Screams and shouts from the bank. They had spotted him. Sure enough, a Mercedes started for him and he whirled, brandishing the Uzi. The driver slammed on his brakes, lifted his hands in the air. Diego fired a burst into the tires. Shouts as he entered the kiosk. He put the Uzi in one of the bags and pressed the transmitter.

This charge was larger and it blasted him down the stairs, falling and bruising his hands and knees. Neither bag had opened. He picked them up and went through the turnstile.

The rented white VW bus was in a parking garage. It was an unsatisfactory choice of vehicle for Paris, which still had a prejudice against German cars, but it was exactly the configuration he wanted.

Diego revisited the Renault a little after one P.M. The first two bags were untouched, waiting. He consolidated the loot in the back of the VW bus into six huge brown suitcases, into which he packed the empty canvas bags, Uzi, beret, baker's cap and coveralls. He emerged from the bus dressed in a striped tie and a business suit, black wing-tip shoes and a raincoat of black cotton poplin.

He drove from there to the Place Vendome and at three P.M. checked into a suite at the Ritz that had gold-plated plumbing fixtures. He left the VW bus with the doorman. He took a taxi to the environs of the Renault and put it in a public parking garage. He returned to the hotel and had dinner alone.

He clipped several copies of the press reports from the papers the next morning.

Maison Laurent called itself a small department store. Consisting of owned men's and women's clothing, dry goods, housewares and jewelry departments and leased children's clothing, electronics, appliances and shoe departments, it took up four floors, each 3,000 square meters. Situated in a good block on the Boulevard Raspail, Maison Laurent carried a limited selection of high-quality merchandise at remarkably low prices that reflected the absence of provenance between the manufacturers and the store. There had been two investigations. "Middlemen, brokers," the owners had said, and shrugged. Diego spotted several items he wished to buy as he browsed and visited the basement. The store was sparsely staffed but unafraid of theft. The ownership was Corsican.

The envelope arrived by express post on the second morning following the bank jobs. It contained a letter, a selection of bank robbery press cuttings, and a swatch of cloth from a purple beret. The letter was short, unsigned and to the point:

"You have been selected to contribute 200,000 francs to the Purple Cadre Revolutionary Fund. Signify your assent by closing the store Saturday. Refuse and weep for your patrons."

M. Laurent's lip curled. He reached for the phone. He had childhood friends living in Paris now who would be equal to the challenge.

The store opened on schedule, eight o'clock Saturday morning, with its normal complement of personnel and some significant additions: three old friends from Ajaccio, six of their children, and three plainclothes policemen. An offhand report to the police the day before had resulted in seizure of the envelope and contents, frantic telephone calls to the store's liability insurer and a quick rump meeting of the national task force on terrorism. The note might, after all, be a hoax, and if they closed the store for the day, they would be establishing an unfortunate precedent. Any crank could close any store with a note any day. Soon stores all over France would be closing.

If they warned the public, they might as well close the store. Besides, the writers of such notes were crackpots, and crackpots frequently acted alone. Perhaps in this case the miscreant was all alone. If he was crazy enough to try something by himself, surely a dozen men could stop him.

Business was light in the early morning but picked up substantially as noon approached. It was crowded by lunchtime. The store patrol began to tire by two in the afternoon. There was nothing in the note that promised action that very day. What if they stayed there till ten P.M. and absolutely nothing happened?

Diego arrived at the Café Le Raspail at 3:05 P.M. There were tables on the sidewalk and the plastic shields were down, although it was not yet officially the springtime. He sat at one of the outside tables in his business suit, coat and shoes, put his *Le Monde* on the table and ordered a citron Perrier.

He looked about, smiling faintly. A small purple ribbon was lodged in his buttonhole. Later, it was the only thing anyone could remember about him. The citron Perrier arrived, with the yellow computer-printed *addition*. Diego thanked the waiter, sipped through a straw. Business was brisk at the department store across the street. With the middle finger of his left hand, he depressed the palm-sized transmitter button.

There were a series of muffled pops in the basement across the street as the four incendiary grenades went off and the tiny plastique charge cut the main water intake pipe, disabling the sprinkler system. Loudspeaker announcements closed the store. Protesting angry patrons fought their way to the streets. Smoke and flames climbed rapidly up through the walls and through the ventilating system.

Diego paid his bill, left a tip in the dish, sipped his drink down to the bottom of the glass and enjoyed the fire engines.

Originally, he had not intended to bomb the restaurant. He had, however, three charges, a detonator and a receiver left over and when the Sunday papers reported the arson, they included a personal interview with M. Laurent himself at the restaurant that he and his wife also owned. His wife ran the restaurant, in the Marée, one of the most successful dining places in the district, according to M. Laurent. As for the catastrophe at Maison Laurent, much of that was covered by insurance.

Diego visited the restaurant that evening. The food was excellent. The tables and chairs were, however, rickety and there was no opportunity to hide anything, certainly not in the tiny men's room. There was a padlock on the door beside it leading to the basement.

Outside, there were relatively few cars parked in the street. It was, of course, still the weekend.

Diego retrieved the Renault on Monday morning.

Chapter 5

ON THE FIRST DAY of school there had been no classes. The students had registered and gone to meetings. Hugo's mother had sent a car for him, and together they had lunched in the Marée, with the twins, who were six.

It had been warm in the restaurant and madame proprietor had left the door ajar. They had taken a front table, near the huge plate-glass windows. Their driver had pulled their car up on the sidewalk outside. They had ordered four Coca-Colas—the girls loved Coca-Colas—and madame proprietor had distributed menus. The girls wore identical outfits. Green. They had immediately decided on omelettes but had difficulty deciding on the filling. Each wished something different, but they were both determined that they would order the same. It was the standard twin obsession. The discussion became heated. First Hugo, and then his mother, noticed one set of knees start to twitch. "Celestine?" Hugo suggested.

Celestine said, "In a minute. Please."

Josephine's knees started to twitch. They had managed to reach agreement on Gruyère and spinach but Celestine wished mushrooms and Josephine *haricots-verts*. Their mother mildly suggested that both were inappropriate with the Gruyère and spinach. The rhythmic knee-jiggling became more rapid.

"*Maman?*" Hugo suggested.

"Young ladies?" she suggested.

Celestine insisted, "I want to agree on the omelette first!"

"I have to go," said Josephine.

"Then you must agree with me," said Celestine, "before you go to the bathroom!"

Their mother exclaimed with impatience and dragged them off to the ladies' room. Hugo laughed. Women!

And then he felt the bomb blast. He seemed to be floating.

The bomb contained three charges of Czech plastic, carefully shaped and placed in the left front door of the Renault Diego had parked at the curb in front of the restaurant. He detonated it from a block away with the same palm transmitter he had used before. The explosion knocked him down, flat and out of breath. For weeks he would have trouble with his hearing. He sat there in a daze on the curb.

The bomb totaled seven cars. The Renault itself was pulverized. The three cars behind it and the two cars in front of it were all damaged beyond repair, including the car sent by Hugo's mother, which was the second car in front of the Renault. Miraculously, no one in any of those cars, including the family driver, was hurt, except for glass and concussion.

Two policemen in a passing car were both killed instantly.

A woman walking on the sidewalk beside the Renault disappeared in the blast, virtually vaporized.

There was a nine-by-seven-meter hole two meters deep in the street and sidewalk.

Every store in the block on both sides of the street had all its glass shattered. The blast also shattered most of the glass upstairs. Four buildings had damage to their foundations.

The blast threw the waiters and restaurant patrons clear across the restaurant in a shambles of glass, stainless steel and porcelain. There were numerous cuts and bruises, sprains, two broken bones and eleven cases of ear damage, sixteen victims of imbedded flying glass—and Hugo. The plate-glass window severed his left leg halfway between the knee and the hip. The stump was pouring blood. Hugo's mother and the girls were screaming.

A block away, Diego staggered to his feet, fingering the purple ribbon in his buttonhole. He removed the ribbon and it fluttered to the ground. He took a taxi to the Ritz, packed and checked out, and drove east in the Volkswagen.

Chapter 6

THE HOSPITAL was in Neuilly, a serpentine two stories of concrete and tinted glass, totally shielded by vines and shrubbery. It nestled into the top of a slope overlooking hectares of empty countryside.

There were two levels of security. The gate was sympathetic, no problem. The desk downstairs, however, was difficult. Hugo's mother had excluded the press and I had not told her I was coming. Sluggishly, I started to function. Hospital regulations permitted visits by parents, did they not? Was I not a parent? No, they told me, indignantly. The Marquis and Marquise were listed as parents. They were even now at the bedside. No one else had visiting permission. I tried again: She was there, would they ask her, please? My name was Michael Collins. Heads shook. Hushed voices remonstrated that it would be inappropriate in view of the tragedy to bother her with problems.

By then, I had seen the room number on the manifest.

"Call the police," I said.

"Monsieur?" Eyebrows lifted.

"He is my son and I am going to see him."

"But we have already explained to Monsieur—Monsieur!!"

She was as lovely as she had ever been. Albeit older and a little wan. The Marquis rose as I entered the room. Hugo was asleep. He was ashen. I could not look at his legs, mercifully under the sheets. The plastic pipes, taped intravenous leads and electronics were horrifying. I stood at the bedside and peered down at him.

"*Bonjour, Michel,*" she said.

"*Il dort,*" said the Marquis.

I nodded and said nothing.

Behind me, the hospital security staff poured into the room and the Marquis halted them with a peremptory wave. They retreated, muttering apologies, and shut the door. The Marquis moved his chair to me. "Sorry. We did not know you were coming."

I nodded, still standing, looking down at my son. What was left of him.

Hugo stirred, opened his eyes and weakly smiled. *"Bonjour, Papa."*

"Hello, kid," I said. "Rest."

He nodded and closed his eyes again. A moment later, they opened again. "Papa?"

"Yes, kid."

"I am still glad I hit him." His eyes rolled back and he was out again.

"Hugo?" My voice must have sounded panicky.

She said, "He goes to sleep like that."

The Marquis said, "It must be the sedation."

I stood there, watching and waiting.

Presently, the Marquis left the room.

"Tactful," I said, looking at the sleeping boy. "Very good of him. How are you, Véronique?"

She gestured and said, "I am sorry, Michel. I do not feel like talking."

Presently, the Marquis returned with another chair. He sat in it. I remained standing.

The Marquis attempted conversation. "He is very proud of some fight he had. Since he returned, he has spoken of nothing else. Not even of the skiing."

"Skiing with me is tame for him," I said.

She said, faintly teasing for the only time, "I have told you before, Jean-Claude, Michel prefers fighting."

"Who was it? Who did it? Some crazy?" I asked.

The Marquis cleared his throat and said nothing.

Véronique finally said, "All right, Jean-Claude. Tell him."

The Marquis said, "I have friends in the SDECE. Do you know who that is?"

I said, "It's your CIA equivalent."

"They say it was some young South American acting on his own."

I made a face, disbelieving. "Independent? Why? What was he doing?"

"I don't know," he said. "No one seems to know. The purple

cadre of something, he says, but there is no such organization. Just him and these things he's been doing. I don't believe it personally but that's what they say. I have no way to check. I don't think they would lie to me, but how can you know nowadays? It does make it hard to track him. Or contemplate a protest of any kind."

"Let alone retaliation," I said.

"Oh, Michel," she said.

"Does he have a name?" I said.

The Marquis said, "Diego is what they call him."

An hour later, Hugo came awake again. He smiled. "Still here, Papa?"

"Yes, kid. I am."

"I don't swim very well. Will you teach me to swim?"

I had trouble speaking. "Of course I will."

"In America?"

"Sure, kid. Of course."

"Or maybe the Caribbean." His eyes rolled back and he was asleep again.

For the next few minutes we watched him. Presently, I cleared my throat and said, "Is he still in France? This person?"

There was a pause. The Marquis said, "They think he went to East Berlin again."

"Again? Then they have some sort of record of him?"

"What are you contemplating? You are a ridiculous man, Michel," said my former wife.

The Marquis lifted his hand to silence her. "What do you wish of us?" he said.

"I don't know," I said.

"But you will want something?" she said.

I said to him, "Will you phone me at the Ritz tonight?"

The Marquis said, "That's where Diego was staying."

I looked at him.

"That's what they told me," he said.

"The SDECE."

"Yes. They have twice just missed him."

"Tell you what," I said slowly. "I'll be there in my room tonight.

Would you please come to see me when you can, and bring your friends along with you, and ask them please to talk to me?"

"I will do what I can," he said.

"Oh, Michel," my former wife said wearily.

"What?" I said.

She shook her head and said nothing.

I had dinner by myself in the room. A cheese sandwich. I ate half of it. An espresso. It was too strong for me. It was a long, long evening. I tried watching television. The moment I flicked the switch, I remembered the last time I had watched television. I wondered if they were coming. At ten P.M., I phoned the concierge to ask if anyone had been asking for me. Was there someone, perhaps, in the lobby or bar? No, was I expecting someone? The Marquis, I told them. Oh, yes, they knew him well. They would phone me on the instant.

The suite doorbell rang at 11:52 P.M.

I went to the door. *"Moi. Nous. Veuillez ouvrir?"* So much for hotel security and the concierge's promised announcement.

I opened the door on the Marquis and two faceless Frenchmen.

We neither shook hands nor made introductions. The three of them perched on the edge of their chairs and refused room service and the minibar.

"Diego?" I said.

The little balding one stirred. "That is probably not his real name. That is what they call him."

"Who?" I said.

"Sources. We do have them. We have learned much about him. He is independent. No one protects him."

"Sources here?" I said. "Or in East Berlin?"

Both of them looked at the Marquis.

He said to them, "I told him he returned to East Berlin."

Both faces were frowning.

The Marquis said to me, "They don't wish to compromise their sources of information."

I said, "I don't want to know them. Can't they tell me anything? I'm the boy's father, damn it. So are you."

The little balding one said, "Everything is confidential in an ongoing investigation."

"Can't you please tell me anything?"

The two of them looked at the Marquis again.

The Marquis said, "Please?"

The little balding one said, "The security services in cases like this exchange information. Nowadays, everyone helps everyone. The airline computer records, of course. Interpol. The Verfassungschutz. The Budeskriminalamt. The Zoll, that's their customs. In addition, we have people of our own."

I said, "And?"

He counted on his fingers. "Origin believed Bolivian. Arrived in East Berlin last month. By plane. The airline was Cuban. He had a Cuban passport. They passed it at the airport but there are doubts about the passport. He went looking for certain types of people. And things. Weapons, explosives, papers. He rented a Volkswagen bus and drove it here. He used the name, 'Purple Cadre Revolutionary Fund.' There is no such organization. He came here with six large soft-sided bags and when he left he took them with him."

"How did he pay his hotel bill?" I asked.

"Cash."

"Stolen from the banks," I said. "Pity."

"Not helpful."

"Tell him about the bus," the Marquis said.

"Abandoned at the airport at Lyon," said the little balding one.

"From where he flew to Berlin?"

"Zurich. Where he changed planes for Berlin."

"And crossed into East Berlin again?" I asked.

Silence. The Marquis cleared his throat.

I looked at him.

"No wall, no checkpoint, one Berlin," he said.

I nodded and looked at them. "Is there anything more you can tell me?"

"No," said the little balding one. "I say that without implying that we know any more, except for who our sources are."

"My boy is French," I said. "What will your government do?"

The little balding one shrugged. His jowly friend with eyebrows spoke for the first time. "What is it that you would have us do?"

"Find him," I said. "Bring him here and put him on trial."

The room was full of silence. They looked at the Marquis again.

"Thank you, Messieurs," said the Marquis.

"Yes. Thank you very much," I said.

They stood. "What will you do?" asked jowls and eyebrows.

"I don't see what I can do," I said.

He said, "That is what we told the Marquis."

The American Embassy in Paris had become far less stolid. I had attended the July Fourth bash twice and liked it. Personnel were no longer the dregs of the State Department Social Register misfit set, the butt of merciless Parisian gossip. They tended to be more friendly and helpful. They were more comfortable on the Paris scene since Lang had redefined culture to include American comics, movies and music. Unfortunately, as they tried to do more, they were able to do less.

Ms. Holyoke, to whom my phone call was referred, saw me in thirty minutes. She took copious notes on what I had to say in a minuscule handwriting with her ballpoint pen and clucked with genuine sympathy until I came to Hugo's mother and the Marquis. She tapped the green form with the handle of the pen. "The boy is French," she said.

"I believe he has dual citizenship until he has elected."

"But his mother and you were divorced before the child was born."

"Nevertheless, I am the father," I said. "That has never been contested. And he has never, to my knowledge, been adopted."

"Perhaps you should see a lawyer," she said.

"What you mean is you won't touch this."

"Not at all. I'll report it."

"But?"

"What is it that you wish from us?"

"Help."

"With what?"

"You might follow the case and be sure they do and, if necessary, file a protest."

Her ballpoint pen tapped, tapped, and returned to the page. Her voice was so soft I could hardly hear, "I have noted what you have requested."

The U.N. commission on terrorism did exist but precisely what they did was difficult to learn by telephone from Paris. They collected some data, wrote reports, spent a bundle, given their limited staff, and might be helpful if a government asked but would not deal with the general public.

At Le Dôme, a lonely haunt from childhood, a place to which I returned feeling lonely again, I found myself thinking of Ross Perot and how much I admired the man and what he had done for his guys in Iran. A private foreign operation. But he had a fixed target to attack. He could make a military plan.

Mine was a moving target.

Should I quit? Was I being ridiculous? Was she right? What could I do?

My son was thirteen years old and had been crippled for life by some Bolivian crazy no one really knew, and no one was going to do anything. My innocent, tender little boy with the perfect foot, and the toes I had played little piggy with, now had a bloody stump instead. I felt the rage in my belly grow. My teeth had clenched, my hands as well. This, too, shall pass, they said, but it would not for me. Where I come from, you take care of your own, and that includes avenging your own. Thou shalt not kill? Turn the other cheek?

Not me. I wanted to kill the son of a bitch.

I would go after him myself.

In the morning.

Chapter 7

THE NEW Lufthansa Flight 1763 left Paris Charles de Gaulle on the dot at 9:35 A.M. First Class was spotless and smelled of coffee. The hostesses smelled of hairspray and the stewards smelled of hostess. I smelled of anger. We went directly to 33,000 feet and held there until we put down at Berlin Tiegel at 11:18 A.M., three minutes behind schedule.

I rented a black Mercedes 190 from Hertz and drove to Checkpoint Charlie. It was gone. I drove half a mile straight up the Friedrichstrasse and left my car with the doorman at the Grand. It was. So was my three-room suite. Luxury had penetrated the former Iron Curtain.

My bank in Geneva had outdone themselves and I had a late lunch in the Golden Goose restaurant downstairs with the head of private banking of the new East Berlin Dresdener Bank branch office.

Herr Gruenbaum, who was in his late forties, had a magnificent head of blond hair and contrasting black eyebrows. He showed me the fax confirming, he translated, that I was a respected and affluent private investor who had been a client of my own bank for many years and was interested in opening an office for one of my companies based in Austin, Texas.

"Yes," I said. "An office for regional sales. We are looking for several people."

We ordered lunch. Herr Gruenbaum ordered five courses: hors d'oeuvres, noodles, brisket, fish, a salad. I ordered a salad.

The bushy black eyebrows lifted.

"American, you know. Diet," I said.

The eyebrows were partially lowered.

I waved and the sommelier approached with his list. I ordered a red burgundy and a Rhine wine for the fish. I had no intention of even sipping either one but Herr Gruenbaum had no way of knowing.

The magnificent head nodded approval.

I handed Herr Gruenbaum three ACA business cards, my personal card, Ferdie Haffenreffer's card, and the card of Peter Flowers. I was a director, Ferdie a vice president and the Frankfurt-based head of European sales, and Peter was the president of Attention Corporation of Austin, Texas. "Feel free to contact either," I said. I did not have to alert them; they were used to calls, from all over the world, wondering if I was for real. Which I was. Whatever I said, they would endorse at once. It was my biggest perk from the business and it was truly helpful.

"Electronics?" said Herr Gruenbaum, lifting his eyebrows again. The cards of ACA bore that intriguing word.

"Small parts," I said.

"High tech?" he asked.

"Yes, but not restricted." I said. "The sort of thing available elsewhere. If we don't sell them, someone will. We buy in quantity all over the world. We always seem to have surplus stock and a need for its disposition."

"And you wish to sell in Eastern Europe?" he said.

"Yes, and we are already selling there," I said, seizing the opportunity to be precise and German, "through nonexclusive sales representatives based in Switzerland and in Sweden."

The captain and two waiters arrived with the hors d'oeuvres cart, and serving Herr Gruenbaum took a full five minutes. He was small and wiry, despite the large head, a Goebbels not a Goering, and I lost my appetite trying to figure out the lack of logical relationship between his size and his consumption. The waiter arrived with my salad.

"Well," said Herr Gruenbaum, "I must say this is certainly perfect timing. The market is huge and starving for everything. Labor is plentiful and wages low. And someday our workers will be willing to work. That is the tradition." He chuckled and continued eating. "And you Americans have always been willing to invest and take chances."

"We are looking for several supervisory people now, in the first instance."

"I see," he said, eating. "We will be delighted to help if we can."

"We expect to pay people very well. And you if you can find them."

"Ah," he said, thoughtfully, as he chewed, digested, forked up some more, and then spoke again with his mouth full, "Good. Good. What sort of person are you looking for?"

"May I be candid?" I said.

"Please," he said.

I leaned forward and said quietly, "Ex-Stasi."

There was silence—and eating—for a full minute.

"Explain," Herr Gruenbaum said.

I said, "We prize good information. And who were the best gatherers of information in the world? The Secret Police, the East Germans."

"It may be hard to find them. Men do not list the Stasi on their resumés."

"But everyone seems to suspect who they are," I said. "And, although I detest generalization, the better they were, the higher they rose, and the higher they were before it disappeared, the more difficulty they are having nowadays in finding new employment."

"Ah, true." He dabbed his lips with the huge linen napkin. "You expect to pay your people very well. What do you expect to pay?"

"Base pay," I said, "Ten thousand Deutschemarks a month. Against three percent of sales, moneys received."

"Ah!" exclaimed Herr Gruenbaum, greeting the arrival of his noodles with delight and a gleam in his eye. "With what sort of limit?"

"No limit," I said.

"None at all?" he said. "Even if there are millions in sales?"

"No. No limit at all."

Herr Gruenbaum looked at me with the same sort of gleam in his eyes that accompanied his noodle eating.

Late the same afternoon, I had a similar meeting with Herr Doktor Inspektor Schmidt of the Federal Police, arranged by Herr Gruenbaum, the banker.

I then returned to my suite to wait.

It took two days.

During that time I had four meetings, three in the suite, one in the Trout Quintet restaurant downstairs, with four men in business suits, whom I categorized by colors.

Red Man had red hair, red-rimmed eyes and heavy glasses with orange plastic frames. We chatted. He made faces and sweated a lot. Herr Gruenbaum had recommended him. He was not all I wanted but part of it. If he had the qulifications I wished, Herr Gruenbaum felt I could trust him.

I asked him about radical politics in Romania. He gave me generalizations. I pursued them. I asked for specifics. He gave me none. I asked for names. He gestured grandly. I should give him time and he would give me all the names I wanted and more. But as for now? He did not have them. I tried Albania next with the same result. He was not my man. He was faking.

Blue Man showed up in a blue serge suit, despite the unseasonable heat of the day. His face was kind despite his record. He admitted that he had run agents in the West. I liked him and I was tempted. Herr Schmidt was a cousin. Blue Man's knowledge of Arab countries was slight. I asked him to explain to me, if he could, the reason for recent terrorism in the West. He shook his head. "Arabs," he said. "They are crazy. Who can predict them?"

"And will they attack new industrial production in the Near East?" I said. "The same people? The same reasons? What do they want?"

He didn't know, but please let him ask a person or two and in a couple of days, he would have an opinion.

I would wait before making a decision.

Green Man wore a green-and-gray houndstooth sportcoat and flannel pants. He, too, was sent by Herr Schmidt. Herr Schmidt said Green Man was brilliant. That was his principal problem. Green Man did not like me, and he was uncomfortably suspicious. "Collins," he said. "Is that a Jewish name?"

"The most famous Michael Collins was Irish," I said. "Why?"

He said, "Jews are not to be trusted."

"I see. And who else is not to be trusted?"

"People who do not tell me what they want. Now suppose you

tell me what you really want, and I will tell you what it will cost
and how long it will take me to do it."

"What I want is for you to get lost," I said.

"*Bitte?*" he said, confused.

I said, "Forget it. Please. You are not the right person."

Number Four was pay dirt.

He was Gray Man. He was small, with a gray suit and the face
of a fox. A predator. A ferret. His name was Werner and he came
highly recommended. Gruenbaum telephoned twice to make sure
I knew it.

Gruenbaum said he was important.

If you wanted someone to run things, who would do absolutely
everything you told him to do, and would use his head otherwise,
and be absolutely ruthless, all the time, he was it. In the first
minute, I knew it. He was perfect.

But.

Why was he here? What were we doing? I was trying hard to
be circumspect after the fiasco with Green Man. We were meeting
in the suite. We had been chatting for a full hour about the econ-
omies of the countries to which we wished to sell and his considerable knowledge of the ruling cliques and who was who in banking, and his eyes never once left my face. Finally, I skirted closer
to the line. I mentioned Paris and the recent terrorism. He knew
a lot about each, he said.

I asked him to explain to me, if he could, the reason for the
recent actions.

Werner smiled impatiently. "Mr. Collins. Sir. You have used
your own name. You have used your own passport."

"Yes?" I said with a slight chill.

"Then let us talk about the job you really want done and dispense with all this nonsense."

I was not ready to buy it yet. "I am sorry," I said. "I don't know
what you're talking about—"

"I know who you really want," he said.

That was blunt and on target. I said nothing.

"He is here. Let me give you the prices."

I waited him out.

He said, "You see? You wish to know what I have to say. I was right. Shall I make a quotation?"

"Look," I said, "let's not make a game of this. I—"

"One hundred thousand Deutschemarks for the whole thing," Werner said. "You may pay it to me in installments."

I said, "What is this? What are you talking about?"

"For ten thousand Deutschemarks, I give you the name. I assure you I know just where he is. He is living with a woman whose roommate is away. She is an airline hostess. Do not waste my time. The name. For ten thousand Deutschemarks."

"The name."

"Danilo von Mehren Mueller Marquez," he said. "Diego in the press."

I went to my attaché case, opened it, counted out the bills, handed them to him and sat down again, the open briefcase in my lap. I said, "More?"

He stacked the bills neatly with his fingertips, and riffled but did not count the pile. "The address," he said, "is fifteen thousand Deutschemarks, with another twenty-five thousand Deutsche-marks when you confirm that he is there, that he sleeps there tonight, that he is there tomorrow morning."

I handed him another fifteen thousand Deutschemarks.

Again, he riffled but did not count the pile. He reached into his pocket and handed me a piece of paper containing two addresses, an apartment on Universitätstrasse in East Berlin and the address of a restaurant on the Zurich Bahnhofstrasse. "The second ad-dress," Werner said, "is for paying me in the event we do not meet again. Have someone sit at the bar and ask for me. They will ask him for a brown envelope. Deliver it, with the cash in it."

I said carefully, "That makes fifty thousand Deutschemarks."

"Fifty thousand Deutschemarks more to get rid of him. Per-manently."

"My goodness, that is hardly my purpose—" I said.

"Please," he interrupted. "I have had two days to do the research and I know about the boy. In Paris. Your son." He waited expect-antly.

"No," I said.

"You are very foolish."

"Still no."

"If you fail," Werner said, "I will sell your name to him. He is certain to track you anyhow."

"How do I know you will not tell him about me anyhow?"

"You have more money than he does," Werner said. "And I may wish to do business with you again."

I studied the Gray Man.

He smiled. "And no, I will not tell the police. That is not how I operate."

"Why did he do it?" I said.

"He has ambitions," said Gray Man, "which are not yet clear. And he has not been tested. As he would have to be, before we could use him."

Thesis: Anyone can kill anyone in the so-called civilized world if he is willing to take the time to properly plan.

Corollary: If he is reasonably intelligent, he has a good chance of getting away with it.

Alone that night. Dinner in the suite. Save the coffee for the morning.

Think of the bloody stump and watch TV.

Think of the bloody stump and read the papers.

My Hartman one-suiter has a false bottom, carefully crafted at great expense, a steel shell so thin it will bend in your fingers. It holds a .32 caliber Walther PPK, field-stripped into two pieces and the magazine, a quick-draw holster, cleaning gear slickly wrapped in plastic, a spare barrel and two spare magazines. I carry all three magazines loaded. X rays will show it as solid. I have carried it all over the world for eight years now and no one has ever stopped it.

I removed the false bottom and assembled the gun.

Early to bed at nine P.M.

Early to rise at five A.M. The cold dinner coffee for breakfast. Out of the hotel and into the Mercedes with a cheery, "See you later" to the doorman. Head north on Friedrichstrasse toward the river, right on Georgenstrasse, left on Universitatstrasse.

I had no sooner parked than a light came on in the third-floor window I had started to watch. I could hardly believe my good fortune.

A taxi arrived ten minutes later. A pretty girl, a brunette, quite tall, came out of the building, dressed in an Interflug uniform. "Schonfeld," she told the driver. She got in and they drove away.

She had left the light on upstairs. I watched it and wondered. It was dawn and the street lights went out. The light upstairs went out.

Diego emerged in a sweat suit and sneakers. He glanced up and down, saw nothing—I was huddled behind the car doorpost—and turned left and toward the river. He was going jogging! It was the best possible setup for killing someone. The jogger is totally vulnerable, even more so than an unsuspecting rider in a car, or a relaxed diner in a restaurant. Diego was small and lithe, a runner. I knew instantly where he was going. He would turn left. Go ahead. He did. He turned left on the Am Weldend and disappeared from my vision. He would run along the parks and the river. It was the perfect route for running.

I started the car and moved out into the Universitätstrasse, fumbling in the glove compartment for maps. I found one, clumsily folded, perfect for the occasion. I put it in front of me, over the wheel, in plain sight, made the left turn and followed the runner. There he was, up ahead, running easily.

I passed him, ostentatiously studying the map, and squinting at the buildings on my left, a lost driver trying grimly to figure out where I was going. I drove out the Am Weldend, along the Reichstagufer along the river. I sped up on the Kronprinzenufer through the parks and halted at the Moltkestrasse corner. A truck went past. Then another.

Then silence.

Here came the runner.

I put on the Mercedes flasher and stepped out, clumsily spilling the map to the ground. I stooped, picked it up, waved and smiled my helpless lost tourist smile. *"Bitte?"* I shouted and pointed with my innocent and empty right hand back toward the downtown area. I held out the map as he approached. He smiled his nervous smile and gestured. He was a stranger, too.

I shot him in the stomach, crack! Then crack! again. He stumbled to his knees, bewildered. "For my son in Paris," I said, "you fuck-ing scum!" and shot him in the stomach twice more.

Gut shot, blood on the lips, he keeled over. Good. He would go slowly.

I got back into the car and turned left on Moltkestrasse. No one about. I turned left on 17 Juni and headed downtown again.

Once there, I parked the car, broke the gun down, put the barrel in my pocket, found a cafe and had myself breakfast. *Kaffee mit Schlag*. Don't let anyone tell you revenge is not sweet. It is. It was for me. Whipped cream was the champagne of the morning.

After breakfast, I went for a brisk walk, cleaned the prints off the gun barrel and dropped it into the river.

Then I went back to the hotel and packed. I cleaned the Walther carefully, paraffined it for traces and cleaned it again. I reassem-bled the spare barrel into the gun, repacked everything into the false bottom and put the false bottom back into the bag. Click. Set.

I checked out and drove out of East Berlin.

I drove all the way to Frankfurt.

I turned the Mercedes in to Hertz there and took the late flight to Paris.

I was delighted with what I had done. Nothing would ever com-pensate for what had happened to my son but I had done what I could to avenge him today.

Tomorrow, I would hug him.

Chapter 8

"PAPA! I am ecstatic!" Hugo reached for me.

I sat on the edge of the bed and we hugged. Behind me, I heard the voices of the frustrated security I had pushed aside. "The other father. The mother said he is harmless. Forget it. Let us leave them." I was tired. I chuckled at the "harmless"—and lost it.

"Papa? Are you all right, Papa?" My one-legged son was patting my shoulder.

I nodded.

He grinned. "Really, it is not so bad. I am in very good health otherwise. And besides, there are advantages."

I was puzzled, as I was supposed to be.

"I am thirteen. I will drive a car in three more years. When I do, I will be able to park in the places reserved for the handi-capped." He chortled.

I felt the tears surge and hugged him again. I desperately didn't want to show it. "Here," I managed to say finally, and reached for the package. "I brought you—" I could not finish.

Mystified, he unwrapped it. "A laptop!" he shouted and clapped his hands. He kissed me.

We explored it, a Compaq LTE Lite/25, a six-pound 386SX, 25 megahertz, 10 meg RAM, a 120 meg hard drive, a 4.5 hour battery and the built-in battery gauge.

"It is twenty-five thousand francs!" he said, "and twenty-five times what I need! How extravagant! I adore it! And you!" He kissed me again and scrambled away. He was already absorbed in the machine. "Windows!" he said. "You installed it!" I got the most beautiful smile. "Games?" he said, at the computer again. "Which?" He manipulated the mouse. "Look what you have on it! Every game I ever heard of!"

There were nurses standing in the doorway.

"Look!" Hugo shouted at them. "Have you ever seen one this small? With every kind of function!"

We played chess. We played the Microsoft flying games. Maybe someday he could learn to fly an airplane. He had his physical therapy and practiced on his crutches. They still hurt under his arms. He could not wait to get back to bed and the computer again.

We started on the logic and quest games and the derivatives of Dungeons and Dragons. Lunch interrupted. You have never seen such a happy kid. I had to keep looking away. We joked and we chattered and we played the games.

Only once did he frown, when he looked at his watch. "*Maman* is usually here by now. Oh, well, later."

We resumed playing with the computer.

In the middle of the afternoon, it was his exercise time. He insisted on walking by himself to the exercise room. They worked him hard for an hour. I told him to figure out the machines he wanted, and when he left the hospital, I would go make the purchase for him.

Later, he bathed, or rather, they bathed him. Hugo insisted I watch him. "I want you to see it. It is good for me to watch your face when you see it."

I watched. They changed the bandage. I felt sick.

"Poor Papa," said my kid, reassuring me. "It is ugly, isn't it?"

I said, "Yes."

My mutilated child laughed at me. "I expected you to lie about that. Do you find it disgusting?"

"No," I said. "I do not. Nothing about you will ever be disgusting."

"*Bonjour, Michel.*"

It was six P.M. when Hugo's mother arrived, wearing an evening dress, and Hugo exploded with excitement. "Look! Look what Papa brought!"

He insisted on showing her everything. For nearly an hour, he demonstrated the computer, insisting she play, and I receded into the background. At seven she looked at her watch, excused herself and kissed him. She flashed a wan smile at me. "We have plans for the evening."

"Do you have ten minutes?" I said.

"For you?" she said.

"Downstairs?"

She nodded. "I have a car and driver waiting."

It was an expensive private hospital with the best of everything. They had a coffee urn and a Limoges service in the drawing room on the ground floor, as a courtesy to those who paid the bills. The piano was a Bechstein. It was in tune. I tried it.

"Play our song," she said with irony.

I played slow Piaf songs.

She said, "Five minutes."

I stopped. "Twice a year is not enough anymore."

"For whom is it not enough?"

"For me, for him," I said. "For years, I have been an embarrassment which you have tolerated. Decently."

"And now?" she said.

"He needs all he can get of all of us. And that includes me, after years of honoring your terms. Look," I struggled to explain it. "You are married. You have two other children. I have no one but Hugo. Only him."

"He loves you," she said. "He is proud of you. We have never tried to interfere."

"I know that, and thanks," I said. "He gives me unconditional approval all the time. Everyone needs that from someone. And I think I can help him in ways that you can't."

"You may be right. What is it you want?"

I took a breath. "Once a month, twice a month. Here, of course, most of the time."

She nodded slowly. "My husband will try to arrange it for you."

What did that mean?

She said carefully, "When you come to France. Your visa problems."

"I see." I did not see at all. But don't rock the boat when it's going your way.

She said, "You may stay with us. We have a guest suite and you and Hugo will have the time you would otherwise have to spend traveling."

"No, but thank you very much. I am afraid we would have a battle royal."

"Which you could not win," she said. She studied me, then checked her watch. "I must go now. Let us speak of the risk."

"What risk?"

"That he becomes attached to you and you are killed. That would hurt him."

"What in hell are you talking about?"

She shook her head. "You," she said. "You are crazy and you know what I mean. Take care of yourself, Michel, darling."

It was as if she knew. But how could she?

Take care of yourself, Michael, darling.

The hospital expelled its visitors at eight o'clock and I drove back to the city slowly. I was fatigued and exhausted.

I had a driver, and soon I was sleeping.

He woke me at the door to the Ritz. I tipped him in cash and said good night. The concierge gave me the key to my suite and smiled as if he knew something.

I took the tiny front elevator and walked slowly along the blond Iranian carpet in the corridor. I unlocked the two sets of doors to the suite.

The first thing I saw was my Hartman bag with the bottom compartment beside it on the coffee table in the living room. On the sofa beyond it were the little balding one and jowls and eyebrows.

"Do come in," I said.

Jowls and eyebrows pointed to the other couch. Sit.

I did.

The little balding one had his hand in a large box. With the other hand, he was holding it slanted down toward the fireplace. It jerked and the explosion was muffled. He withdrew my Walther and put it on the coffee table. "Nicely cleaned," he said. "No sign of firing recently." He disassembled the box, fumbled with the innards and came up with a slug. He put it in a plastic bag. "For the German Federal Police," he said.

"He could have changed the barrel," said jowls and eyebrows.

"No," said the little balding one. "I am sure he would not have thought of that."

"He did change the barrel," said jowls and eyebrows. "Look at him."

I sat there, motionless.

Jowls and eyebrows shook his head at me. "Amateur. How could you?"

Silence.

"And what will you do now?" said the little balding one. "Wait till he gets out of the hospital and this time shoot his kneecaps out?"

"Do you not believe in killing? Is that it?" said jowls and eye-brows.

I sat there.

"He doesn't know," said the little balding one.

Jowls and eyebrows was shaking his head. "With small caliber like a .32, you must go for the head. Even the heart might not be fatal some of the time."

"Let us be fair," said the little balding one. "He had good luck. You had bad. The liver is bruised. The spleen is clean. You missed the spinal column all four times. He will lose six inches of intestine, that is all. And of course, you told him who you are." He shook his head. "You have an ego problem."

I was hearing another voice, far away now. "If you fail, I will sell your name to him. He is certain to track you anyhow." My bank had paid Werner the twenty-five thousand Deutschemarks that afternoon at the specified Zurich restaurant.

Jowls and eyebrows was saying to me, "You will leave Europe, please, tomorrow."

I was not sure I had heard him correctly. "What?"

Jowls and eyebrows repeated, "Tomorrow. Go home."

"And as for him," said the little balding one, "there has been intervention on his behalf. The German Federal Police will let him go."

Again, I was hearing another voice: "And he has not been tested." Now he had been tested. He had survived. And I had failed.

They both stood. The little balding one said, "There have been interventions here on your behalf. You will be permitted to return to see your son. After the situation cools down a bit."

"How long?" I said.

He shrugged. A Gallic shrug. "A week. Two weeks. A month. Who knows?"

Jowls and eyebrows could not resist it. "You will, of course, have to be careful wherever you are. You have shot one of the most dangerous men in the world. This may have impressed him un-favorably. I cannot imagine that he likes you."

They were right. I was in trouble.

Sooner or later, he would come after me. And probably sooner. Even worse, Hugo was totally vulnerable. It was clear, therefore, what I would do. I would indeed go home the following day. And then I would go to Plan B right away. Plan B was the hard way. Help from others, big complications. I had always had Plan B in reserve, in the event Plan A was unsuccessful, and it had been. Worse still, it had been an option before. Now I had no choice.

Kill or be killed.

Kill him before he killed me and even thought about my son.

Same objective, new motivation.

Chapter 9

THE Sheraton-Prudential in Boston was by now one of the city's older hotels. It attracted a somewhat more business-class clientele and significantly less attention than the Ritz, Four Seasons, Westin and Boston Harbor, all of which were vastly more expensive. Discretion was a prime objective and the Hospitality Suite in the Sheraton-Prudential Tower contained three sumptuous bedrooms and a living room decorated by this year's New York best, two conference rooms, a communications center and separate security, service and support rooms. It was accessible by its own locked elevator only from the lobby and mezzanine and from a section of the basement-level garage, and could be entered through locked overhead doors from the ramp beside the hotel.

The Hospitality Suite was always paid for and seldom used. Oliver Nelson Brooke used it maybe twice a year when he wanted a Boston meeting. Brooke had been nicknamed Beano by his Exeter classmates who reversed his initials and called him Brook No Opposition. He had homes in Seal Harbor, Pride's Crossing, Palm Beach and Palm Desert but kept a penthouse in the Prudential Center apartment house next door for Marge when she came to town with him. She could walk from there to Symphony on Friday afternoon. He would go with her and they would hold hands sometimes. Or he could walk over to the Hospitality Suite unseen through the garage for a meeting.

He was tall and angular, lanky said some, Lincolnesque said Marge—she was an original wife—and he stood before the huge plate-glass windows at the northwest corner of the small conference room overlooking the Charles River, Harvard and M.I.T., and the industrial slums of Cambridge and Somerville which the two universities had helped him create. The city was varying shades of gray and silver in March, the blue-gray of the river since the ice was out, a patch of dark green-gray off to the right, the Common. Brooke spoke quietly into the telephone as he waited for the others to join him.

Brooke, a rural minister's son, had parlayed some inherited New England farmland into a property empire in seven countries on three continents without ever selling a single property at a loss or missing a single mortgage payment. He was not a director, officer or trustee of anything and was by choice unknown to the public. Brooke's anonymity was essential to his avocation. He was known in political circles as The PacMan. Political Action Committees controlled by him were responsible for more than 11 percent of Republican expenditures in presidential and congressional elections and a smaller but growing percentage of Democratic Party collections. Indeed, if real power in the country rested in a dozen hands, Oliver Nelson Brooke's were two of them.

He turned and flashed his cat smile at the others, who were now arriving. " 'Cats with their arseholes wreathed in smiles,' " muttered Lieutenant General Aaron Steele, U.S.M.C. Special Forces, five feet, six inches of spit, polish and the horrors of war and soon to be one of the Joint Chiefs. Steele had resented being forced to come and felt immediately better both at being able to recall the World War II song and at having the wit to invoke it.

Price Santry remembered it. He grinned as they were sitting down in the overstuffed teak and black leather dining room chairs. Assistant Director of the CIA, Santry's trademark was openness and his policy on covert actions was to eliminate them. Price Santry was a survivor.

Lewis Noyes, at his elbow, *summa* from Michigan and first in his class at the Stanford Law School, where he had been called behind his back "the Fascist," was twenty-seven, bespectacled, and had perfect visual and auditory recall. He was Santry's protégé and worshipped him.

The fourth man, Robert Pettigrew, had played guard on three great late-forties Alabama teams and carried 285 pounds of beef and blubber on a five-foot, nine-inch frame. Pettigrew, a Bubba with broad horizons, had extensive interests in wood, pulp and paper in the South and West and had investments in numerous producers of newsprint, which was intermittently in short supply. This gave him valuable media connections and enhanced his value as chief fund-raiser to a certain colorless Senate member of the Armed Forces Committee and the Joint Committee on Oversight of Intelligence.

Brooke continued to speak on the telephone. The mouthpiece was sheltered by a concave plastic guard so they could not hear the words. He gestured at the coffee and rolls on the sideboard. Santry nodded and Noyes fetched, black for everyone, a bran roll for Steele; for Pettigrew, cream and two sugars and two cinnamon and raisin buns.

Brooke hung up and joined them. "How kind of you to come," he said. No one laughed. "I didn't expect you all to run up here, where there's one of me, four of you. I expected to come down to Washington."

Steele said, "The White House said it was important."

"And we're here," Pettigrew said. "What's the beef?"

"No beef," said Brooke. "But a problem. Let's discuss it. As you know, I have good relationships with a number of major contributors, and six of them, three couples, took Marge and me to Israel this month. It ws the first time we had been there. An impressive country, with all its problems." He looked about. No one said anything. He continued, "My friends are concerned. They no longer trust us."

There was silence.

"Now," Brooke said and looked around again, "whether we like Jews or not, they are the only reliable friends we have in that part of the world. Let's not kid ourselves about the Arabs. Even the

Saudis and the Egyptians. Even the Kuwaitis, despite what we've done for them." Santry made a gesture of impatience. Brooke went on, "The point is, the Israelis can't trust us anymore. Which will sooner or later raise in Mr. Santry's mind the question of how far we can trust them."

Santry was shaking his head. "I resent that statement. They get a hell of a lot from us, whether or not they trust us."

Brooke stared at him. Pettigrew looked at the two of them. What was happening in front of him did not seem to affect Alabama politics, the South or West, wood, pulp or paper. He said, "What's the point?"

"Exchange of intelligence," Brooke said.

"Oh, come on. They're not exactly forthcoming," Santry said, "and we continue to do our share."

Brooke said, "Our share? Fine, let's talk about terrorists."

"What about them?" Santry snapped. "There seems to be dissension among the terrorist groups, fighting, assassinations."

Brooke said, "What about the new training camps?"

"What new training camps?" Santry said. He looked at Noyes, who was studying Brooke. Santry said, "There's nothing."

Pettigrew stirred. Steele took a deep breath. He looked from Santry and Noyes to Brooke again.

Brooke said, "Libya 2, Syria-Lebanon 7."

"What's that? A soccer score?" Santry laughed.

"The new training base locations," Brooke said.

Steele shifted in his chair and said to Santry, "We told you we heard something."

"There is no clear evidence," Santry said. Pettigrew and Steele looked at him. Brooke moved and they all looked at him. Brooke was reaching under the conference table for his briefcase. He removed a large brown envelope and handed it to Santry. Santry did not touch it. He gestured with his chin to Noyes. Noyes opened the envelope. He glanced at Santry. Santry was motionless. He said, "Describe the contents."

"Satellite photos of terrorist training camps."

"Our photos?" said Steele.

"Where did you get them?" Santry said to Brooke.

"Where do you think? The Israelis gave them to him!" Pettigrew exploded.

Santry said to Brooke, "Are you telling me that they have admitted infiltrating our satellite operations?" Brooke was searching through his briefcase. He came up with a business-size white envelope and pushed it across the table to Noyes. Noyes opened the envelope, took out a single sheet. He looked at Santry. Santry said, "What?"

Noyes cleared his throat. "The names of the Romanians who supplied the photos and the amounts the Mossad paid them." He turned to Brooke. "Where did the Romanians get them?"

"From their own files, of course, their prior administration. The Mossad doesn't know who gave it to them," Brooke said. "The KGB, the Stasi, who knows? Who cares?" He was staring at Santry. So were Pettigrew and Steele.

Santry said to them, "I would have told you riding back on the plane—" but their heads had turned back to Brooke again.

Brooke was looking at Santry. He said, "The camps are there. We know they are there. We need a way to stop them. My Mossad friends tell me that they are almost entirely funded by Germans. Through secret accounts in Austrian banks. If we can prove it, we can stop the flow of funds, and the camps won't be able to function."

Santry sucked his teeth. "All right, that's a tough one—"

"Come on!" Steele snarled. "You do know something!"

"This goes no further," said Santry. "We're not certain what is going on, but the Stasi—who were even more potent than we feared—have disappeared, gone underground, and, with the German unification proceeding so rapidly, we suspect—that's all, there's no proof—suspect, that there are continuing operations."

Pettigrew exploded, "What sort of operations?"

Santry said, "We don't know."

Steele glared. "You don't know?"

Santry chose his words with care. "Our regular Agency sources seem to have a feeling, that's all, that something grandiose may be being planned. But they have no idea what it could be. And our special source insists it is rumor, that's all, that there is nothing of consequence being planned, by the ex-Stasi, the Arabs, or anyone else, and as for the Germans funding the camps, that is Israeli paranoia, that's all, Israeli disinformation."

Brooke said, "Our special source? Austrian?"

Santry said, "German."

Brooke said, "A particular person?"

Santry nodded, uncomfortable. "Is there more?" he said.

Brooke said, "Is it possible that your source is covering up?"

"No."

"No? Then let's move on," said Brooke. "Why don't you tell us what you know about special terrorist training in those camps for American operations."

There was a moment of shocked silence. Pettigrew said, "Well, that's blunt. All right, Santry, what do you say to the man?"

Santry was blinking. "American operations? You mean terrorist attacks here?"

Brooke said, "Two of the camps in Syria and one of the Libyan camps now specialize in American accents, American clothes, movies, music, sporting events, politics, gossip, customs."

"Oh, fine," said Santry, and they looked at him. "I don't expect you to believe me now but we have no such information." Brooke nodded. He kept nodding.

Brooke said, "Is there some sort of secret protocol between the CIA and the people in charge of these camps that there will be no terrorist attacks against Americans here as long as we ignore the camps and pressure Israel to take no ground action against them?"

Santry exploded, "That's a lie! A provocation!"

"Makes sense to me," Steele muttered.

Santry shook his head. "No evidence, unproven."

"And if it's true, and they break their promise?" said Steele.

"That is just too farfetched to respond," Santry said.

"Aw," Pettigrew gestured, impatient, "but what if it isn't? What if they warn us in advance? What if they say it's some fundamentalist crazies, totally out of control, please don't hold them responsible? They'll help us if they can but the guys on the loose are poor suffering buggers, willing to die, inspired men, religious men, wild men? And then they blow up an airplane? What are you going to recommend when it happens?"

Santry looked from him to Brooke. "What do you want?" he said.

Brooke said, "I don't want us to sit on our collective butts. I want to do whatever we can. I want to cooperate with our friends and exchange information. I think there is something in the wind, notwithstanding your informant's fine German hand, and I want to know more about who it is and what in hell they're planning. Frankly, terrorism frightens me. Can you imagine it being run by Germans? It has been bad enough up to now, but it has not been happening here, thank God, and I don't want it here in my lifetime. Hell, I don't want it here after my lifetime. Look, I want to know who is driving it where. I want to take them apart first. I don't want it to happen!"

Chapter 10

IT WAS EARLY when I awoke in my New York hotel room. The light blanket was some kind of new mesh. Was it acrylic, wool or cotton? I was warm and my mind was wandering. I always let it, first hour in the morning, until I had jogged and eaten breakfast.

It went to the indefatigably cheerful child I had left in the bed, trying so hard to show me that he was tough and not stricken by panic. Some defiant ones did learn to ski on one leg. I would take him if he wanted to go and try not to weep, watching. Could he ever learn to like swimming? I would hug him, teach him, stay with him. And meanwhile, I had to protect him, and myself, from the man they were calling Diego. I had lost the first round, thrown it away. I would be lucky to survive the second.

I would have to move swiftly and carefully. I needed access to an intelligence service. The SDECE would do nothing further for me. That was clear. The CIA was inaccessible to me. The KGB was a ridiculous thought and my Stasi fling had frightened me.

"And he has not been tested." By whom? I had no answer. Some private organization? Who else was there? Interpol? I knew no one in Interpol, I didn't even know who Interpol was, or if they still existed.

Israel.

I realized that I had known from the first it would come to that. They did have the best intelligence, with their Mossad, Shin Bet and Aman, but why should they help me? Because I was Jewish?

That would not be enough.

I was, however, important in that singular Jewish-American sense of the word: I was a Big Giver. I had the plaques on my wall to prove it—from a museum, a university, a library, a kibbutz. I had framed letter from public figures. That would get me in the door. They would at least humor me.

What was I going to ask for?

To help me find and kill Diego before he killed me or my son.

And to hide Hugo in a safe place in the meantime.

I had the beginnings of a plan.

What I needed was a contact point. In Washington, I had my friend the flack, and he was sure to know someone, but how well would he know them? I would see him over the weekend. And here in New York, I had fat Sidney Rosenbloom.

I was in New York to renegotiate my bank lines. I would make the deals over breakfast, go see Sidney at ten o'clock, tell him to close the deals with the banks—and then pop the other question.

Fat Sidney would know whom to contact. He represented the Israeli Ministry of Defense. He had bragged to me about them.

Okay, clear the head, think of nothing. Abruptly, I sat up on the edge of the bed. The blanket was in fact cotton. I liked the hotel, refurbished, small. It cost an appalling $425 a day for a small suite. That was inflation and bad for the dollar, but when the dollar went down I sold it short and made money from the inflation.

I put my feet on the floor. The rugs were pale peach and a few months old, soft still with the faint smell of institutional disinfectant. I went barefoot for the towel in the bathroom, an enormous bath sheet, heavy pile on both sides, not one of those cheating things with one side flattened. I took it back to the bedroom and spread it neatly on the rug. I did my push-ups, 100. My sit-ups, 100. I rolled to my feet, went to the wall, put my back against it and sank slowly down; knees at right angles, I counted off the seconds: 100, my thighs were starting to strain; 130, painting; 150, trembling; 180 seconds, done.

Sweating lightly, I donned my paean to patriotism, my white cotton briefs from Hanes, my crew-necked T-shirt from Van Heusen, my blue side-pocketed Speedo running pants, my white absorbent Thurlo running socks, my old red Nike Air-Flex cushioned running shoes and my red-and-blue-striped rugby pullover from Land's End. Watch, wallet, keys—where were the keys?

I crossed swiftly through the sitting room and found them on the marble foyer table.

The corridor was empty.

I held the door behind me open while pausing to check. I had suddenly become cautious. Corridor clear, I released the door. Behind me, it clicked, caught. Locked. How many elevators were there? Four? For fourteen floors? What did the temperature of my finger have to be for the elevator button to respond to my touch? Ping. It worked; the button light came on. A chime. A red light over elevator number four. How long should a hotel guest have to wait before it became a problem?

Whoa. Suppose it opened and there was someone there. What should I do? What could I do? A man alone could not check elevators.

The hell with it. Go for the run. I was on edge this morning.

The lobby lights were still on.

Outside, it was false dawn; the light was faint orange. I fumbled with the buttons on my rugby shirt, looking about, taking my time, checking the elderly concierge behind the bell desk, the single clerk at Reception. The lobby was otherwise deserted, the newsstand not yet open.

"Good morning, sir," the concierge called. "My, we're up early this morning!"

I smiled faintly, said nothing. I knew the man. Brendan. The

Reception clerk forced a smile as I walked past. It was too early for talking.

The front doors revolved and a vision in a long green St. Laurent cape swept inside, followed by the doorman holding her matching green garment bag and carryon, both of them new Hartmans. The lobby exploded with warmth and greetings, the Reception clerk flashing his teeth in a smile and Brendan bustling forward with a hearty, "Ms. McDonald! Welcome back, ma'am!" Brendan seized the bags from the doorman.

She was instant California, long brown hair streaked discreetly gold, slim, energetic and capable, right off the red-eye and ready to go, busy, efficient and sure of herself, but sexy, available and present. As she breezed past me toward the Reception desk, her blue eyes scanned me from head to toe. Click-click-click, man-place-clothes, was I worth a whirl? Time interval available? The atmosphere crackled with evaluation.

She signed the register. I finished with my buttons. I had a sudden hunger. It had been so long. Should I try? Time was a problem. The doorman dashed back outside. Brendan burbled. The Reception clerk pushed computer buttons. There was a pause. Silence. No one spoke. It was my move.

My move was no move.

It was the right one. The lady hesitated. "Is the cafe open?" she asked the Reception clerk.

"Not yet, ma'am, forty minutes—"

"Just coffee?"

"Not yet, ma'am, but room service is open."

She turned to me. "That's not what I want." She smiled.

"Perhaps they can bring some down to the hall—" offered the Reception clerk, snatching at the phone.

"Please do."

I cleared my throat.

The staff all turned.

"Perhaps you'd like to go jogging?" I said.

"I beg your pardon?"

"While you wait."

She had a sense of humor. "I never run," she said.

"Never? From anyone?"

She laughed.

"Brave woman." Could I juggle the time? My bankers were on their way over to the hotel for a 7:30 A.M. meeting. She was not the quickie type. What if I were late, say, 8:30 A.M.? One banker would wait, two would leave. I would have to pass. What a shame. I tried do it gracefully. "I love it," I said. "I go every day. Around now."

"Then enjoy it today," she said. "By all means." There was the slightest derisive edge in her voice.

"Perhaps later?" I said.

"I'm booked right through." She grinned. "That's the way it goes."

"Pity," I said.

"Oh, there's no telling." She swung away to the elevators, Brendan, with her baggage, following. Alas, it was not to be some enchanted morning.

I pushed through the revolving doors to the street and left them still revolving.

I adjusted my collar.

There was the doorman and no one else about. I was quiet. The streetlights were blinking out. The sun was not up and the light was weird. In the east it was bright but no pink yet showed.

"Have a nice run, sir," said the doorman.

"Mmm."

"And please be sure to stay out of the park this early in the morning."

I started jogging.

I headed north along the wide sidewalks on the east side of the street across from the park, running lightly, smoothly, nine-minute miles, five blocks, ten blocks.

I was perspiring more freely now.

It was still dark under cloudy skies. I jogged across the street and into the park. I remembered a reservoir with a cinder track somewhere in the trees, half a mile ahead.

It was darker under the trees. Threatening. I shivered. Was someone watching?

Uphill, now, and over the rise. Why were there no other joggers? There were three, coming toward me, white men in their twenties, pounding down at me, running. As they came abreast, I said, "Hi! Could you please tell me—?"

They went past, without pausing. The leader never looked. The second man was wary, and the third, openly contemptuous, as if I were asking for money or something—and then they were gone, their footsteps fading. Maybe indifference was a good thing. The less people cared, the greater the freedom to be left alone.

Mine were the only footsteps. I speeded up. Was someone really watching? I cut precisely up the middle of the path, which opened suddenly into a clearing and a paved cross street winding east and west. I slowed, looking both ways. There were no cars on the road, no taxis. Why not? Oh, yes, the park was blocked early in the morning.

I jogged across the street into the park on the far side. It was gloomy but a bit brighter, the trees less dense.

There was the reservoir, up ahead. Up the stairs, through leaves, up more stairs, up one more final flight of stairs. At last, my oasis.

Onward, the track narrowed. Something glinted in the trees! Was it moving? No, it was not.

Angrily, I cleared my mind screen. The first rays of dawn lit the treetops and faded in an instant into murk. Far across the reservoir, a distant jogging couple disappeared. I was alone with my nerves again.

I jogged along, checking the trees. Nothing moved.

There was a noise behind me. I glanced back. It was a runner, a black man, big, running not jogging.

The footsteps were closer. The black man was overtaking me. He was going fast for a big man. I was doing nine-minute miles, he must be doing sevens, overtaking at two miles an hour, a mile every thirty minutes, an eighth of a mile, a 220, every three minutes and forty-five seconds. We were approaching the halfway point.

The footsteps were close on my heels. He sprinted, speeding up to pass on the left and I held to the outside edge of the track.

Suddenly, I saw a puddle in front of me. I cut toward the center of the track, in front of him. He steadied me with his hand, passing, grunted, " 'Scuse" and moved on.

I watched him pull ahead of me, a big man radiating presence. He had apologized. And he hadn't tried to hurt me. Relief. So why was I still feeling uneasy? Up ahead, the black runner pulled away. Another thought, suddenly—I felt for my pocket and my wallet was gone! Of course. The son of a bitch had touched me. My wallet had been taken.

I started running at top speed, legs churning, fists pumping, driving, bouncing from the arches, adrenalin. The man ahead was holding speed, running steadily. I pounded after him, catching up with him.

He heard my footsteps and glanced back at me. Seemingly pleased at being overtaken, he grinned, speeded up. Did I want to race? We would race all right—

"Hey, man—" The other man was grinning wickedly as I came abreast and tackled him.

We crashed into the brush beside the path. He was heavier and stronger, built like a football player gone to beef and flab. I kept him off balance, driving with my shoulder. He swore and swung a massive elbow at me. I smashed the heels of both hands against his nose and jaw, driving upward for blood and bone break and then, even before the strangled grunt, I slammed the bony outside of both my hands down hard on his left collarbone.

Bruised, I thought, but not broken.

His mouth opened, half moan, half scream. I fumbled in his pockets and came up with the wallet. I squatted on my heels beside him, shaking it in his face.

He was in agony and I didn't care. I wanted to smash his teeth in.

Silence.

My anger ebbed. I got it under control again. He had stolen my wallet, not bombed my son. He was not the man I wanted to kill. I stood, looked down.

The black man looked up at me.

I turned away and resumed jogging.

"Did you have a nice one?" asked the doorman.

He ushered me through the revolving doors and into the lobby, where the concierge handed me my *Wall Street Journal* and *New York Times*.

"How far do you run?" smiled the Reception clerk.

"Four," I said.

"Really? That's a good run. I admire a man with discipline. Shall I let Room Service know you're back, sir?" The Reception clerk was looking at me quizzically.

"Yes, please," I said. I entered the elevator, pushed the button.

I came out of the elevator and glanced up and down. The corridor was empty. What did I expect at quarter to seven in the morning?

I had cooled and stopped sweating. I would have the first cup of coffee before my shower. I walked toward my door, fumbling in my pocket for the key.

My door was properly locked. I put the key in the lock. The key turned, I heard the tumbler flip, the bolt slide back. I took out the key, turned the knob and pushed the door open.

On the table in the foyer was my wallet.

I closed the door behind me and reached into my pocket for the wallet I had taken from the man in the park. The two wallets were nearly identical.

I stood there for a moment.

Then I picked up my wallet and walked into the sitting room.

I put the two wallets side by side on the desk and sat there, thinking. What to do? The two wallets were slightly different. Mine was more worn. I had not noticed that in the park. I had not looked for a difference. No wallet, empty pocket, jostled, black man, boom!

Way to go, Michael Collins. After all those years of searching your prejudiced soul, you still think reflexively, black—thief—animal—get him.

The man had presence. Who was he? His wallet was full. I tickled my middle finger through the credit cards in their neat plastic envelopes. Oh, perfect, a black executive, vice president-finance of CompuLink Investments, offices on the twentieth floor, a good address, a river view, I had been in the building. American Express platinum, MasterCard, Diners, Discover, Visa gold. Home was a penthouse on the West Side, rent controlled, another good building. Driver's license, the Harvard Club, M.B.A. Four hundred dollars in twenties. I finished thumbing the billfold.

I put it down and looked at the telephone. I do not believe in wallowing in guilt. I would have to do something.

Phone the man. Hello, this is Michael Collins. We just met in the park. I thought you took my wallet. We had this little misunderstanding. I'm sorry about your nose and collarbone. I hope your jaw isn't broken?

No.

What the hell, shut up and keep the money? Shit happens all the time.

No.

Why not?

Because I couldn't.

Chapter 11

LAWYER Sidney Rosenbloom exploded with laughter.

Sidney was sixty-five, good at what he did and a pillar of the Jewish community who had managed to make a great deal of money doing what he loved for clients he did not like very much, most of whom did not like him.

I did. He did my banking. He was fast, he did the work himself—no delegating to the overworked, undertrained young one of the moment—and he never once billed me. He let me bill myself. He would phone and say, "Send me money," and I would. I once asked if he treated all his clients that way and he snickered and said, "Are you kidding?"

"Then why me?"

"I saw you coming."

"From where?" I said.

"From where you come from," he said. "Have we ever had a problem?"

"No."

"Why not?" he said.

"Because I always overpay you."

"Right," he said. "And that's where I saw you coming from. And don't you ever tell anyone else. It would ruin my reputation."

In fact, he had a weird reputation. He had had numerous client problems. He would bill them on whim whatever he chose, without time records or explanation. If they did not pay their bills promptly, in full, they either cut Rosenbloom in for a piece of the deal or he ceased representing them. Out. But he had never sued a client. The bottom line on Rosenbloom—how I hated that awful phrase—he was exactly what he seemed, he had crazy ideas about billing and he had worked for Israel for many years and they seemed to like him.

He laughed, and I sat there. He was as fat as I remembered him. I looked at him, laughing away, tears in his eyes, shaking, rich, arrogant.

I wondered why I liked him. Because he had flattered me with the billing nonsense? No. His redeeming factor, I decided, was the quality of his laughter. It was neither cruel at the black man nor a put-down of me. It was his recognition that the world was sick. It pure enjoyment.

All right, it was funny to him, not to me. He was calming down finally, wheezing. He started to speak, but looked at the wallets on his desk and lost it again. There were tears in his eyes. He took his glasses off and wiped them.

Rosenbloom took a breath. "No, I will not call the police," he said and choked down more laughter.

"Why not? There are places in the world where the police would help."

"Oh, yeah? Name one."

"Home," I said.

He said, "That's different. You're special there. Here you ain't shit. Here they'll fucking bury you. What you need is an ash can, not a lawyer or a policeman!" He emptied the black man's wallet onto his desk and dropped it into his wastebasket. He picked up my own wallet and held it out to me, announcing, "Done! End of problem!"

I took my wallet and pocketed it.

That left the cash on Rosenbloom's desk. Rosenbloom chuckled, enjoying the situation. He picked the cash up and held it out to me.

I shook my head.

"Why not? You earned it!" he said and burst into raucous laughter again.

I sat there in stony silence.

Rosenbloom flapped a ham hand on his desk in disgust. "Aw, come on, what do you mean, no? That's four hundred dollars in cash, man! What is this, virtue triumphant?"

"It's his."

"Not now it isn't. You want I should give it back to him?"

I said nothing.

Rosenbloom cocked his head. Did I mean it?

I did.

He was incredulous. "Come on, man, be serious! You want to be arrested? You want to risk litigation?"

I stared at him.

"Schmuck!" Rosenbloom snapped at me. "All right, I'll send it! In a plain brown bag by messenger, and he won't know nothing. All right?"

I said, "No, it isn't."

"Oh, Christ, are you a problem!"

"The man was an innocent victim. He was not looking for trouble. I broke his nose, maybe his collarbone, maybe even his jawbone. What's that worth if he sues me?"

"How's he going to sue you? How's he going to find you?"

"Please answer the question."

"You want to pay him money, too? What kind of muscle are

you?" Rosenbloom chuckled at the idea, imagine, voluntarily paying! "And where did you learn to fight like that?"

"In grammar school. I majored in street fighting. Just give me a number, please. What would a court give him?" I said.

"If he sues you and if he wins?"

"If he sues me and if he wins."

"You are very foolish," Rosenbloom said.

"Rosie," I said. "Like in the book. When you call me that, smile."

He looked at me. "You are very foolish, sir," he said, smiling as if he had ulcer pain.

"That is, after all, my privilege," I said. "Now, do I get my answer?"

Rosenbloom gestured. "On the high side? I don't know, maybe fifty thousand. Minimum? Five, maybe ten. That would be low, ten thousand."

"I'll give you a check for thirty thousand."

"You will not!" Rosenbloom glared at me.

I looked at him. He missed the point entirely like so many lawyers. He was so used to telling people what to do, and to people paying him to tell them what to do, that he had forgotten how to listen. He did not get the message. I said, "I don't ask my lawyers what I can do. I tell my lawyers what I'm going to do. I ask lawyers how. Not if. So I'll give the money to you, and you get the money to him, okay? Those are your instructions."

Rosenbloom laughed. "I love it," he sputtered. Once again, his eyes were tearing.

I ignored him, took out my wallet and pen and wrote out a check for $30,000. I held the check out to Rosenbloom. "I made it payable to your firm, of course. You pay him in cash, any way you want."

Rosenbloom sat there and let me drop the check on his desk. He looked at me carefully. He reached for the wastebasket. He daintily picked the black man's wallet up, took the paisley handkerchief from his suit breast pocket and started wiping off the fingerprints.

I watched in silence.

Presently, he said, "I tell you what. Give me ten, max. Any more is saying you're a rich man. He might hire a detective, you never know. You know what I mean? It's generous. Please? Schmendrick? Ten thousand dollars?" He tried to sound serious but started laughing.

I reached for my check, tore it up, picked up my wallet and pen and wrote out a second check, this one for $10,000.

"How about your fee?" I asked.

"No," he said.

"I'd prefer to pay you."

"No."

"You want me to say thanks?"

"You want to pay me, you'll pay me. You'll add it to the next one." Rosenbloom took a deep breath. "And let me sit, not send the money right away, see what he does when he gets this." His knuckles rapped the black man's wallet. "Please?" I said nothing.

Rosenbloom went on, "There's trouble I got position. You see, I still got the $10,000. Anyone know you were running? The hotel, maybe the doorman?"

I put away my wallet and pen.

"The doorman," said Rosenbloom, and pushed his lips out prissily. "He knows. Oh, Michael. Please."

I thought, wildly, that's a moue. Look at it, a goddamn moue; the man's grandfather must have been Viennese. I wondered if it was genetic.

Rosenbloom was droning on, "All right, all right, it is what it is. Say nothing to the doorman. We'll send the wallet and contents first. Then we'll wait, a month, maybe two, three months. To see if he finds you and sues or what. You can always change your mind. Let's talk about your banking."

"Fine. Here." I handed him a list of the banks, currencies, amounts and terms.

He studied them. "You can do better than half a point over prime."

"I know," I said. "Leave it alone."

"Why? You know the trouble with you?"

"I am about to learn."

"You want people to love you," he said. "You try to make them love you by always overpaying. Well, they won't. They got no respect, banks. You're a schmuck for overpaying. Let me earn my keep. Take it down."

"No," I said.

"You want I should leave it alone."

"Yes," I said. "And one other thing."

"What?"

"You used to work for Israel?"

"You want to give them something?"

"Not exactly. Not entirely. It may go that way. I want to meet someone."

"Who?" he said.

"Mossad. Shin Beth. Aman."

He sat back. He was not smiling. He could not sidestep this one. I was, after all, a Big Giver, as well as one of his clients.

I said, "Oh, do you know the Mossad man?"

"Their intelligence presence in the United States is really very limited, you know."

"I know. I hope so."

"The United States is a friendly power, you know?"

"I know," I said. He waited. I said, "Can you get me to someone up in the chain? Someone who can make decisions?"

He was considering what to do. I watched and waited.

If you want something, you go as close to the top as you can get. I knew that and so did he. If he sent me far enough up the line, something might happen which he might not like, and they would hold him responsible for it. I could feel Rosenbloom's fine-tuned brain sifting the options and consequences.

He said, "Where are you going to be the next couple of days?"

I told him.

Chapter 12

I WENT TO Washington the next morning.

The avenues were empty, the taxicabs underpriced and the cherry trees would blossom in another three weeks. On street corners, the lounging underclass wondered what to gossip about and missed the former mayor.

It was good to be home.

My condominium was on a wharf with a harbor view. Inside, everything was white; walls, furniture, appliances, dishes, bedding. Decorators baffled me and my place was a statement, my reaction against the age of accumulation and the excesses of too-free-spending. I kept it spare and almost never cooked. I hated novels where the men cooked. They made me feel inferior. I made coffee with chicory and various beans, and suzette sauce from scratch with orange juice, and every once in a while I rolled pasta—from high-gluten flour with a sensuously thin rolling pin—but that was it. I thought most men were terrible cooks. I knew for sure that I was. Which was a blow to my macho image: It had somehow become more masculine to acknowledge a yen for the domestic.

My condominium was sanctuary, *querencia*, a place for heavy thinking. And rest. And yet it was isolated and underprotected. Should I hire guards? Probably useless. What could I say?

Safety lay in the counterattack, the unexpected.

Get moving.

A plain brown envelope, covered with stamps I did not recognize, arrived in the mail the next morning. The lettering was Arabic. Saudi? Turkish? Syrian. Express Mail. No return address. I turned it over and froze.

Under the flap was a scrap of purple ribbon.

I studied it for a long moment.

It was too flat to be a letter bomb.

I slit the flap with my pocket knife and opened the envelope with the tip of the blade. A newspaper clipping. French. With two fingers, I pulled the clipping out.

It was the story of the Paris bombing.

The paragraph naming the casualties was circled in purple magic marker. Numbly, I noted Hugo's name. At the bottom of the page, in capital letters, the purple edges blurring into the newsprint, were the words "HIM FIRST, THEN YOU. YOU TOLD ME ABOUT HIM."

I telephoned Rosenbloom.

I said it was urgent, get him out of the goddamn meeting.

They did. He sounded harassed when he came on the line. "Hi, Michael, I made your call to my other clients—"

"Today," I interrupted, "Rosie, I need them today."

"That urgent?"

"Life or death."

"Whose?"

"My son's." I heard my voice trembling.

"Where are you?"

"Home."

"Stay there. They'll contact you."

"When?"

"Let me get off now, I'll get on the horn. Can you give them a day?"

"Do I have a choice?"

"Michael, please understand what I say. I can ask but that's all, and I will ask, but Michael, I do not control them."

" *'Allo, Michel.*" Véronique sounded weary and pressed for time. They were about to go out for the evening.

"I have had a threat," I said, "about the boy."

"How?"

"By mail. From Syria. A newspaper clipping about the explosion. Hugo's name was circled in purple ink."

Silence.

"Do you have any idea how sorry I am?" I said. "It's all my fault!"

"You did what you felt you had to do. We have four guards around the clock at the hospital and we do not see what else we can do—"

"I will pay," I said. "Will you let me?"

"When you are here, you will speak to my husband. Hugo will be home the week after next, and then, the recuperation, and the school, and the vacation—" She broke off, her voice strident. "There is no end," she finally said in a small voice.

"There will be an end, I promise," I said.

"When?"

"I have asked for help."

"From whom?"

I hesitated. "I will tell you when I know what they are willing to do."

"We do not wish you—or them—to do anything at all, without the permission of me and my husband."

I sat there and looked out at the water all day. The phone did not ring.

The messenger arrived at 5:10 P.M. He had a small white envelope. I signed for it. It looked familiar. It was an invitation to a cocktail party that evening. The envelope had been familiar because I had received one in the mail. It had been in the pile that I had opened the day before.

This was a second invitation. By messenger.

It was a command, not an invitation.

Chapter 13

THE PARTY WAS THROWN BY Alex Black, whom I have uncharitably referred to as my friend the flack. It was a sought-after invitation. Alex stocked the party with single lovelies recruited months in advance, the hottest new faces in politics and media specialists in celebrity. It was the first major party of the nascent springtime, crackling with energy and buds about to burst. Into the heady mix, Alex dropped a half dozen of his biggest accounts and government procurement officers and staff from the Hill. The meanings of "procurement" were multiple, according to my friend the flack; public relations included introductions. Alex would grin and I would hate him. But one of his accounts was now Attention Corporation of Austin, controlled by Peter and Emily Flowers, and I had brought them to him.

They were two of the closest friends I had. Once I had even taken a vacation with them and, when it was over, I still liked

them. I had gone to school with Peter: three years of promise and
excitement and then we all went back where we came from with
a few stray friends from dissimilar backgrounds. Peter's father ran
a Greek restaurant. Peter had gone to Cal Tech and then back to
Austin, where he had also struggled, but not with the same passive
acceptance.

He had founded ACA with all the money they had in the world
and all they could borrow. ACA made the tiniest bugging devices
and a miniature compressed gas implantation gun. You could bug
a room in ten seconds. I had made an investment. Initial sales
were promising. Then budget cutbacks were threatened for the
littlest members of the military-industrial complex. Alex had an
unspecified "triple play" planned to reverse the cutbacks.

It was much too early in the season for a large party to be held
out of doors. It had snowed an inch two weeks previously and then
rained three days in a row. Alex had invited five hundred guests
to the Philippson estate for four o'clock. He had provided neither
tent nor heaters. By all rights, it should have been cold. Instead,
it was the first warm day of the year. All the early flowers were
out, supplemented by white, pink and purple florist tubs and trel-
lises. The temperature was perfect, brisk not sharp, a clear blue
sky and a suggestion of a southern breeze. The divinity had, as
usual, smiled on Alex.

Four of us, myself, two blond ladies and an older man, arrived
at the bar tables simultaneously, faced the four bartenders and
studied one another out of the corners of our eyes. The two women
seemed friendly, interested. The man was foreign and wary but
somehow also interested. I wondered in what. I was on a Bombay
gin kick. I had had three, neat, earlier, before coming over. Frustration made my heart no fonder. And who knows what evil lurked
in the hearts of men at Alex's? Here was my bartender. He was
my age, with a wispy mustache. "What would you like, sir?"

"Gin," I said.

"With what, sir?"

"Just gin."

Blonde on the left laughed. Blonde on the right turned a shoulder. The man beside her was determinedly colorless. Blonde on
the right asked him questions. The man was evasive.

"Michael?" It was Emily and Peter. Clutching my gin, I kissed her.

Alex instantly descended. "Emily! Michael! Peter! So glad! Here's someone you have much in common with! This is Meredith Slater! Meredith is Bureau! You know, the Task Forces? O.C. and Special Operations. Meredith is procurement coordinator. And there's someone else you must meet if I can find her!" He irradiated us with his smile and vanished, leaving behind a pinstripe in a Brooks Brothers shirt clutching a drink that was ice cubes and amber. Ice tea? Or bourbon?

"I'm sorry, I don't know what he's talking about, but I am Mac Slater." He wheezed bourbon laughter.

Peter introduced himself and Emily and me. The two blondes and colorless hung there on the fringes. The Organized Crime Task Forces? Slater smiled, patiently. Peter said, "You might have heard of my company, Attention Corporation of Austin?"

"Ah," said Slater, "I get it. The teeny little devices. I'm a fan. I wanted to buy the product. Would that we could, but the budget, you know? So we make do as best we can."

"No," I said, and they looked at me. "You're not making do as best you can."

"Oh, Michael!" Emily was embarrassed.

"Are you with the company?" Slater asked.

Peter said, "He's one of our investors."

I said, "I try to look at the figures."

"Oh, good!" said the blonde formerly on the left. "So do I."

"Genevieve!" said Alex, who had reappeared. "Wonderful! You found her! Genevieve's very important. She's with the General Accounting Office!"

"Genevieve Wilson?" said Slater. He turned to Peter and gestured helplessly. "She's the witch who cut us."

"This is my friend, Dorothy Morrison," said Genevieve, introducing the blonde on the right. "Dorothy teaches at Georgetown. And this is?" Foreign and colorless smiled, not understanding, and shook hands with all the men in turn, Peter, Slater, me. Genevieve went on, to me, "What's this about figures?"

Alex beamed at me. This was it. The triple play had started. The FBI and the General Accounting Office. But that was two, not three. No time to worry about it. "What are your ten biggest successes in the last ten years?" I said to Slater.

"Why?" he said.

"Because eight of the ten were based on taps," I said.

"Oh, come on, not eight—"

"Exactly eight. Based on what has been published."

"Is he correct?" said Genevieve.

"He could be," said Slater and looked nervous. "Why?"

She frowned and I told him, "It's her job to figure out what is cost-effective." I said to her, "Call it a reduction in forces. That's what we're after, internationally speaking."

"And speaking of internationally, I would love to see these devices," said the extraordinarily handsome dark-haired man beside him. He was wearing a stunning summer-weight suit, expensive English tailoring. "And I have a big open to buy and no budget problems." The slang was business school, the accent Brit.

Alex was proudly clutching him by the shoulders. "This is Bassam Ben Hassan from the Embassy of the Republic of Syria. Bassam means 'Smiley' in Syrian. Bassam, I would like you to meet Peter Flowers, and this is his wife, Emily, Mac Slater, Gen Wilson, Michael Collins and Dorothy—where is Dorothy Morrison?" The blonde on the right had somehow receded.

"We are serious about the products," said Ben Hassan, apparently the third leg of Alex's triple play, the threat of hostile foreign purchase. He was anything but smiling. "Perhaps if we came to Austin?"

"That would be fine," said Peter. "Michael?"

"Are there any restrictions on export?" I said.

"No," said Slater and Alex together.

"Are you sure?" said Genevieve? "What does Langley say?"

Alex said, "They haven't put us on the restricted high-tech list yet. They haven't paid us enough attention."

"Let us make hay while the sun shines, then," Ben Hassan said. "I don't have your list of products and specifications and perhaps you could provide them?"

I backed away. Had I financed a company that was going to export high tech to Syria? I could imagine against whom they would use it. I turned and there was Dorothy Morrison. "Uncomfortable, Mr. Collins?" she said. "I understand you are Jewish."

"Are you an agency consultant," I said, "or do you only teach at Georgetown?" She grinned and did not answer. Foreign and silent stirred, restless. "How do you do? I'm Michael Collins," I said to him. He smiled and shook my hand. "And you?" I said. He smiled again. "you must speak some English," I said. "Where are you from?"

"Israel," he said, and gestured, uncomfortable.

"Some sort of embassy posting," Dorothy Morrison said to me and to him. "Then you don't like what's going on, selling electronics to the Syrian Tyrone Power over there?"

He said, "What can I do?"

"I don't know. What do you do?" she said.

"Economic section," he said and stuck out his hand. "My friends call me Shima."

"Ah," I said.

"What a pregnant sound," said Dorothy and turned to him. "Are you Mossad? Or what? Something secret?"

"Do you know," I said to her, "that this is the only country where it's polite to ask that?"

"We're in Rome," she said, "and we're the Romans."

"You're right, and that's the problem," I said, and my gins surged. "Civilizations seem to last two hundred years and we've now had more than our share so let's hold hands and go down the drain together."

"Are you trying to provoke me or impress him?" she said.

"Both," I said.

"You are one for two. I don't think you impressed him." She went off.

"Clever woman." He smiled, turned away, scanned the scene and sipped his drink, a Coca-Cola from the look of it. "What do you want from us?" he asked, not looking at me, his voice so quiet that I was not sure I heard him.

I swallowed. "It's my son—"

"You mentioned him to our friend."

"I don't know where to begin—"

"You don't have to begin. Your lawyer friend called two days ago. That started the file on you. We have offices in Europe. I know about Paris and East Berlin. Has something else happened?"

"A threat. In the mail. Against my son." My mouth was dry. I sucked on a piece of ice. I was having trouble speaking. "I want you to protect him."

"Mmm," he said, still looking about. "So pretty in the spring-time. And?"

"I want you to help me find him. Diego. Before he can get to me. He knows where I am. And where Hugo is."

"So soon?" Shima's voice was thoughtful.

"There was a man I hired in East Berlin. I told him too much. He shopped it."

"Ah," he said. "Agents, agents. They are a problem in this busi-ness." He glanced at me. I had prodded something. He turned away. he drank some more of his Coke again. "What can you do for me?" he said.

"Money," I said.

"That would be a useful quid pro quo. My organization never has enough."

"I know how you can get it."

"That is what you were supposed to say. Tell me, how?" he said.

I was careful not to look at him. I sipped my gin. "You are operations?"

"And if I am?" he said.

"You want major funds, you have to ask," I said. "And it doesn't come out of the budget. You're getting your funding somewhere else. Foreign accounts, that sort of thing. Special contributions. From special people. And you have to ask for those funds, too. You would prefer not to ask. You would like your freedom."

"Correct," he said. "And are you going to give it to me?"

"I will help you make it."

"Good," he said. "How?"

"How much would give you freedom?"

"More than you have. Twice what you have. Twenty million dollars." And he smiled, looking about, dreamily.

I froze. He was right. He knew what I had. A bit more than $10 million. So much for Swiss bank secrecy. "Look," I said, recklessly.

"I'll give you half now. And I'll make the other ten million for you. I will teach you my system."

"Your system for trading currencies? Your gambling system?"

"It has worked for me."

"Lucky man," he said. He cleared his throat, studied me. Finally, he said, "The person who is causing you such concern is in the Bekaa Valley training camps. The threat is not immediate. But we will put the boy in a safe house. I assume the parents are willing?"

My voice was thick. "I will call them. Thank you."

"I will get my money's worth. I will contact you."

"When? How?"

"Soon. I will send you someone."

He walked away without looking back.

I tried hard not to watch him.

Chapter 14

"THAT IS RIDICULOUS," Véronique said. "With whom?"

"I don't know," I said.

"Where? And for how long?"

"Isn't it better that we don't know?"

"What about his schooling?" she said. "And the physical therapy? And what will happen in the event that he needs further medical attention?"

"I am sure they will call you."

"You are sure? Tell me, Michel, how can you be sure? And what about visitation?"

"I am sure they will permit it if you want. Please?"

"There have been no threats here yet, Michel. Stop being melodramatic for once."

"Do you still have the guards?"

"Yes. And they are fine. And my husband prefers to pay for them. He has friends here as you know. Everything that can be done is being done. Hugo's home is in France and he is safer in France than with your Mossad wherever they would take him. We appreciate your concern and thank you—"

"Véronique, please. It's a mistake. It's too dangerous."

"He misses you," she said. "Come and see him."

"Véronique—"

"No," she said. "No, no, no. Jean-Claude has taken care of everything. I have the confidence in my husband."

Chapter 15

DIEGO WAS passionately heterosexual and Latin. There were men in the camps who were neither. He was light-skinned and good-looking. Most of them were not. The gunshot wounds in his stomach from which he was recovering, albeit slowly, were mysterious, attractive, a badge of courage. Many of his camp companions were more relaxed in their sexual orientation and more casual about expressing what they wished than Diego was prepared to understand. He resented their suggestions. He expressed his resentment violently twice.

The Bulgarian failed candidate for a degree in psychology was hospitalized for slightly more than a month. He was luckier than the North Yemenite.

The North Yemenite was a discharged policeman. He was huge and weight-lifter muscular. He carried a knife with a seven-inch blade. He considered Diego's nonresponse insulting. It was. The North Yemenite managed to slash Diego twice—across the ribs, reopening one of the bullet-wound scars, and also in the upper arm—before Diego got a grip on the knife hand and wrist. The North Yemenite dropped the knife when Diego broke the wrist.

The North Yemenite groped for Diego's eyes with the fingers of his functioning hand. Diego slipped the thrust, rolled and slammed the heel of his hand against the North Yemenite's jugular, just under the ear. That stunned him. A kick to the groin dropped the North Yemenite to the ground. Diego did not hesitate. He strangled the man.

Diego's intestinal pain recurred as he rose to his feet and resulted in a grimace read as a smile by observers. His overreaction was within the rules and permitted. As a consequence there were no further approaches.

Unexpectedly—to himself as well as to everyone else—Diego promptly fell in love with a German girl, a blonde with violet eyes, sultry moods, a long, lean body with clean lines and a classical education. It occurred the very night of the demise of the North Yemenite. She had witnessed the fight with some excitement and the initial coupling was her suggestion. Diego had been in love twice before, first with a wild and beautiful Bolivian girl who had lived next door to him in La Paz and who had been banished to the neighborhood convent, and second with a lissome Serb classmate at the Sorbonne who used to study while they were making love. Neither had been savagely animal and he found the German intoxicating. The Syrian instructor in charge of the camp wondered in his evaluation report whether there was some sort of psychological connection—relief, sublimation, projection or whatever—between the killing and the affair with the girl. Their attachment to each other was palpable. Wherever they went, eyes followed them, two young prowling panthers. She nursed the wound on his stomach. As it rescarred, she loved to lick it. She would hug him fiercely in the middle of the night when he had his intestinal twinges.

He even told her about East Berlin, his vacation mood, his carelessness, his lack of concern as he approached the lost American tourist, the empty pointing hand, the voluminous map and then the Walther concealed in it, the shout about the son in Paris. It had been so totally unexpected. Diego had even wondered in the hospital if it could have been a mistake in identity, although he had just come from Paris. There had been no American in either of the banks, the department store or the restaurant, according to

what he had read in the papers. And then he had received the
visit from the cold ex-Stasi, with the face of a fox and the gray suit,
who had given him the explanation and the name and address of
the American and the son—and had recruited Diego for the camps.

Even so, Diego had not liked him.

The training exercise following the sixth week of the weapons
course consisted of a nighttime infiltration of Israel from the Bekaa
base and a rocket attack on a bus at dawn. A bus has no defense
against a rocket attack. Diego was chosen to operate the rocket
launcher. His aim was perfection, three direct hits with three rockets, not a single miss. Nine passengers, including two children,
and the bus driver died in the flames.

The attackers melted into the desert brush and reached the
border without incident. There they split into two groups. Four
men, including Diego, created a diversion with a grenade and
rocket attack on the Israeli patrol group in charge of the sector
while the other six attackers crossed the danger zone. The diversion was a complete success. The Israeli patrol took cover and
returned their fire. The four attackers then withdrew two by two,
Diego bringing up the rear of the second two, and dropping his
scrap of purple ribbon.

The six attackers who crossed the border first had the bad luck
to be spotted by a low-flying Kfir which made two passes before
the attackers dispersed, strafing and hitting two of them and killing
one.

The deceased was the German girlfriend. Diego showed no response when they told him, except that his stomach twinged.

He grimaced. They thought it was a smile.

They thought he was fearsome.

Chapter 16

SHE WAS twenty-nine and would look it until well into her fifties. People described her as dark and sensual but *dark* did not do her justice. Her skin was light olive. She had black hair, green eyes and a wicked grin.

It was focused on me.

I had seen the grin approaching my table and it was all over for me instantly. Incredible as it sounds, I knew it. I never learned a thing about her that I did not know in that first instant. The French called it a thunderclap, a *coup de foudre*. I had always laughed but they were right. It did happen, there, to me. It was definitive, overwhelming.

There I was, sitting beside her, at one of the front tables of the Combined Jewish Philanthropies Big Gifts Luncheon Meeting. In view of what Shima was doing for me, I could not duck the invitation. The hotel ballroom was overflowing with overeating, overdressed people, excitedly laughing and joking. She had arrived with Sidney Rosenbloom and the rest of the heavyweights from New York, in town as this year's liaison with us local yokels. Rosenbloom was seating himself on her left. She was wearing a ring. She was married! Oh, no! To Rosenbloom? Apparently not to him. The room vibrated with high-decibel social chitchat. I was numb from the noise and the emotional wallop.

"Well, hello, there!" she said and introduced herself. Her name was Sarah Ravitch. She seemed to be having a wonderful time. She was sensuous. And gleeful.

I said, "Hello." Kick in, brain.

She laughed. "You're Michael Collins. I've heard of you."

I smiled politely, quivered at her voice and stared fixedly at the rostrum.

"Speak to me," she said. "What are you thinking?"

I sipped my ice water and steadied my hand. Rosenbloom and the others were chatting away. Waiters of uncertain origin fluttered around the table.

"Mr. Collins?" she said softly. "Do you read me? Michael? Earth to Collins?"

"I'm looking at your upper lip," I said. "You have the most beautiful upper lip."

"What?"

"And I'd like to see your breasts."

"Now?" she said. "It's an intriguing thought, but I have doubts about the occasion."

"That's a wedding ring," I said. "Isn't it?"

"Yes."

"Shit."

"I'm a respectable married woman," she said. "Arnold is a pillar of the New York community."

"I see."

"With prostate trouble and a girlfriend."

"I'm smitten," I said.

She said, "Aren't we susceptible!"

I heard my voice say then, "Here, take me. Take it all. Take everything."

That set her back. "Well!" she said. "That was original."

I blinked. Had I really said those words?

She said, "You know what?"

"What?"

"I believe you."

"Good."

I looked away to regroup.

Behind me, she was chuckling.

Up on the rostrum they were calling cards. It was an effective but barbaric fund-raising game, fun laced with a touch of the cruel—but the cause was just. Jews take care of their own. I wanted to take care of my own. I had endless admiration for those who subjected themselves to the indignity. My own giving was anonymous. My life was anonymous. Years before they had pressured me: "It is something all of us have to do. If you opt out, everyone will." I had opted out but increased my contributions.

Sarah patted the table beside my hand. I said, "I'm afraid to look at you. I'm trembling. I meant what I said."

"Take it all?"

"Everything."

Somewhere in the distance, far away, voices were running a meeting. Nearby, old Jews and a fat lawyer from New York tried hard not to listen. The faces reeled, the room spun. She said, "You're good, you know. You do this well."

"Do you think it's a line?"

"It doesn't feel that way. So now what happens?"

I smiled dreamily. "We leave here as soon as we can and go back to my apartment."

Sarah whispered in Rosenbloom's ear. Rosenbloom glared at me and spilled his wine. Sarah efficiently mopped it up, using her napkin, then Rosenbloom's. "It wasn't that outrageous, Rosie," she said. She sprinkled salt on the spot on the tablecloth.

"Salt?"

"It absorbs. You bleach the rest out."

"What did you tell him?"

"Where I was going to spend the afternoon."

I managed to say, "Wow."

She laughed. "My plane leaves at seven."

We drove through the city in a collector's item, my 1984 Datsun 300ZX, one of the few without the T-top.

I hated foreign cars. They had destroyed the dollar and our confidence in our ability to manufacture. I had bought this car to abuse it. I changed the oil once a year, not the filter, never brought the car in for maintenance, never even balanced the tires, and when the time came to trade the car two years later, there was nothing wrong with it. I had gotten used to it and I couldn't find anything else I wanted. So I painted it fire engine red, knowing I would soon get tired of the color, and tried to run it into the ground. It was still running strong 180,000 miles later. Sarah put her hand on mine. I looked at her hand. "Where are we going?" she said.

"My place?"

"Okay."

I had been holding my breath. She laughed. I said, "I'd like to get to know you."

She groaned. "If you want to go to bed, say you want to go to bed, and spare me the euphemism."

"Yes, ma'am."

We drove into the lot beside the building. Silence. We parked and got out. Silence. It was, as usual, deserted. We entered and took the elevator. Silence. We walked to my door. Silence. We opened it. Silence. We went in. I locked the door behind us. She prowled. "Coffee?"

"Espresso."

"Got it," I said. Delicate. I went to get the grinder.

She slid open the terrace door. "Pretty." She got the harbor smell. "Phew." She slid the door shut. "I suppose you get used to it."

"You should smell it at low tide." I finished grinding the espresso beans.

"That's sweet of you," she said, "but forget it." She was looking at my books. I finished pouring the water and flipped the switch. She said, still looking at the books, "Ready?"

"The coffee?"

"No, dummy."

"Oh," I said. "Sure."

"Come here." I walked over to her as commanded. She turned and we kissed, our light first kiss. Her lips were warm and a little dry. I breathed her scent. I felt a flutter at the base of my spine.

"Goodness," she said. "You're trembling. Are you sure this is something you want?"

"Yes."

"What is it that worries you?"

"What's going to happen next," I said and kissed her again. It was our second kiss and it lasted longer.

"Let's find out," she said.

I was willing.

It was tender. It was everything. And yet there was something not quite right. I realized what with a start: She was laughing at me.

A man does not like a woman to laugh at him while they are

making love for the first time. She might be laughing at his love-making. Was I clumsy? Unimaginative? Was this woman too much for me? Too elusive? I felt sixteen.

Afterwards, we basked and held each other close.

"Coffee?" she murmured.

"I'm sorry. I forgot." I went to get it. "I hope I didn't burn it."

I poured two in my tiny espresso cups. Black. When I brought them, she was sitting up in the bed, knees under the sheet, waiting. I handed her hers and stood there. She smiled. I sat on the bed. "I love your breasts," I said.

"I'm glad," she said. "It didn't take you long to see them."

"No," I said and delicately reached out and lightly touched, then kissed them. She was irresistible. We kissed again. We put our cups down on the table beside the bed. Then we continued kissing.

It was wonderful. And bewildering. Something was going on. A gossamer connection. Why couldn't it last? It wasn't fair.

I was yearning for it.

"Call a taxi?" She was getting dressed.

"I'll take you," I said, getting out of bed.

"I'd rather you didn't. Do you mind?"

I shook my head and stayed in the bed. "You don't want to show me to your friends?"

"I want you to be lonesome."

"I can take you and still be lonesome."

"I can't say what I have to say in a car and walk out on you at the airport." She was putting on her lipstick. "Can you guess?"

I shook my head. "I have no idea what's coming."

She said, "Sex is serious."

"Oh. Was it that bad?"

"That's the problem. You see it as good or bad."

I slowed my pulse to keep calm. "Explain. Are you really going to sit there and evaluate my performance?"

She put her lipstick back in her purse. "My, you do use all the words. Tell me about performance."

"Mine? Yours?"

"Either."

"Frankly," I said, "I'd rather not."

"Do."

I said, "I thought it was pretty good. I thought I was good—"

"Expert," she said.

"Competent."

She said, "Expert. And you came."

"Of course. And so did you. Each way. Every time. Is that bad?"

She smiled the faintest of smiles. "You're sweet, but you know from nothing. Call the cab."

I picked up the phone put it down. "The hell with it. I'm driving. And come on. Let's have the rest. You can't leave it there."

"Okay," she said and perched on a chair. "You're a typical product of the times."

"Meaning?"

"You are very proficient—"

"Thank you, ma'am."

"Let's dispense with the interruptions. With the hands, you know what you're doing. You know lips. You know where to use them. You understand sensations. You know how to vary pressures. For a man, you understand noises. You kiss, hug and croon, touch neck, tits, tum, caress back, bottom, inside of thighs, you have a reasonably complete repertoire, but the moment I don't respond like you want, you tend to get frantic."

"I suppose I do get upset," I said.

"No, frantic. When I don't do what you want me to, you go right up the walls. You panic. You want to manipulate me, control me, make me sing."

I said, "Scream."

She laughed. "You mean come. Scream and scream and come and come. That's what you mean by performance. You're good with your mouth. You know you are. You've heard it from other women. You give great head," she said, mock mimicking, "but when I didn't respond, a couple of times, just to see—what happened?"

"All right, I got upset. And you know what? I've had it."

"Fine. I hope you learned a thing or two."

"Why? In case there's a next time? I doubt that there will be a next time."

"Oh, of course there will be," she said. "Don't be dumb."

"Oh, shit, lady—Look, I don't know who you are, or how I ever got into this, but I'm not enjoying this discussion—"

"That's just it. You don't know how to enjoy yourself," she said. I stared at her. "You come when you feel like coming. You do what feels good and forget about me, and forget about what you can do for me, and what you can do with me and make me do. In short, you forget about fucking me and concentrate on fucking. What are you laughing at?"

It was dark outside. I went into the closet to get dressed and said, "I can't believe this conversation."

Chapter 17

WE RODE DOWN in the elevator in silence.

The parking lot was dim. Several of the lights were out. I would have to report that to the building. Sarah drew me out into the middle of the lot, where it was brighter. Behind us, headlights flashed by on the street. Then it, too, was dark and silent.

Our footsteps were timid on the asphalt, Sarah's heels like knuckles on hollow oak. Was there someone lurking in the dark behind a car? We walked on past it. A truck blasted by on the street behind us as we approached my car. The truck disappeared. I was slowing. Sarah reacted, hearing it now. She turned to look behind us.

I did not have to look. I looked at her.

Her eyes widened.

A man had moved out of a doorway, the service entrance to the building. He was clean-shaven, young. He looked Cuban, I thought, hungry but very good-looking. I glanced in the other direction, at the end of the lot on the harbor. A second man appeared from behind a car, pale white skin, even younger, maybe eighteen, this one, a knife showing in the belt at his waist. Both men were smirking.

Sarah pulled at me.

I looked about.

Sarah's voice quavered, "Oh, Michael—no—"

I was looking down the line of cars. "Well well well," I said.

A third man had appeared from between two cars. He had been the one lurking. A thug, that was the only way to describe him, a big swarthy brute with a mustache, two thumbs in his waistband. He sauntered toward us.

I took Sarah by the arm and planted her firmly behind me in the slot between my car and the next one.

The three now had us surrounded, Cuba out in the light in the middle of the lot, both hands still empty, Whitey with his knife now in hand, coming cautiously down the line of cars from the direction of the harbor, Thug coming toward us down the line of cars from the street end, drawing his blade from his waistband.

I smiled.

The three of them halted.

"Hey, guys, we got a little problem here," I said. "A mixed situation. Some good things, some bad things."

They looked at me.

"First of all, the good things. The cash I got. Six hundred plus. Nothing over twenties. How about it, man?"

They stared as if I were crazy.

I went on, "And she's got that little gold Patek watch and those green emerald earrings!"

They smelled blood.

Sarah moved closer behind me. I turned. Her hands were shaking. She unfastened her earrings. "I—"

"Quiet, dear." I patted her arm and pushed her back where she belonged. She should stay behind me, say nothing. I turned back to the three of them. "Now then, guys, the bad news. I'm not going to give you a fucking thing. Not shit. Not anything. You're going to have to take me."

They were wary but they closed in.

I kept on trucking, "Come along. Try me. Hey? Now you may be asking, what is it I got that you don't see?"

Cuba had produced a knife. That was three. I could feel Sarah's terror behind me. Why were women so afraid of knives? The pain, the blood, the scars, or what? Forget her, they were the problem. Push them. Harder. They were close enough. Now. My hand flashed back along my belt.

They froze.

"Look at you," I said. "Show and tell time."

"Michael, please—"

"Shut your mouth, darling. All right, guys, what you see is what you get. Right? Or is there something you don't see? Huh? That's the problem."

They waited.

I went on, "Am I carrying, say, a Colt .45, the officer's special? The little one? On cock and safety and ready to go, one in de chamber, six in de clip? On de belt in de middle of de back on de butt? And can I shoot? Say a grapefruit? From the hip? Seven for seven?"

They were frozen.

I said, "Of course, I may be bluffing. Who shoots fruit? Splat!" I clapped my hands and they jumped.

So did Sarah behind me.

I put my hands on my hips. "No moves? Come on. Not one move? Well, I'll tell you what I'm gonna do. You!"

I shouted it at Thug, who flinched.

"First, I shoot out your kneecap. A .45 will gimp you. Then I shoot your balls off. Then I shoot your face off, not enough to kill you, but folks will puke when they see you."

I certainly had their attention.

I went on, to Thug still, "Then I'll ask, you wanna live or no? You may ask me to croak you. Beg, I'm gonna ask you. I may walk away and leave you. Or I may look at your ugly mouth and shove in the muzzle. Well?"

They didn't like it.

I laughed.

"You—" Cuba started shakily.

"You! So it's gonna be you! Fine. Pretty boy, eyeing my woman. Let's make you the example! I'm gonna count to three real slow and then I'm gonna blast you. Now! Uh-one! And uh-two! And—"

Cuba could not handle it. He backed away. Whitey and Thug moved slowly after him.

Take it up one more.

"Run! Run, you assholes!" I shouted, reaching around for my belt at the back. "Run, you chicken assholes!"

They ran.

I turned toward Sarah. She was trembling. I put my arms around her and hugged her. She was rigid. I unlocked and opened the car door. She got in. I closed the door after her and walked around to the driver's side. She was still trembling. I closed the door and locked it and started the car engine. "Hey, it's all right," I said.

She gestured, "Go."

We drove until we approached a brightly lit service station. "Pull over," she said.

"Are you all right?" I parked at the curb, in front of the service station.

"Wise ass. Let me see it," she said.

"Oh, you mean the gun."

"Yes."

"It's all right. I have a license."

She had turned to face me. I have rarely seen a woman more angry and I have seen my share of angry women. She said, "I am not going to ask you again. Pull it out."

I sat there, not daring to make a joke of the words.

"That was my life you were risking."

"Do you think I'd go out after dark down there with you and without a weapon?"

She said nothing. Her face was working.

I counted slowly to ten. Then I hunched forward, reached behind me and unsnapped it from my belt. I put it in her lap, quick-draw holster and all. "It's on cock and on safety, like I said. Do be careful if you take it out."

She took a deep breath and put it back in my lap. "Sorry," she said. Her voice was trembling still.

"That's all right." I slipped the gun down between the gearshift and my seat and drove off toward the airport.

She was looking at me. "How long have you had a gun?"

"Forever," I said. "I believe in guns."

"Do you shoot much?"

"I practice all the time."

"Where?"

"The police station."

"Are you any good?"

"Yes."

"That's modest."

"It's accurate."

"I'll tell him," she said.

"Who?"

She looked at me. "Haven't you figured it out yet?"

"No."

"Shima."

I stared. "He sent you here?"

"He told you he'd send someone."

Book II

Chapter 18

HUGO WAS STRONGER. They had fitted the prosthesis. He was working with it for hours every day, trying to progress to a cane from the crutches.

He insisted that he could learn to walk without any support at all. It was just a question of enough practice.

I took him to Paris for the afternoon with the head physical therapist—and two laconic bodyguards—and spent six grueling hours testing exercise machines. The lower body selections were difficult but we finally purchased five machines. I charged them to my platinum American Express card and arranged to have them delivered.

We had a wonderful time, or rather Hugo did. I had a problem, all day long. Where was the Mossad? I kept looking about. Francois, with the mustache noticed. "They are there," he said.

"Who?" is said.

"The Jews. They are okay. They have notified us. It is all okay. Madame is unhappy. We are not. Please call her from the airport."

I nodded. I would.

"It is fine, Papa," Hugo assured me. "Do not worry yourself. The Marquis says Maman has to accept it."

I hugged my son.

But if they were there, why hadn't I noticed? If anyone were out there, watching us, shouldn't I be able to sense them?

You feel it in the places on your body you cannot see, from the base of your spine to the back of your neck. Particularly between your shoulder blades.

"Are you all right, Papa?" Hugo asked me.

I realized that I was shrugging my shoulders.

Hugo, the physical therapist, the bodyguards—and the invisible Israelis, for all I knew—drove me to Charles de Gaulle. The ramps circled, twisted. "Good-bye, kid," I said. "You're doing great, I'll see you soon." We halted at the curb. I got out of the car.

For the first time, the voice wavered. "Papa?"

I dropped my bags, got back in and held him. Steady, Michael. Think of the kid. He sobbed. I hung on. Don't, Michael, don't.

"You'll be all right, kid. We'll be all right." Meaningless words. I patted his back. He held me tight.

Steady.

Finally, he took a deep, deep breath. He seemed to smile.

I looked.

He was in fact smiling through the tears. He said, "The good thing is I get to see you more."

I managed a laugh and tousled his head. "It's been good for me, too. We have all learned something."

I did phone Véronique from the aiport.

"The situation is truly ridiculous," she said. "He will be home from the hospital early next week and then what will we do with the guards? Will they have to sleep here? Two of them? And another two downstairs with the concierge? How long do you expect us to live like this?"

"As long as there is danger and you keep him there."

"Explain this to my neighbors."

"I'm sure you can explain it to them."

Chapter 19

SHIMA SHOOK HIS HEAD. "She is being very foolish."

He was meeting me with reluctance late at night in the elegant lounge on the second floor of a London club, a place I had selected. It was a converted stately mansion. The ceilings were high, the oak woodwork rubbed to a deep polish. The furnishings were new and expensive Victorian fake. A lavishly appointed bar occupied one wall perpendicular to the draped windows. The six stools at the bar were empty. The two bartenders were busy mixing. Black-tied waiters with silver-plated trays shuttled to and from the adjacent ballroom, which had been converted to a roulette, craps and baccarat gaming room.

Beside the bar, the lounge had eight tables serviced by a ster-eotypical butler with a crafty long face. He looked like he had done it. Several times. Shima tasted his burgundy marc—and made a face.

I sipped my Boodles and said, "I agree."

He said, "Our people are there, as you know."

"I know."

"But they say they cannot protect him there. The apartment, the school, the daily life. Against an enemy who is clever."

"What else can I do? Kidnap the boy?"

"Frankly? We recommend it."

I shook my head. "I've thought of it. But no. Not yet."

"If we fail, you will not get your money's worth."

I shrugged.

He went on, "Twenty million dollars?"

"He's all I've got. I want you to do whatever you can to see he's protected."

"All right," he said.

"It's a deal. Let's do it."

"Mmm. Your friend is back in Europe."

I felt numb. "Where?"

"Yesterday, in Zurich."

"And today?"

"We don't know. All we have is an unconfirmed at the airport in Zurich."

"Could he have gone to Paris?"

"I don't know. It's possible."

"Can you flood the place for the next two weeks?"

He hesitated. Gestured. Unclear.

"I will transfer the funds tomorrow, okay?"

"Twenty million dollars?"

"Ten. That's all I have. As you know."

He said, "You have no respect for money, do you?"

"That's not true. I know how to spend it."

"And how is that?"

"I spend it on what is important to me."

"That's fine," he said, "and I respect it. But what about the other ten? Where am I going to get it?"

"I told you. I will show you how to make it."

He shook his head. "You said that you would make it for me using your trading system."

He was right. I had said it. I told him, "All right. I will."

His head was still shaking. "You promise but I am not convinced. Suppose you fail."

"I will not fail."

"How do I know that?"

"I never have," I said. "And you have ten million to prove it."

"Which you will immediately put back into the market at risk."

"No," I said. "I will provide the funds at risk. The ten is yours, you keep it."

"How did you make it? On one lucky trade? That's how it happens with speculators."

"You asked someone. A mathematician? An economist? Who? I am delighted. I have your interest."

He looked at me sharply. "It's gambling, isn't it? That's all it is."

"Yes, and no," I said. "It's gambling but that's not all it is. It is risk management. That's more of what it is."

"Risk management."

"Yes."

"And you bring me here, to a casino, to prove it?"

"Come." I stood.

He looked up at me. "Where?"

"Inside. I want to show you how I make it."

"I don't care how you make it."

"You will," I said. I stacked ten-pound chips in six piles of six. "What's your favorite number?" I said. "Pick a number between one and thirty-six. Or zero."

"Seventeen."

"Great." I picked up two piles of chips and put them in my pockets. I picked up two other piles in my hands. I gestured for him to pick up the other two piles.

"Ten million dollars?" he said.

"That's what we need."

"And you are going to convince me by playing roulette that you know how to make it? And that I should bet on you?"

"Gamblers have systems," I said. "Their systems work for them. They believe in them with passion. The gods of gaming want you to protect my son. And to understand what I do. What I believe I do."

"You make it sound like a religion."

"Not quite," I said. "Call it faith, not religion."

"*Faîtes vos jeux, faîtes vos jeux, faîtes vos jeux, rien ne va plus!*" intoned the croupier.

I put one ten-pound chip on number 17. The croupier spun the wheel and flicked the ball. I enjoyed the tension. The wheel slowed, the ball dropped, click click click click. Number 22. The rake slithered out over the felt and swept the losing chips from the table. "Now what?" he said. "It's thirty-six to one each time."

"No. Thirty-seven," I said. "Thirty-six numbers and a zero, don't forget. One in thirty-seven."

We played and lost. And played and lost again. Shima made a face. "How many times will you play? Thirty-six?"

I put a ten-pound chip on number 17. Shima was staring at the spinning wheel. The ball dropped, click click click, number 32. The croupier swept the table clean. "Cheer up," I said. "We've only lost three times."

Shima looked at me. "It's your thirty pounds."

I said, "Yes, but it's all yours if we win." That got his attention.

We lost three more times and returned to the bar. Shima ordered another marc. He said, "The wheel does not like you tonight."

"Good. You're learning. First principle, luck is streaky. If you take a perfectly balanced coin and keep flipping it one hundred times, you expect it to be heads about fifty times, and tails the very same fifty times, and you would think, if you graphed it, it would go up down, up, down." I traced the zigzag pattern in the air. "But that's wrong. That never happens. Instead, it goes like this." My finger sketched big zigzag streaks. "Sometimes when you stand at the tables, the night feels good, the room feels good, the money and chips are warm in your hand and you know you are going to win, and you do, and you keep winning."

"But?" Shima's voice was sardonic.

"Sometimes the room and the faces around the table are cold. You have that cold feeling in your stomach. When that happens, you pick up your chips and walk away."

The butler brought his drink. Shima took a sip. "And how can you be sure if you're hot or cold?"

"You define it mathematically," I said. "Six losses define a losing streak."

Shima was nursing his marc now. "Which is why we left the table. What if you had won?" he said. "How long would you have played?"

"The probable length of a winning streak is seventeen games," I told him. "Why? I can't tell you. I've put it on a computer and done simulations. You get occasional runs of seventeen, but almost never runs longer than that. So you don't play more than seventeen times."

"Do you always bet the same thing? Or do you increase your bets? Bet all you win?"

I said, "If you win, you want to win something meaningful, even if your luck should change. So you pyramid each win three to one. On the first win, you triple your bets and put the rest in your pocket, and even if you lose the next six bets, you still have eighteen in your pocket."

"And if you win again?" he pressed. "You triple again?"

"Yes."

"Let's try again."

"We're cold tonight."

He pressed me, "Let's go back to the table."

We played and lost six more chips.

But Shima had the hunger. He insisted we try one more time. So we did.

"Faîtes vos jeux, faîtes vos jeux, faîtes vos jeux, rien ne va plus!" Shima was staring at the whirling ball, willing it to fall on number 17. The wheel slowed, the ball dropped, clicked, stopped on number 22. The croupier swept the table. I placed my chip. Shima put both palms on the table. The croupier chanted, spun the wheel, flipped the ball. Twenty seconds of tension, the ball dropped, clicking noises, and the number—5. Shima took a deep breath.

We played and lost, played and lost again and played and— number 17 came up.

There was an instant of shock and Shima shouted, "Damn! We won! We did it!"

People laughed. The croupier swept the table. He left my single chip on number 17 and counted off our winning chips from the bank stack. He pushed them forward with the rake. I took seventeen chips from the winnings and made one pile of two chips and five piles of three chips each. I gave the rest to Shima who stuffed them into his pockets. I put the two chips on top of my single chip on number 17. "Michael?" said Shima. "We have three hundred seventy pounds now, and even when you take your one hundred eighty pounds out—" All about us, people were placing bets.

The croupier picked up the ball. *"Faîtes vos jeux, faîtes vos jeux, faîtes vos jeux, rien ne va plus!"* I reached out to take my three chips back. Shima suddenly barked, "No!" I left the chips on the table. The croupier spun the wheel, flipped the ball. Click click click. The ball dropped on 12.

I placed my next three chips. Shima tensed. The croupier changed, the bets stopped, the wheel spun, the ball was flipped, around and around. It was going to fall. It fell. Clicking, clicking, clicking—number 7.

Shima grimaced. "My lucky number."

"Do you want to shift?"

"No. Go! Seventeen! Again!"

I bet my thirty pounds. Others bet with us. The croupier chanted, spun the wheel, flipped the ball. Round and round and round she goes and where she stops nobody knows. The ball dropped, click click click, teeter, click click—zero. A groan from those assembled. The rake snaked out from the croupier's hand, gathering lost chips from the table. Shima scowled. I gave him the remaining three piles of three. "Want to quit?" I asked.

Shima shook his head and placed three chips on number 17. The croupier chanted, spun the wheel and flipped the ball. Shima muttered in Hebrew. Ball, come on now. Drop for me. The wheel slowed, the ball dropped, the clicks, one two three four five—and the ball stopped on number 17.

Shima shrieked, "Damn, that's more than a thousand pounds!" He hugged me and whooped. A table of smiles. The croupier pushed the winnings over with the rake. Shima gathered them, counting, astonished at the total.

"Want to quit?" I said again. Shima was dividing the chips into piles, six piles of nine chips each. I stacked the remaining chips in front of me. He put the first pile of nine on number 17. I asked, "Do you mean to let the others ride?" Shima did not understand. I reached for the three chips from the prior winning spin of the wheel remaining on the table.

He said, "Oh. Those are ours, too?"

"You bet them, you didn't lose them."

"And we only want to bet nine, now. I get it. I guess I'm a little slow." He nodded at the chips in my hand. "Take them off the table."

"You can feel it when you're going to win, can't you?" Shima said. The wheel was spinning one way, the ball circling the other. Shima had lost once and replaced his ninety pounds.

I said, "Oh oh."

Click click click, the ball dropped on number 12. The croupier swept the table. Shima said, "Oh oh?" He put his ninety pounds on number 17. "Well?" All about us, people placed their chips.

"Faîtes vos jeux, faîtes vos jeux, faîtes vos jeux, rien ne va plus!" The croupier spun the wheel, and flicked the ball. The ball slowed.

"I'm going to win," said Shima. "Now. Now!" The ball dropped, click click click, into—number 17! Shima raised both fists into the air with a howl of triumph. He turned and pounded me on the back. "That's three thousand pounds!" he shouted. "We're hot! It's a winning streak! I told you!" The croupier swept the table and counted out Shima's winnings in the larger plaques. I divided the chips into six new piles. Shima was staring at the six new piles. "That's two hundred seventy pounds in each pile!"

I said, "Do you want to quit? How many spins of the wheel so far?"

"Twelve." He turned away from me. People were placing their bets now. Shima picked up his first pile. The croupier looked at Shima and reached for the wheel. He chanted, picked up the ball and spun the wheel. Shima said, desperately, "Have you proved whatever you want to prove?"

I said, "Twelve is not seventeen spins of the wheel."

"But it isn't their money, it's mine now!"

"Then quit," I said.

Across the table, the croupier spun the ball. Shima moved the pile of chips toward number 17—and then took them away and put them in front of him. No bet. The croupier laughed. Shima scowled. The wheel slowed, the ball dropped, and click-click-clicked, and stopped—on number 7. Shima took a deep breath. People laughed. Shima left the table.

The butler brought his marc and my Boodles. Shima took a belt of his marc and choked. "Risk management makes it exciting."

I said, "Yes."

"It doesn't feel senseless, like gambling should."

"No."

"And I learned something. I respect what you do." He laughed. "And I learned that I like to gamble."

"You like to win," I said. "You like it enough to put up with the gambling."

He said, "Let's review. In a way, it's simple. You look for a payoff of six to one. Or six tries at thirty-six to one. Pick a number and stay with it to the end. Lose six, you've defined a losing streak. You're cold. You quit. Off the table. Run. And seventeen bets and your streak is done. Manage the risk, lose a little or win a lot. If you win, you triple your bets. If you keep winning, you keep tripling. Those are the essentials."

"So now I know all about gambling." He grinned and tapped the table with his snifter. "All right. Teach me currencies."

"I have."

"You mean it's the same thing? You look for payoffs of six to one, and the rest?"

"In a way, it's cleaner," I said. "And easier, too."

"In what way?"

"For one thing, the vig is less."

"Vig?"

"The house cut. In roulette, on some European wheels, the house pays thirty-five to one, and takes half your bet on a zero. The vig, the house cut, is 1.4 percent. In the U.S., they take your entire bet on a zero or double zero. The house cut is 5.3 percent, or more if they pay less than thirty-five. The house commissions on currency trades are less, and even those are negotiable. A lot closer to zero."

He took another sip of his marc and this time he did not choke. "You said, 'and easier, too.' "

"The wheel is a random bet. Same with the crap table."

"You can manage the risk on craps, too?"

"Yes, same rules, six to one and all, but the throw of the dice is random, too. Currency moves are not random. You have economic data from all over the world."

"Balance of trade? Flow of funds?" He smiled. "Whatever that means."

"We call it the fundamentals. And there are programs for what the traders do. We try to call those in advance, too."

"So it's predictable."

"By some of us. Some of the time," I said.

"By you."

"I like to think so."

He studied me. "What did you mean when you said, 'Oh oh?' "

"Do you remember what I told you about sometimes you stand at the tables, the night feels good, the room feels good—"

"—and you know you are going to win, and you do? I felt it tonight. That's the streak feel."

"You felt more than that. When you know you're hot and you're going to win, and you feel you are making it happen—that your number will drop because you are willing it to drop, that it's magic and the force is yours—you're wrong. You have lost your judgment."

"I see." Shima cupped the snifter in both big hands and grinned. "Then I was right to leave the table!"

I said nothing.

"Risk management, huh?" he said.

"That's what I do."

He laughed. "I don't think so. That's what you tell yourself you do. In reality you love to gamble. You'd like to bet it all."

"Every time. But I don't."

"You'd bet your life if you could put it on the table."

I waited him out.

"Maybe I know you better than you know yourself," he said. "The question is, do I bet on you?"

I sat there.

Finally, he gestured, slightly smiled. "Go make my money. I'll help you."

Chapter 20

THE NEXT DAY I was in my office at 6:30 A.M. I ran the program on my Northgate 486-33.

I was proud of that program. I had developed it myself with some initial help from an expert in program trading, a statistician and a genius in APL, the computer language we found most efficacious for speedily manipulating masses of numbers—like the opening, high, low and closing prices over five years of gold, the Swiss franc, the Deutschemark and yen. That computer was my Tinkertoy, and tinker I did.

It was my Foucalts Pendulum for currency speculation.

We had asked a number of banks and traders we knew about the computer trading programs in most common use, and had studied them, looking for patterns, chewing through vast quantities of price data, number crunching on a grand scale. We had liked the sound of that, crunching. Such a healthy sound, like oat bran. At first, we had found nothing. Then we did. Armed with the first clues, we had ultimately found patterns in a number of different programs.

We had assembled our analysis of the patterns, weighting them in accordance with the frequency with which the patterns correlated with market action and our guesstimates as to the dollar volume with which each of the various underlying programs was being used by program traders throughout the world. The results were intricate so we translated them into graphs which were easy to use. Instantaneous recognition. Running the program on a 33 mhz 486 would take less than six minutes, plus another two for printing.

Our program would predict, one to three days in advance, what the underlying programs would tell their users—the commercial banks, individual traders and managers of funds—to do in gold and our three currencies, and would give me the equivalent of a weighted consensus each day. It was very short short-term trading. A long-term trade was three whole days, the maximum length of our prediction. Our short-term trading was in-blip-quit. But with program trading growing at an escalating rate, and even the biggest commercial banks, like Citibank, reporting huge quarterly currency speculation gains, I had figured that over a couple of years, the system's predictive accuracy might well increase. And what do you know?

It had happened.

The program told me which currencies would move up and down. The roulette rules told me how to bet. I simply moved them to the currency markets.

First, I looked for payoffs six times the risk.

Currencies were priced in units per dollar in Europe. For example, a Swiss franc price of 1.500 meant the dollar was worth one and a half Swiss francs, or one Swiss franc and fifty centimes. and 1.5001 meant one Swiss franc, fifty centimes and a "pip." The dollar risk and the average daily range determined the size of my contract bet. For example, if the average daily swing, top to bottom, for a month, was 120 pips, I would be prepared to risk 30 pips for each dollar of risk. I would buy or sell a 500,000 Swiss franc contract. If I lost, I would lose 500,000 Swiss francs multiplied by .003 and divided by 1.5, or $1,000.

My objective, of course, would be six times the risk, or 1.8 centimes, 180 pips, and I would not bet unless my system said that I had a good chance to make it. If I lost 30 pips, I would liquidate, quick. If I made 180, I would liquidate, quick, achieving my $6,000 objective.

European contracts were "spot," purchases of currency the same day, or "forward," purchases in the future, with the prices determined by the spot prices adjusted by the difference in the two currencies' rates of interest.

American contracts were called "futures." They were purchases in the future and they were all priced in dollars. For example, if the European Swiss franc price were 1.500, the spot price of the Swissie here would be $.6667. The last two digits were called "ticks." Since contract units were 125,000 Swiss francs, each tick was worth $12.50. If the average daily swing, top to bottom, were 80 ticks, I would be prepared to risk 20 ticks and I would buy or sell four contracts. My objective would be six times that, or 120 ticks, but if I lost, I would lose 20 ticks multiplied by $12.50 and multiplied by four, or $1,000.

I would close out my position if I made 120 or lost 20 ticks, and I would close out all but one of my positions at the end of each day. I refused to hold more than one position overnight. Prices could fluctuate wildly overnight and I was afraid of the Far East markets. So I seldom lost my full limit or made my full objective. Nevertheless, I won many more bets than I lost, while staying within my objectives and limits.

Out of every three bets, one would fail and I would win two. And I would make the amount of my loss limit twice as often as I lost it. That was an enormous advantage, unbelievable vig my way. So I had developed a strategy to parlay the wins. A money-management system. Manage the risk. Win a lot, lose a little. Translate roulette to the currency markets.

I did.

I had made the rules. I could define the terms. Monopoly where I could name the streets. "Game," "set" and "match"—I defined them.

Winning or losing the dollar risk defined one game.

A cumulative five games won or lost defined a set. If the chances of losing a game were 1 out of 3, the chances of losing a set were 1 in 81.

At that point, I had further extrapolated from my roulette rules: the probable maximum length of a winning streak was seventeen sets. Never in my numerous roulette wins—and I had been a gambler all my life—had a streak run more than seventeen spins of the wheel. If the same magic number was applicable to commodities—and why shouldn't it be? It might well be all bullshit anyhow—and there was only 1 chance in 81 of losing a set, there would be only seventeen times as much, or a 21 percent chance, of losing a match of seventeen sets.

There is no believer quite like the willing number-deluded. Since I would have no idea why it worked if it worked, I could be a mystic, deceiving myself into faith in the system. Furthermore, if it worked in accordance with the odds as I had calculated them, I could reasonably expect to win at the start and to keep on winning for a considerable time. The validity of the calculation, of course, would always depend on the system continuing to win two times out of three. I realized how chancy that had to be—but what the hell, I would go for it!

The win would be ridiculous.

I went back to work on the money-management rules. A match would be defined as over when seventeen sets were won, or any set was lost. When a match was over, I would take my money out, and take a vacation.

I could pretend it was all mathematics. Even the vacation. That pretense was another key element in the psychological trickery needed to control the tension I adored. I had convinced myself that tension made me sharp. Managed risk and limited tension nourished.

Back to the money-management rules again: If I was on a roll and winning set after set, I had to raise my bets progressively in a geometric escalation consistent with roulette. In the first set, I would bet it all. In the second set, I would bet it all again. If I was correct in my calculation of the odds, there was only a 2.5 percent chance of losing in the first or second set. In the third set, I would take three times the first set risk. In the fourth set, four, in the fifth set, five. Thereafter, over the next twelve sets, the risk would be 50 percent of the cumulative stake. When I figured the cumulative win after seventeen sets, I couldn't believe the computation.

The first time I had played, my initial match risk was $5,000, all I could afford. My initial game risks had been a fifth of that, each $1,000. I had won at first. In the third month of play, I had lost the first five games in the fifth set, a loss in the set of $25,000. Gloom. Game, set and match over, I had cashed out and, dispirited, I had counted up.

I was shocked. Even after the loss, I had still had $30,000.

A month later, I had returned to the fray, and decided on a total $10,000 stake. I had won six units, I would risk two.

Later, I would wish I had bet it all. Or at least tripled to three units.

When it was over, and I didn't even go the full seventeen-set route, I had $4 million and a tax bill, and the knowledge that I would never have to work again.

That was the first of my three big wins. I had played the system eight times in all and I had not won the same way every time. Once I had bombed out on opening day. Twice I had lost in the early rounds. I had been appalled at the size of the last round losses, enormous amounts of money which had brought me down to a third of what I would have had if I had won.

But I had still had huge net winnings.

The system had its own rhythm and it mocked the normal words of caution. "When the horses aren't running, don't bet," that is, do not play choppy markets where there is no trend. That was a well-accepted aphorism. My system seemed to laugh at that; it consistently made money when there were no trends. "He who fishes for a bottom comes up with mud"—do not bet against a trend where there is one. But my system consistently called major market turns, both the tops and bottoms. Yet some days for no apparent reason, with all the signals clear as a bell, it would lose a major fortune.

I had made the bulk of the money in the three big wins, without ever risking much of an original stake, and in less than two years I had made $10 million in after-tax net.

Incredible.

I had truly beaten the system. Or rather, my system had beaten the system.

And now I had given it all away, the entire $10 million.

Hell, I had done even more than that. I had pledged to double the first ten mil. I was giving the fruits of my system to Israel.

Talk about anonymous giving!

Okay. It was a clear, cold and cloudless day. The program finished printing. I phoned Zurich for Hong Kong and Tokyo, the morning gold fix in London and the day-to-date ranges in the currencies I was about to start trading. I noted them at the top of the printout and hung up. I was alone and in my element on the twenty-seventh floor of my building. I felt good. What did the computer say? Buy gold. Oh, no! Gold had been weak three days in a row and the morning fix was down $2 an ounce. Was it appropriate to start contrarian on opening day? It would be humiliating to start with a big loss. Come on, Michael, go for it. Don't second-guess the program.

I had $100,000 to play with. Yes, I had a little more than the $10 million I had given away, but the $100,000 was a good chunk of my mad money. All right, $100,000 to play with meant that $20,000 was the game risk. Today we play gold. The average thirty-day range was $4.20. Divide $20,000 by $4.20 and the quotient by 100 ounces, and that meant forty-eight contracts on the Comex. All right, buy them.

What next? The computer said bonds, sell. They had been coming down, fast, for the last three weeks. The computer said hit them. Let's see, were the two plays consistent? Buying gold in the face of rising interest rates? If bonds were down, interest up and the dollar strong, gold could well move down. Damn. But maybe the markets were saying no, bonds down and interest up in the face of economic recovery meant a big new push at the wrong time and inflation resuming. That would be consistent with a gold buy. I had to laugh. You could rationalize anything. Mine was not to reason why. Stop thinking and start trading. Twenty-thousand dollars divided by the 34-tick-range game risk divided by $31.25 a tick was an even twenty contracts. Sell at the Chicago open.

Well? The currencies were all running soft. Should I take a third position? What the hell. Ask the computer, the currencies were dropping. But the computer said no, don't sell. Leave the currencies alone. I was disappointed. I loved to sell the currencies short when I could. Buying the dollar felt patriotic.

So, two phone calls now and I would be done for the day.

"Welcome home, sir!" David exclaimed.

I gave him the orders and the tick range on which I would want executions. We had never met but I liked the voice, the executions were selectively expert, particularly in nursing the biggest winning trades, and the house was one of the very few solid surviving old ones. They could trade in the forward markets, too.

"No stops, just executions?" David said.

"If you were trading in this sort of volume, would you put in stops?"

"That depends."

"On what?"

"Who else is in and what's going on."

"My trades first?" I said.

"Of course. Every customer's trades come first."

"Would you buy a used car from you?"

"Sir?"

"You don't remember that one?"

He said, "No, sir."

"How old are you, David?" I asked.

"Twenty-two."

"Did you ever hear of Richard Nixon?"

David called me at eleven o'clock. Gold was down from the opening by nearly $3.

"So?" I said.

"I thought maybe, first trade and all, you might want to cut your loss—"

I said, "David, have I ever cut a loss?"

"No, sir, sorry to bother you, please let it go, forget it—"

"You were right, sir!" David trilled.

"Which?" I said.

"Both," he said. "The bonds have been soggy most of the day, they're down twenty-seven ticks, right at the low now, and gold, that's what's remarkable. It's come back, up $1.20 on the day. And now?" I consulted my watch. He went on, "One position only the overnight rule?"

"Yes."

"Hold the bonds, sell the gold?" he said.

"No."

"Most people let their most profitable trades run."

"I'm in the business to take profits and run," I said.

"Buy the bonds back?"

"At the close, David, please. Only at the close."

I hung up knowing David would fight to catch the low.

I knew I had done well when David did not call.

At four P.M., I phoned him. "Well?"

He said, "They were twenty-six ticks down at the close. I didn't like it so I hit the aftermarket. I got out down two. Twenty-eight ticks, no extra commission."

I ran the calculation on my computer and let the kid swing in the breeze. "That's $31.25 times twenty-eight ticks times one hundred contracts, less $22 a contract for commission and fees, is $17,060 right?"

"Yes, sir," he said.

"And what was the low?"

"To date, sir, two ticks down."

"Good boy. We caught the low. And gold?"

"Still $1.20 up for the day in the aftermarket, too," he said.

"David?"

"Sir?"

"That's good work. And thanks."

"Thank you, sir. Thank you very much."

I hung up, knowing full well that David had matched my bond trades for his own account and was probably long gold overnight, too.

There was joy in Mudville. A war risk!

Iran threatened Iraq again early the following morning. Gold opened $12.40 higher and ran. The only thing better would have been another Russian revolution! David gleefully followed the price with trailing stops and sold for a $16.50 gain. Gold fell back and closed $12 up for the day. Meanwhile, the computer said to short the currencies, they had all weakened severely following the new outbreak of German terrorism, so I sold the Swiss franc, the Deutschemark and the yen at the opening. Iran explained its position—and the currencies moved down steadily all day long. I took my $20,000 profits in the Swissie and the Deutschemark and held the yen short overnight.

As for the gold, the $13.60 gain multiplied by the ounces was $64,224, which moved the total profits for the two days well over $100,000 and there was only the overnight yen position to worry about.

The next morning, the computer said stand aside and I did. In fact, gold was sharply lower that day, and the yen opened higher and was closed out at a loss, but the net win was over $100,000 anyhow.

The match was in the second set and the next bets were doubled.

I would win or lose $40,000.

Chapter 21

DIEGO SLOUCHED IN HIS SEAT.

The Peugeot upholstery was uncomfortable. He had been here for most of the past two days.

Except for the move from the hospital home, Hugo never left the apartment. He was guarded around the clock. There were four six-hour shifts every day, two in the apartment upstairs, one always with the concierge, one out front in a car parked on the street.

There seemed to be others circling, in cars, and still others in the cafe down the block. Not French.

Diego would wait. They could not keep this up. Too expensive. And sooner or later, the boy would go to school. They could not tutor him at home indefinitely.

Diego would try again some other day.

He smiled his nervous smile. The American had received the package in the mail and was worried about little Hugo. Which was fine.

Meanwhile, Diego had plenty to do.

It would be his first for-hire mission for someone else. That thought intrigued Diego.

Chapter 22

THERE WERE THREE Shima matches in all. I started with a grub
stake of $100,000 each time. I considered parlaying the winnings
and taking higher risks but after each match, the winnings were
not my money anymore. It was bad enough that during the
matches I was gambling with funds that belonged to the State of
Israel.

In the first match, we went slowly. We won steadily, eight sets,
and then lost spectacularly in the ninth set. I never broke the
trading rules, with one exception. In the fourth set.

I was massively long all the currencies the day of a one-of-the-
biggest-ever dollar collapses. I put in trailing stops to protect the
win but the currencies kept running. Particularly the Deutschemark. It ran and ran, much, much farther than it normally would.
I was so outrageously ahead at the end of the day that for once I
held everything overnight. It was not really a violation, I told
myself, because I stayed awake and followed the markets around
the world and finally closed the positions out in London the next
morning. When I added it all up, I had $1,700,000, more than I
would have if I won the fifth set. Was I going into the fifth set or
the sixth set?

I decided I was going into the sixth set, took my $1,700,000 and
went back to the tables again. And phoned Geneva to ask my
questions again: Had there been many sales of banks? Or bank
control? In Switzerland, Germany, England, France, in recent
months? The markets were continuing to behave so peculiarly.

This time they did have something. But not much. A few small
banks had been sold, they said, but they still thought the whole
thing fanciful. The currency markets were so huge nowadays that
no one could control them. Not the Fed, not the central banks,
maybe not even the Japanese! I realized that that was the Swiss
idea of a joke and I laughed.

Presently, I found myself in the ninth set with $5,400,000 in my
pocket and half of it at risk. I was restless. I need to travel a bit.

Too much nose to the grindstone. I would lighten up, make only one play at a time. I would try to see Sarah in New York. And I would go to Paris and see Hugo again. I was phoning him regularly twice a week.

I certainly did miss him.

Chapter 23

"HE ASKED WHAT?" The old man was shouting into the phone.

Werner hunched over the desk telephone. "I read from my notes. Quote, 'Have there been many sales of banks? Or bank control? Here, Germany, England, France. In recent months?' Unquote. And when Herr Barisch asked him why, he said, quote, 'One of our clients, an American, who trades currencies extensively, feels that the markets have been behaving peculiarly.'"

"*Scheiss!*" said the old man. "Shit! And this is the same Geneva bank who asked our bank in Basel?"

"A month ago," Werner said.

"Didn't I tell you—"

"Yes, sir, you did. And I did twice. In New York, in the park, but he attacked that man, you remember, the Negro executive, and our people said he was a crazy man, they did not know what to do when he did. And in the capital, in the parking lot—"

"I remember. The Cubans," muttered the old man.

"It should have worked," Werner said. "But he had a gun. I might have anticipated that he would. Perhaps I was careless."

"Not careless. Wrong. Do you know what worries me?"

"Sir, there is no way to trace it back to us."

"But he keeps going to the District of Columbia."

"Yes."

"Where my foolish, trusting friends are."

"You mean the government persons?"

"Werner, this is an open line."

"Sir, you think he might speak to them? He has no such connection."

The old man said, "I cannot take the chance, Werner. It is too bad, the man is very smart. You should see his trading record. We might have become associated. Under different circumstances. Even now, perhaps. But not with what I have in mind. No, he is American. Unfortunately."

Werner said, "And Jewish."

The old man said a surprising thing. "Perhaps that is the source of the genius."

"Sir?"

"Werner, I want someone new for this. Someone with talent who will do what he is told. Someone who is ambitious and likes this work."

"Fine. Someone with a motive, in addition?"

"Yes." The old man was intrigued by a thought. "Someone who will do a series of these things just for me. Someone—someone special."

Chapter 24

HELMUTH LEFT the East Palace partway through the meal at 11:10 P.M., pleading indisposition. Abdul the Camel Driver drove the white Cadillac Fleetwood hard, arriving at Helmuth's gate at 11:35 P.M. "Stop," said Helmuth, consulting his watch. The Camel Driver stopped outside the gate. "I'm feeling somewhat better," Helmuth said. "I can drive myself. We'll drop you off here. Good night."

"But Excellency—" said the Camel Driver.

"I've got to see a man about a falcon."

"Sir, I can drive you and wait—"

"No, you cannot. Out, please. I'll be back by dawn. Have my coffee ready at eight A.M." Helmuth smirked and adjusted his tie.

"Ah," said the Camel Driver, understanding. It had something to do with a woman.

It did not.

Helmuth drove directly to the Abu Dhabi airport. He left the Cadillac in "Live Parking," crossed the ramp swiftly, trying not to run, pushed his way through the air-conditioned terminal doors. He arrived at the Swissair counter precisely at midnight. Flight 375 for Zurich left at 12:05 A.M. He had no baggage, no reservation and no passport. The last had been picked up by the police three weeks previously, early in the problem. Helmuth presented the special platinum American Express Card and the special Swiss Travel Club Card with the emergency name prudently provided by the prudent head of security of the third largest and most prudent Zurich bank to its prudent head of private banking in the Emirates. The two male clerks duly noted them. Eyes flickered, buttons were pushed and they led him behind the counter, through the office doors, through a first set of offices, down a labyrinthine path through corridors, through another set of offices and out a door onto a remote corridor past customs and passport control and next to the gate. It was 12:04 A.M. The gate had closed. They reopened it. He entered the plane as the cabin door was closing, squeezing under the partially lowered door, went forward and settled into Seat 1-2. The First Class cabin was two-thirds full but he recognized no one.

The DC-10's doors thumped closed. The engines immediately started. A moment later, the big plane rumbled from the gate. Helmuth closed his eyes and started counting. This was it. Let my people go. Let me go, Emir. He felt a stir. The plane was rolling. It gathered speed, thrust. He counted, thirty-two seconds, thirty-three, thirty-four. Up. Up. Up! Takeoff!

He had won the first round.

The flight from Abu Dhabi to Riyadh took twenty-five minutes. The flight was uneventful, the landing smooth. They rolled to a stop at the gate at 12:35 A.M.

Round Two had started.

The plane door growled and thumped up and open. Helmuth

heard voices, Passenger Service from the sound of them. A dozen passengers disembarked. There was a pause. No one boarded. Helmuth pretended to doze. There was nothing he could do. He was helpless. He was traveling under a false name, without a passport, ticket or papers. The old devil could have called ahead. He could be arrested. The Saudis would honor a request. Eyes closed, he listened.

There were no untoward noises. Nothing.

The new passengers boarded at 1:20 A.M. First Class was largely full now but there were still a couple of empty seats, including Seat 1-1 beside him. Helmuth found that comforting. He did not want conversation.

The call came for the flight attendants to prepare for departure in Arabic first, then in French, then in English, then in German. The chief attendant's accent was German. A moment later, the door growled and thumped—and then came startled voices. They calmed. Quiet laughter. Helmuth's mouth was dry. He would say nothing, try to send a message if he could, if they would permit him. Here they were. He heard the voices from afar. A hand on his shoulder.

Helmuth opened his eyes. It was the hostess. Behind her were the men in uniform—but they were the male cabin attendants. Helmuth slowly focused. A new passenger had boarded, holding Seat 1-1. Helmuth sleepily but graciously rose to his feet.

It was a woman in a chador. She moved past him, excused herself in Arabic, a murmur. Black flashing eyes. Slender. Sandaled feet, a tiny straw carryall, a faint scent of jasmine. She settled into her seat. Helmuth resettled into his. The plane was taxiing. He was going to be all right. He was going to make it. Round Two, near the bell, and he was still on his feet. At the head of the runway, the jet turned and paused. Go. Go. Please. Now. Go. Helmuth closed his eyes again for luck, holding the Perrier in its plastic glass. This was it. He felt the stir and opened his eyes as they rolled. They gathered speed. Thirty-three seconds, thirty-four seconds, thirty-five seconds, enough for the thrust. Thrust! Up! Take-off!

Helmuth felt himself sighing.

The hostess offered the passengers champagne a few minutes later and Helmuth downed his at once. The hostess smiled and refilled his glass.

Helmuth felt the desire to explain his life to some other person—no drinking, no women for months at a time, not a moment of safety in the Emirates, not for an executive in private banking—when he realized that was no longer what he was. He would never return.

What had he abandoned? Clothes? Books? He would have a new life, without the fear of sudden death at the hands of the old fanatic. There must be something he would miss. His sterling silver cufflinks from London? His new cravats from Paris? Perhaps he would miss the tension.

Beside him, black flashing eyes stirred slightly in her sleep and turned toward him. Her scent was delicious. The long legs were tucked under a delicate haunch.

Helmuth hungered for them.

Two more glasses of champagne later, he fell asleep, somewhere over Ankara.

He awoke with a light hand on his knee and an erection. He blushed. Black flashing eyes was standing, holding the carryall. *"S'il vous plaît, monsieur?"* She wished to pass. Should he stand? He could not, not without—he blushed again, think of something else, discipline! Carefully, he tucked his knees up toward him. She moved past, lithe legs, slender hips, tall for an Arab. And amused, he thought. In the black eyes, he read something. Was he imagining it? She moved off.

He slept again.

He awoke with the slightest pressure against his shins and looked up, startled. She had changed into a designer original, Lebanese from the look of it, stunning; cobalt blue silk, clinging close, the nipples a faint suggestion. She wore a single strand of pearls around her neck, a single pearl in a gold setting in each ear, a pearl ring on her left middle finger, and she was young, twenty-five at the most, coal black hair cut pert, short and gleaming. She was lovely, she was delicate, and he had been right when he read amusement in the eyes.

Helmuth scrambled to his feet with an apology and she slipped past, her thighs brushing him. She moved lightly, holding the carryall and an airline pillow and off-white blanket. She bent slightly to put the carryall down, the cloth arcing over a graceful back down to a tiny rump and Helmuth felt the rush again. She seated herself, adjusting the pillow, smiled up at him, tucked the blanket around her head and disappeared into it.

Helmuth seated himself. He was unable to fall asleep again. It was, of course, the tension.

At five A.M. the hostess appeared with the cart and an elaborate breakfast. "Is Madame asleep?"

Helmuth said, "I think she is."

"Would she care for breakfast?"

"I don't know. Perhaps you should come back later? Perhaps in a few moments? I wouldn't be fair to wake her—"

But the voices had wakened her. She blinked, emerging from the blanket with a smile. "Monsieur is very courteous and Ileana thanks him."

They had coffee and rolls together and refused the rest of the breakfast. Ileana retrieved a small purse from the carryall, extricated an American product he had never seen before, a Johnson & Johnson baby washcloth, from a silvery foil packet, lightly dabbed her face and reapplied lipstick and no other makeup. Helmuth was enchanted.

She was Romanian and visiting an uncle and aunt. She would be staying in Zurich for the next few days at the refurbished Hotel Ascot. Helmuth told her about the hotel's wonderful restaurant.

The flight arrived in Zurich on the dot at 6:20 A.M. Two faceless young men from bank security were waiting with a limousine, having expertly covered in advance the missing passport problem. They dropped Ileana at her hotel and took Helmuth to the office, where Herr Barisch assured Helmuth it was not his fault, the full explanation was in his record, the customer was a lunatic who would pay in the Swiss manner for the trouble he had caused. The bank was about to bill him. Helmuth should pick up his mail and take a few days off, perhaps spring skiing, there was still good snow in Zermatt, or he should go to the Riviera, or wherever he wished. These things were best forgotten.

Helmuth took his mail home to his apartment. It was spotless, as usual, with its closed, musty smell. Helmuth opened all eight of the windows. It was chilly, fifteen degrees centigrade, that early in the morning. Helmuth sat in his chair and thought about what to do. All he could think of was the woman. He closed the windows, showered and changed his clothes.

The limousine had waited.

Helmuth took her to "brunch"—he liked the word, she had not heard it before, one of his few Americanisms—at noon at the Ascot. The restaurant was still one of the city's best and they remembered Helmuth, which flattered him. He sat at his favorite quiet table in back and nursed a Campari and soda until she appeared in a canary yellow replica of the cobalt blue dress, both of which he complimented.

She thanked him and ordered Campari and soda, too. She was comfortable and they chattered. She was so young. And exotic, too. She had been born in Ploesti, had spent most of her life in Bucharest. She was a graduate student at the university there, working on her doctorate in the classical literature of England. He loved the way she pronounced "England." It was the way she used her tongue and teeth. She had changed the color of her lipstick. Her father was in the consular corps and stationed in the Emirates. Her mother and brother lived with him. She tried to visit four times a year but it was so expensive, wasn't it? And such a difficult place for a woman. And why was he in Abu Dhabi?

He explained that he was a banker and she seemed disappointed. He asked her if she was.

"I expected something, I don't know, romantic," she said with a little grin.

"Why?" he asked.

"Older man, younger woman." He smiled. She wiped the smile

away quickly. "And then there was your fear," she said. "What should a banker have to fear?"

"How could you tell?"

"I don't know. I have a sense for men. I thought you were running. Were you running?"

"Yes, from one of the emirs," he said. He excused himself. Outside the hotel, he dismissed the limousine. He had decided he would tell her everything. He so needed to tell someone who was uninvolved, contact with a normal person.

She listened, captivated, through onion soup, a mushroom omelette, veal piccata and the salad. The white Dole was crisp. She had two glasses and he had four.

Helmuth had been in the Emirates for thirty-seven months and nine days, a shade more than three terrible years, and he had enjoyed much of the work, notwithstanding his life's strange rigors.

"No alcohol, women, gambling?" she said.

"Not safe. Not for a banker. Not for a moment."

"Not once?"

"Not there. Never."

"But?"

"In Europe," he said. "Four times a year. A week each time."

"An orgy?"

He said, "Nobody is perfect."

"But the good ones like you keep trying. And it worked? The bank prospered?"

"The most profitable profit center we have. After all, we bank some of the most wealthy sheiks and several of the emirs."

"Including this one? And you handled him?"

"I dealt with him. No one will ever control him."

"And you had to flee?"

"Yes."

"Tell me why?"

He looked at her searchingly and said, "I will, but you must promise me you will never tell anyone."

She put her hand on his and he shivered. She smiled. "I promise."

He told her what happened.

"You have 11,800,000,000 Swiss francs," he had told the old pirate in the huge tent, which he considered an affectation.

"Yes, but how do I know?" the Emir had said.

Helmuth had laughed and then realized from the stony look that the old man was serious. This was suddenly a big problem. "From the statements here—" Helmuth had tried to insist.

"They can be falsified."

"But they are on the bank's letterhead!"

"Banks are not immune to temptation."

Helmuth had then said carefully, "What is it that you wish, sir?"

"To count it."

"All eleven billion."

"Closer to twelve."

"How? How do you wish to count it?"

"Here," said the Emir. "In cash. In my tent. I will myself do the counting."

Helmuth had nodded. "We can arrange it."

"Do."

Helmuth had nodded again. "Sir, to liquidate an account that size will take days—"

"How many?"

"Two weeks."

"Take a month."

"There will be costs," Helmuth had said. "Brokerage, bank charges. Other things. And some of the positions are very large. The sales may disturb the markets."

The hawklike face had appraised his. "How much cost? As a percentage?"

Helmuth had gulped and calculated. "Five, maybe six percent?"

The Emir had slowly nodded. "It is worth it to be certain. And the cost, of course, you will guarantee. Five percent."

"May I phone my Zurich office?"

"No. I asked for a man to be the bank, here, not in Zurich. You are that man. You guarantee. You said five percent."

"Yes, sir. All right, I will do it."

The Emir seemed pleased. "And in an effort to keep the costs down, you may arrange with the bank and the brokers not to charge again when I buy thing back."

Helmuth had blanched. "Sir, I do not know that I can do that."

"Then I might not buy the same things back. I may not redeposit with the bank."

"That would be your privilege, sir. And sir, if you do buy back—"

"Yes?"

"It would again disturb the markets. We might have to buy at higher prices."

"Then again I might not do it."

"Yes, sir."

"Go. And you be here for the counting."

Helmuth had phoned Herr Barisch in Zurich and tried to explain. It was difficult. Herr Barisch had laughed the first time Helmuth had said it. Then he had understood and screamed. Was Helmuth serious? Helmuth was. Herr Barisch, stunned, had not approved the guarantee, he would speak to the bank's directors. Helmuth had booked himself out on the next day's flight to Zurich to supervise the liquidation. Forty minutes after his secretary had called Swissair, the police had arrived and picked up his passport.

Ileana was stunned. "So quickly?"

"Just like that. He had someone in my organization."

"Your secretary?"

"Someone."

The bank had liquidated expertly, assisted by rising prices in world markets. The net cost was a hair under 4 percent from the total on the Emir's statements. Relieved, Helmuth had had the cash flown in, in 10,000 Swiss franc notes. He had phoned ahead to the Emir's assistant and suggested that they bring their own expert in, anyone they chose, anywhere, to verify the currency. Helmuth need not approve him.

The currency arrived in steamer trunks. Helmuth met the plane with two assistants, two armored cars and a police escort provided by the government. They whisked everything into the desert, down the long, empty roads to the desert tent. There they waited for two full days, all of them, bankers, armored cars, drivers, police, sending for meals and snatching sleep where they could, in the cars, on the ground, in the flanking tents.

The Emir appeared at sunrise on the third day. They brought the trunks into the big tent. The Emir sat in the elevated chair on the slightly raised platform and they opened the trunks in his presence. The Emir sat there, silently, and gestured, once.

Helmuth and Weiscz, one of his executive aides, a frightened young Swiss a year out of business school, arranged the notes in pile after pile. Finally, it was all there, nearly 11,400,000,000 Swiss francs in notes of 10,000 Swiss francs. It did not take up all that much room. It was impressive but not that impressive: 1,140,000 bank notes in piles of 100, 11,400 piles, each bound in two rubber bands, 100 rows of 114 piles. Helmuth and Weiscz stepped back.

The Emir sat there motionless, minute after minute. Helmuth was exhausted. Finally, he could stand it no more. "Sir?" he said, looking about. "Your expert?"

The Emir gestured. "You would not cheat me. I do not need one." Helmuth would later learn that the Emir's assistant had made numerous calls but somewhere between the questions asked by the experts as to the extent of the verification wished—occasional notes selected at random? Laboratory testing of every single one?—and the fees quoted, a million Swiss francs and up, the Emir had lost interest.

Meanwhile, they sat there and waited. Nothing. "Don't you wish to count, sir?" said Helmuth.

The Emir nodded. He did. He slowly lumbered forward and sank to his knees. His courtiers rushed to him with cushions, rugs. The Emir adjusted himself comfortably and reached out for the nearest pile. It toppled, taking with it several other piles. The Emir laughed. Everyone present, other than the Swiss, laughed. They did not find money amusing. The Emir scowled at Helmuth, who forced a smile. The Emir pointed. Helmuth retrieved the pile, gathered it, neatened it and handed it to the Emir. The Emir produced a knife and slit the rubber band. It skittered across the room and the Emir laughed. His people laughed. The Emir looked at Helmuth, who obediently smiled. The Emir cut the second rubber band. Again, the skitter, the laughs, the look at Helmuth, the smile.

The Emir counted.

He took his time, three full minutes. There were exactly one hundred notes in the pile. The Emir took a deep breath. All the others present took deep breaths. The Emir resumed counting— the same pile again!

Again, he took three full minutes, and again they all waited, but this time, he lost count partway through. He scowled. No one moved a muscle. The Emir resumed counting the same pile a third time.

Three minutes later, he finished. Again, he took a deep breath. All the others present took deep breaths. The Emir smiled. All the others smiled. The Emir said to Helmuth, "I was right. You can be trusted."

"Sir." Helmuth waited. The Emir sat there. Helmuth said, "Thank you, sir." The Emir gestured dismissal. Helmuth gaped. "I may go?"

"Yes."

"That's it?"

"Yes."

"Sir." Helmuth turned with his people and walked to the door.

"One moment."

Helmuth froze at the Emir's voice. He slowly turned. He said, "Sir?"

"Take it. Back to Zurich. And reinvest it again."

Helmuth focused again. "Sir? Invest it in what?"

"Oh, the same sort of thing."

"But sir, we did well because the market is strong and then we were a seller, and now the market is still strong but we will be a buyer—"

"I was right. You can be trusted."

Helmuth said, "Yes, sir. Thank you, sir."

"The same investments."

"Helmuth, do you know what the loss will be?" Herr Barisch's voice on the telephone was strained.

Helmuth said, "Sir, I told him the market was rising."

"Helmuth," said Herr Barisch, "did you guarantee?"

"Not the repurchase, sir."

"Are you sure?"

"Yes, sir. I am very sure."

"Will he say you guaranteed it?"

"He may," said Helmuth. "His last words were 'the same thing.' He knew what he was saying."

"Oh, my God," said Herr Barisch.

"I'd say that about sums it up," Helmuth said. "And remember, he has my passport."

"Yes. We will have to do something."

The markets had continued strong and the repurchases pushed them up further. The bank had delayed, waited, parceled orders out to several houses a bit at a time, but still the prices had edged up and up.

Trying to hold the line was hopeless. In addition to the 472 million Swiss franc liquidation cost, the net loss on the repurchases, after outside commissions but nothing for the bank, had been slightly over 800 million Swiss francs. The total cost of the exercise, without any repurchase charge by the bank, was therefore 1,272,000,000 Swiss francs, or 10.78 percent of the original 11.8 billion Swiss francs. It had not been completed by the end of the month, and when the Emir's assistant had phoned to ask, Helmuth told him that. The Emir's assistant had hesitated.

"What's the matter?" Helmuth had said.

The Emir's assistant had croaked, "We have your passport."

"I know you do."

"I know you are trying to do your best and I do appreciate it."

"I know you do, but does the Emir?" Helmuth said.

"I have told him."

"I see." Helmuth sighed.

"He has less appreciation."

One week later, the Emir's assistant had phoned again with the summons to the palace dinner. Helmuth had of course accepted. "And the repurchase?" the Emir's assistant had said.

"Completed," Helmuth had said.

"The statements? You will please bring them?"

"I can't," Helmuth said. "We made purchases in seven different

currencies, in sixteen different markets. Each with different brokerage houses and management fees and they all have to be converted to Swiss. And we have credited back to the accounts all of
our normal commissions. I will need another three days. Maybe
four. Would you like to postpone the dinner?"

"No!" the Emir's assistant had said. "He is pushing me."

Helmuth had said, "I will hope to see you at the dinner."

"Yes. You should know that he has telephoned Herr Waffen."

"Beg pardon?"

"Who owns the bank. He told me to tell you that."

Helmuth had been confused. "I regret but I do not know that
name."

"I see. That is a puzzle perhaps. Please try to bring some of the
statements."

Helmuth had raised the matter once more but Herr Barisch had
been adamant. "Give him nothing until we finish the statements."

"Yes. Do we have a Herr Waffen in the bank?" Helmuth had
said.

There had been a pause. "Not that I am aware of."

"Perhaps a director or something."

"No."

"He has phoned Herr Waffen," Helmuth had said, "according
to his assistant. He told the man to tell me that."

There had been another pause. "And what did you say when he
did?" Herr Barisch had said.

"I regretted that I did not know that name."

Herr Barisch had said thoughtfully, "I see."

"Was that the correct thing to say?" Helmuth had said.

"I assume so. I do not know him."

The actual dinner had been calm enough. The Emir had de-
voured five kinds of lamb, each one of his favorites. Helmuth had
been unable to eat. "Pressure, my boy?" the Emir had jibed.

"I hope you will be pleased, sir," Helmuth had said.

"But it has all been completed."

"Yes."

The Emir had nodded. "The cost selling out was only four percent and you guaranteed five and did better than that. This time the cost will be less, of course, because the commissions will not have to be the same because I sold and bought back the same thing, which should be one, not two charges, and the bank will waive commissions. And I know you are to be trusted and you understand my position."

"Yes, sir. Thank you, I appreciate your trust and understanding."

"No. You have reversed it. I have the trust. You have the understanding!" The Emir had laughed.

"Yes, sir."

"All the same," said the Emir, "when the statement is here, we will all feel better. Certainly you and me."

"Yes, sir."

The Emir had laughed uproariously. "I know you will feel better, eh?"

Helmuth had left the dinner shortly thereafter and phoned Herr Barisch at home.

Ileana licked her lips. "What a story!"

"Yes."

"You are very brave."

"I had no choice," Helmuth said.

"And the statement from the bank is where?" Ileana said.

"Delivered today to the Emir."

She laughed. "Even I am glad to be here not there."

"Where we cannot hear the thunder." Helmuth smiled.

"You are a good man," Ileana said.

Helmuth said, "And you are a good listener. Would you like some dessert?"

"Do you know what I would like?" She smiled at him. Helmuth shook his head.

"It makes me excited, the danger," she said. Helmuth could not believe where this seemed to be heading. She went on, "And you have not been with a woman for twelve weeks?"

"Eleven weeks and five days," Helmuth said.

"That is a long period of sexual inaction," she said.

"Even for a Swiss," he said.

Ileana smiled and lightly touched his hand. "The abstention is also exciting. Order me raspberries and espresso, darling?"

Helmuth did not know what the raspberries and espresso had to do with her excitement or their plans or anything else, but he ordered them for her. He ordered an espresso for himself, too. It was the jolt he needed. And presently they were in her room upstairs, and she was removing his tie, then his suit jacket. She kissed him lightly on the lips and withdrew when he attempted to clutch her. She disappeared into the bathroom. He went to the window and looked down at the street. Zurich in March had never seemed lovelier.

When she emerged from the bathroom, she was naked. Helmuth nearly went mad with desire at the sight of her. Her skin was pale, almost luminous, and her figure, to his taste, was perfect, her breasts large, some would say excessive, but as high and firm as any he had seen, the aureoles small, the nipples stiffened. He wondered if she had used cold water on them. He took her gently by the arms and kissed her.

It was slow and exquisite and unbelievably, ecstatically erotic. He told her he would do as she wished, over and over as she wished. He had no wishes at all of his own, except to be passive. She smiled as if it was expected. He lost track of the number of times he came. He lost control of his own noises. It went on for hours and hours. He was only dimly aware of what was happening and knew he would never be able to describe it. He knew there would never be anything like it again. Late in the afternoon, he dozed, but only for a few minutes. She disappeared into the shower. Immediately, he missed her. She laughed at the look on his face when she returned. "Well?" he said, defensively.

"I'm trying to decide if you would be comfortable. I want you to be comfortable." She kissed him. "You might think it a bit exotic."

"What?" he said.

"Have you ever tried a little bondage?"

That shook him. He said, "You mean you want me to tie you up?"

She laughed. "You have it backwards." She stooped and reached into the satchel and he shivered at the sight of her slender buttocks. She returned with a filmy nightdress and two pairs of handcuffs. He stared at the handcuffs. She said, "Would you like to try it? We'll quit if you get nervous."

He said, "I don't quite understand it."

"It has to do with being passive and putting yourself into the power of someone else. Into the hands of someone else."

"Your hands are delicious."

She held out the cuffs. With an effort, and very slowly, he held out his hands. She cuffed his wrists to the brass rails at the side of the bed. They made love again. Or rather, she did, to him. She caressed him with her hands and mouth and slowly guided him into her, crouching over him, holding his face in her hands, kissing him, riding astride him, slower, and slower, until he started to scream, at the first sign of which she slowed still further, and he drifted into the haze of the exquisite, the peak of imagined pleasure. He screamed at the release.

Afterward, they lay there. Presently she stirred and shivered and he felt himself again becoming rigid. She asked, "May I escalate? We don't have to. Whenever you want, we can stop it."

He felt reassured. But.

"Your ankles."

"Oh," he said.

"Believe me," she said, "You'll feel it. Helpless."

"I'm already helpless." She got up—and again he reacted—and she brought the satchel to the bed. She affixed two more cuffs to his ankles and the brass rail at the foot of the bed. She was right. He did feel helpless. He felt it in his penis. She smiled when she saw it.

She sat astride his thighs and took him in her hand and slowly, unbelievably, stretched and caressed him, from his testicles to the tip of his penis, up, and up farther, first with one hand, then the other. It was wild. He thought he would lose his mind. She laughed at the look on his face, reached out for the nightdress with her free hand, she never stopped with the other, and dropped the nightdress over his face. Again and again and again the hands, and he moaned, and moaned, a sob, a near scream, as she went far beyond what he thought he could take. He went over, no, almost over, no, she brought him back, those hands! Those hands!

In the distance, he heard noises. He felt her lips and heard her murmur. He was squirming, thrusting with his thighs now, she had asked him to be passive, but he could not help himself, thrust and thrust! "You're a nice man," she said, "you deserve all you get." Thrust and thrust again. He screamed! She brought him to the edge! She was pressing down on his face and the nightdress with something, what was it? A belt? What? It was down around his throat now, how in the world could she do it? With her hands on his penis? And her lips? Had she slipped it over the rail at the head of the bed? "The loss of air," she said, "escalates the fear, which escalates the pleasure." He half moaned, half giggled, he could not care. It was tight, it hurt around his neck, he squirmed but of course could not touch it. She pulled it tighter and, at the same time, voluptuously caressed his penis. "It was the Emir," she said. "He sent us." He smiled at the joke and felt a flash of fear which did enhance the pleasure. He was going to come again now! Almost! Thrust! Thrust again! Harder! "He gives us money," she said. "We do what he says." He thrust and almost came and did not! He could not breathe! Thrust! Hard! Harder still! And thrust again! He started to come!

Helmuth did not panic until the last moment of his life and as he died, he ejaculated.

Diego screwed a large metal hook into the ceiling beam. He wiped the two hotel keys and put them on the table. He put the copy he had made in his pocket. He sat in the chair while she showered. He remained motionless. She finished showering, toweled dry, swiftly dressed, went to the bed and removed the handcuffs. She put everything back in the satchel. He watched her. He shook his head. She looked at him. He stood and said nothing.

They hoisted the body up together. Diego looped the free end of the nylon cord around the metal hook and tied it with two half-hitches. Helmuth hung there, twisting, naked. Ileana placed the chair on its side below Helmuth's feet, as if he had kicked it over. Diego examined the dried sperm on the thighs. It was copious, which was perfect. It would appear to be a sexual accident, not a suicide, and no one would think of murder. The room was in the girl's name. Afterwards, she had fled, panicked at the thought of the questions. The passport number was someone else's. Swissair personnel would recall the woman on the flight, but they would have have have no clear record of who she was; she had paid in cash for the ticket when she arrived at the airport. The bank security men would describe her but she had been sleepy and silent in the car. The police would wonder if she was a prostitute whose passage had been arranged by Helmuth himself. Helmuth had certainly been in charge of things as he whisked her away from the Zurich airport. Ileana paused in the doorway and looked about the room. "What is it?"

Diego was looking at her curiously. "Does it bother you to do things like this?"

She shrugged. It was French and appealing.

"Things like this for things like the Emir?" he said.

"The Emir is one of those who pays our bills."

"He sells his oil to the Americans. They are the source of his great wealth. They are the ones who support him."

"His paying our bills with their money is amusing."

"There are also Germans who pay our bills. Are you willing to do their bidding, too? Whatever it is, no questions?"

She smiled.

Diego slowly looked away from her to the hanging body. He said, "Bank charges."

"What about them?"

"His Excellency was angry because the bank charged for something. That's why he had us kill him."

Ileana looked at Helmuth and said, "The man at the end of the table calls the tunes."

"And you like dancing."

"Among other things."

A beat. "You liked it with him." He indicated the hanging corpse.

She said, "I liked him."

"I see."

She smiled. "Don't tell my brother," she said and went out the door. It clicked.

Diego looked at the door. He was not smiling. He took a piece of purple ribbon from his pocket and dropped it on the floor. His signature to her show. But he had done the killing, after all. He wondered if it would confuse things. He hoped it would.

Even better, Fox Face had mentioned it twice and Diego knew it would irritate Fox Face. A lot. Diego's stomach twinged and he grimaced.

Diego took his handkerchief from his pocket and carefully opened the door. There was no one in the corridor. His stomach tweaked again and he smiled his brief smile. It appeared, flashed and vanished. Still holding the handkerchif in his hand, he went out and closed the door behind him.

There was an impenetrable Rhine fog rolling in. Diego walked off in it. He liked walking by himself in that fog. He would regret leaving Zurich tonight.

But perhaps there would be fog in Paris.

Chapter 25

I WOKE UP EARLY in the morning, still holding hundreds of gold contracts, with the plane to New York scheduled for three P.M. I would arrive after the markets closed but it felt pretty safe, what the hell. I was excited about our dinner date.

She had, I felt, invited the phone calls. She had specifically promised that there would be a next time. I had called her on the telephone every three to ten days.

I reached JFK early, as the market closed. Gold was down a little less than a dollar for the day, which was unpleasant but unimportant. Ho.

I took a yellow cab to the hotel.

Sarah.

At 8:30 P.M. we were on the Upper West Side in the world's
worst expensive Mexican restaurant. It was not going well. Sarah
had picked the place. She loved the chip dip. I did not. She had
a nice smile. I was overcharged. My head was clear. I had eaten
lightly and drunk next to nothing for days. I was in the best physical condition of my life. I would sleep until noon the next morning
following, hopefully, my favorite tranquilization. And, this time,
hopefully, no humiliating postlude. The quesadilla shell was soggy,
the contents glop and we dropped into a conversation about political values. We shifted to "Who are you?"

"Where do I come from?" she said. "Aco."

I said, "Isn't that Arab?"

She said, "It used to be."

"Up north?" I said.

"On the coast," she said.

"Brothers or sisters?" I said.

"I have two sisters. I'm the oldest. Jeanne married a flamboyant
leftist lawyer in Paris. Tamara married a publisher from Buenos
Aires who disappeared during the troubles, leaving her with one
boy and three girls. She has remarried a brain surgeon from the
university hospital, who was divorced, with two children of his
own. I seldom see any of them anymore, except for the Paris sister
and her lawyer."

I said, "Who is flamboyant. And adores you."

"He's French. It's polite, not serious."

"Oh. How would you like to see them again?"

"What is that all about?"

"Tomorrow."

"You are going over there?"

"Have another margarita," I said. I waved at the waiter. He came
at once. I ordered two, up with salt, Cuervo Gold. "I am going to
see my son."

"In Paris," she said.

"You know?"

"Some. I would like to know about it."

And so, I told her. Everything. The marriage, the birth, the
attempts to stay in touch, Gstaad, the bomb, Diego, East Berlin,
the threats, the plea to the Mossad. She put her hand on mine. I

looked at it. I said, "That's the first time I have told it." I stared at her.

"What is it?" she said.

"The marriage."

"It's none of your business about the marriage," she said. "Yet. I'm sorry. I know you want to know but I don't want to talk about it." The waiter arrived with our second margaritas. She took a healthy sip of hers. She licked the salt. "On the other hand, if you keep getting me refills—"

"I'll always get your refills."

"I'll say this, I'm comfortable." We clinked glasses. I had this sudden chill. She knew at once. "What's the matter?"

"Why?"

"Your face," she said.

"It's my stomach that seems to be a problem."

"Then don't eat," she said. "You don't have to, we can leave, I'm sorry if it's the food—"

"It isn't," I said. She waited. I was embarrassed. I told her anyhow. "Gold."

"What about it? Do you have a position? Are you long or short?"

"Long. Big long."

"Overnight?" she said. "You told me you hate to hold overnight."

"And now my stomach is resonating with the price. I don't know why. There's no reason."

"But the market is closed."

"The markets are never closed anymore. They're always open somewhere in the world. Right now, Hong Kong is trading."

"Is there someone you could call?"

"Would you mind?" I said. "I hate to leave you."

"The lure of the chase. The smell of blood. The call of the wild. Your game," she said. "Go. I hope it isn't too awful."

It was.

There was a rumor that the Russians were selling. Gold was down $27 an ounce. I was long a full position. Overexposed. I was abstracted when I got back to the table. She took one look at my face and called for the check. She stood.

"Hey, I pay," I said.

She said, "Sure. Do you have a separate phone in the living room? You can talk all night if you have to, without preventing me from sleeping."

We went back to the hotel. I did spend the night on the telephone. The price was down another $9 and looking weak even there when I finally took my loss and sold. They skinned me on the execution. What was worse, I made the bottom. I lost $2,700,000 of my cumulative win.

Two million seven hundred thousand dollars belonging to Shima and the State of Israel!

"I feel I cost you that," Sarah said. "The excitement of seeing me."

"No, no, no."

"That's the wrong response," she said.

"Sorry," I said. "Let me try again. I couldn't think of anything except for you and it was worth the money."

"Now that's what I call gallant. Let's make it worth the $2,700,000."

We did.

Afterward, we had breakfast, and held, and dozed, and made love again, and this time had champagne, and did it again around noon, and this time finished the eggs, and afterward had coffee and held and dozed again. The next time as I started to come, she seemed to take charge herself, with vaginal contractions, progressively tighter and more prolonged, and I came and and came, with everything, I kept coming, and she kept prolonging me. She was making me come, more and more. She was moaning now. Screaming. No, she wasn't. It was someone else. What the hell. It was me! I never scream! I panicked. More! More!

And then it was over and I was sleeping.

I awoke to the smell of cold coffee. Yes, it does smell good, even cold.

She was sipping hers, sitting on the edge of the bed. She poured a cup for me. I blinked and did not move.

"Well," she said. "My favorite word. What's yours?"

"Spent," I said.

My lady chuckled. "I'm going to shower and go home and pack and then I'm going to meet Hugo."

"You're coming with me?"

She looked at me. "Of course."

Chapter 26

SARAH INSISTED I spend quiet time with Hugo first, before she made an appearance.

The bodyguards picked me up in front of the Ritz in one of the Marquis's limousines. The little one with the mustache nodded, "*M'sieu.*" I looked about the square. "There will be four of them," said the mustache helpfully, "two of them in the car before, two in the car after."

I could not spot them in the traffic.

Hugo struggled toward me on the crutches. The other kids watched. Two boys and three girls came over. Hugo introduced us. *Au revoirs.* We drove him off. The two bodyguards rode in front.

Hugo was tired. I waited. "May we go to your hotel, Papa?"

"Sure. How about the bar off the lobby downstairs. We can sit there for hours. Do you have a lot of work to do tonight?"

"Too much. We should eat not too late."

"I have a suite, you could do your homework there. Or I don't mind taking you home if you wish. What do you say? Your call."

"The bar. Papa?"

"Yes, kid?"

"Just Papa." He put his head against my shoulder. His eyes were closed. I put my arm around him.

The doorman tried to help Hugo. Hugo refused. He struggled into the Ritz with the crutches. The bodyguards discreetly disappeared into the woodwork.

It was the cocktail hour. The bar had started to fill. Hugo had a Pepsi-Cola. I ordered a Campari soda.

"You drink gin," Hugo said.

"I'm with you. I want my head clear."

He cocked his head and said nothing. The drinks arrived. We clinked our glasses. "Ooh la la," he said.

I put my glass down and followed his look.

Sarah stood in the doorway. She was smashing in her beige St. Laurent. She waved. "Ooh, Papa," said my Hugo. "*La tienne?* Yours?" She came to the table. I introduced them. They grinned at each other. They kissed, two cheeks. Sarah smiled and sat and Hugo, before the waiter could get there, crutch and all, held her chair. She thanked him, in French, naturally. He was delighted. He chattered at her excitedly.

And they were off.

Smiles, jokes, chuckles. They were animated, charming. They flirted. They enchanted each other. He responded to her. She responded to him. I responded to them. Family. Warmth. It was working. Sarah ordered a Vermouth Cassis. I ordered my Tanqueray rocks. I nursed it for an hour. Hers was untouched. So was Hugo's Pepsi-Cola. They were too busy. Occasionally, they included me. Most of the time, they ignored me. Sarah was not above talking about me. She told him we were "recent." Ah, he said, but we had promise. She said "possibly." He laughed. Told her I was lucky. She blushed, thanking him. He wished me the best, he told her, always. They looked at me, smiling. They were the lovers. I was the beard. For an instant, I was jealous of Hugo.

I paid the check. We got up to leave. Sarah went to the ladies' room. "I love her," he said. "She is wonderful."

As we got into the taxi, she whispered to me, "I love him. He's delightful."

We had dinner at a tiny restaurant she knew in Montmartre. I did not ask who had taken her there. "The lawyer brother-in-law," she voluntarily told me.

The food was good. I ate a lot of it. Both of them ate lightly. He told her about school, what he liked, what he didn't, what he planned to study. She told him about her languages. He asked her which ones and she told him. I had never asked her. I was staggered by the number. She spoke most of the European languages, Norwegian, Swedish, Finnish, Danish, Turkish, Russian, Georgian, Mandarin, Cantonese, Japanese, Hebrew, Arabic, Pharsi, Coptic. She had a masters from Harvard and had dropped out because it ws limited. She was stating the facts, not boasting. Hugo was fascinated. They tried each of Hugo's languages. He had three. She told him of her ambition to develop a multiple-language program they could use in schools internationally. I was interested; she had never told that to me. He told her about his family. He told her about his friends. She teased him lightly about the girls. I cringed. He asked her if she were married. I protested. She put her hand on mine. She told him, "In name only." He said he was pleased. She was pleased that he was pleased.

When we dropped him off at 10:30 P.M., he started to shake hands, withdrew his hand, and they did the two-cheek kiss bit. He made his speech. The evening was lovely. It was such a pleasure to meet her. It was such a pleasure to see me so happy. À *bientôt*, soon, hopefully. "Hugo?" she said.

We paused. I was walking him to the door. "Madame?"

"What are you doing tomorrow?"

"What would you like to do tomorrow?" I said.

His eyes gleamed. "A picnic in the country. The races of horses, I have never been. A movie in the late afternoon. Dinner with you two, naturally. And a *boite*, perhaps?"

I said, "I will phone your mother in the morning."

I did phone. At 9:30 A.M. La Marquise was distant, amused, cooperative. That made me uneasy.

The day was sunny. We had our picnic in the country. I lost 1,000 francs at Longchamps. Hugo won a little. Sarah won more. We saw a double feature movie. We had dinner at Hugo's "favorite." The nightclub had both music and comedy. We dropped him off at 1:30 A.M.

He kissed Sarah good-bye and hugged her again. He hugged me for a long time.

"Today was perfect, was it not, Papa?"

"*Oui*. Is there anything you want to say to me?"

"Only that I am ecstatic for you, Papa." He grinned at me. "And Maman will be ecstatic, too."

He was inside the house before I could reply.

The bodyguards must have been exhausted.

Chapter 27

VÉRONIQUE INSISTED on taking Hugo and the Marquis's nephew, Charles, to the tennis matches together. The boys did not know each other very well but the Marquis felt it was important to convey a greater sense of family to Hugo.

The bodyguards consulted. They protested. It was too public, too many people. Véronique stood firm. After the excursions with Sarah and me the day before? Their position was unreasonable. The bodyguards then made two mistakes. They said that they could not be responsible.

Véronique said, "And who asked you to be responsible?"

The bodyguards then asked to speak to the Marquis.

Véronique stared at them indignantly. "I am going with the boys to the tennis today, with you or without you."

Hugo and Charles had a marvelous time. Every one of their favorite players won. They watched three different matches from beginning to end. They each had four hamburgers, loaded, and the extra-low alcohol beers that Véronique permitted. There was no sign of danger. Véronique felt vindicated.

They returned to the apartment for dinner at six P.M. The bodyguards got out of the front seat. They waited patiently, profession-

ally, until the Mossad cars positioned themselves at each end of
the block and the bodyguard waiting in the lobby signaled that the
building was clear. Only then did they open the rear doors of the
limousine. One held the door on the left side for Véronique, the
other the door on the right for the boys. Charles got out of the
right rear door first, backing out and reaching back so he could
take Hugo's crutches. He straightened up with the crutches.

The three shots from the Kalashnikov shattered his spine and
smashed him against the car. The bodyguard beside him pushed
him into the car. The bodyguard on the far side shoved Véronique
back into the car, jumped behind the wheel and drove away.

Diego had fired from the window on the fourth floor of the
building two doors down the street. He dropped the assault rifle
with the scrap of purple ribbon on the butt and disappeared down
the stairs, through the courtyard, through the service entrance to
the alley in the rear, down the alley and into the busy cafe. He
nursed an apéritif and listened for the sirens. They arrived within
two minutes of the shots.

The Israelis had been utterly helpless, which amused him.

Chapter 28

THE TELEPHONE chattered on the bedside table of our Geneva
hotel.

It was Shima. The Mossad had notified him in London. Véronique was hysterical. Would I call her? Please?

I did.

The Marquis answered. *"Un moment."*

Véronique had been sedated. *" 'Allo, Michel."*

"I am sorry," I said. "Shall I come there?"

"No!" she shouted. The Marquis must have taken the phone. I

could hear him speaking to her. When she next spoke, she was calmer. "I am sorry. *Je me rend*. We can take no more."

"Let them take the boy. Please."

"I don't know," she said. "Just a minute."

Hugo came on the line. "Papa?"

"Yes, kid. I am so sorry."

"He died, taking my crutches. It should have been me."

"You can't feel guilty about that, Hugo—"

"It is agreed." It was the Marquis, who had taken the phone again. "He will go with the ones who wait downstairs. You may tell us later the details."

I said, "Yes," and added, "thank you."

Hugo took the phone again. "Can you send me a small computer, Papa? And some games? I do love the games. They will give me something to fill the time."

I swallowed. "I will try, Hugo."

Chapter 29

SARAH WOULD GO with Hugo. We had all had the same idea. I had asked, Sarah had offered and Shima had suggested it. Sarah and I bought the computer and games on the way to the airport.

We killed time until they came for her in the expensive chrome and formica restaurant on the second floor of the airport. Where were they going? I was need-to-know. Did I need to know? Forget it.

Sarah ordered a Croque Monsieur, lean and trimmed, with very sharp mustard. And a Heineken.

"Two," I said.

The waiter gathered the menus. He said, in German, "The ham is not lean."

"Trim it," I said.

"They won't let me in the kitchen."

I looked at him.

"*Ja, ja,*" he said. "I will do it."

She smiled at me. "I think the time is right for a little unfinished business."

Portrait of a failed marriage. She was twenty-two and Arnold was thirty-eight when they met. He was wealthy, literate, energetic, accomplished and passionate.

I held up my hand. "You know, you don't have to do this."

"Yes, I do," she said.

Arnold was self-made, he insisted on telling her; only a portion of his wealth was inherited. He loved her and he was the classic good provider. He had three children by a prior marriage whom she liked. He understood her need for a life of her own and her desire to keep learning languages. It would require travel, but that was fine, they would travel together until the children came. They would have two children together.

It should have been a good marriage.

It foundered. In fact, he turned out not to understand her need for work. They didn't need the money. She was already recognized as accomplished. Why did she need any more of the same? He resented the time it took. Travel became possible only if he were with her. When she traveled alone, he became jealous.

One day she awoke and asked herself, where was the affection? Had it ever been there in the first place? She no longer remembered. She became progressively more restless. She wanted a grand passion and always had. He could not provide it.

Ultimately, her great need for intensity scared him into other relationships. Almost as soon as it started, she knew it. Indeed, she wondered if she had unconsciously pushed him over the edge. In a way, it made things better. They accepted what they had and did not divorce. Instead, she sardonically built a life for herself around her own personal assets.

"Sardonically?" I said.

"Yes, I admit it," she said. She had finished her beer. I waved at the waiter, pointed at her glass.

She had always treasured her Israeli contacts. One day she met a high official in the Mossad.

"Shima?"

She nodded. Somehow, almost casually, she did an "errand" for him. It was innocuous. She carried a paper. Afterward, when she reported in, her understanding of the place she had sort of shocked the local head of station of the Mossad.

"Shocked?" I said.

"Yes." She smiled. "Staggered."

She nibbled at her Croque Monsieur. Did I mind if she talked with her mouth full?

No, I said and gestured.

They had used her again, elsewhere. She loved it. Her reports were thorough and accurate. She was willing to help with whatever they asked and she quickly became a resource. She was rich and distinguished in her own right and even if her marriage had failed, her husband was a well-known and respected man and a Big Giver. She smiled at me. "You were once a Big Giver."

"Still am," I said. "Anonymous. The sandwich is fantastic. Talk."

She did. Arnold gave even more in a sense. His not getting a divorce from her became Arnold's contribution to the cause. As his wife, Sarah's cover proved impeccable. She could travel wherever she was needed. Now a free spirit, her time became her own. She could do whatever she wished to get the information she needed. "Go ahead, ask."

I hesitated.

"Ask," she said. "Go ahead, you chicken, ask."

I finished my beer.

She waited.

"All right," I said. "Have you ever, in the course of your business?"

"Say it," she said.

"Resorted to deliberated seduction," I said, "to accomplish an objective."

"Once."

"Me?"

"No. Not you."

"Oh." I made a face.

She was lost in the reminiscence, prodded by the beer. "I liked him. A lot. I still like him. He was exotic. It happened in Rome."

"Of all places," I said.

"Don't mock it."

"Then what's the issue?"

"Guilt," she said.

I said, "Frankly, I think it sounds healthy as hell. Blessings on you. Forget it." I paid and left a 20 percent tip and we went for a stroll in the airport.

We held hands. My left in her right. That left my right free for my 9mm Star as I scanned the crowds, Secret Service-style. I did not tell Sarah. I was too busy being romantic. We walked along. She looked confused. "It's like we've been together years. Let's see. What's unfinished?"

"Don't," I said. "Let it sit where it is."

"Arnold needs something on the side," she said. "He probably always did." Her eyes searched me.

"Me?" I said. "I am the opposite imperfect. I am tempted, as we all are from time to time, but I keep looking for exclusive relationships. Like now."

"Oh," she said and we walked again. "That sounds serious."

"Yes," I said. "There isn't anyone except Hugo in my life and there hasn't been for months now and that's the way I want it. I don't want to make you uncomfortable. I suppose I shouldn't have said it."

"The last of the great romantics," she said. She stopped. I turned. She kissed me. Tears in her eyes. People shied away, embarrassed.

"What is it?" I asked.

She shook her head, took my hand. There was a bum on a bench with newspapers. He cleared away the papers. We sat.

She said, "My eyes are red."

I sat on the edge of the bench and looked about. There was no one who seemed suspicious.

The bum beside me cleared his throat and said, in German, "May I have ten francs? I would like a cup of coffee."

I turned and felt for my wallet. It is against the principles of the religion to refuse a beggar if you can give. Beside me, Sarah protested. "Ten francs for a cup of coffee?"

"Five?" The man was grinning, negotiating.

I gave him five francs.

The man was delighted. He stood.

I said, "There are no beggars in Switzerland."

He said, "I'm not a beggar. I'm respectable. I'm fashionable. I am a homeless person."

We laughed.

He walked away.

We watched him.

Sarah said, "I like the boy. I will enjoy the time with him."

"Do you have any idea where you will be?" She hesitated. I said, "Forget it. I think you should divorce Arnold and marry me."

She laughed. "I would lose my cover."

"I will protect you. I always will. After this? It's the least I can do—"

She kissed me. We sat there. She said, "I'll think about it."

"Do."

"I'll be in New York in a couple of weeks," she said.

"And what are my orders, messenger girl?"

She said, "Pack and stay ready to move. And I'm not a girl. I'm a woman."

Chapter 30

THE Athens airport was bedlam.

In addition to the well-publicized lack of security—too many passengers, too few guards, too few X-ray stations and inspectors, no provision for examining baggage—they had scheduled excessive departures and landings at peaks throughout the week. Ground personnel were indifferent to the needs of both airlines and passengers. Computer operation shut down frequently due to the vagaries of Greek telecommunications. Various terminals seemed to have been constructed without any sound insulation. Air travel here was an effort.

Diego arrived on the flight from Paris late on a Monday afternoon wearing mirror sunglasses, a lightweight beige gabardine suit with a tiny purple ribbon in his buttonhole, a beige Panama hat and beige Italian slip-ons. He had spent the flight stabilizing himself after hearing on the taxi radio the shocking news of the wrong-boy failure. These things would happen, he had kept telling himself, over and over.

Ileana and her twin, Roman, arrived seven minutes later on a Syrian Airlines flight from Damascus. They arrived at customs as planned within minutes of each other. None of the three had checked any bags and they cleared customs and immigration and emerged from departures separated by fifty yards and twelve seconds.

At the taxi stand, Diego sensed that they were being watched. He removed his sunglasses and put them in his outside breast pocket. A moment later, he entered the first taxi in the line of cabs. It drove off. Roman and Ileana remained in the line of passengers. Four taxis later, Roman reached the head of the line. He got into the taxi by himself and Ileana went back into the airport. There was a sudden flurry of activity outside. Roman, driving off, ignored it.

Diego had been uneasy at the airport. He was uneasy on the taxi ride into the city, uneasy checking into his *pension*, although it was nice, uneasy on the elevator trip with the porter to the room and uneasy as he entered. The room was unexpectedly large and clean, freshly painted an absurd shade of light pink and with a minimum of furnishings, all wood. There was a mirror over the bureau set in the wall, instead of an armoire with the mirror inside its door. He wondered if he was being observed or televised. There was no bug on the telephone so far as he could determine.

He lay motionless on the bed and wondered what had happened at the airport.

They phoned up from the desk at eight P.M. Should they come

up? No, he would come down. They were waiting in the lobby and rose from the stuffed chairs when he appeared, a Slav with a horse face, Russian, he thought, in a coarse brown suit, his hands behind his back, and of course, Fox Face. They looked at him. He nodded. They preceded him out the door and into a waiting cab, which drove off as soon as they entered.

Diego sat between them in the back. The seat was crowded. Still without saying a single word, Fox Face placed a manila envelope in his lap. It was the promised 150,000 Deutschemarks in old bills. Diego was pleased at not having to ask and determined not to show it. He put the envelope in his inside breast pocket.

The restaurant was making him nervous.

Greek music was being played on classical string instruments by three old men in peasant dress and a thin, wild-haired woman of indeterminate age with a clear singing voice and some sort of flutelike pipe woodwind. The restaurant had two different levels and occupied the entire rooftops of two adjacent buildings. It was a popular restaurant and crowded. It was cool this evening.

To the right of the small performing combo was a semi-open kitchen with four busy cooks. In front of it was a salad and dessert buffet with three salad chefs. The remaining space was pretty and open. There was a glorious view of the city lights. There were eighteen tables with checkered cloths. There were huge potted plants and flowers and a vine-covered arbor covering the service and waiting bar. Diego noted a checkroom girl, two bartenders, two maître d's, four captains, eight waiters and six busboys included in the large staff. It was late but the restaurant was still two-thirds full. In addition to the two at the table with him, other hard-faced men in business suits occupied the adjacent tables. There were windows in the building overlooking the restaurant and, on the rooftop of the other building, there were men sitting on the parapet. A dozen in all, Diego decided. Were they trying to impress him?

Each of the others ordered retsina as soon as they were seated. Diego abstained. Fox Face lifted an eyebrow. Diego was unmoved. The waiter suggested mineral water? Imported, perhaps? San Pellegrino? Evian? Diego said, "No." The waiter waited still. "Thank you," Diego added. The waiter disappeared.

Fox Face almost smiled. Horse Face scowled, disapproving. "Well," he said. "Let us begin. Do you have any questions first?"

Diego said, "I will ask whatever I have to ask when I know what is wanted."

Horse Face said, "We wish to know why you decided to come over here. What is your objective?"

"To avoid seeming foolish."

"And?"

"Answering that would be foolish. I am here because you like my work. Surely you remember Zurich?"

Fox Face smiled his predator smile. "And Paris. We know about Paris."

Diego's stomach twinged. He grimaced. "There is something I should have asked you before."

Fox Face said, "About the American tourist? He is now of interest."

Diego paused to digest it. "Have you met him in person?"

"No."

"Too quick," said Diego. "When and where did you meet him?"

"I did not."

Diego smiled his stomach-twinging nervous smile. "Was it before he came for me?"

"Do you mean did I know it and let him?" asked Fox Face.

"Yes."

Now Horse Face smiled. "Telling you 'yes' would be really foolish. This is not going at all well. We are not making progress—"

Diego stopped him with a wave of his hand. "Then let us do business normally. You have names?"

Horse Face sat there.

Fox Face said, "We have names. He is Sergei. I am—who am I?—Gunther."

Diego studied him carefully. "I believe you. I think your name is Gunther."

Fox Face Gunther's eyes widened slightly but he was otherwise impassive.

Horse Face Sergei was irritated. Gunther put his hand on Sergei's arm and said, "Can you tell us anything about yourself?"

Diego said, "It is too late now for a job interview. You saved me from the Berlin police and sent me to the camps."

"Speaking of which," Gunther said, "tell us about the others."

"Who? Which others?"

Sergei flushed. "We paid you the money for the others, too. Are you offering to return it?"

Diego was expressionless.

Gunther said, "The man will be reaching his hotel about now. We have had him psychologically tested."

Diego's intestinal smile flashed and disappeared. He said, "Intelligent, unstable, likes to kill and abnormally attached to his sister."

They looked at each other. Sergei made a face. "Obviously, we should have asked you first and saved the time and effort. What about the girl?"

Diego said, "Have you tested her? That would excite my interest."

Silence.

Diego said, "Do you have the girl?"

Gunther said, "We had three cars waiting in the line outside but we are embarrassed to acknowledge that we were not prepared for her to go back into the airport. No, we do not have her. Will she contact you?"

Diego said, "I can never predict what she might do. It would be useful to have her tested."

"Yes," Gunther nodded. "If we return you to your room by half past ten, when do you think she might appear downstairs? Midnight?"

"Is that when would you like her?" Diego said.

Gunther said, "Yes."

"I would like to return to my hotel now," Diego said. "I might be able to arrange it." He started to rise but Sergei gestured. Diego perched on the edge of his seat.

The waiter brought the retsinas and produced his order pad. Sergei waved him brusquely away and the waiter promptly retreated. Diego was looking about.

Sergei said, "What is it?"

"How many of you are there here?" Diego said. "Twelve?"

Sergei appeared pleased. "And why do you think we brought you here?"

"I don't know. Because someone else likes to come here?"

Sergei now seemed impressed as well. He looked at Gunther and back at Diego again. What else have you observed?"

Diego said, "I am being videotaped and recorded."

Silence. "You could not possibly have observed that," Gunther said. "And by the way, Gunther is not my real name."

"I believe you," said Diego and nodded his head. "But you should not have said it for some reason."

"Wunderbar!" exclaimed the old man as he watched the end of the tape. He looked at Gunther, who was pressing the VCR rewind button. Gunther was exceedingly nervous. The old man smiled. "And the little purple cloth in the flower hole?"

Gunther said, "It's his trademark he always leaves behind, for the Purple Cadre that does not exist. Childish, a sort of posing."

"And, speaking of childish, why in the world did you choose that name? Of all the incredibly stupid things to say—why not Werner, your own name? Or Heinz, or Franz, or Ludwig or anything at all?"

"I am sorry," said the wretched Werner, for that was in fact his name. "I made a mistake. I have no idea why I did it."

The old man looked at him. Werner squirmed. The old man laughed. "You are remembering the banker, Helmuth."

"Yes, sir."

"That reminds me, I want to watch that tape again. You brought it with you, too?"

"Yes, sir," said Werner, and fumbled in his attaché case. "Here."

The old man took it and put it on the lamp table beside his chair. It was an ugly leather reclining chair. The room was dark and furnished like the rest of the sumptuous two-bedroom flat in pre-World War II Berlin taste, the way the old man liked it. "How long have you been with me?"

Werner considered. "One way or the other, more than thirty years?"

"Thirty-two, your entire adult life. Within the East German Secret Service, but working for me. With your life at risk. And how many mistakes have you made in that time?"

"Many, sir, I am sure," said Werner.

"Not true," the old man said to him. "You have made remarkably few errors. Play the tape again, starting at the airport."

Werner started the tape again.

The old man chortled when Ileana went back into the airport. "I wonder if she went into the ladies' room or to some other airline counter right away and out some other exit."

Werner shook his head. He was not prepared to guess.

They were watching the restaurant now. The camera zoomed in on the purple ribbon in his buttonhole as Diego refused the retsina, then the water, refused to answer questions, challenged Werner about meeting the American and asked their names. "Sergei!" said the old man. "That was an appropriate name for Grigor. What did Grigor think?"

Werner said, "He found the boy a strange mix of crude and sensitive. Rude, intuitive, unexpected. He thinks the boy handled himself remarkably well."

"Would the KGB have used him?"

"In a minute. With the same qualification I reported before," Werner said. "The KGB has found South Americans dangerous in the long term. In the short term, steady, effective, notwithstanding the Latin temperament, and then poof! No warning, erratic."

The old man chuckled. "Here it comes, the brother, 'abnormally attached to his sister,' " said the old man, cueing Diego's analysis of Roman on the screen. The old man laughed. "Perhaps we shall see if he is right."

Werner said, "That is the way the brother tested."

The old man was studying Diego on the screen. "Here comes his guess as to how many of you were there. Were there twelve of you?"

"Fourteen," said Werner, "including the two of us."

"Then it really was accurate, eh? 'Because someone else likes to come here?' I love it! He somehow got a sense of me. Did you hear that one, Werner?"

"Yes, sir," said Werner. "I did."

"And now the very last thing he said—here it comes. How did he know you should not have used the name 'Gunther'?" the old man said.

"I don't know," said Werner. "Something on my face, I suppose."

"All right! He's my boy! Bring me the girl."

"Yes, sir," said Werner.

Ileana phoned Roman at half past nine.

"Hi!" she said.

"Three," he said.

They both hung up together.

Ileana phoned Diego a moment later.

"Hi," she said.

He said, "Five."

There was a moment of hesitation and she said, "Will you be there?"

Diego hung up on her, irritated.

Werner played the call tapes to the old man over the phone. The old man chuckled and hung up without a word.

Werner was waiting in the lobby of the *pension* when Ileana entered. He rose and checked his watch. "You are a minute late," he said.

Ileana said, "Your watch should be adjusted."

Difficult as the evening had been, Werner found her unbelievably attractive. She was wearing a clinging sheath of pale blue silk with nothing underneath it. She studied him, and he realized she was reading his reactions to her on his face. It was the second time that day it had happened to him—Diego had read him the same way—and Werner did not like it. He gestured and two faceless trenchcoats entered.

She smiled at Werner and said, "Do you really wish me to go with them?"

Werner found himself blushing furiously. He gestured, she should go.

With a mocking look, she exited with the two men.

Werner waited until the car drove off. Then he phoned upstairs. Could he please come up?

Diego said politely, *"Bitte."*

"Where is she? Did she come?" Diego asked.

"As scheduled. Yes," Werner said. "Someone is talking to her."

"I see. And you wish to talk to me."

"Yes," said Werner carefully. "That is the purpose of this visit."

Diego gestured.

Werner sat carefully in one of the two wooden chairs. Diego sat in the other.

Werner counted the points on his fingers. "One, please open a bank account. Any bank you wish, you pick it. If you wish, we will help you with it. Otherwise, we are prepared to pay in cash, which is a nuisance, but we will do it. Two, we will pay you one hundred thousand Swiss francs each month. That is a retainer, not for the work you will do. Three, you will remain in the Bekaa camps available to us and will not join any of the formal groups or defect to Baghdad or Libya. We will clear it each time with the head of camp. Four, we will pay you for what you do each time, a substantial bonus. The amount depending on what it is, of course. Five, we expect four to six assignments each year. Six, you are free to refuse any assignment you wish. Seven, you may terminate at any time. We will give you a telephone number to call. You need only phone us. Eight, we may terminate if we wish. We will advise you if we do it. Nine and last, we may wish to talk to you about the situation in the places where you are. That should not cause problems for you since the people in charge where you are will be aware that you work for us, too, and can be expected to talk to us. Questions?"

"One," Diego said. "The American."

"To be terminated. You will do it."

"Good. First?"

"No. When the time is right."

"I am not sure I like that," Diego said. "What of the brother and sister?"

"We intend to employ them each at a separate retainer half of yours. We respectfully suggest that you do not tell them that, although, of course, you are free to do it. Well?"

"Who will we be working for?" Diego said.

Werner said, "That I cannot answer. There is no formal organization or group as such. Just persons who are restless with what they now do."

"Which is what?"

"Lots of things. Oh, in your area of interest? They have been using little boys from Beirut. Each time, a new little boy from Beirut." Werner made a slight face. "I would like you to make your mind up tonight."

Diego said, "I will do it."

Chapter 31

THEY BLINDFOLDED Ileana in the car and she unhesitatingly submitted. They drove for less than ten minutes and pulled over to the curb. She heard the door of another car open and they helped her out of the first car and into the back of the other car, still blindfolded.

The second car smelled like a Jaguar, wood and leather, expensive.

The second car drove five minutes and stopped. She could tell they were outside a building. She listened to the murmur of voices. They helped her out of the car, onto the sidewalk, up two stairs, through a door, up more stairs, down a short corridor smelling of jasmine and paused. There were elevator noises.

They entered the elevator with her, and rode up for a creaking twenty seconds. The elevator stopped, the door opened. They helped her out. She heard a distant door buzzer. She heard footsteps within an apartment, an opening door. "*Danke*," said a pleasant mature voice. Hands helped her forward.

She entered. Two steps on parquet, a new firm hand steadied her and she stopped on what felt like an Oriental carpet. She heard the door close behind her. The pleasant voice said, "You may remove that."

Ileana removed the blindfold and exclaimed in Romanian.

He was wearing a black oval mask over his eyes and nose. He was older. Nondescript. Definitely older.

She looked about at a large, well-furnished apartment, full of old things, Germanic.

The older man's pleasant voice said, "My, you are indeed attractive. May I offer you something to drink?"

Ileana laughed, knowing instantly what she had excited. "Yes, please. I could use a drink."

"What would you like, Fräulein? Wine, beer, hard liquor, some sort of tea? Perhaps one of the coffees—Western, espresso, Greek, Turkish?"

Ileana said, "That depends on what you have in mind for me."

He said, "First, we will watch a movie."

"I see. And then?"

"We will probably talk a bit."

"And then?"

He said, "I cannot predict it."

Ileana said, "In that case, coffee. Turkish."

It was Helmuth!

Ileana could not believe it. "I know him!" she exclaimed with a smile to the masked older man beside her on the couch.

His look was steely, curious. He gestured at the television screen.

Ileana turned back to watch again and curled her long legs beneath her. She stiffened slightly as she realized what she was watching but otherwise said nothing, not a single word.

The older man beside her pushed the pause button when her Turkish coffee arrived. The maid, in her seventies, pattered in on slippered feet and put the coffee on the table in front of Ileana. Ileana murmured thanks. The maid half-smiled and disappeared.

The older man beside Ileana said, "Drink it."

Ileana hesitated.

The older man reached forward and poured. He handed Ileana the tiny cup and saucer.

Her hand shook slightly and the cup and saucer chattered.

The older man smiled.

Ileana sipped her coffee and said, "Do we have to do this?"

The older man said, "Yes. I want to watch you watching."

They watched it.

Ileana made love to Helmuth. It seemed to go on for hours. Even Ileana found it erotic. The older man beside her kept studying her reactions. She waited for him to touch her.

He did not. He sat there beside her.

Finally, she poured herself a second cup of coffee.

He said, "Aren't you a bit afraid of being overstimulated?"

Her hand shook again as she sipped from the cup and he reached out his hand to steady hers. "Thank you," she said and finished her coffee down to the dregs. Turkish coffee. Thick. Sweetish.

She put the cup and saucer on the table again and sat back, brushing his shoulder.

It was electric but he still did nothing.

Before them, on the television screen, she made love to Helmuth forever.

She was startled when Diego entered the room. When he strangled Helmuth, she grimaced. She watched her own face in close-up as Helmuth climaxed and died.

She took a deep breath and murmured with surprise once again as the camera photographed her in the shower.

She and Diego strung the corpse to the light fixture and arranged the chair. Finally, she and Diego had their little talk and she exited, Diego watching her. She was amused when he dropped the purple ribbon. The television tape finished and flickered.

The older man beside her flicked the rewind button. Diego said again, "There are also Germans who pay our bills. Are you willing to do their bidding, too? Whatever it is, no questions?"

Ileana on the tape smiled again. "The man at the end of the table calls the tunes."

The older man stopped the tape and turned the VCR and television set off. They sat there in the darkness.

Ileana said, "Are you the man at the end of the table who calls the tunes?"

He said, "Are you willing to do my bidding? Whatever it is, no questions?"

She said, "There are things I will not do. But I have not yet drawn the line. I think I would like a brandy now. You have made me nervous with this self-examination."

He grinned. Then he gestured, she should go get the drink herself.

Ileana turned her head. She saw the bar built into the wall. She rose and went to it. She could feel his eyes on her. She scanned the bottles before her. Delamain. Vintage. She half filled a snifter and turned. "May I get something for you?"

He shook his head.

She sniffed, sipped and drank a bit. The brandy burned, slightly choked her. She shivered. His faint smile was mocking her. She returned to the couch and sat beside him, her back straight, her eyes black and flashing, her legs curled beneath her.

He said, "Do you know why I wanted us to watch it?"

Ileana considered, "You hoped it would make me excited?"

The older man laughed and said, "Yes, and it did. And?"

She said, "You want me to do something for you tonight?"

"Not with a noose around my neck. Come on, now, think, that's not the reason." His voice was impatient.

"What? Did you want me to ask how you got the tape? From the Emir?" Ileana said.

He gestured, more, she was on the right track.

She said, "You were somehow involved in it?"

Another encouraging gesture. "More."

"You did it? You ordered it? But it had to be the Emir! You work for him? No? He works for you?"

The masked older man was delighted. He said, "It is complicated. But there is more. What other reason for watching the tape?"

"You want me to know you have it?"

"And?"

"You want Diego to know you have it?"

He said, "Yes" and grinned at her.

"But why?" she said.

He said, "No more talking."

Ileana said, "You want me to wonder and him, too?"

The older man beside her grinned.

She shivered. "I will have to tell my brother about you. This man in a mask. German. Older. An apartment. Wherever this is, I don't know where it is."

He said, "And he will wonder."

"About—?"

"Yes?" he said.

"What we do. If we do—anything."

"Will he wonder whether or not we do anything? Is he likely to be jealous?"

Ileana, said, "I don't know."

"Then that's the point, in a way."

She said, "To find out?"

"I wish to know his weaknesses," he said. "Stand up."

Ileana hesitated, and stood.

Slowly, still seated on the couch, he removed every single thing she wore and left it in a pile on the floor. She had never felt so little in control in her life. She stood there, quivering.

He watched her. Enjoying it.

He removed his own shoes and socks and struggled out of his pants and shorts. He kept his dignity despite the mask. He was erect and remarkably well endowed, she thought. She had not known many older men. She shivered. He had excited her. She wondered how he would take her. It looked as though he wanted her to sit over him—

"Kneel down," he said.

It came as a surprise as she realized what he wanted. She knelt down between his knees.

He laughed at the look on her face. "I am too old to worry about what you want and I have very simple pleasures."

She took him with her mouth and hands, slowly, deftly, expertly, three times in forty-five minutes. She was exceptionally good at what she did and what is more, she always had been. She knew she had the touch of near genius. She loved what she was doing.

The first time he exclaimed. The second, he screamed. The third time, he shouted.

He stood. "Wonderful," he said and walked out of the room. "You may dress," he called back to her.

She partially dressed. She heard water running.

He returned with two clean towels, one damp, one dry, both luxurious pile. She mopped and dried herself where he had spilled. She reapplied her makeup. He redonned his shorts, socks, trousers, shoes and sat again on the couch. She finished dressing.

He watched her.

She looked at him and smiled.

He was holding her bindfold in his hand.

She said, "Shall I leave now?"

He said, "Yes, there is a car downstairs. I will summon someone to take you down. I wish to give you something." He removed an envelope from his pocket and paused.

Her lower lip was trembling.

He seemed puzzled, *"Bitte?"*

Ileana managed to say, "I have never, ever, in my entire life, been paid for a sexual episode—"

"And you are not now being paid for that!" he said. "I am not paying you for what we did. I am paying you to tell him."

She stared.

He laughed.

She tried to smile but she couldn't. She was afraid of him.

In the elevator on the way downstairs, blindfolded, between the two of them, whoever they were, she realized that he had never removed the mask and she had no idea what he looked like, or who he was, or where they were, and she had no intention of trying to learn. Ever.

It would be dangerous, possibly even fatal.

Chapter 32

THE SECOND MATCH started uneventfully. I took $100,000 back
to the tables.

I was using the new AST notebook. At 25 megahertz, the program took a little bit longer to run. On the other hand, it weighed
less than seven pounds and fit neatly into my overnighter. I could
play while I was traveling.

I continued to play. I won steadily. But.

There was a yen problem.

I did not understand it.

The yen felt unreliable. The overall price trend was clearly up
but it kept selling off in spasms. The system was working two times
in three and it worked with the yen eight times in eleven, which
was fine, but there were those three spectacular dumps when the
price collapsed in those spasms. There was something wrong.
Something new was happening.

I had long since concluded that the yen was not a currency. It
was a managed number. The government and the major corpora-
tions were working together to control the yen price for the good
of the Japanese economy, and individual citizens were going along.
No one was protesting. Further, I believed that the central bank,
or MITI, or whoever it was, had a group working on information
close to mine, on the assumption that there was someone like me
out there with a program predicting what the systems would do,
in addition to all the pitiful souls playing the underlying systems.
It was the mission of that group to take me and I had no illusions.
If I continued to play the yen enough, sooner or later, I would
lose a big one. That was not, however, the current situation. I was
playing small. I had difficulty understanding what felt wrong. It
was as if the market was testing me. The moment I took a yen
position, it went wrong. Then it went further wrong. Then it went
right, then it went wrong again. Ultimately, it seemed to correct
as it should but the experience was unnerving. I came close to
liquidating prematurely twice. I wanted to, no question. The only

reason I didn't was that if I had quit, and it turned out that I should have held, I would have lost confidence in what I was doing.

The positions I was taking were far too small for the MITI killers to be paying attention. Was there someone else out there watching me? Focusing on the yen and trying to discourage me? Or focusing on me and my trading in yen? Trying to figure out what I was doing?

Notwithstanding the yen puzzle, I eventually won the first five sets on the initial set stake of $100,000 and game stake of $20,000. At that point, I was sitting with just over $1,600,000 net. I had a set risk of $800,000 and a game risk of one fifth of that, or $160,000. The computer market analysis program said to buy yen again. There were four conforming signals. Four. Count 'em. Buy. I almost ducked. I wanted to. Could I? I was afraid of yen. Should I risk $160,000 in a bet on the yen? Discipline? Or trust my instincts? Which?

Discipline won.

I couldn't not play.

All right. Where to play? Chicago? I hesitated, reluctant to risk it. It would be a 57-tick game play, 224 contracts. That was a lot but really not too much. It was safe to play futures in Chicago. I generally preferred trading forwards in London. It would be safer if there were turmoil. Unfortunately, this time the time zones were wrong. I was on Mountain time in Snowbird. My trading would have to start at midnight if I were going to trade forwards in London. And at midnight, I would be tired from the skiing.

What the hell. I would play in Chicago.

The computer also said buy Swiss, sell bonds. That would be three positions, even more risky although permitted by the rules. Three risks of $160,000 each. A big risk, $480,000. Maybe I should amend the rules. Make me pick the single best position. A dangerous thought, amend the rules. You don't amend while playing. And anyhow, the unamended rules would force me to trim to one game risk for overnight, so maybe I wouldn't have to hold yen overnight. If I were lucky. So what the hell. That had become one of my favorite expressions. What the hell. Do it, stop whining. In for a penny, in for a yen. When you start a match, you play it out, or you find yourself eating your heart out. The moment you quit on it, of course, the system is bound to run wild, winning.

I split the order among three floor brokers.

It went well.

The markets had been quiet overnight. The Swiss franc moved up smartly from the opening bell. Bonds moved down, then stabilized, then collapsed half a point at noon following the Fed intervention. The yen moved up 11 ticks. The bonds rallied somewhat by two o'clock, New York, so there I was with the close coming up, sizable wins in both Swissies and bonds, and the yen ahead decently, but the yen win comparatively small. I groaned. The rules were clear: I was in the business of taking profits, contrary to the usual shibboleth about taking your losses and letting your wins run. I would have to close out the Swissies and bonds and hold the yen position.

I did.

I checked the aftermarket twice around dinnertime. Nothing much had happened.

I went to sleep.

A frantic phone call woke me shortly after midnight. The Tokyo branch of one of the large German banks had announced an acute Japanese shortage of oil fifteen minutes before the Tokyo close. All hell broke loose on the financial markets, with the yen collapsing wildly past my stops. I sold at once in the London market, hedging my contract position to the extent I could, not certain what the exact numbers were, knowing that I could not possibly get fair executions, but trying desperately to cover as best I could. The sell orders were coming from everywhere, far beyond all reason. Some huge player was determined to hammer the yen.

Meanwhile, I had lost $800,000 of my fund belonging to the State of Israel.

On the other hand, I had only lost part of what I had previously won.

And I still had $800,000 profit on the second match. That made $3,500,000 of the $10 million objective.

Chapter 33

AND THE NEXT TIME OUT, we went all the way.

We started with $100,000 again—and a negative report on the dollar from the London branch of a German bank; I had started to pay attention to reports from the German branch banks—and won and won, the whole shebang, in just nine sets. Forget the match, forget seventeen sets, I was done. What I had hoped to do and more.

I had $8,100,000 more, $11,600,000 in all!

It was beautiful. We rode the dollar to hell and back. It was shooting fish in a barrel time. We sold dollars for Deutschemarks and the dollar promptly went down and down and down, until the computer said it had bottomed, so I bought back all the dollars I had sold, and went long, buying dollars with Deutschemarks, reversing the prior position. I went even longer, buying dollar options, and guess what? The same branch of the same German bank reversed its position and said buy dollars, and people did and the dollar went up up up.

And there I was, sitting pretty, with all my dollars and dollar options.

I never traded yen. Not once. I was still suspicious of the yen.

I never took a gold position. Not one. I remembered the loss I had taken on gold.

Why take risks if you don't need to take them?

Book III

Chapter 34

THE CRUISE SHIP *Empress of Corinth* sailed from Piraeus at eleven A.M. and was hijacked an hour later about thirty nautical miles from Athens.

Two "honeymooners" traveling in First Class had invited to their cabin for cocktails a "tour group" from Bremen. The automatic weapons had come aboard with the newlyweds in an oversized steamer trunk trailing pink and purple ribbons. No one was ever able to explain convincingly why it had not been opened, let alone examined.

The hijackers burst from the First Class cabin, dressed in combat fatigues, and split into six pairs. One seized the engine room, one the bridge, one the radio room and one the lounge, and the other two rounded up the passengers from the recreation areas and cabins. There was no suggestion of resistance. The ship was owned and operated by the Italian Line. The crew was motley and couldn't care less. The officers were apolitical Italian.

The passengers were for the most part European, French, German, Austrian, Danish, Swedish and even a few Finns. There were groups from South Bend, Indiana, Toronto, Canada, and the north coast of England. The search parties gathered them all in the lounge.

Diego, the honeymooning "husband" wearing a purple ribbon armband on his upper left arm, smiled at them pleasantly and read his demands: release of a long list of "prisoners of war" in England, France, Germany and Israel, and payment by each of those countries of a large sum in dollars, cash, a total of $120 million. The passengers listened, uncomprehending. He said he would start executing prisoners at sundown in the event his demands had not been met by then. They listened in silence. He left them there and went to the radio room and broadcast his demands and the threat to Athens.

The Greek government dutifully relayed them to the respective governments.

There were hours of consultations and requests for clarification. Diego repeated his demands in the same words and again threatened the executions.

The U.S., British and Italian navies each sent ships toward the area with instructions to coordinate a possible attack at mid-afternoon the following day but otherwise nothing happened.

Diego rejoined the passengers in the lounge just as the sun began to set.

In the gathering shadows, the distant land mass was barely visible as the sun sank on the horizon, turning the sea red and glowing. The orchestra stage was in the process of being rebuilt. Diego ordered Ileana and Roman to take the largest, longest planking outside and lash it to the rail of the fantail. It projected out and over the side. The passengers watched uneasily through the lounge windows.

Ileana and Roman reappeared. *"C'est fait, Diego. Et maintenant?"*

Diego turned toward the prisoners. They shriveled. "Out!" Diego shouted at them. *"Vite, vite, vite!"* The prisoners stumbled outside and gathered on the stern facing the disappearing sun. "You!" said Diego to a dark English boy. "You are a Jew?"

"No, sir, I am not a Jew. I am English."

"That is good. You walk the plank."

"What, sir?"

"You know, walk the plank. Like the famous Sir Henry Morgan." Diego grinned. The unhappy boy blinked. Diego went on, "English pirates, they make people walk the plank. All Jews, we will make them walk the plank. You go first, show the others. Now!" Diego leveled his assault rifle. The boy's mother whimpered. The father, a private investor, with extensive holdings in continental banks, known as an angry, difficult man, clutched his wife to his side. "Now!" Diego shouted. "Out on the plank!"

The youngster clambered up onto the plank. He walked unsteadily out and stopped short of the rail. "It's too high, sir. I can't. I won't have a chance."

"Go!"

"But, sir—"

Diego shot him. He toppled. "No!" howled the father and rushed to the rail.

"You now!" shouted Diego. "You join him!" The father climbed over the rail and jumped, disappearing into the sea below. Diego fired a burst from his automatic rifle after him and turned, now shouting, "You! You! You and you!" He moved through the passengers, slapping shoulders. "Run! Quickly! Over! Now!" The four selected went up the plank and over, or over the rail. Diego quickly picked eight more, including two women. "Go!" The six men and one of the women jumped but the other woman collapsed, hysterical. Three of the hijackers seized her by the arms and legs and threw her, screaming, over the side.

Diego abruptly left the deck for the radio room. He reported the executions, repeated his demands and threatened to scuttle the ship with everyone on board if the demands were not met in full by seven A.M.

The gathering navies moved up the time of attack to dawn but at three A.M., without warning, a fast powerboat pulled alongside the ship and the terrorist contingent disembarked by ropes. Diego was the last one over the side. As he disappeared, the passengers rushed to the rail. He laughed and fired his assault rifle at them from below. They screamed and ducked back and he fired again. The powerboat vanished into the night, trailing a wake that was phosphorescent.

Four of the hapless passengers were picked out of the sea at dawn, barely alive, including the wounded English boy. His father drowned. His body and those of three others were washed up on shore over the next two days and four others were later recovered by boats. The other two bodies were never found.

The survivors were interviewed for days and were unable to describe any of the terrorists except for the one called Diego— that smile, those eyes, the hard edge to his voice—his wife, so incredibly attractive even in fatigues, and the one who looked like her whom she called Roman. Probably Balkan, the survivors all agreed. The other nine hijackers all seemed German.

The English boy and his mother were discreetly approached by a small City bank specialist firm on behalf of one of the small Austrian banks, who expressed condolences and suggested a price for the portfolio of bank securities owned by the deceased. The estate solicitor investigated and concluded that the offer was fair. Six weeks after the drowning, the estate quietly sold all its continental bank holdings.

Chapter 35

THERE WERE no further incidents for weeks. Then, without warning, it started again.

This time in Düsseldorf. At six o'clock in the morning, as usual, a chauffeur picked up the president and sole owner of the second largest private bank in the area. The black 800-series BMW was brand new and had a number of experimental features. The owner-president read the morning papers.

Two blocks from his home, an unmarked delivery van came out of a cross street without pausing at the stop sign and drove in front of them. The chauffeur jammed on the brakes to avoid smacking into it. The owner-president lurched nose-and-newspaper-first into the back of the right front seat. He cursed. The chauffeur angrily blasted his horn. The van stopped. Two heavily armed men and one woman surrounded the BMW. The woman held her assault rifle against the window beside the chauffeur's head. One man entered the right front door of the BMW. Another entered the back. In his lapel, he wore a tiny purple ribbon. The woman returned to the van. The man in the back of the BMW ordered the bank owner-president to telephone the bank on his car phone. The manager of the main branch had just had arrived, had he not? Call him and instruct him to open the vault and assemble 10 million Deutschemarks.

But the vault was a time vault, the owner-president protested. The man insisted. The bank had that much cash in the overnight vault for the payrolls going out early in the day. The owner-president denied it. The man repeated the order once more, call the bank. The owner-president attempted to argue. The man put his pistol against the head of the owner-president. The owner-president was stubborn. He refused. The man pulled the trigger.

The chauffeur screamed. The man beside him shoved his revolver against the chauffeur's mouth. The chauffeur whimpered. The man ordered him to drive the BMW back to the home of the owner-president. The chauffeur did so. The van followed.

At the house, they ordered the chauffeur to get out of the car. He did so, shaking. They then told him to dump the body on the front lawn. He did as he was ordered. They ordered him to get down on his knees. He did so. They asked if he wished to live. He said he did. They asked him to beg. He begged. They laughed. They got into the van. They asked if he was sure he wished to live. He said he was sure. They pointed guns at him. He closed his eyes. They told him to beg again. He begged again. They drove off and left him on his knees begging.

The chauffeur described two Balkan types, one of the men and the woman. They looked alike. A brother and a sister, there was that much resemblance. The other man was a South American, the one with the purple ribbon.

No group took credit for the crime. There was speculation about the identity of the terrorists but the Federal Police had in their files a prior reference to a purple ribbon.

Three weeks later, the bank was sold to a consortium of other small banks. At a fair price, the widow was reported to have said. The central bank praised her for her prompt decision to sell and assisted in the negotiations.

Chapter 36

NO WORD from Hugo or Sarah.

No word from Shima. Nothing.

I had packed. I stayed by the phone. One morning it rang. I answered, "Collins."

"Me." It was Shima. I sat up straight. He said, "I am here. I am coming."

I let him in.

The three men with him did a walk-through of my condo. One waited on my balcony. The other two waited in the corridor outside and closed the door behind them. I offered Shima coffee. He shook his head. He sat on my white couch in his raincoat. He said, "Congratulations. About the money."

"Thanks."

"Someday you must teach me money. Meanwhile, things are moving. Fast. And I am worried about something."

"My boy?"

"He is safe. And Sarah is still with him. Have you read about the *Empress of Corinth*?"

"That was our man?"

"And also the Düsseldorf shootings."

"I see." I took a deep breath. "Better them than me."

Shima said, "I have a favor to ask."

"What?"

"Think. What is the connection?"

"I don't understand."

He reached into his inside pocket and came up with a memorandum. "For you. What do you think?"

I scanned the memorandum. There were five short translations of attached German newspaper clippings. In Stuttgart, the prior Thursday, the same brother-sister Balkan team and the same South American, this time wearing a purple armband—Diego, they were now calling him—had robbed another private bank, downtown. They had shot and killed three persons, one teller, one guard and one fifty-six-year-old customer, a woman.

They had apparently driven directly from the bank to the suburban home of a major manufacturer of auto parts. They had arrived in the early evening. They had rung the doorbell and methodically shot the man, his wife, a bodyguard, the maid and two of his three young children. The third child had hidden in a cabinet in the kitchen.

Once again, no political group had taken credit for either crime. There was speculation about the motivation.

In Frankfurt, at three the following afternoon, three unidentified persons, two men and a woman, had shot their way into the executive offices of a chemical machinery plant, killed the president, vice president, treasurer, four clerks and two guards, and bolted with the week's payroll. One of the survivors had mentioned a purple armband. An hour and half later, the same killer trio had circled around through fields and woods and ambushed from behind the police roadblock south of the city, killing five.

At eight A.M. the next morning, the three had burst into a major resort hotel in Baden-Baden. They took the room keys from behind the desk, charged upstairs and assassinated in their vast bed the chairman of the board of the second-largest German insurance company and his wife.

The killers were believed to be heading south toward Switzerland. No group took credit for any of the incidents.

On Sunday, there had been another flurry. The police had trapped Diego in a Munich hotel. He had shot his way out of it, leaving behind four dead policemen. They had not known who he was until they had found the ribbon in the room.

I looked up. "What is the question?"

Shima said, "Your Diego was trained in the camps. He was sent there by someone in Germany. He is working for some German. We do not know who. Or where. Or why. Or what is the plan or program. We have a potential contact in the camps. We are using your money to pay him."

"What does he say?"

"Nothing. Yet."

"And Langley?" I said. "Surely you have asked there?"

"That is the reason for my presence here."

"And?"

"I am a paranoid hunter of Nazis, they say."

"And what else do they say?"

"Nothing," he said. "Can you help?"

"Why me?"

"We have reason to believe that support for the camps is coming from someone in German banking."

Chapter 37

IT WAS A SLICK OPERATION from the very start. Grigor enjoyed the American words. Piece of cake. Like a breeze. Went like clockwork. Everything happened almost exactly as planned, on schedule.

Diego had not made problems, which Grigor appreciated so much that he had said it. Diego did not know what to make of that; he was suspicious. Grigor was amused. Indeed, except for the woman, and Grigor considered that part of the plan an irritating bit of nonsense, it was as perfect as an exercise can be. No, Grigor would go further than that. It was magnificent.

Any new woman was brought to the desert tent for a week, bathed, perfumed, examined by physicians and prepared in every way required for the Emir's first visit. The requirements varied according to the Emir's shifting tastes. The Emir would make it clear to the harem master what he had in mind but he did not plan the length of the visits. Sometimes he came for a day or two. Once or twice, he had stayed for a month. That—according to the Emir's assistant, who had cooperated, motivated alike by hatred of the Emir and fear—had not occurred for years. The assistant had opined cautiously that this woman would not be worth it. she was Yemenite and very beautiful but darker than the Emir had expected. Three days, the assistant had predicted. In fact, he had hesitated to go so far, but if pushed to say exactly what he expected, he would say that, according to (a) form, (b) what he knew of the woman, (c) the Emir's physical condition and (d) his recent mood, the Emir would leave in a huge rush at the crack of dawn on the fourth day of the visit.

The assistant had been precisely correct and Grigor would see that he was paid as promised with an unasked 25 percent *pourboire*. Good work deserved a bonus.

There were six in the group, plus Grigor. Diego and the Romanian brother-sister were three. The other three were Palestinian, typical Bekaa camp fodder, but well-trained and highly recommended. The group had deployed in a huge van and an old Citroen. They parked by the side of the road. They waited. On the morning of the fourth day, the Palestinian in the hills behind the desert tent radioed shortly after five A.M. Here they come.

The soon-to-be-funereal cortege was arranged in its customary manner. First came the lead Cadillac. One thousand yards behind it came two large Lincolns. Close behind those came the stretch Cadillac. The armored Mercedes brought up the rear. The waiting ambush group let the lead car pass unimpeded. At a signal, they hit the Lincolns and Mercedes with rockets, and the stretch Cadillac with 150 mm recoilless rifles. All the rockets connected. All the target cars exploded. They hit the burning hulks with follow-up rockets. That was it for the Emir's bodyguards. The attack group machine-gunned the walking wounded.

The assault on the stretch Cadillac proved more difficult because of the need for survivors. The recoilless rifles had flat trajectories; the attackers just pointed them and fired at the engine block, wheels and axles. They hit the engine block, two wheels and the front axle. Two of the doors were off their hinges. They did not have to use the plastic. They dragged the Emir from the wreckage, stripped him stark naked, manacled him in steel shackles and dragged him off to the van. Grigor and Diego in front drove the van. The girl rode in the back with the Emir. Roman and the Palestinians waited at the attack scene for the lead car to double back. It did not return.

Roman and the Palestinians left the scene. The bodyguards had heard nothing, they later insisted. They had been slow to realize that they were no longer being followed. At that point, they had in fact returned. The bodyguards found the terrified driver, two secretaries and assistant lying face down in the sand at the side of the road beside the carnage.

Roman drove the Palestinians in the old Citroen to the rendezvous with the exit contacts. He left them there and rejoined the others in a filthy warehouse on the city outskirts. It was a Saturday. The area was deserted. They celebrated with coffee and waited for the girl to emerge.

In the back of the van, Ileana did as instructed.

She removed her watchcap and shook her hair loose. The ugly little lecher had a potbelly and more hair on his upper back than he had on his head. He did have large genitals. He had dribbled on himself as they had wilted. Ileana found that most unattractive. The Emir perked up when he saw that she was a woman, as predicted. Ileana then cheated. She smiled at him. He responded. He said to her, "You are extraordinarily attractive." Ileana was pleased. She had won the 10,000 Swiss franc wager. Roman had said the Emir would offer her money first.

The Emir now proceeded to do just that. "How would you like

ten million dollars in a Swiss account and a villa on the Italian Riviera?"

Why the Italian Riviera? Ileana wondered. He must think she is Italian, she decided. She said provocatively, "For what?"

"Ah," said the wizened old Emir. "You understand my interest. One million dollars for here and now."

"In fact, that is not impossible," said Ileana, encouraging him. "We will discuss it when we get to it. I have a fixed agenda."

"A which?"

"An assigned list of topics to discuss and the order in which I must discuss it. How do you propose to pay us?"

"I will pay you, not the rest," said the Emir. "I realize that it will take money to get rid of them, but you will arrange it."

"How?"

"I will give you a letter," said the Emir, "to a very important man."

"A banker?" said Ileana.

"Much more than a banker. A man who owns bankers. Who will do anything I tell him to do. Including eliminating—no, forget all that. Give me a piece of paper."

Ileana said, "Eliminating what? Bankers?" The Emir squinted at her. Ileana said, "What is the name of this banker?"

"I will write him a letter. You will see it on the piece of paper."

"Has he told you that you can mention his name?" said Ileana.

"Quite on the contrary. It is a secret," said the Emir.

"I should tell you my instructions. If you speak his name, we will cut your tongue out. If you write it, we will cut your hand off. If you see it, we will remove your eyes." The Emir was stunned. She went on, "Why do you think you are here?"

"For the ransom."

"Don't be foolish."

The Emir slowly said, "He is the one who sent you?"

"You had a good man eliminated."

"A banker. Only a banker."

"Yes."

"And for this, he kills my people? For this he has me kidnapped? They were charging me for counting my money!"

"Because you were making too much trouble."

"Were not you the one who did it? One of the ones who did it for me?"

"And you talk too much."

"Me?" said the Emir.

"You mentioned his name to the banker. Although you knew it was a secret."

"Indeed," said the Emir and thought about it. "That is true. I did. I was angered. I suppose it is just that I pay for this slip. How much shall I pay for it?"

"I do not know. I have not been told. What you must do now is the next item on the agenda," said Ileana and smiled at him. "I will free your right hand and give you a pen. You will sign six blank pieces of paper."

"Which he will then complete as he wishes. And if I refuse?" said the Emir.

"I will cut off your hand," she said. He looked at her unblinking. Ileana produced his scimitar. The Emir recognized it. He felt a stirring, a genital response to fear. She smiled at him and licked her lips.

The Emir felt a stirring of a different order. "And if I do sign?"

Ileana said, "We will then proceed to the next item on the agenda?"

"Is that the one which interests me?"

"Sort of," Ileana said.

"Then I will sign the papers," said the Emir.

Ileana brought Grigor outside the van the six blank signed pieces of paper. Girgor opened his thin flat leather case and removed a control sheet, a sample of the Emir's signature. "Very good," he pronounced. "You have succeeded."

"Thus far," said Roman.

Diego snickered.

"Stop it," said Ileana. She returned to the van.

The Emir was sitting up in the corner. He was, of course, still manacled, except for the hand she had left free. "Well?" he said eagerly.

"You have a choice," Ileana said.

"What is that?"

"If you wish, I will invite my associates in and they will shoot you in the head."

"I find that unattractive," said the Emir.

"You have not yet heard the alternative. You and I can have sexual intercourse," said Ileana. "You will remain bound except for the hand. I will hold a pistol to your head."

"And shoot me if I fail to satisfy? Or perhaps if I do!" The Emir laughed. "Sold. Let us do it."

"My friends will watch," she said.

"So be it."

"And afterwards, I will castrate you. With your own scimitar. My friends will put your genitals in your mouth. They will bind your head with a piece of your robe and hang you by your ankles overnight."

"What an ugly thought," said the Emir.

"You must choose," she said and waited.

"What happens the next day?" said the Emir.

"Oh," said Ileana. "I forgot that."

"I do not think I am going to like it."

"We will give you a choice again."

"Explain it?"

"I will cut off your head if you ask it."

"Or?" said the Emir.

"We will hang you up by your ankles for another night."

"And ask me again the next day?"

Ileana nodded. "And now you must choose at once."

"Easily," said the Emir. "I choose to die as I have lived."

Ileana said, with a sinking heart, "How?"

"I always choose the sex first."

Ileana emerged from the van. She leaned against it. They surrounded her. She shook her head. They waited. She said, "I cannot do this."

They groaned.

Diego said, "You can do anything."

Roman said, "My poor weak sister."

Grigor said, "You agreed."

"I did."

"Well?"

"I should not have. I find myself disgusted."

Grigor said, as he had been instructed, "He will be very disappointed."

She said, "I am sure."

"And you will forfeit the one million Deutschemarks."

"So be it."

"Not so fast," said her brother. "I think it is fair that she should forfeit, but what of us? We have done what we were told to do. Why don't we do it?"

"Do what?" said Diego drily.

"Not that!" Roman said, laughing. "Not the first. The rest."

Grigor was impressed with how close they came to what the old man had predicted. Grigor said evenly, "He wants her to do it. He was clear and explicit."

"That is easy," Roman said. "Let us divide the money between us and tell him she has done it. Then he will not be disappointed in her and what he wants done will in fact have been done."

"Except of course," said Diego, "for who did it. I don't know. I am undecided. I find it all foolish."

So did Grigor although he never said it. Grigor told them, "The money must be kept in boxes. All of it. By each of us. He monitors bank deposits."

"Good idea," said Diego. "I forgot."

Grigor was shocked that he would admit it.

They confronted the Emir with the scimitar. The Emir protested, he had been given a choice, and absent the sex, he chose to be shot. They argued with each other. He had elected the sex. Should they not castrate him, hang him upside down and cut off his head? Those were their instructions.

Ileana pleaded, Shoot the old rascal. And in the end, they did.

As agreed, they told the old man that Ileana had performed as he had wished. The old man had Grigor pay her. She gave the money to the others. They divided it among them and put it in safe deposit boxes. So far as the rest knew, the old man never did find out.

The old man, of course, did find out. He was immediately told by Grigor.

"Predictable," he said to Grigor.

The bank set up an *anstalt* for the benefit of the Emir's wives and sons, and their wives and sons and so on for five generations down the line. The bank had discretion as to who would get what and the bank would control the investments.

No one at the bank ever knew what had taken place. From the point of view of the unknowing bank, however, it would keep the money for one hundred and fifty years. The operation certainly succeeded.

Chapter 38

SHIMA WAS SEASICK.

He had been delighted with the invitation and had changed his schedule so that he could accept it. Oliver Nelson Brooke was the most powerful American non-Jew Shima knew. Thanks to the lunatic American election laws, no national campaign could be funded without the support of Brooke, or someone like Brooke, and the fact that no one had heard of the man was something Shima admired.

Unfortunately, Brooke's idea of male bonding was a day-sail together in a small boat, and Shima was a weak sailor.

Halfway Rock was more or less halfway between Marblehead and Rockport. It was totally covered with guano. Brooke had happily called it Shit Island as they had passed it this morning. They were coming up on it again, on their left side now, returning. Marblehead to Rockport and back. Brooke had said his old 110–the first boat he had ever owned, and lovingly refurbished more than a dozen times—was his and Marge's favorite.

What Brooke had not said was that his boat was rigged with both its own recording equipment and sensitive devices for detecting other broadcasting or recording devices in the event a passenger was wired or wearing. Shima was neither, but the upper red light on the sonar depth machine panel indicated that Brooke was recording whatever they said. And Shima knew this because his locals, his *sayanim*, had boarded and searched the boat the night before. Accordingly, Shima had watched what he was saying. Brooke's hand had flickered toward the switch twice. Shima found that fascinating. Brooke had considered turning off his own recording.

Shima was seized with another wave of nausea. The wind had picked up and the sky was turning gray. The swells were huge, ten feet or more, and the whitecaps seemed to be getting closer. Shima shuddered and repressed a heave that would not have been dry, and would have left him embarrassed.

"I'm so sorry," said Brooke in his nasal twang, the voice of cold roast Boston. "I had no idea. It is most unusual on sailboats, you know. It only happens on stinkpots. You know, ships with engines."

Shima nodded wretchedly. He gestured off at the island. To port. "Isn't it getting worse now?"

"Yes," said Brooke, "and the wind is shifting. We'll be coming about in a moment. In fact, enough. Ready about! Head down!" He scrambled forward, holding the tiller in his fingertips, and loosed the jib sheet. "Hard alee!" He shoved the tiller down.

The bow swung left, into the wind and swells, and froze there, the sails furiously fluttering, the bow riding up, down, farther up, farther down, pounding, pounding.

"My goodness!" screamed Brooke. "We're not turning!"

He pulled the tiller back toward him, eased it away and sawed it back toward him, hard. The bow eased to the right, slightly, then swung wide as the sails filled and the boom slammed to the right, grazing Brooke's head.

Brooke laughed. "No fool like an old one!" he chortled, lashing down the jib, watching the sails as they picked up speed, reaching back for the tiller.

Shima stared at him. The man is going to drown us, Shima thought, and look at him, he's happy. Crazy man. Goyim.

"Hard alee!" Brooke shouted. He loosed the jib and pushed the tiller down again. The bow swung hard left, into the wind and swells again, the sails furiously fluttering again, the bow riding up, down, farther up, farther down. Brooke sawed the tiller away from him. The bow swung tighter into the wind and hung there, pounding. Water crashed over the bow, soaking Shima and wetting Brooke, who cursed this time.

Brooke gave up and started sawing the tiller toward him. For an instant, nothing happened. The boat hung there, in irons, and another heavy wave piled in. Shima was helpless. Brooke grinned his crazy goy grin, sawing, sawing. The bow eased to the right, slightly, and finally swung wide. The sails filled and the boom slammed to the right, and this time Brooke ducked it.

Shima looked about. The swells were horrible, huge, black-green, foaming at the tops, churning at the bottoms. The island ahead was nearly on them.

Brooke lashed down the jib, watching the sails, reaching back for the tiller, as they picked up speed.

"Hard alee again!" Brooke shouted again. He loosed the jib and pushed the tiller down. The bow swung hard left, into the wind and swells, the sails furiously fluttering, the bow riding up, down, farther up, farther down. Brooke sawed the tiller. The bow swung tighter into the wind and hung there. Water crashed over the bow, soaking them. Brooke cursed and sawed—and sawed again—and they seemed to be turning! An inch! Another inch! And—they turned!

The sails filled as they came about, heeling over hard. Brooke reached forward for the jib sheets, playing them. The sails filled as they came off the wind and suddenly they were running free for the shore. He lashed down the sheet. "Hooray!" shouted the grinning goyim. "That was a bit of a tight one."

The swells were now behind them. They seemed to soar, smoothly planing. Shima took a deep breath. "What would have happened if we didn't turn the third time?"

"We would have had a choice," said Brooke. "We could sail the ship to the Azores or try to swim to the island."

Shima stared. "If you were gone, they'd postpone the election."

Brooke smiled and looped the coiled line over the cleat.

Shima realized that the mal de mer had left him. He took another deep breath, then another one. He was cold and wet and shivering. The boat was soaring on the crest of the waves, powering ahead, aquaplaning.

Brooke fumbled beneath the seats, coming up with a bottle. Mount Gay rum. He handed it to Shima, who uncapped it and took a swig. It was fiery and Shima began to choke.

Brooke said, "Remind me to tell you someday how my great grandfather made his fortune."

"Rum?" Shima was again croaking.

"The triangle trade—slaves, molasses, rum. Your color is better. Is your sickness gone?"

Shima nodded. The man was not unkind. Brooke's visit to the Holy Land had been a huge success.

Brooke threw the rocker switch on the depth machine, turning off his recording machine, and promptly caught Shima watching. "You knew," Brooke said.

Shima let it go.

"Really, you might have said something."

Shima said nothing.

Brooke had reddened. "I must apologize for treating a guest like that. It is not my style. Not at all." He repeated it, "Nottattall," and added, "Arthur Santry kept insisting. His rude CIA training."

Shima grimaced and shrugged with his hands.

Brooke was shaking his head. "Santry says you're way off base. The terrorists are acting on their own, not for some big European," he said. "And each attack is a separate event, no plan, no connection or coordination."

"I know," said Shima. "For months, that is what he has been saying."

"As I see it," said Brooke, "there are three parts to this. First, the German connection. You have to stop pounding that one. You hurt yourself. Our source is better. He even tells us what you are doing." He held up his hand to forestall the questions.

Shima felt dizzy with frustration. What did he mean? What had their source told them? Source singular, a person.

"I know I stepped over the line there," said Brooke. "I deliberately gave you something. I need all the help I can get. I've been such a pest that they are cutting me out. I believe in what I am doing."

"All of which we appreciate," Shima said, "and that is the reason I am here today. Please feel free to ask what you want. I will do what I can. Within reason."

"In a moment. Second," Brooke was continuing with his orderly summary, "there is the terrorist thing. We know it is very serious. And we know they are planning something. They are always planning something. But what? Can you tell me? We would help if we could. Even Santry would help. I think I have seen to that one. Third, your insistence that it will happen here. That is most important."

"To you."

"What is important to me is important to you. If we can call the event in advance, we will win. Even if it happens. Is there anything you can give me to work on? Otherwise," Brooke paused and shrugged. It was a tight, pale imitation of Shima's shrug. "Otherwise, we are whistling in the dark, and no one will pay attention."

Shima felt his nausea returning. He said, "A large number of people will be either killed or taken. Mostly Jews, we are sure of that. A major social function."

"Where? What function?"

"I regret that we do not know that. Yet."

Brooke grimaced. "Then I regret very much telling you that we feel that we can do nothing."

The boat crested over the top of the swells and now they were heading down, a terrifying rush into the trough, like a submarine diving. Were they going to sink straight to the bottom?

Brooke was paying it no attention.

Shima gathered himself and said, "General Steele said that? You asked him?"

Brooke said, "My goodness. You know about him, too."

"Marine Special Forces. You trust him."

"I do. Odd you should find that out. And here I thought I was no one. The invisible man in Boston. Well. It just goes to show you. Nothing is ever certain." He shifted into explanation. "Steele says we're just too big. Too many airports, too many borders, too much coastline. For practical purposes, we are defenseless. When you leave here, where are you going?"

The question came so smoothly that Shima almost blurted the answer out. But he was too well-trained. He restrained himself for a moment of hesitation. The boat was deep in the trough now. Would the rising green torrent swamp them? Nothing was happening. They rushed along. Relief. "Los Angeles," Shima said, uncharacteristically. Why on earth had he told him?

Brooke made a face. "Bad," he said.

Shima said, "Why? Too many great big weddings, bar mitzvahs, charity functions?"

Brooke said, "It's the biggest port in the country now for travel and immigration. It's our new Ellis Island. And in addition to the port, there's the border, there's the coastline."

"So you feel you can do nothing." The wind had picked up and Shima was wet and cold.

"There's an alert to all airports and borders but let's face it, that is nothing. Would you like police help in Los Angeles?" Brooke felt impotent and he was trying.

Shima said, "I would love police help if I knew what to ask, but what am I going to tell them? We hear there are terrorists coming to town? Something is going to happen?"

"Mmm," Brooke grunted. "Well. Here we are."

They were soaring past some small islands. Moments later, inside Marblehead habor, the wind died. Shima felt warm for the first time since noon.

He watched Brooke pick up their mooring.

Chapter 39

GUNTHER INSISTED they meet in Bonn. He had to see the politicians.

Grigor flew in with Diego, Ileana and Roman. They checked into the Hotel Bristol. It was the only four-star hotel in town.

Gunther himself did not come to the meeting. He had an apartment in Bonn, too. He had Grigor bring Ileana to him.

Meanwhile, Werner met in the hotel suite with Diego and Roman. "Well done," he said.

Diego snapped his fingers at Roman. Roman, smiling, handed Werner a gift-wrapped package. Werner opened the package. It was a glass jar.

It contained the Emir's private parts.

"It is a present," Diego was saying.

Werner managed to control his features. When he was certain they were impassive, he said, "I will give it to him."

"And when do I get to meet him?"

"Not yet. After the next assignment."

"Too bad. Because the one we just did," said Diego, "was the last assignment."

"Not quite."

"Quite."

"Wrong."

Diego's temper flared. "You promised me the American."

"Yes. You are going to London."

Diego said, "For him?" He was at once alert.

"Listen carefully." Werner leaned forward and dropped his voice. "A senior Mossad person is at the Savoy Hotel in London. He is sniffing at our operations. Your man is at the Connaught."

"Collins," Diego said.

"Yes. The two of them are meeting."

"And?" said Diego.

"You do both. But only both."

"Fine."

"And only when they are together," Werner said.

Diego made a face. "That is not so fine."

"But those are the conditions. It is critical that it happen exactly that way. It must appear like an attack on the Mossad man, your man an innocent victim."

"Why?"

"We do not wish to call attention to him. He has been asking certain banking questions."

Diego glowered. He looked at Roman. Roman shrugged. Diego looked at Werner again.

Werner said, "Do you want Roman to come with you?"

Diego said, "I am in charge? I do the kills?"

"Of course."

"Then send Roman."

Chapter 40

ILEANA WAS rapidly losing control, to the limited extent she had any. He insisted that she urinate on his chest, squatting over him. He masturbated with relish in the meantime. She concentrated on the good things. It was his chest, not his face. It was on him, not on her. They were on the bathroom floor, not in the bed, a hopeful sign. He was such a meticulous man. There had been no mention of defecation. Yet.

When he finally ejaculated, and it seemed as if he never would, before he could recoup, she hugged him, notwithstanding the urine. He was in a semitrance. She insisted on washing him in the bathtub. He lay there, passively, until she was done. She got down on her hands and knees and washed the bathroom floor with a sponge and pail, using a combination of water, detergent, disinfectant and deodorant she found under the sink in the kitchen.

She showered when she was done.

He watched her the whole time.

When she came out of the bathroom, toweling herself, her heart sank. He was sitting on the bed. On it, beside him, were several sets of handcuffs and the old English sailor whip, the cat of nine something. The old man's eyes were gleaming.

This was her chance.

She sat on the edge of the bed. "Sir?"

"You will call me Gunther."

"Yes, sir. I mean Gunther. Sir. Herr Waffen."

He grinned. "What?"

"Do you really want to do this?"

A beat. "What do you mean?" he said. "I want what I want."

"Of course." She stroked his belly, between his legs, lightly. He quivered and responded at once. She licked her lips. "Only, you are such a clean man."

"And you are a clean woman. I will never forget you there on the bathroom floor. On your hands and knees. Your tail in the air. You smell of the disinfectant."

"Oh," she said, concerned. "Shall I wash my hands again?"

"It wasn't your hands I was remembering."

With both hands, Ileana stroked him. She leaned forward, kissed him, pushed him down. She moved over him, knees lightly straddling him. She reached down and fondled him. "Did someone once make you do this sort of thing? Someone very dear to you? At a time when it wasn't working? I mean between the two of you? And then this, and you felt unclean? You felt it was a perversion?"

He stiffened. He studied her. She could not read him. "Well," he said. "You certainly are a strange one." She caressed him lightly. She bent down and kissed him on the lips. She smiled. He forced his hips up against her. She made sounds of contentment. He caressed her breasts. She blushed. She sat back. She took him in both her hands. She stroked him. "Stop," he said in a faint voice.

She did, knowing he hadn't wanted her to stop. Ask, she pleaded silently. Ask. Ask me what do I think you want. Go ahead. Ask.

He did ask. "What do you think I want?"

Ileana told him.

Chapter 41

SHIMA HAD SUMMONED me to London but he was in no hurry. I cooled my heels at the Connaught for two full days. In the late afternoon, of the third day, I was seated at one of the tiny tables in the bar. I had two native-born Tanquerays. Gin from the home of gin. I was rapidly losing all the rest of my dwindling stock of patience.

"Please don't turn," said the voice behind me. I did not turn. "You have been waiting several days for someone."

"Yes."

"He is here but there is a problem. Please be very careful all the time."

It is amazing how sober you can suddenly get. "That sounds ominous."

"It is. Do you enjoy theater?"

"What does that mean?"

"The hall porter has the ticket you ordered."

"For when?"

"Tonight."

"I am free tonight," I said.

"A car will be waiting. Don't dawdle outside the hotel here or outside the theater entrance. You will leave at the end of Act II, Scene 1. Don't run but move quickly. The same car will be waiting."

I heard rustling noises behind me, coins on a plate. He was paying his check and leaving.

"Hello, there, don't I know you?" said Shima.

I froze, standing in front of my seat, my coat over my arm.

"Collins? Michael Collins?" He had a seat in the row behind me.

"How do you do, sir," I said, and shook Shima's hand. I seated myself and turned. "How is he?"

"Fine." That was it.

I turned away. The play began. I felt alert, alive.

Shima leaned forward and said in my ear, "Don't you just love the theater in London?"

I left as the curtain went down on Act II, Scene 1, clutching my coat and bolting up the aisle. Two men met me in the lobby outside. One took my coat. The other handed me a heavy trenchcoat. I was putting it on before I realized what it was. "Kevlar? Bulletproof?"

They did not deign to answer. They were wearing huge, floppy, weapon-concealing greatcoats themselves. One produced a walkie-talkie. He clicked it on. He spoke into it, Hebrew. He held my arm. We waited. He heard what he wanted. "We go."

They hustled me out of the theater, one in front, one at my side, a Secret Service special. My car was waiting. They got in with me, and off we drove. I saw wooden horses, a roadblock, police vans and bobbies searching cars all over the place. "Bomb scare?" I said, mystified.

They gave me no explanation.

Our car pulled over to the curb a block from the hotel. Strong and silent was on his walkie-talkie again. He spoke to the driver. "They chased him off, go!"

They circled the block and paused at the Connaught door. They got out first, scanned and pulled me out of the car. My favorite night doorman was most impressed. They pulled me through the lobby with them. The hall porter and reception saw no evil.

The tiny elevator was waiting.

Up.

They checked my hotel suite and left me there with a fond farewell: "Don't go near the windows."

"Sure," I said.

"Very good," one of them said. "We'll come for you in the morning."

Chapter 42

DIEGO DID NOT MUCH LIKE the Kalashnikov, even this specially-modified sniper version. It was too big, too clumsy and not all that accurate in his opinion, which was not humble. At this range, however, he could not miss.

He had rented a Humber because it was such a stable car. It was parked across the street from the theater and fifty meters away. Diego was going to do it as instructed, first the Israeli, then the American. In case the American was not killed, Roman was across town covering the Connaught Hotel entrance. It was a good plan, not perfect, but they were after all only the two of them. Finding out about the theater tickets had been a stroke of luck. They owed thanks to the Arab hotel-employee grapevine.

There were less than ten minutes to go before the final theater curtain. Diego was loading the automatic rifle when he heard the noise.

Sirens.

Was it the police? A fire? What?

Three police vans careened into the street and past him. Unarmed bobbies in their ridiculous uniforms poured out. They set up wooden-horse roadblocks at both ends of the street. They started on the parked cars, one by one, using metal detectors, opening, searching.

It was a bomb scare.

Diego cursed.

The American's car across the street started its engine. It pulled out from the curb and rolled forward, obscuring the theater entrance. What was going on? The bobbies let the car remain there. The American came out of the theater, flanked by two Israelis and wearing a strange coat. Diego's car window was open. He had two seconds to shoot. He did not. The American and his companions jumped in the car. Off it went.

Diego cursed again. The bobbies were moving toward him down the line of cars. People were coming out of the theater now. Where was the Mossad man? Come on. Come on now. Wait. The bobbies were close. Wait some more. Ten more people, twenty, still no Mossad man. The bobbies were on him. Diego grimaced, put the Humber in gear and drove off, studying the crowd at the theater entrance as he passed them.

There was still no sign of the Mossad man.

Diego decided to go around the block and try again. He paused at the wooden-horse roadblock; the bobbies moved it away. Diego drove on and got stuck in traffic at once. Hopeless. Nerve-wracking. It was twelve full minutes before he returned and of course, the theater had emptied by then.

It was a bad night for Diego.

It was Roman's turn. Could he rely on Roman?

In front of the Connaught Hotel, three streets come together. Cars park on all sides and beside the triangle in the middle of the street. Roman was parked across the street opposite the hotel entrance.

He looked around startled. The bobby had rapped on the window with his knuckles. Roman cranked down the window.

"Restricted zone, would you kindly move along, sir?"

"Oh. What about those cars over there, in front of the hotel?" Roman said.

"The ones in front of the hotel, sir? There are six live spaces for the hotel. Would you like to wait for one of those, sir? That would be fine but you must keep moving."

Roman drove away. He circled, ran into a one-way pattern, doubled back and tried again.

The bobby was waiting. There were still no spaces free. Roman felt like he was making a fool of himself. He drove off.

He left a note for Diego at Diego's pension.

The long-haired elderly banker, the alternative target they had given him, according to his dossier lived a block and a half from the Thames and took long walks on its banks at midnight.

Seething from the theater fiasco, Diego went to the banker's home at 11:30 P.M. He needed to do well what he knew how to do. Diego stood in the shadows. He had to wait less than fifteen minutes. The banker came out and went for his walk. Diego followed him. It was a waltz. On the banks of the blue-black Thames. He had a 9 mm Beretta in his belt, the new military weapon.

The banker heard Diego's footsteps. He turned his head. Diego smiled his nervous smile. He said, "Hello?" and lifted his hand with the gun. In the darkness, he couldn't see the three dots of the sight, so he just leveled the gun, sighted along the barrel at the eye and fired. Crack! The eye disappeared. The puncture was

neat. The man collapsed. A neat kill. London was no longer vir-
ginal. The eye hit suggested something. Diego ignored the exploded bloody mess at the back of the head, reached down and
shot out an upper front tooth. Make it look like a revenge hit, an
eye for an eye, a tooth for a tooth. The second slug smashed
through the jaw and collarbone and angled into the pavement.

Diego hauled the body to the riverbank. He pushed it in. He
field-stripped the gun. He threw each of the six pieces separately
into the river along a one-mile stretch with five reverse twists. He
thought about going to the Connaught. Roman was there. He did
not feel like facing Roman yet. He took a long slow walk back to
his pension, his crummy bed and breakfast.

It was too bad about the American and the Mossad man. He
would be patient and get the two of them another time. Bad luck
did happen.

He thought about the kill he had made.

There was one thing about it that bothered him. It was the color
of the hole in the head. You would think that it would be gray
from the lead, or white from the bone, or red from the blood.

It wasn't any of those.

It was black. Why? It didn't seem logical. Diego would have to
ask someone. Fox Face?

No. The Russian.

Diego wanted an explanation.

At the bed and breakfast, there was a note on his door. Roman
had called.

Diego went back into the street. He hailed a cab. He went to
Roman's hotel and they compared notes. Roman shook his head.
"That is too much bad luck."

Diego gritted his teeth. He did not want to talk about it with
Roman.

It got worse. When they phoned in the morning, the targets had
each checked out.

Diego and Roman remained in London for six more days trying

to pick up the trail again. It was fruitless. Diego made the check-in call.

"Leave town," said the anonymous German accent.

"Why?" Diego said. "We like it here."

He heard a snort, then the single word, "Go."

"Sorry," Diego said, "we are not ready to go. We have two people to do."

"You are a fool," said the voice, "you have lost them. You will do as you are told. Today. Now."

"Thank you very much. Who is this?" Diego said.

"Someone who is clever enough," said the voice, "not to tell you who I am. Go to Frankfurt and make your next call. A mutual friend wants to meet you."

"How can we have a mutual friend," Diego said, "or a mutual anything else, when I don't know who you are?"

The voice said, "And you never will. Have you figured out as yet why the police were there?"

"I don't know what you are talking about."

"The bomb scare."

"Oh," said Diego. "Is that what it was?"

The voice grunted. "Good for you. No. That is not what it was. MI-5 received a warning call. And the monkeys chased your tail around the flagpole."

"What?"

"That is an old American saying."

Roman flew back to Damascus and the camps.

Diego flew to Frankfurt and made his phone call. The person who received the call patched Werner in. He summoned Diego to Berchtesgaden.

It was a spectacular day in the mountains. Gunther arranged to be alone except for the two old servant women. Werner brought Diego, introduced the two of them and left. The old women brought coffee to the terrace. Diego looked at the mountains. It was serene. Diego was not.

He told Gunther in detail what had happened. Diego was impassioned. He was angry, frustrated, impotent. He raged at Werner for the instructions. At Gunther for the impossible condition. At the American. At the damned Mossad man. At the bobbies for appearing. At the person, whoever it was, who sold them out.

There was one odd element. Gunther held up his hand. "We know there was a call to MI-5 about an attempted assassination. But as I understand it, you think they knew it was you."

"It felt like that."

"You have no proof. They let you drive away. You cannot be certain."

"No," said Diego. "Maybe they did not know what I looked like. Maybe they had no description. Maybe they had heard that I was dangerous and decided it was prudent to let me go."

Gunther said ambiguously, "I am inclined to trust your instincts."

Diego whirled. "What else do you know?"

"I know nothing. But I shall take steps to ascertain if there is a leak of some sort. I will plug it if there is one."

Diego was raving. "I had a shot. I could have shot him!"

"At sixty meters, with men on both sides of him?"

"I had support, the window of the car, and an automatic weapon! I kept thinking the Israeli would follow him out. I could pop the Israeli, shift to the car. And shoot! And keep shooting!"

"Don't be hard on yourself," Gunther said. "Your accomplishments have been brilliant."

"I failed! And I wanted this!"

"True, but it is not final."

"You find the son," said Diego, "and I will kill the man!"

"All in due course," said Gunther, "you will get your chance. Meanwhile I will have to see if there has been some sort of betrayal."

Chapter 43

IT WAS PEACEFUL. The peace that comes with survival.

There we were, at dusk, sitting on the terrace behind some-body's five-hundred-year-old Welsh cottage. It was ours for the weekend, period. The terrace was fieldstone, the lawn vast. To get a lawn like that, you roll it. And roll it and roll it. It was somewhere near Harlech. I remembered the battle and the song. All those spearmen and bowmen, those knaves and hinds and yeomen, had they died and become fertilizer for this lawn? Or survived and spent their lives rolling it? Shima's warriors of the present day were out of sight in the forest. He could not go anywhere anymore unless he was protected. Especially in England now after what had happened in London.

They had told me what had gone wrong. MI-5 had sent the bobbies out unarmed. A little failure of communication.

Shima was wearing a double-breasted Savile Row blazer with sterling monogrammed buttons, flared charcoal slacks, knee-length wool socks and rich dark cordovan loafers. Unfortunately, being Israeli, he wore a flowered open collar sport shirt. In honor of his tielessness and sport shirt, I wore a nine-year-old T-shirt. Also my fifteen-year-old and most treasured Levi's, frayed and stringy at the left knee, both ankles tattered. He was an undercompensated bureaucrat and liked to spend big money on clothes, whereas in my laid-back middle-class America, the richest affected the oldest.

Shima tasted his champagne marc and told me about his new kibbutz in the Negev. I sipped my Jack Daniel's English-style, no ice and crushed mint leaves I had picked myself in the bushes surrounding the terrace. It was one of those rare occasions when it was polite to smell my fingers. I did.

He abruptly stopped talking.

"Tell me about my son," I said.

"He's doing well."

"And Sarah?" I said.

"Still with him."

"In Europe?" I said.

Silence. Shima sniffed his marc and did not answer me. "I told you about our informant?"

"Yes."

"He says you were specifically targeted by the people in charge," Shima said. "Not by Diego alone."

"Ah. Then I'm right."

"About what?" Shima was as alert as I had ever seen him.

"The banker's program."

"Go on," he said.

"I have no proof, but I've been guessing. And asking around. There is someone controlling currency rates by controlling the brokers and the banks who trade and who has huge funds for trading."

"Go on."

I said, "I suspected it in my trading. I've been asking my banks, and your bank, too—"

"Herr Barisch?"

"And they all know nothing. But you remember the question you asked last time?"

"About the connection, if there was one, between the terrorist incidents and banking?" Shima said.

"Remember the Englishman on the *Empress of Corinth*? He owned bank stocks on the continent. When he died, the family sold them. To a small bank in Vienna."

"Düsseldorf! The victim owned a bank."

"Which was sold to a consortium of other small banks. Now watch this," I said. "Remember your clippings? Stuttgart, Frankfurt, Baden-Baden?"

Shima was excited. "In Stuttgart, they robbed a bank. But none of the people killed were banks. They were industry, insurance—"

"They all owned stock in the robbed bank. Controlling stock, between them."

"Are you sure?" he said.

"That's what my bank said. After checking. The auto parts business one of them owned was the largest single borrower from the bank, a one-man business. The sales collapsed, the bank called the loans at the end of the month, the business could not pay, the bank had to take the loss on its books and the impairment of capital made the bank marginally insolvent."

"And?"

"Get this," I told him. "One of the regional banks stepped up with new capital in exchange for control of management and a debt-and-stock arrangement. The central bank praised everyone because it all worked out without government intervention."

"That's it." Shima was pacing. "You got him. So that's what he's up to, the old man, the German. We even have the name from the informant. He's fucking the sister of the informant. Now we have to prove it to Santry.

"Who?"

"The CIA Langley." He sat on the stone wall. "And I made a mistake. Unfortunately."

"What?" I said.

"I told Santry about him," Shima said. "So now he knows that I'm onto him."

"And he knows about me because my bank has been asking questions about sales of banks and bank control and funny stuff in the markets, price manipulation—whoa! What do you mean, you told Santry, and they told him?"

Shima said, "They felt they had to confront him."

"How come?"

"He has been their best source for forty years of European banking information."

Chapter 44

KLOTEN Airport in Zurich was a depressing lake of tiny black rubber floor-covered buttons, ingeniously designed for cleanliness. They were easy to install, easy to maintain and easy to replace when needed. They were washed and machine-buffed once a day.

The black absence of color on the floor hid dirt. The low level of lighting from above hid dirt. There were no reflections.

Diego approved of the dimness. He had arrived on the early flight from Istanbul. He cleared immigration with his new Turkish papers and walked toward the Air France First Class lounge. There were convenience chairs in the corridor, made of black leather and chromed steel tubing. An elderly couple dozed in two of the chairs, the man slovenly in a green acrylic shirt, the woman with hairy facial moles, an unfortunate matching mustache and a lapful of plastic carrying bags containing gift-wrapped packages. Duty-frees. Roman was lounging in the eighth chair down, an Air France flight bag on his lap, another on the seat beside him. He was checking his watch.

Diego asked him the time, in Turkish.

Roman told him, in Turkish.

Diego thanked him, in Turkish, and glanced about.

"She isn't here," said Roman. "She is with him." He spat the word "him."

Diego took the small Air France flight bag from the chair next to Roman and entered the First Class lounge.

Roman said nothing.

Inside the lounge, Diego handed his ticket to the plump platinum blonde female clerk at the desk, Anna, according to her white-trimmed blue enamel name tag. She said she would check him in, if he pleased.

He nodded slightly. He would be pleased.

She would call him in advance of the flight, she said, at least thirty minutes.

He smiled his brief nervous flash of smile and went over to the huge plate-glass window. The view was bleak. The window was less than clean. Neither the coffee table nor the end table between the right-angled couches had been cleared. The couches were brown leather overstuffed and too deep for comfort. Werner-Fox Face and Grigor-Horse Face sat on one couch, reading the morning Swiss papers. Diego sat on the other couch, the Air France flight bag in his lap. He zipped it open and examined the contents. A small Czech machine-pistol. Three extra loaded banana clips.

And a gift from Roman, his joke of the day, a tiny can of Binaca. The two of them had wrestled the week before, and Diego had suggested that Roman try to get the Listerine concession for the Balkans.

Diego flashed his quick smile again and zipped up the flight bag. Werner and Grigor were reading their papers. That was fine. Diego did not mind waiting.

Outside, in the corridor, two Hasidim were approaching, complete with broad-brimmed black hats, glasses, spit curls, beards, black capes and black carpet bags, babbling to each other spiritedly in Hebrew, engrossed in each other's problems. The elderly man in the green shirt opened his eyes and looked at them with droopy distaste. His wife adjusted her packages.

The Hasidim stopped at the coffee machine. They examined it and discussed how it worked. They were confused by the directions. Eventually they pumped in the requisite coins. Their first cup dropped, its coffee dripped, they exclaimed with pleasure. They conferred and decided to share. They sipped, slurping, chuckling. They deposited both the cup and some food trash from their carpet bags in the black steel refuse container. They wandered off, still animated, still chuckling. The elderly coupled watched them.

Roman struggled erect in his seat, stretched, checked his watch and rose to his feet. He searched his pocket for coins and found some. He walked across the corridor to the coffee machine. The elderly lady down the line disinterestedly adjusted the packages in her lap but otherwise paid no attention.

A pager in Grigor's pocket beeped. He shut it off.

Werner said, "Your friend outside makes me nervous."

Diego glanced at him. "How?"

Grigor appeared to sink deeper into his newspaper. "He was not where he was supposed to be."

"Twice," said Werner.

"Sex with someone?" said Diego.

"That is likely, knowing him," Werner said, "but with whom? And why leave without permission?"

Grigor said, "We have not asked him for an explanation."

Diego was motionless.

Werner said, "He has a bank account. A different name. And quite a bit of money in it which did not come from us. We are trying to trace the source."

Diego said, "And?"

Grigor said carefully, "In the corridor outside this room. Something has just happened."

"That was the pager," Werner said.

Diego said, "Kill him."

The room seemed very quiet. The two of them watched him. Werner said, "This is no time for joking."

Diego looked at him.

Grigor said, "The group is still in Istanbul. Their flight does not leave until morning. There is time to abort. But I am unwilling."

Werner said, "Yet."

"Go outside," Diego said. "See what happened there."

Grigor rose, tucked his newspaper under his arm and walked out of the lounge.

Diego watched him.

Werner said, "You would need to send everyone back to the camps and train for a week with someone else."

"Less," Diego said. "Forty-eight hours."

Werner shook his head. "I don't believe it. It is Roman or we abort it."

Diego said, "And the sister?"

Werner thought about it. "That is delicate. Because of the person whose name we do not mention."

"Will she be on the plane?"

"So far as I know."

Diego said, "That was the plan."

"It is still the plan."

Grigor was approaching. They waited. Grigor sat. He said, "How much does he know?"

"Roman?" said Diego.

Grigor gestured, answer the question.

Diego said, "Why? What has happened?"

"Does he know where it will happen?" said Grigor.

Diego said, "Not from me. You haven't told me where."

"Does he know your destination tomorrow?" Werner said.

"I don't know my destination."

Grigor said, "Where do the rest of them think they are going?"

"Los Angeles," said Diego. "That's what you told me to tell them."

They studied him. Werner glanced at Grigor. "Well?"

Grigor said, "I don't know. I don't like it."

Werner handed Diego an Air France ticket.

Diego studied it. A ticket to Lyon.

"That is the assembly point," Werner was saying. "And this is the man we told you about." He handed Diego a manila envelope.

Diego examined the contents, photographs. The subject individual was named M. Gilet-Cohen. A tiny, balding, elderly man.

Diego turned to Grigor. "Outside, what happened?"

"We have videotape," said Grigor. "You may see it."

Diego said, "When?"

Grigor shook his head. "We have to identify two persons."

Diego was incredulous. "Here? He met with someone?"

Grigor said, "You will tell him nothing. The same with the girl. You will ask them no questions. You will not let him out of your sight or permit him access to a telephone."

"I cannot watch him all the time. You know that."

Werner said, "Do the best you can."

Grigor said, "I don't like it."

"Neither do I," Diego said.

Werner said, "Just stay with him this evening."

Ileana was having a marvelous time.

She had taught Gunther to make love Chinese-style.

"What does that mean?" Gunther had said.

"We train you not to come," she had said.

"Ever?" he had asked.

She had said, "Only when you wish it."

"Why?"

"So you can go indefinitely. So you can really give pleasure to a woman."

Gunther had resisted the idea. At first. "Don't you remember what I have told you? I am too old to worry about what you want."

"And what if it were not me? What if it were some other woman?" she had said. "And maybe more than one woman?"

He had said nothing but she knew she had intrigued him.

They had had three Chinese sessions as she wished and he had learned to sustain his erection indefinitely, just as she had predicted he would. He was immensely pleased that he could do it and her ecstatic responses excited him. Still, he had doubts.

"Don't you like it when I come?" he had asked.

"Of course I do."

"Well?" he had said.

"You can fake it," she had said. "A woman can't tell, and she gets just as excited."

She had, of course, deceived him. She could tell by the ejaculate, or its absence, although there was never very much of it with him, except for the first time. She was, however, careful never to let him know and she did not have to fake her excitement. She had grown to love being with the man. That was sufficiently exciting for her. That, and his delight in what he was learning, and in the pleasure he knew it gave her to teach him.

They had had a near catastrophe at dawn in the third session when he could not come when he wanted and panicked. She had held him, shh-ing him as one would a child. "You're fine," she had said, "we will try something different."

"What?" he had snapped. "Drugs? Stimulants? Never!"

She had giggled, "No, not stimulants. Most of them are ejaculate suppressants."

"They are?"

"Yes," she said. "You just lie there. You leave it all to me. It happens to most men who have been learning what you have learned, and doing it so well, and so often. It always seems to happen."

"Explain."

"Well, the way I see it, first you worry that you will, then you learn and you don't, but somehow you don't stop worrying. Right?"

He had said, "I think I still worry about something. Why?"

"You have learned to associate sex with worrying. So when you don't, you worry that you can't have sex and then, of course, you panic and you can't."

"An anxiety reaction?" he had said.

She had said, "Although you are not by nature an anxious person. See?"

He had started to recover his erection. "That? That is soft," he said. Contemptuous.

He needed further encouragement. She said, "It is what all the famous studs do."

"Studs?"

"The great lovers. They do Chinese. You must have wondered how they do what they do. Many different lovers, all night long, perpetual erections?"

It had helped. She had reached him. He said, uncertainly, "At the moment, however, I would settle for one small ejaculation."

She had laughed, reassuringly, and hushed him and made him lie there passively. She had taken some lightly scented hand cream and caressed him languorously with both hands, extending him, caressing him, first with one hand, then the other, extending him, caressing him, starting below his scrotum, extending him further, until she knew she had him.

He had shouted with the explosion.

It was the fourth Chinese session, tonight, in Zurich. In its honor, Gunther had produced an heirloom, an illustrated *Secret Garden*, a rare private edition that had belonged to his grandfather.

"Was he like you?" she said.

He said, "Wilder." They lay there, nude on the silken sheets, and turned the pages one by one, and tried the positions one by one, each until Ileana had her orgasm. She had them each and every time, about that there was no question. She had moaned, squirmed, shouted, even wept. She had wanted to claw and bite, too, although, of course, she couldn't.

Gunther never came, not once. He didn't seem to mind at all anymore. In fact, he had gone from not minding to enjoying not coming. In between her orgasms, he had held her, caressed her, kissed her with long lingering kisses that made her melt.

"I hope that doesn't bother you," she said, concerned. "I mean, your liking kissing me. I wouldn't want you to turn on me because you had some crazy idea that liking me was weakness."

"Amazing," he said.

"What?"

"That you read me so well. More," he said.

She reached, delighted, for the book.

Some of the positions were contortions. He especially loved them. Hours later, he came for the first and only time in a long, slow, shuddering spasm. She felt like weeping, it was so delicious. Afterwards she lay there very still. She hoped he was as pleased as she was. She did so want to please him.

Gunther liked expresso in the morning, so Ileana made it for him. They had it on his secluded terrace, overlooking the roofs of the old city, the downtown visible but distant. It was early and very quiet. Everywhere they met, he seemed to have a penthouse apartment with a quiet, secluded terrace.

It was cold, about 15 degrees centigrade.

He wore a luxurious Italian bathrobe. She was naked. He laughed. "How you please me."

"I try," she said.

He hesitated, musing. "How do Diego and your brother get along?"

"Roman?" She smiled. "He is crazy, Roman."

"Is he happy?" Gunther asked.

"My brother has never been happy. Killing is as close as he ever comes. In a way, I am surprised he has lived this long."

"What an extraordinarry thing to say."

"Because he is my twin?" Ileana said. "I always tell you what I think. Otherwise, you will get impatient."

Gunther considered, "And speaking of impatient, there is something which you once said to me, and which I have never mentioned up to now, but perhaps the time is coming soon, perhaps even our next time."

She said, "More than one woman?"

Ileana, Diego and Roman took the Air France flight to Lyon at nine o'clock in the morning.

Roman boarded first, as was their custom.

Diego boarded with Ileana. "Well," said Diego, "you look lovely this morning."

She smiled serenely.

Diego said, "You are flushed and your lips are swollen."

She said, "Oh."

"Did you get any sleep at all?" he said.

"I don't think I'd better answer that," she said. "Are you telling me you didn't?"

"I spent the night worrying about you," Diego said.

The black eyes flashed wickedly and she said, "With Roman in the next bed?"

Diego said, "Roman was snoring."

Roman was traveling up in First Class. Diego and Ileana were in Coach Class, Row 32.

The Airbus reached altitude at ten thousand meters. The seat belt sign went out. Diego stood. He beckoned and walked toward the rear of the plane. Ileana rose and followed him.

Diego was standing at the telephone on the wall just short of the row of W.C.'s. He turned to watch her approaching, then looked pointedly at the door of the W.C. at the end of the plane.

Ileana knew what was coming. There were two hostesses chatting in the last row of seats. For one wild moment, she thought of speaking cheerfully to them. She wondered if that would stop him. She decided it wouldn't. She decided not to risk his response. She walked past him, reached the rear of the plane and reached out to push the folding door to the W.C. open.

Behind her, she heard him hang up the phone and then she felt his body pushing hers into the washroom compartment.

He locked the door behind him, lifted her up on the counter beside the sink, reached under her skirt, yanked her panty hose and shoes off, dropped his pants and took her twice, violently, in one continuous sexual passage.

Ileana had three thoughts in rapid succession. First, she had showered and douched before dressing, thank God; she found mixing men disgusting. Second, Gunther would be amused if he knew. She did not understand the reasons but she knew that he would be and the realization hurt her. And third, this was definitely not a rape. Ileana had been raped twice and this was different. This man was crazy for her.

And she for him.

If only for just this moment.

As for the act itself, she liked it. A lot. She even came. Each time he came. Jealousy in a man can be aphrodisiac to a woman. When he was done, he held her. She listened to the two of them breathing.

Presently, she kissed the tip of his nose and said, "I can't wait to get there. Will my little gray horse be waiting?" She smiled her little cat smile at him.

Diego was chilled. She knew where they were going. And they hadn't even told him yet the target destination.

Innocently, she spelled it out for him. "You have heard the rhyme from children? 'À *Paris, à Paris, sur mon petit cheval gris*'? Isn't that where we are going?"

Chapter 45

HUGO READ the newspapers daily. They were sent to him on the island. Until he left Paris, I had telephoned him twice a week and we had long talks about French politics. Now we both missed those conversations. When he grew up, Hugo had decided, he would go into politics. The injury had given him an acute awareness of who in the world did what to whom. And the fact that he was crippled could prove to be a political advantage.

Cynical?

French.

Astoundingly, Hugo was happy on the island. Being there was giving him the time to learn to walk properly and he was working on his swimming. He loved being with Sarah. He liked her and she liked him. One day he appeared in the kitchen door, smiling at her, with a branch he had trimmed.

She recognized it as a cane immediately.

"*Oh, Hugo, la canne, c'est fantastique!*" she said. "*Où sont les bequilles?*"

"The crutches? I have thrown them away," he said. "And the cane, I can twirl it." Gleefully, he demonstrated, barely missing an end table. "Like Gene Kelly and Fred Astaire. Madame?"

Sarah was teary.

He swarmed all over her. "Oh, Madame, it is good, is it not?"

"Your father would say it is terrific."

"Don't cry, Madame!"

She kissed him. She said, "I have to blow my nose." She retreated into the bathroom and closed the door. She turned on the cold water. She washed her face and looked in the mirror. She started to weep again. She cursed. She would have to stop this.

Through the door came chortles.

Sarah had had them send her the Microtec translation programs for German, Italian and Spanish and one of her few remaining copies of the paperback Richards' *Spanish Through Pictures*. Hugo was wildly excited. He couldn't wait to load the programs on his notebook computer. "Could Madame please get it in Greek? I am studying Greek."

"That would be classical Greek," Sarah said. "Modern Greek? I'll have to write it."

They turned pages and chatted nonstop for an hour. Hugo struggled to his feet and walked over to the computer.

"Is it difficult?" she said. "The cane?"

He gave her the exaggerated, full-court press French shrug—hands, mouth, shoulders, elbows. "A simple question of balance," he said.

"And yours is good?"

"Better and better. You should see me on a how you say, *un fil de fer? En haut?*"

"A tightrope wire!" She wanted to laugh but the tears started again.

"Oh, Madame!"

They worked hard on his languages. They played games on the computer. They discussed current events. Most of what follows is based on Hugo's collection of clippings from the newspapers.

Chapter 46

IT WAS ALL SO UNEXPECTED.

There had been other incidents in Paris, more bombings, a few shootings, but they were all in the past, were they not? Two months? Now closer to three months? Time marches. Paris had quieted.

Most of those present at the party had read the French press reports of a shootup in an Ankara synagogue. They remembered it only dimly. The two weeks since it had happened were more than simply time passed. It was a full frenetic generation of reassembled television news teams. Also, it had happened in Turkey, which was a thousand miles away and exotic.

Even its Jews were exotic. They were Orientals, living amidst Ottomans.

This was France, highly civilized and good to its Jews. They had acceptance, if not assimilation, and they had culture if they had the money these guests had. Nearly all of them lived in Paris or the nearby environs.

Ah, Paris in the springtime.

The air throbbed with promise. It was the annual spring garden dinner dance of the Society for French-Israeli Cultural Understanding.

The special elegance of the Tenth Arrondissement was for the occasion further heightened by the designation of even more than the normal glut of one-way streets. Rue Hubert Lèvy was one way for the evening. The organization had quietly arranged it. Access to the complex of tents ballooning huge on the garden lot between the buildings was permitted only past the ticket taker tables and through the single main tent opening. That access became progressively more difficult as dusk deepened into evening. The chauffeured Mercedes, Rolls, Cadillac and Lincoln limousines backed up two and three deep, then six deep, then a dozen. There was no provision for the cars to wait after discharging their querulous passengers into the maw at the fete entrance, so they double- and eventually triple-parked on every adjacent street.

The six gendarmes who were moonlighting by special arrangement with the prefecture blew their whistles and swung their batons and then blew and swung harder as they progressively lost any semblance of control. Ultimately, the only stretch of clear street was the portion of the rue without function: the end abutting the avenue down to the drop-off point in front of the garden.

On the avenue and the tiny parallel streets, the chauffeurs leaned against fenders and limousine doors, smoked and quietly listened, enjoying the music. Laughter pealed, wine flowed, eyes sparkled and the dancing became more animated with every set. In the immortal words of the last French queen, the cake was being eaten.

Down the avenue came three monster Mercedes tour buses with double quartz halogen headlights, all their window glass darkened. They slowed as they came abreast of the Rue Hubert Lèvy—and then turned the wrong way into the empty end of the street.

Two of the limousine chauffeurs moved out into the street, waved and shouted, "Hey!" The four gendarmes up the street by the entrance blew their whistles and waved their batons, and one of them charged down the street, toward the buses blocking the way. The lead bus slammed him out of the way, knocking him against the wall of the building.

The other three gendarmes angrily shouted and pounded the side of the lead bus with their batons. The two gendarmes inside the tent entrance appeared, running forward, whistling and waving.

The buses did react, seemingly.

They slowed, swerved right, but then turned left, rammed their huge tires over the curb, scattered the people, overturned and crushed the ticket taker tables, and swerved even more sharply left into the tent flaps and poles as they virtually took out the entrance, injuring a dozen guests and attendants and seriously crushing two jeweled older women.

People screamed.

Black-watch-cap-clad terrorists poured out of the right side bus entrances, three men and women from each bus with automatic weapons, leaving similarly clad drivers with handguns at the wheel of each bus.

The terrorist team from the first bus, led by a slender, good-looking Latin with a nervous smile, circled the inside perimeter of the tent to the left, driving the party guests into the center, while the companion team from the second bus circled the tent to the right, joining up with the first team at the rear with sufficient speed to prevent all but a few frantic celebrants from escaping under the tent, and driving their captives back toward the buses.

Simultaneously, the team from the third bus split, each pair running in a different direction around it, one of them running gracefully, a woman. They confronted the policemen in the street.

Stunned, the gendarmes froze. They were outgunned and unable to shoot, covered by the terrorists' automatic weapons.

"Drop the guns!" shouted the woman, and instantly killed with an automatic rifle burst a slow-reacting policeman.

The onlookers screamed, "Don't! Don't!" and the remaining gendarmes reached into the air, hands far from their holsters.

Inside the tent, the terrorist teams from the first two buses forced party-goers at gunpoint into the buses, hysterical husbands reaching for wives who, in turn, attempted to calm their husbands with hushing and hand-patting gestures. The doors closed. The first bus, nearest the gendarmes, started to back into the street, its doors still open. The young Latin leader swung aboard.

The terrorists on the street backed against the open doors of the first bus and Diego personally pulled them aboard, one man, two, three, Ileana last, the bus doors closing.

The third bus, the second and finally the first rolled slowly toward the avenue.

Frightened faces on the curb watched them.

The first reports made no sense.

Three busloads of crazies, for that's what they were—that's what terrorists always were—had kidnapped 338 of Paris's richest, most of them Jews. The bare statement of what had happened elicited French smiles, from the police, the army, even some of those at the Élysées. Only the intelligence forces took it in with faces showing no expression.

What did the madmen plan to do? Drive the Jews to Libya? Guffaws.

Meanwhile, they were in the open, rolling slowly south through Paris.

If it were not for the single dead gendarme—and he was moonlighting, not on duty at the time, and should he really have been assigned as doorman for a party?—it would have been possible to dismiss it all as pure farce.

But the man was dead.

And he was a non-Jewish Frenchman.

It was the lead story on the evening news at both six P.M. and eleven P.M. on all three U.S. networks. CNN had it even earlier and kept running up-to-date flashes all night long, every twenty minutes, throughout the world, including the Arab countries. In the camps from which the attackers came, there was rejoicing and excitement.

It was the late afternoon headline in all U.S. newspapers and the morning headline the next day in every newspaper throughout the world: "Terrorists Kidnap 400 Jews From Gala in Paris!"

No one would pay attention to one little banker among them.

Chapter 47

IT WAS AN ESPECIALLY BEAUTIFUL NIGHT. The Paris suburbs were unseasonably warm, the sky clear, black, sparkling.

The buses rolled out of Porte de Bercy and headed south, uninterrupted. French army helicopters hovered cautiously overhead, while the nation secretly savored *le panache* and *l'audace*, two of its favorite romantic conceptions.

Two more helicopters arrived, news teams from television.

It was hard to take it all seriously, except for the dead policeman.

The buses were within seven miles of Orly before the SDECE made the connection.

The forces regularly stationed at the airport were three army squads and a special police antiterrorist force. No one bothered to alert them until the SDECE insisted, but when the SDECE finally did, their response was magnificent. They rolled into place, including the tanks, in one minute and thirty seconds.

They seemed to be fully adequate to cope with anything that might be attempted that night if, indeed, the airport were a target, and they could certainly hold the line for a sufficient time if it were necessary to summon reinforcements.

The airport was functioning as usual, planes taking off and landing with only normal delays. It was a busy spring weekend.

The army and police attempted to stay out of the way despite the heavy security. Under the command of Captain Petitclerc, a survivor and a grizzled veteran of '54, the four tanks and four armored personnel carriers and two squads of men on foot with rockets and automatic weapons were stationed in the darkness by the side of the road at the entrance from the highway.

As the buses were approaching the outskirts of Choisy-le-Roi, the airport appeared to be their planned destination. But what was planned?

Were they going to drive up and demand an airplane?

Three more squads of soldiers were deployed throughout the terminal buildings.

As the army squad trotted into place, one man every twenty meters, flanking the mouth of the Air France arrival and departure pier, the loudspeakers quietly called the evening flight to London.

An escorted tour of schoolchildren, twenty-five boys and girls and four nuns, moved through the hand-baggage and metal-detection checkpoint under the eyes of four machine-gun-toting policemen. Étienne, a homesick twelve-year-old with glasses, was playing salsa on a ghetto-blaster loud enough to cause vibration in gold fillings. The pretty, bored control woman with the sulky mouth, Marguerite, according to her Air France name tag, snapped at the boy to turn it off. He did and put it on the moving belt. There was a deafening silence.

A group of four East Bloc businessmen joined the line, among them a Romanian killer in a blue pinstripe business suit, whose dead eyes registered everything, told nothing, and an East German from Dresden with a trenchcoat and a fat neck. The Romanian, Roman Belasco, would have been identifiable as the twin of the woman killer on the bus, but no one at the airport had seen the woman; the brother at the airport was an equally good-looking and vastly more deadly version.

"Go," Roman ordered Heller, the burly German, who promptly went into action.

"No, no, no! Computer!" Heller howled. He clutched his large Compaq portable with both hands and refused to put it on the moving belt.

Sulky Marguerite had met the problem before. "Give it to me, please," she told him.

"*Nein*," he refused, hugging the Compaq to his chest. "*Ist* program. Must not ruin program."

"Put it on the table, please?" she asked him, more or less pleasantly. Marguerite did not much like Germans.

"What you do to it?" the stubborn East German asked her, suspiciously.

"I will open it and turn it on."

"*Nein. Ist* not possible." Heller shook his head, determined.

"Then, M'sieu, you cannot take it on the plane," she said, self-righteously, and summoned the two nearest police guards.

"If I open, I turn it on?" Heller offered.

"*D'accord*, but I must look at it," Marguerite explained. She was rapidly losing patience.

"*Ja*, but you no read program?"

She laughed. So that was the problem. Ridiculous, stubborn Germans. "*Ja*, okay," she told him. "I no read program."

"*Gut, gut*," Heller told her, relieved now, and smiling. He put the computer on the table and reached for the catches, Marguerite and police guards watching.

Down the ramp, Étienne retrieved his ghetto-blaster and turned it back on, full volume. Salsa reverberated off the narrow walls again.

The two police guards looked around at the boy and laughed. Marguerite exclaimed with annoyance and shouted at the boy to turn it off.

The startled boy did, but in the process he dropped it and started to cry, falling to his knees and hugging the radio much as Heller had hugged his Compaq.

The police guards felt sorry for the boy.

Beside them, at the security checkpoint table, the East German opened the cover of his Compaq case. The police guards and Marguerite turned to examine it. They never got a chance.

Roman and the two men behind him produced machine-pistols from inside their coats. Roman shot and killed the two police guards, one crisp three-shot burst for each guard.

The other two police guards, shocked, slowly spread their hands in surrender, unable to unshoulder their machine guns, but Roman's companions unhesitatingly cut them down anyhow, one burst for each policeman.

The children were screaming. Marguerite crawled under the table. The fatnecked Heller produced two more machine-pistols from his dummy Compaq case and whirled, one in each hand, firing up the pier at the nearest soldiers, who dropped to the floor and fired back, too high, because of the people, the shots neatly stitching the ceiling.

Roman and his two machine-pistol-carrying companions had charged ahead, vaulting the barriers. They swiftly herded the children and nuns in front of them, *"Vite! Vite! Vite!"* down the ramp and past the terrified Flight Attendants. Roman shoved the Flight Attendants ahead of him at gunpoint after the screaming children, who were fleeing down the ramp toward the Flight Crew of the waiting stretch 727. The Flight Crew were now reacting, but much too late, trying to close the doors of the plane.

Roman fired a warning burst, two shots smashing into the fuselage and the third slamming the Steward in the cheek. The man went over backward and lay on the cabin floor on his elbow, face smashed bloody, mouth open. The frightened children trampled past him.

Roman scowled. Kill when you have to, do not wound, were Diego's clear instructions. Roman's two companions hurried past him, drove the last of the children into the plane and sent them scurrying down the aisles. They confronted the Flight Crew in the cockpit. Back on the ramp, in the terminal, Roman rejoined Heller, the East German, and now crouched beside him. Over the heads of the cowering travelers, they exchanged fire with the dozen soldiers and police guards who were coming up fast, charging their position.

Roman was an artist with the machine-pistol. Despite its famous inaccuracy, he killed one soldier and wounded another badly with two neat three-shot bursts. He paused. Heller fired covering bursts. Roman reloaded his magazine as the East German emptied his. Then Roman fired and Heller reloaded.

They each fired a final burst and retreated down the ramp toward the plane, pausing at the final twist in the ramp just short of the plane entrance, where they could cover with their weapons the entire length of the empty ramp corridor stretching up into the terminal before them.

Behind their backs, Étienne's ghetto-blaster had shifted from salsa to loud rock. It was the only sound from the airplane.

Roman produced a walkie-talkie from under his coat, turned it on and started talking.

"Plane to Diego! Diego, come in!" Roman's voice crackled over the walkie-talkie in Diego's hand.

Diego pushed the transmit button. "I hear you. We have arrived at the airport. What is your status?"

"We have secured the plane. We are waiting," Roman said.

"Fine."

"Would you like a demonstration?" Roman asked.

Diego smiled grimly. "Not quite yet."

The passengers heard the words with dismay.

The walkie-talkie crackled again with Roman's gravelly, threatening voice, "We are ready for the demonstration when you wish, repeat, ready for the demonstration." And he laughed.

The buses turned off the highway toward the airport entrance.

"What sort of demonstration?" Captain Petitclerc snapped at the radio man in the back of the open communications van who had monitored the conversation.

They were shown live on French television.

There was pandemonium at the airport entrance. The captain's men had set up a wooden-horse roadblock, trapping half a dozen cars west of it. The three buses slowed, approaching the roadblock from the west.

"Attention!" Diego snarled into the built-in bus loudspeaker. "Get those cars off the road! Cars off the road!"

The buses had to halt behind the cars. To the east, the tanks rumbled closer.

Diego then preceeded to make a major error in public relations. He ordered, "Go!" The lead bus slowly crunched into the parked cars. The occupants screamed and abandoned their cars, shaking their fists at the bus. It ground forward, slowly, inexorably, pushing the cars in the rear into those parked ahead, crushing bumpers, fenders, trunks, crumpling cabs, pushing free engines, popping lights, gradually clearing the first of the wrecked cars from the road.

A Renault burst into flames, which spread instantly to the Jaguar alongside. The fires lit up the ominous buses, their darkened sides gleaming orange, looking spectacular on television, as they pushed the remaining wrecked cars through the wooden-horse road-block—and totally lost the sympathy of the viewers watching on French television.

The miscalculation was essentially political. The vast majority of Frenchmen have a passionate romance with leftist causes. They adore revolution. "Let's go, children," says the national anthem, celebrating the "day of glory," a day of inspired rebellion. Furthermore, trading with the powers of the left and giving asylum to the exiles on the left has been traditionally both lucrative and, for the French, moral.

Given a chance, therefore, the typical Frenchman will always embrace a cause on the left, but then he will hesitate. It is part of the national character, first the enthusiasm, and then that moment of doubt.

At that moment, that instant of dénouement, some enthusiast in the movement of the day always seems to miscalculate, go just a hair too far and do something that clutches at the nation's soul, like burning cars on live television.

The problem is one of the bourgeois soul, full of sincere empathy for the possessive instincts of like-minded people. Those dramatically burning cars give them pause. The average Frenchman loves himself, first, and next to himself his country, and then his car, in third place, and then his children, most of the time, and then from time to time, his wife, consort or lover.

Consequently fear shivers through the nation at the televised sight of burning cars. And the heart goes out of the movement.

The balance of power in French politics has several times depended on the election-eve display of burning automobiles on television.

There was a hush when the two cars burned. Then the tanks roared onto the asphalt, blocking any further forward motion. There was a brief silence.

Diego said politely into the loudspeaker, "We request permission to move ahead."

Captain Petitclerc had his own electric loudspeaker in his hand where he sat in the half-track. "No. Permission refused. You will descend from the buses, hands in the air."

"I am sorry, that will not be possible, sir." Diego was calm, although his smile was nervous.

"Please listen," said the captain unexpectedly. "I have no authority to permit any further forward progress."

"That cannot be true," Diego suggested.

"Why not?" the captain asked.

"You must have authority as the man in charge on the scene to deal as best you see fit under all the circumstances whenever human life is threatened."

The moment was pregnant. It was playing live on television. In the studios, the news staffs were ecstatic.

The captain said carefully, "I want to be sure you know what I will do."

"I am sure you will tell me you will storm the bus."

"The moment you kill anyone, I will. Yes."

Diego chuckled, on live television. "No. You will not do it."

The captain sighed wearily. "You are on television."

Diego said into the loudspeaker, "One rich man here, one child on the plane. You are forcing me to kill them."

The onlookers were immobile and silent.

Diego gestured and the bus door opened.

The watchers readied their weapons.

Out of the bus came a tiny, balding, elderly man, M. Gilet-Cohen, the banker. He was wearing a smashing blue custom-tailored tuxedo. His hands were on his head and trembled. He stumbled in the blast of searchlights, falling to one knee.

"Up! Up!" snapped Diego over the loudspeaker, his voice irritated, commanding.

M. Gilet-Cohen daintily brushed the dust from his tailored knee, put his hands back on top of his head and walked shakily toward the tanks.

"Halt!" Diego commanded over the bus loudspeaker.

The elderly man stood there in the lights, hands on his head, blinking uncontrollably.

Roman prodded the little girl in the back with his gun muzzle. She was pretty, with short brown hair and bangs, and large, bewildered brown eyes in a face, and what a face! A piquant oval. Wearing a pinafore, she moved hesitantly forward, one step, a second step, and stopped.

Roman grimaced, irritated. He started forward, changed his mind. The loud rock music came from the plane. The little girl was too far into the open. They would have a clear shot at him if he moved farther forward.

Police and army shouted into walkie-talkies from behind the barrier at the other end of the ramp.

"What is your name, chld?" Roman demanded.

The child was too terrified to speak. Her right thumb slowly entered her mouth. The cameras caught her in close-up, all pinafore and tears and fist in front of mouth as she trembled with sobs. She was tiny and fragile. She was seven.

"Name!" shouted Roman.

"Marie-Claire," she squeaked and her mouth opened and she burst into uncontrollable tears.

"Silence!" commanded Roman.

Marie-Clair did control the tears. She put her thumb back into her mouth.

"Marie-Claire, you will now walk up the ramp. I will let you go all the way up the ramp to the men with the machine guns. Do you hear?"

Marie-Claire, eyes enormous, nodded.

"Go!" Roman shouted, and she ran from him.

"No. No. No," the captain murmured to himself as he waited at the back of the communications bus. There was dead, terrible silence, except for the sound of the child's footsteps on the ramp, hollow on the radio, echoing.

M. Gilet-Cohen stood in the glare of the headlights, hands on his head, his blinking even more uncontrollable.

A shout, "We have her!" came the voice over the radio.

The crowd broke into wild cheering.

The captain whirled, commanded, "Silence!"

In the bus, Diego grinned and flicked the loudspeaker switch on. His voice rang out, reverberating. "Now you know what it will feel like. All France knows what it will feel like. The man and the next child will now die. Send out the child!"

At the head of the ramp in the terminal, television crews filmed Marie-Claire, hugging the paratrooper, people crowding around, smiling, in tears.

Down the ramp by the plane, Roman had his arm around Étienne, the homesick twelve-year-old boy with glasses and the ghetto-blaster, still playing rock, too loud.

Outside, at the gate, it was over.

Grimly, the captain waved the buses through, past the tanks, which were reversing off the road. The buses rolled past the army and police, who were helplessly holding their weapons, and past the tiny terrified man, waiting at the side of the road, still with his hands on his head, barely comprehending that he was still alive. The lead bus paused. The door opened. Diego said, "Moneylender, you will lend no more. Close your banks and move to London."

M. Gilet-Cohen gaped at him.

The bus door closed.

The little banker was free but did not understand that he was until the bus engaged its gears and slowly rolled past.

There was total confusion at the head of the ramp. Army and police still clutched the freed Marie-Claire. They looked cautiously down the ramp toward the plane.

Etienne stood there alone, crying. Roman had disappeared back into the plane, holding the boy's ghetto-blaster which was now playing country and western on the station chosen by Roman.

The plane door thunked closed.

Inside the plane, Roman slid the door bolt shut. He put the radio down and shut it off. The Pilot stood and confronted Roman. He absolutely refused to move the plane from the gate. "I can't, I have no permission—" he was saying at the point when Roman shot the Steward lying on the floor.

The children started screaming. Roman snarled and they quieted. Roman said to the Pilot, "You have my permission. Do you understand? Start the engines."

"Sir," the Pilot started to protest and Roman shot him, too.

Again, the children screamed and wailed as Roman dragged the body out of the cockpit and flung it on the Steward's corpse.

"Silence!" Heller commanded the children.

They obediently fell silent.

"*Gut.*" The East German was immediately pleased. Heller entered the cockpit, strapped himself into the pilot seat and reached for the engines.

They coughed, sputtered, whined, blasted, roared.

The buses drove slowly around the edge of the field toward the extreme north end of the 360/0 north-south runway. Across the tarmac, the stretch 727 moved toward the same rendezvous.

The buses arrived first and waited. The 727 lumbered alongside, turned and halted, engines screaming. They quieted to a faint whistle. The door opened, the stairs came down.

The buses had maneuvered closer and were now surrounding the plane stairs, shielding them, like gathered wagons. The bus doors opened. Two terrorists descended from each bus and covered its open doorway.

The hostages emerged, hands on their heads. The terrorists herded them off the buses.

The nuns and schoolchildren came off the plane. The terrorists herded them into the first of the buses.

The terrorists herded the Jewish hostages toward the plane. They stumbled up the stairs into the plane, crowding each other, pushing. They poured past Roman to the rear of the plane. When all the seats were full, the line of hostages halted. The terrorists had them turn and march down the stairs. They clustered at the foot of the stairs, hands on their heads, waiting. The terrorists ran up the stairs and into the plane.

Diego stood in the doorway and covered the hostages with his weapon. They cowered. Diego laughed and entered the airplane. He spun the door wheel closed.

The hostages on the tarmac watched.

It had been a perfect operation.

Chapter 48

THE Vienna airport was churning bedlam.

The searchlights, the military vehicles, the Austrian army, the state police and the federal antiterrorist strike team were photographed, interviewed and televised by the top reporters covering hot spot news for every major newspaper and television station in the Western World.

They had surrounded the control tower at the rumor that the Air France 727 had radioed in and announced its arrival.

There was much too much noise on the ground to hear anything in the skies overhead. The searchlights could not penetrate the low clouds but the operators kept on trying, swinging them back and forth, back and forth.

It was entirely useless.

It was the interval just before false dawn.

Up above, there was no sun. The mist, as thick as Rhine fog, blended into the lowest of the low clouds. One stratum higher, the faintest of light streaked the darkness.

The poor weather contributed to Diego's good mood. It gave him mystery. What could be more perfect? He was there but they could not see him.

He had the media world in the palm of his hand now, the world that mattered. He could do anything he wanted and everyone would take note of it. He could do nothing and the world would wait. He could speak and the world would listen.

It was even rather beautiful there in the clouds and darkness. You could not see a thing but the reflections of your own lights, except that from time to time the searchlights did glimmer through the black sky all about the airplane, turning the world opalescent.

Diego took the microphone and spoke terse, guttural German, ignoring Heller's wincing. Diego delighted in mangling the German language.

"Request permission to land," he said. "We are the Air France 727 from Paris you have been hearing about. We shall land in three minutes."

"Clear the area!" bawled the chief air traffic controller into his microphone, gesturing wildly as if that would communicate, too.

The room was packed with army, police, the special strike team and four television cameras.

"Head due east at once and maintain altitude four thousand meters! Repeat, you must head east, oh nine oh, altitude four thousand meters!"

Diego was having a wonderful time.

"You will have closed the airport," he said. "We are directly overhead and circling, repeat, directly overhead. Please designate the runway for landing, repeat, designate the runway for landing."

Back in the tourist cabin, Roman and Ileana had made their selections, a terrified woman in an evening gown and an incongruously eager little girl in glasses. They took them from the arms of their companions and escorted them toward the front of the plane.

Diego instructed his men, "I want everyone's belt fastened now, before the doors are opened."

Roman and Ileana arrived in the front of the plane and positioned themselves in the jump seats, fastening their seat belts. Heller reached behind him and closed the door to the cockpit.

Everyone was now belted in except for the woman in the evening gown and the little girl with glasses.

Diego switched on the microphone again. "Do you hear me?" he said, his voice now sharp. "You will select a runway, please. Otherwise we will land on runway oh-one-two in exactly one minute, repeat, oh-one-two in one minute."

The chief air traffic controller looked about him at the uniforms and cameramen, all milling around, leaderless.

"Air France 727 from Paris," he shouted. "Calling Air France 727 from Paris. Permission to land refused. Do you hear? Permission to remain refused, do you hear? Leave the area immediately! You are a danger to yourselves and everyone else! There are other planes in the area! There is a jumbo behind you half a mile at six thousand meters! Come in, Air France 727 from Paris, please!"

"Air France 727 from Paris calling Vienna Air Traffic Control." Diego's voice was sugary. "We seem to be having a failure of communication. We have told you what we are going to do but you do not get the message. We will send you a message you can understand. How old are you?" he asked the little girl in glasses, loud enough so the microphone would pick it up.

The acoustics in the control tower were perfect.

"How old are you, little one?" Diego's voice shouted. His voice was especially harsh with the static caused by the low-pressure area moving in.

"I will only ask you one more time! Do you hear, child? How old are you?"

"Nine," came the voice of the little girl.

"Boy or girl?" the general in charge in the control tower asked his aides, and many voices answered at the same time, a few saying "boy," most of them "girl," all of the speakers and the general promptly lapsing into silence, embarrassed.

"And you?" Diego asked the woman.

"Thirty-seven," she said.

"Your attention, Vienna Air Traffic Control. The message consists of two Jewesses. One nine-year-old child and one thirty-seven-year-old woman. In a black dress, the woman," he said. He turned to the woman. "Who made it?"

"Balenciaga," she said.

"Wearing a black Balenciaga and jewelry worth millions," Diego said. "Good luck to those on the ground who find the jewels. One child with glasses, one woman. How about it? Would you like to meet them?"

He paused.

There was silence on the radio.

Diego smiled his nervous smile and spoke quietly, deliberately speaking away from the microphone so his voice would be faint. "Open the door, please, now," he said.

The lady was frozen. "No," she whispered. She started for the passenger cabin but Roman held her back.

"No! No! No! No!" she shouted, struggling.

Diego smiled and extended the microphone toward the woman who continued to scream, "NO!" He glanced at the child and met contempt. The child turned from him to the woman in the dress.

"Shut up!" said the little girl to the older Jewess.

"They're going to throw us from the plane!"

"So be brave and keep your mouth shut," said the little girl.

"See, the door is open!"

"Hold your head up! You are French!" said the child.

"I don't want to die! I don't want to die!" Diego let the woman seize the microphone. "Let them land, please! Just let them land! What difference does it make to you if they land?"

Diego beamed at her.

She was, indeed, a perfect selection.

Her voice reverberated throughout the control tower. "Please let them land! Please! Please! They're going to throw us from the plane! I don't want to die! I have children!" Her voice paused. They listened to her sob.

The little girl's voice was cutting and clear. "Don't you want your children to be proud of you? These animals want you to weep like that. Can't you see that your hysterics are foolish? Here, you," she said to Diego. "She is in a panic now. Let me go first, before the woman."

The child's voice elicited approval from many of those listening. The military stirred. Let the brave child die first. It was the better way. One had to have courage. Stand firm. Die well! The child before the woman!

Diego loved it.

He took the microphone. "No. We shall let the little one live. We shall now throw the woman from the plane. Then a man. Then another woman. And then we start on the children. Don't forget the jewelry on the corpse of this woman, let's see, a necklace, two bracelets, ear and finger rings, emeralds set in platinum, diamonds and more diamonds—"

"Noooo!" bawled the frantic woman, struggling toward the microphone. "You are forcing them to kill me by not letting them land!"

Diego could not have written better lines. He extended the microphone toward her.

Thus encouraged, she did even better.

"You are killing me! Not him, you! Why do you insist on killing me? Won't your government tell you to stop it?"

They listened in silence.

They heard a noise, the rushing noise of air, and the muffled scream, "They are opening the door now! They are pushing me! The door is open!"

The quality of the picture on my rear-projection fifty-inch Mitsubishi television set was extraordinary, cable-sharp and clear, the colors brilliant. I was home. Lonely. Waiting again. Restless and impatient.

CNN showed a live picture of the hijacked plane as it dropped through the low overcast, touched down on the distant runway and rumbled on the ground toward the Vienna airport terminal.

As it wheeled in a huge half circle to a bumpy halt, left side toward the control tower, the American announcer in the upper right corner of the picture told the story in a flat, matter-of-fact Midwestern voice. "The hijacked French airplane has been permitted to land at the Vienna airport, but only after the hijackers threatened to throw from the plane one wealthy French woman and one child, a girl of nine.

"Unofficial sources have attributed to the child some sort of extraordinary act of valor.

"The same two sources say it is possible the two were in fact thrown from the plane but there has been no confirmation and no reports of bodies being found, or of any search being carried on. There is a high degree of confusion here.

"The terrorists, whose organization has not been identified, have demanded the release of a woman and five men being held in an Austrian prison.

"Austrian authorities have surrounded the plane. The tower is in radio contact. We are advised that they have just now demanded release of the children, but—there! Something is going on—the door of the plane is now opening! There!"

The television cameras had zoomed in and indeed, the plane door was opening, and the folding stairs came down.

The nine-year-old girl with glasses appeared at the top of the stairs, pushed from the plane at gunpoint. She looked back over her shoulder with anger and contempt.

"It's a little girl!" shouted the television announcer on CNN. "Oh, no! They are pushing her with their weapons! No! It's only a child! No!"

"Go!" The voices from the plane were faint. "Little girl, go!"

The child blinked in the glaring lights.

The weapons of the antiterrorist team covered the door of the plane.

"Come, child, come!" the green-overcoated Austrian general commanded over his bullhorn in his raspy French.

Slowly, with dignity, the little girl descended the stairs of the plane and walked across the open tarmac.

There were cheers and the child looked up at the cheers. The television cameras switched now to the waiting people jumping up and down, smiling, laughing. The child walked slowly toward them.

A burst of gunfire came from the plane.

The child stopped in her tracks.

The crowd fell silent. Then they screamed, nearly in unison, "Run, child! Run! You can make it! Run!"

The little girl looked over her shoulder at the plane.

The gun muzzles projecting from the plane door were tilted at angles up into the air.

The child smiled timidly.

The terrorists fired into the air again. It was their salute to a little girl.

The crowd screamed, hysterically, for the child to run, run, run!

The Austrian military held their fire.

The little girl, a little shy, now, walked slowly through the nearest door, into the Vienna airport and freedom.

Book IV

Chapter 49

I KEPT SWITCHING CHANNELS, from CNN to CBS to ABC to NBC and back to CNN again.

And my door buzzer buzzed.

I switched the TV off and went to the door. Careful, Michael. "Who is it?" I said.

"Look," said the muffled voice through the door.

I had a pinhole in the door. It was Shima and three other men. Shima came in, looking grim and holding his unlit cigar. The others remained outside and pulled the door shut behind him. Shima walked past me into the living room.

Shima sat heavily on the couch. I sat on the edge of an upholstered chair. Shima said, "You're going over. Sarah will meet you. I brought you your tickets. Are you packed and ready?"

I murmured yes. Shima looked weary. I said, "Where were you?"

He said, "At a bar mitzvah."

"Where?"

"Los Angeles. We went to the wrong address," Shima said. "We were off by one day and seven thousand miles."

"Paris?" I said.

He said, "We knew there was something imminent but we didn't know what or where or when. We had a report, Los Angeles. There is a bar mitzvah there, tomorrow, a big one, one thousand people."

I was incredulous. "He was going to try one here?"

Shima said scornfully, "And why not here? Grow up, Michael." He got up and walked away from us and looked out at the city lights, lost in thought. I went to my bar and poured us two brandies. Shima said, out the window, "I was misinformed about the location."

"Was it deliberate?" I said.

"I don't know. The source may have guessed and tried to help, or he may have been given wrong information." He gestured with his cigar, turned from the window and sat on the couch again. He noticed the brandy and picked it up from the coffee table.

"Is it who I think it is?" I said.

Shima said, "Yes, your friend, Diego. He let the children off the plane. They let the six killers and the plane go with the adult hostages still on board and he's taken off for Tripoli."

"You're going to try a rescue?" I said.

"No."

"Disappointing. What then?"

"We will meet his demands."

"And what then?" I said.

"I want to kill him. And you know how I'm going to get at him?" Shima said. "I'm going to make him come after you."

"How?"

"My German banker will send him."

"And how are you going to arrange this?" I said.

"You will meet a prominent Jew in a public place. He will give you an envelope. You will bring me the envelope."

"The contents?" I asked.

"Bank files."

"Proving what?"

"My banker's support of the camps. And use of killers from them."

"I see," I said. "These bank files, how did you get them?"

"The man you will meet is in publishing. He has investigative reporters on his payroll. They have bank connections." Shima studied his brandy.

I studied him. "How did they know what accounts to track?"

"Good question. We deposit funds in a bank account for the informant I have referred to, who transfers them to another account. We have obtained reports on the second account. And on other deposits to that account. A computer expert has traced those back to the account of origin. The account from which the funds come has several times made payments in parallel, to accounts for the sister of the informant, who works with him and Diego, and to accounts for Diego in the same bank. The same source of funds has paid larger amounts to a Syrian army special account."

"For the training camps?" I said.

"We can prove that. What we need is proof of the source of funds, the man who controls them."

"Your banker."

"Right."

"I have no interest in him. My interest is purely personal. My boy, I want to protect him."

Shima swirled the dregs in his snifter. "Let me tell you the sort of thing the banker has been discussing with Diego. We know some of the details. This one wasn't just another attack. It was the beginning of a new wave. This one was a sample." Shima took a deep breath and went on. "Planes, boats, buses, trains, subways, cars. Overpasses, bridges, ferries, tunnels."

"Transportation," I said, "so nothing dares to move."

"Utilities, gas, electric, water, sewer, phone," he said.

"Infrastructure."

"And crowds," Shima said. "People. Sporting events, theaters, movies, concerts, fireworks shows, temples, churches, even schools. Supermarkets. Wherever lots of people go. Pick a country, shut it down."

"Which country?" I said.

"First Israel. And then, who knows?"

"When I bring you the files, will he know it?"

"Yes. You'll be dangling out there, tempting him."

"So that's the plan," I said.

"Part of it. Make him angry, expose you to tempt him. Make it irresistible—in a place of our choosing." He finished his brandy.

I said, "How do you know he will send Diego?"

"His favorite weapon," Shima said.

"He has used him before?"

"At least five times. And besides, who is the target?"

"Me."

"Who would you send after you? If you employed him?"

I had to agree. "And that is part of your plan?"

He said, "The rest will seem inconsistent. We will pursue it at the same time, two plans that are inconsistent."

"Explain."

He gestured with his glass. "He's alone, my old German. He has no one to talk to. No trusted colleague, no son, no woman. We think that you might interest him. He might wonder if you would work for him."

I could not believe it. "But I'm Jewish," I said.

"In a sense. I would not call you observant." He sniffed his empty glass. "And if you were to raise some doubts by what you do, deliberately confuse things . . ."

"That is crazy."

"Not entirely. Perhaps you should go to work for him. He would call his killer off you and your son. And you could find out what his plan is and tell me what he is doing." He grinned.

I said, "I do not find this amusing."

"You wanted a plan. Now you have one. Good luck."

"I am going to need it, out there dangling."

"Yes," he said. "These things are amorphous, all the time. You can start them with the best of plans. But you never quite know where they are going."

Chapter 50

I PAUSED at the overstocked sundries store on the departure level of the International Terminal at JFK to pick up the New York papers. I read them in the tiny Austrian Airlines First Class lounge. I was taking the six P.M. direct to Vienna, Flight 502.

The headlines were reasonably uniform. The *New York Times* boxed the story in three adjacent columns four inches high at the bottom of the first page, center. "French Jewish Prisoners Released in Tripoli. Huge Ransom Reported." A picture of Diego with a tight smile graced the adjacent two columns, two inches high, four column inches. They had interviewed him at the Tripoli airport.

He was going on vacation now, he said. Where? the reporters asked him. Where he could encourage the most speculation, he said.

A choice thought.

"And did he have further ventures planned?" the reporters asked. " 'There is much unfinished business,' he said, thoughtfully," the obliging *Times* reported.

It was nine A.M. when I came off the plane in Vienna. It was cold.

There seemed to be soldiers everywhere in their green Austrian army greatcoats. Everyone else was wearing loden coats. The entire population was in uniform green.

I felt eyes. I looked about. No, no one was watching me. At least, no one I noticed was watching me.

But I could feel the eyes.

And there was Sarah!

I held her.
"How is he?"
"He is fine."
"Wherever he is."

"There is a wonderful woman with him while I am away."

"Sarah, I love you."

"For taking care of him?"

"For being you. For everything."

"You're a sweet man and I like him."

There was more of the same in the baggage area, soldiers and loden coats everywhere. I shivered, scanned the scene and saw nothing.

Sarah said quietly, "Yes."

"Yes what?" I said.

"I feel it," she said. "I feel something, too."

"Anything specific?"

"No."

"Languages?"

She made a face, looked about. "Accents, but all German."

My bags arrived. She had a porter with hers. He took mine. He was wispy and ancient.

Outside, aggressive Austrians in loden coats scrambled with padded elbows, heavy shoulders and hips for the taxis. It seemed hopeless. Our mouse of a porter seemed helpless.

I held up a one thousand-shilling bill, New York-style. Bad manners. It worked. Three taxis screeched to competitive stops, missing each other by inches. Two of the drivers jumped out and raced for our bags. The third one merely shouted.

The two older drivers scrambled with the porter for our bags and shouted at him in broken English. I picked the younger man who had remained in the car.

Was it a setup? They had put on a convincing show. There was no way to tell if the young one was in on the act. The others were surly giving up my bags. I tipped them as an insecure American should. One of them thanked me. The other did not. I remembered the day when the dollar was strong and no one wanted shillings.

"Do you speak English?" I asked our driver.

"*Nein,*" the man smiled.

"Why did you pick him?" Sarah asked. "Younger?"

"Yes."

"Less aggressive?"

"Right answer, wrong reason."

"Oh," she figured it out. "You didn't want to wonder where they were back when? Gee, it was fifty years ago."

"Hate makes time pass, time does not make hate pass," I said.

"It's love, and you have it backwards," she laughed. "It does pass."

"Don't be pessimistic." I slouched in the corner of the taxi. Below us, the tires rumbled.

We went to the Opera.

In Vienna, in season, it was the thing to do. Excessive lights blazed everywhere, radiating the shockingly overfed and opulent crowd with lumens of glitter.

I helped Sarah out of our battered Mercedes taxi and stood there on the street with her. I was stunned. I was wearing my midnight blue Brooks Brothers off-the-rack suit with a crisp white shirt and a midnight blue bow tie with small Liberty's of London swirling foulard figures. I had thought I looked elegant; I had glanced into the hotel lobby mirror. Sarah had laughed and hugged me there. Now I felt shabby. Nowhere had I ever seen such jewels, not at the Academy Awards in L.A., not at the opening of the New York Metropolitan Opera. I looked at Sarah.

She was, as always, stunning, in a white mink stole, a cream-and-emerald-green floor-length dress, her emerald earrings and a small matching emerald necklace.

"You're wrong," she said. "I'm just as under-dressed."

"Come on," I said. "You look smashing."

She kissed me. We stood there. We were making people nervous.

We mounted the sidewalk and milled about in the mob, elbowing our way toward the entrance doors.

Parsifal was playing.

The production was just like the audience and opera house,

overlit, overstated and oddly dead. Sarah whispered, "You know what?"

"I know I like being with you," I said.

"There's no heart to this performance," she said.

"Maybe there's none to Wagner."

She held my hand. Laughter and applause swept the audience, waves of louder laughter, ponderous, heavy, pretentious laughter, self-aggrandizing false laughter, from redder and redder faces on fatter and fatter necks. I loved her, I was alone with her, I was ecstatically happy being with her, two nonpersons holding hands, surrounded by the hostiles.

The crowd hushed for the aria. The tenor dramatically placed his hand on his chest and waited out the introductory phrases. I laughed. "It reminds me of what Verdi said to Wagner," I said.

"What?"

" 'Why can't you laugh, you fucking clown?' " I said.

"*Ridi*, Pagliacci," she said and hugged my arm. "Verdi did not write Pagliacci."

"I know. Go ahead, ask me."

"Who?"

I said, "Leoncavallo."

"Very good. I'm impressed." She grinned. "What else did he write?"

I made a face and she laughed. I said, "You win. I know nothing else about him."

At intermission, we stood in the lobby and sipped expensive sparkling water.

"Champagne?" I asked.

"I don't feel like it. Beer. No, I don't even feel like beer." We settled on seltzer. It sobered us even further. We were breathng sticky self-satisfaction in the smug superior atmosphere. We were outsiders. *Ausländer*.

"At least there are no Arabs," I said.

"No."

"Are you listening to the languages?"

Sarah gave me a ghost of a smile.

The overhead lights blinked off, on, off, on, and I found myself blinking, close to tears. "I was thinking of the kid."

Sarah kissed me. "Don't? And please be careful."

The audience was filing back into the hall. People pushed past us crowding too close. She put her hand on my arm. I breathed deeply. "You know what?"

"No," said Sarah, "you tell me what."

"I've had it. I don't like the last act."

"You want to leave?"

"I want to leave. You remember who gets the Holy Grail?"

"Who?" she said.

"One of these assholes."

It was quiet.

Back in the hotel suite, Sarah hung up her stole and put her jewelry back into its case. I stretched out on the bed and recovered. Sarah looked at me. I shuddered. "That bad?" she asked. I nodded. "Take a shower," she said, "you'll feel better."

I closed my eyes.

She sat beside me on the bed. "Where are you going to meet him?"

"Who?" I said.

"The publisher."

"We're in Vienna," I said. "Where do you think?"

"The Sacher?"

"Bingo."

I awoke to her chuckle.

Sleepily, I murmured, "What?"

She hummed and moved against me. Sensuous. Sensual. Voluptuous. Slow. Presently, she was straddling me, on top of me, her cheek against mine, her arms around my shoulders, her knees at my hips, her pelvis against mine, my erection where it ought to be, and more, gently gripped, extended, by muscles deep within her. "Oh, my God," I said and pushed up, in, up farther, driving into her.

"God?" she mocked. "Is that all you ever have to say?"

"I do love the position," I said.

"They call it the rabbit position," she said.

"They?"

"People," she said, and moved. And gripped. And moved. And moved harder. I had slowed. "Did you think I was thinking of someone else?" she said.

"What you said was 'people.' " I recovered. "I understand why there are so many rabbits," I said.

"They call it the people position," she said.

I laughed.

"Ah, it laughs. I like the laughter," she said. "You know what I really like in you?" We thrusted, gasped and the talk did help to maintain it, prolong it. "No matter what, you're always there for me. Like now."

"Grab," I said.

She did. I groaned, pleased, then ecstatic. She said, "I did all the work to get us here. Say thanks." I did. "Harder." I did. Harder. She was pleased. "You want to know how I learned this?"

I froze again.

She laughed. "It slows you down every time."

"Figure out another way to do it."

"Do you mind?" she said.

"What?"

"My taking charge?"

"I have no brain, I'm not here, I've disappeared."

"You're losing it again."

"No!" Frantically, I ground into her.

"There, that's better. Poor bewildered man. Answer the question."

"Which?"

"Do you mind? My controlling it? Do you mind, do you mind?" she said.

I said, "I like it, I like it!"

Pronging, prolonging, pleasure. Agonizing. Together we came. Somewhere, someone was screaming. Her? Me?

It was me, groaning.

Chapter 51

THE Sacher was sumptuous.

I arrived by taxi. I was holding a small attaché case. I paid the driver and stepped out of the cab. I tipped the doorman holding the cab door. It gave me a chance to feel my surroundings and I sensed something. I turned to ask the cab to wait, but he drove off.

And what do you know? There were two somethings, one down the sidewalk to my left, one ahead of me. A big blocky blond man was studying the pharmacy window down the block. A dark man, nicely dressed, inconspicuous, invisibly blending, was standing outside the hotel front doors, pretending to take the air. He caught me looking at him and went back inside.

I followed him into the hotel. I walked through the lobby, past the man. He was at the newsstand, buying a German magazine. He looked German. Maybe he was.

Onward into the dining room and Herr Doktor Grossbart.

Hyman Grossbart was seventy-six years old.

He dabbed his fat, sneering lips and luxuriant mustache with his white linen napkin and blinked beadily through his thick spectacles.

I spotted him at the choice table by the window and decided on sight that Herr Grossbart was not a nice man and that I did not like him. There was another problem: There was someone else in the room watching us, in addition to the stocky blond man on the street and the lobby German coming up behind me. I could sense the additional presence.

I beamed, approached Grossbart, extended my hand.

"You are late three minutes," Grossbart told me.

"A lifetime," and shook the man's hand.

"What?" he said.

"I've been so looking forward to meeting you—"

Grossbart preened. "Worth a detour, I am, in the Michelin!" He laughed and gestured expansively for me to sit.

Smiling, I sat at the table and I put my attaché case on the floor by my feet. Grossbart waved for the maître d', who responded to the great man instantly, beckoning and calling two waiters, one with a tray, one with an elaborate cart on wheels. There were no menus. Either Herr Grossbart had ordered previously or they had standing orders how to serve him. The waiters piled enormous breakfasts on our plates. The standing orders were to serve everything.

I lifted my eyebrows. "I see you know the menu. It is a privilege to dine with you."

Herr Grossbart, forking eggs past his mustache, managed a grandiloquent chuckle. "Eat, eat, *essen*," he gestured with his knife and dripping fork. "One of the sights of Vienna, I am! Is this your first visit?"

I sipped my coffee. "No."

"You must spend a day in the *Kunsthistorische*, excuse, you are American, you could hardly know—" he said.

"The Art Museum?" I said.

"More, much more. It is a symbol of the treasure here, the soul of Austria is cultural," he expounded. "And you must go to the Opera! It is the world's greatest opera today! And the world's most knowledgeable audience!"

"I saw," I said.

Herr Grossbart continued to talk through his food. "You must see them. Last night was superb, *Parsifal*, a true work of genius, one of his later operas—"

"Wagner's last opera," I said.

"Ah, yes! Wagner. Richard. Brilliant moments, boring hours!" Herr Grossbart roared with laughter.

Actually, the eggs looked delicious, a sort of soufflé. I permitted myself a forkful. "That was Rossini, right? The quotation?"

"Huh?" Herr Grossbart was flustered but only for a moment. "Yes, Rossini, but he was wrong. Rossini was a fat Italian. He was a cook with no sense of history. You cannot expect such a man to understand a German."

I said, "I left before the ending."

"Typical," said Grossbart.

"Of what?" I said.

"Americans," he said. "Wagner requires education. You can't understand *Parsifal* unless you've studied Schopenhauer. *The World as Will.*"

"*—and Representation,*" I said. "Wasn't that the full title?"

"Huh?" Herr Grossbart stopped eating. He was squinting at me. *"The World as Will and Representation?"* I said.

Herr Grossbart mopped his plate and regrouped. "Yes, it's the pessimism of the romantic theme that the renunciation of desire is the only possible salvation."

"Oh?" I said.

"You do not agree? Why not?"

"Because the hero, the Aryan hero, is only able to renounce desire after he has seduced the Jewish whore," I said. "And abandoned her to die in bliss. Because she has had his innocence. Only then does he get the Holy Grail. Now is that fair? I mean, fair to our women?"

Herr Grossbart's eyes blinked wetly. He produced from his waistcoat pocket a tiny black notebook and a tiny gold pen, put the notebook on the table and made tiny notes. He mumbled, "Hmm. I must remember that. A novel interpretation."

He was old, I must respect him. He was successful, I must respect him. He was probably a Bigger Giver than me, I really must respect him. He reached into his briefcase, produced a folder of papers and handed them to me. "Here—here is your order, for your latest model MiniMagnum."

I studied him. The man was nervous. He was perspiring and there was still the froth of whipped cream on the full, fluffy mustache.

I signed the top copy and gave it back to him. Herr Grossbart seized it. I put the papers into my attaché case.

Herr Grossbart became both expansive and gloating. "That will teach him to sneer at me. That banker. That politician. With his fingers into the central banks. That master of manipulation. Dealing with the terrorists, that rotten anti-Semiten—"

The maître d' arrived with more coffee and whipped cream in a silver bowl on a silver tray and Herr Grossbart fell silent. The

maître d' filled our cups and spooned whipped cream over Herr
Grossbart's. Herr Grossbart sighed.

"*Schlag*, sir?" the maître d' asked me. I shook my head. No
schlag, ever again. "Anything else, sir?"

Herr Grossbart was suddenly angry. "No, he doesn't eat a thing
and you are interrupting—"

"I would like an entire big Sacher torte," I soothed, "wrapped
to take with me. And the check."

"Don't be silly, I will sign the check. I can buy and sell you.
And your company in Austin. And the other company," Herr
Grossbart said and preened.

I stared at him. Mossad in Hebrew meant company. It was an
incredible lapse in front of the maître d'. Incredibly, Herr Grossbart was laughing. Was he an amateur out of control with relief,
now that he had passed the papers to me? Or was it something
worse than that? A deliberate provocation of someone listening?
It was time to get out of there. I was suddenly too heavily dangling.
Casually, I told the maître d', "Bring a check for the torte separately, please?"

The maître d' looked at Herr Grossbart, who nodded, with a
show of reluctance. The maître d' departed.

Herr Grossbart smiled, still pleased with himself. He sipped and
looked owlishly at me through the whipped cream in his coffee
cup. There was another dollop on his mustache. "Maybe I will buy
your company," he said. "I mean the one in Austin. You would
benefit. You could work for me. I could make you rich and teach
you much."

"But I'm so slow learning. I am sure you would become impatient."

The maître d' returned with the wrapped Sacher torte—they
must keep them ready and packaged—and the two checks on tiny,
discreet silver trays. Herr Grossbart signed his, making no further
effort to take mine. Good.

I deposited the necessary cash shillings in the tray and rose,
thinking of something to say. Temptation. Give them something
to call home about. Let's justify the recording. Come on, Grossbart, cue me.

Herr Grossbart looked up over his coffee cup at me. "Well? Say the word. I will make you rich."

I smiled agreeably. "Hitler was very stupid."

"How?"

"He could have conquered the world. All he had to do was ask, and you would have explained it all to him."

Chapter 52

"YOU MEAN YOU ACTUALLY SAID IT?" Sarah was incredulous. She paused in the process of serving the torte from the coffee table in the suite living room.

I was opening a bottle of champagne, standing by the window. I looked out through the curtains.

There was a dark Mercedes at the curb.

Dangling, dangling, dangling.

I stepped away from the window. I had the foil off the bottle and the wire nearly clear. There. I dropped it in the ashtray. I started working the cork up with my thumbs, carefully holding the bottle at the requisite forty-five-degree angle.

"He's sure to report it to Shima!" she said.

"I wouldn't be surprised, an ego like that." Pop! The cork flew against the curtains, dropped to the floor. I held the bottle steadily. The champagne foamed up and, as always, did not drip a drop.

Sarah was glaring.

I sat beside her on the couch. I reached for the champagne glasses on the coffee table. I poured.

Sarah forced herself to resume serving the torte. "How could you! He's important!"

"Is he a Big Giver?" I said.

"Damn you! Stop joking! What happened? You were all right when you left here."

"He started speaking. He is the most obnoxious man I have ever met."

She eyed me coldly.

We ate bites of the torte and sipped champagne.

"He is an old man and a rich man and you might at least respect him," she said.

"Old?" I needled. "Do I respect old? And rich? For that you respect him?"

"Forget rich. He is an old man who has done good things."

Here we went now, over the edge. "He gave me a new perspective on the Holocaust," I said.

There was a moment of harsh silence. Sarah put her glass down firmly. "Don't you dare say it!"

"What?" I said.

Her voice rose. "What I think is coming."

"I mean, suppose they were all just like that," I said. "Not just the rich, the upper crust, but the middle class, the intellectuals, the professors, the doctors, the lawyers, all of them, even the businessmen—"

She controlled herself with difficulty. "Go ahead, you bastard, finish the thought! Your new perspective on the Holocaust. You wiseass, you coward, go on! If they were all like that, like Grossbart, what? Say the words! You can understand killing them?"

She glared at me.

I was silent.

She said, "You can understand wanting to kill them?" She slammed down her fork and went to the closet. She reached in and tore out her suitcases. She threw them on the bed and opened them. She stormed back into the closet.

I said, "They were not my words. You said them."

She opened the suitcases and started to pack.

"You said them, you must have thought them."

She turned to me. "I never thought I would get angry enough to walk out on you. But here I am!" She resumed packing.

"Look, where are you going?"

"I don't know," she said. "Yes, I do know. I'm going to go to Athens."

"Ah!"

"In fact, I'm already ticketed there," she said. "I'll move it up a couple of days."

"I see," I said. "Shima's in Athens."

She picked me up on it. "Yes, Shima will be there. And you're a mess. All over the lot. You know what? I find you disgusting."

"My goodness. Will you see me there? When I come?" I asked. "Assuming that I do come?"

Sarah shut her suitcases. "You have the papers," she said. "Come with me. Let's leave. It's this place. It must have gotten to you—"

I said, "My grandfather is buried forty miles from here. I am going to put flowers on his grave. Why don't you come with me?"

"No. You come with me!" she said. Stubborn.

I shook my head. "No. I can't. Good-bye, Sarah. I love you true. And I'll take you to the airport."

"Don't bother!" she said.

I said, "Of course I will. You used to be my woman."

She rushed into the bathroom and shut the door.

I listened to the water and looked at the bathroom door. I shook my head and looked about without appearing to do so. It was in the elaborate light fixture in the center of the room. I studied it while shaking my head, mournfully watching the door.

The coverage was comprehensive audio but limited angle video. I took a deep breath and sighed for the video. With a heavy heart I took Sarah's suitcases from the bed and lugged them over to the doorway—out of the eye of the video. Silently, I placed my attaché case on the high table beside the door. I opened it and took out the papers. I reached down to Sarah's smaller suitcase and carefully opened it. I delicately maneuvered the inner frame, released a flat false partition catch and slipped the papers into the compartment. By tomorrow, they would be safely in Athens.

Tight-lipped was the word for her.

The porter loaded Sarah's bags into the trunk of the taxi standing underneath the ornate overhang outside the hotel entrance. It was busy. The noises seemed far away. The stony-faced doorman held the right rear taxi door, and the love of my life got in.

Holding my attaché case ostentatiously, I tipped the porter. A big tip. I entered the taxi gingerly.

Halfway down the first block, an old white Mercedes diesel pulled out from the curb as we passed. It moved into the traffic behind us.

From time to time, the taxi driver looked at us in the rearview mirror. Was he in on it? I hoped so. He checked his outside mirror. Stuck behind an old BMW, he slowly pulled onto the Autobahn.

The taxi picked its way through the traffic on the departure ramp. It pulled up in front of the Olympic Air signs.

There were porters all over the terminal this morning.

The driver and I both jumped out. I held my attaché case under my left arm and flagged a porter ostentatiously, with my right hand waving a large bill. The nearest porter responded instantly, eyes on the bill.

I gave it to him. He reached for my attaché case. I shook my head. I indicated the baggage in the trunk, which the driver was now opening. I walked around and opened Sarah's door. I reached for her. She got out of the taxi and avoided my hand. She stood on the curb and fumbled in her purse for her money, passport and tickets.

The porter put her bags on his trolley and held the baggage checks. Sarah offered him money. The porter told her in German that I had already taken care of it. She gave him the money anyhow. He reached for her tickets. She gave them to him. The taxi driver stood by the car.

The porter asked Sarah if she was going to carry one bag or check them both through. Sarah gestured irritably, what the hell, check them both. The porter gave her bags to the captain on the curb. Sarah watched sullenly. I watched patiently. The porter stapled the baggage checks to her tickets and brought them back to her. Sarah tucked her tickets into her purse. I reached for her with my free hand. She recoiled.

"Wow," I said.

"Wow to you, too."

"See you," I said.

Sarah grunted. "Sure."

"Soon?" I said.

"I doubt it," she said.

"Whenever. If ever it happens. I do love you."

Sarah went into the terminal building.

I looked after her. I took a deep breath. Helplessly, I got back into the taxi, still holding the attaché case under my left arm.

The taxi driver looked at me in the rearview mirror. He asked where I wanted to go.

"Hmm?" I said, unhelpfully.

Did I want to go back to the hotel?

I gestured, we might as well. I looked out the window.

On the way out of the terminal we passed the old white Mercedes diesel. We approached the access road to the Autobahn. There was an old BMW up ahead. I wondered if it was the same one.

Chapter 53

I CHECKED OUT OF THE HOTEL the next morning. By now, Sarah would be in the Plaka having a late lunch of feta and olives.

I made the maximum fuss in the lobby, questioning the un-questionable phone bill, challenging the charges for long-distance calls.

Outside the hotel entrance, a porter and the hotel doorman loaded my one bag into the trunk of the rented Mercedes 500. I put the attaché case flat on the right front seat. I got in, closed the doors, started the engine and opened the electric front windows. Across the street, a horse-faced Slav in a brown suit was standing with his hands behind him against a shop-front window.

I looked at the hotel. Everyone stood at attention. I smiled. They smiled at me. Off I drove.

It was a spectacular springtime day.

Traffic was light. I reached the Tyrol, the trees green and budding, the fields fresh-plowed. I felt like singing. Soon I was, for the benefit of anyone with a bug in the car.

I didn't mind dangling on such a beautiful day. A half kilometer behind me, an electric utility truck followed. I speeded up slightly. So did he.

Through the greenwood, through the greenwood, through the greenwood greenwood tree. The song shouldn't end with tree. There was something wrong with the rhyme there.

Whither do I follow follow follow?

Half a kilometer, half a kilometer, half a kilometer.

I reached my destination late in the afternoon: Bad Ischl, a small, pretty town, picturesque.

I drove through it slowly, enjoying the sights, remembering the stories. I had been there before, twice. I pulled over to consult a map. I asked directions of a passerby. I had spotted all the following cars. There were three, the electric utility truck, a relatively new Volkswagen and the same old BMW.

The Jewish cemetery was north of town in the middle of a forest on a small dirt road.

I sat on a grassy knoll, the attaché case beside me, contemplating the graves. Mine was the only car. I seemed to be the only one there. They, whoever they were, were out there somewhere — they had to be. Maybe they were waiting up the road. Or maybe they were around me, in the trees. If they were, they were certainly quiet. As a tomb.

I somberly drove back into town.

There was no utility truck on the road, no Volkswagen or old BMW. There were two outdoor cafés in the main square. Each could be watched from windows. The waitress was slender and cheeful. I put the attaché case beside me on a second chair. I ordered *Kaffee schwarz*, without *Schlag*, in honor of Herr Grossbart. I studied the map, thoughtful. I sipped the coffee slowly, missed the schlag, played for time. Shima had asked for forty-eight hours. I was running ahead of schedule. They had followed to see what I would do, who I would meet, where I would go, and the cemetery visit had answered all that. Here I was. Vulnerable. They could, if they wished, pick me off now. Maybe Shima had men out there covering me but somehow I didn't think so. I would have a better chance of surviving if I could draw them out in the village. I would be helpless once I got on the road. Here at least there were people.

But I would be helpless if they picked me up and made it look official and took me with them out on the road.

Stall. They would wait till I got in the car again. The side streets were safer.

I went for a walk in Bad Ischl.

There was a park four blocks from the main square. I headed toward it. Briskly. Hefting the attaché case by the handle. I could feel them closing in. I paused at the park entrance, read the signs, looked at the ugly statue. If I entered, that would be perfect. For them. I hesitated. They had to hesitate. Again, I checked my watch.

I turned and headed back toward the main street, holding the attaché case under my left arm. I could hear someone behind me approaching fast. I turned. A large man in a gray suit paused to examine a shop window. Across the street, a car door opened. Up ahead, I saw a tall, well-dressed, elderly man, who must have been in his seventies, holding a wooden cane as he approached me. I studied the map, looking puzzled. I looked about, looked at the map again. I was lucky. Now there were other people. The elderly gentleman smiled politely. He wanted to be helpful. He said something in German. The footsteps behind me had stopped.

I managed to look awkward. *"Bitte?"* I said. "Excuse me, sir, do you happen to speak English?"

The elderly man said, "A bit," and introduced himself, "Scharnhoff!"

I shook his hand. "Collins. Could you tell me, please, where is Hauptstrasse?" I presented the map.

We consulted it together. Herr Scharnhoff babbled, "I know

where it is! I know it well! It is here! Look! There!" He pointed to the map, then up the street and rattled off directions in German.

I looked at him, helpless.

We both laughed.

"You are what nationality? English?" Herr Scharnhoff asked.

"No," I said. "American."

"Ah, that is very good for you. Look, I will take you there, where you wish to go, the two of us, we can walk it."

"Oh, no, sir," I said to the nice man, "I couldn't let you—"

"Come! It is near, I would like it to do." Herr Scharnhoff put his arm under mine. He drew me along, through the crowds on the sidewalks, his cane tap-tapping up the street. Footsteps followed us. Up ahead, I saw a familiar horse face. A brown suit. Hands behind him. Back against a shop-front window. Ah, yes. Across the street from the Vienna hotel, same posture, another window.

"You come here from Vienna?" Herr Scharnhoff was saying. Brown suit's hands appeared from behind him. Firmly, he started toward us. His hand disappeared beneath his coat, along his belt. There were other footsteps behind me. Herr Scharnhoff said, "What brings you from Vienna?"

"A visit to my family." How would he react? Badly, I hoped.

"I must know them. What is the name?" he said.

I said, "My grandfather is dead now. I have visited his gravestone."

"Oh. I must have known him. What did he do?"

"He had a factory," I said. "He made boxes."

Herr Scharnhoff stopped cold. He turned on me. "Cohen? Horst? *Juden!!*"

Perfect. I smiled at him. People on the street were stopping.

"*Jude!*" He lifted his cane, spat in my face and struck at me. I moved inside, blocked the cane with my left forearm and slammed Herr Scharnhoff hard in the face with a clean right cross, banging his elderly head hard into the building behind him. Herr Scharnhoff sat down heavily, dropping the cane. His hands feebly patted his broken face. People gathered about us muttering "hospital" and "police."

Well!

I turned on them. I shouted, *"Polizei! Ja! Zetst! Polizei! Zetst!"* They stared. Some of them spoke to the pharmacist, who disappeared into his pharmacy.

Wee-waw sirens sounded. The police arrived with an ambulance. The ambulance crew examined Herr Scharnhoff. The police tumbled out of their police cars. Two officers approached me.

"Excuse," said one. "This is Officer Wallens. I am Officer Dietrich. May I please see your passport?"

I gave it to him.

Officer Dietrich studied it. He made notes.

The old BMW pulled up across the street. Inside it were two obvious security men, a small thin driver with a Gestapo face, and a ruddy-cheeked blond my age, with a loden coat and presence, obviously in command and the more dangerous one. He beckoned to Officer Wallens.

Officer Dietrich finished his copying. He handed my passport back to me, hesitating as he did so, noticing the BMW for the first time.

Officer Wallens was standing beside it, signaling. Officer Dietrich turned to me. "Would you mind signing a statement?"

I looked across the street and made eye contact with the man in the BMW. Hello, there, so you're the boss man. Exasperated, aren't you, being flushed out too soon against your will? Now you will have to take formal charge of a confusing situation. "Yes, I would mind," I said.

"I am sorry. It will be necessary," said Officer Dietrich. "Please?" He reached out for my attaché case.

I protested.

He took it anyhow.

Dusk had softly settled on the town by the time they released me.

Officers Wallens searched my car and baggage. The boss man searched my attaché case. He was not lacking in humor. "It was the woman, of course," he said.

"Who? Frau Ravitch?"

"Cherchez la femme. And we let her go," he said.

I said, "I don't know what you're talking about."

His mouth twisted. "It was such an original fight."

"Which is that?" I said.

"Your view of the Jewish Holocaust," he said. "And your words to Herr Grossbart."

I drove back to Vienna. No one followed.

Chapter 54

SHIMA PHONED Brooke in Boston. "I understand you've been looking for me?"

Brooke was groggy. "What time is it? Where are you? Still in Athens?"

Shima said, "This is an open line."

"Can't help it. This is urgent," said Brooke, "First, Mr. S. is ripshit. He does not believe what you sent him. He put his bright young man on it and told him to study the problem."

"Mr. N."

"Every time you do that," said Brooke, "I conclude that we must be leaking like a sieve, to both you and the Russians. Yes. The conclusion is, we can't tell. We need more. It establishes support for the camps but not the identity of the key supporter."

"What else?" Shima said.

"There's nothing in what you sent concerning your nightmare about currency rates and banking. And Mr. S. is frightened," said Brooke.

"Ah," said Shima, pleased.

"If you are right, and you may be right, do you realize the implications?"

"For the dollar?"

"Yes, for the dollar and more," said Brooke. "It would wreck our whole economy. The collapse of the ruble brought down the Russians."

Shima said, "He won't cause the dollar to collapse. He'll just cut its value by a third. Or a half."

"And reduce our standard of living."

"Ask Santry what could happen."

"How close is he to having the power now?" Brooke asked.

"Close. We have no idea how many banks he controls, or the assets they manage or the markets they are in. And we know he has currency dealers as well. They and the banks do the trading."

"And we can't confront him," said Brooke. "He's our own man."

"He would simply deny it," Shima said.

"And we have no proof. But if he's got the power you say he has, we have no choice. We will have to stop him."

"Take my word for it. He's well on the way."

Brooke grunted. "We need evidence."

"A witness."

"Yes."

"Close to the subject himself. Someone in whom he confides," said Shima.

"Yes."

"No such person may exist."

"I know," said Brooke. "But perhaps you will create him."

Chapter 55

SABAUDIA WAS 120 kilometers south of Fiumicino on the Mediterranean coast. It had been built by Mussolini for elite Fascists. The villas south of the town on the beach road were sedate, aristocratic.

The Cadillac limousine parked in the circular drive behind the house. The two Italians in the front seat jumped out and opened the rear doors. Werner helped Ileana out of the car. She stretched. The jump seat was shallow. Werner admired her posture.

So did Gunther, circling the car. He saw Werner looking. Werner looked away. Gunther spoke to her, for the first time in two hours. "Are you stiff?"

"I am fine," she said.

He nodded toward the marshes east of the road. "Circe turned men into pigs there."

She said, "Are you telling me why I am here?"

The old man did not laugh. And he could not look at her. He was looking at the marshes. "There are still wild boar hunted there. And the mountain," he indicated the mountain to the south, nestled against the water, "is Monte Circeo, named after her. The myth is quite symbolic."

Ileana said, "Perhaps it is history not just myth."

But Gunther was walking into the house without her.

What was the matter?

Ileana knew that there was another woman in the house the moment she entered the marble foyer. Was it perfume? Instinct? Or her awareness of Gunther's discomfort?

Werner led her to her own quarters. They were elaborate, a substantial sitting room, an enormous bedroom with a huge bed and a combination dressing room-bath, truly Roman in its fixtures, with a magnificent view of the beach from the tub. She watched the people on the bench and realized that they could not see her. One-way glass. Ileana was delighted.

She drew herself a bubble bath. As the tub filled, she inspected the closets. They contained a full wardrobe of quality clothes, Italian designers, her sizes. Someone had done a superb job. It was thoughtful of Gunther.

Ileana decided to enjoy herself.

She returned to the bathroom. Playfully, she undressed. She sat in the tub and let the bubbles rise around her. She knew from the closed-circuit TV pictures the old man so loved to watch with her that unseen cameras were recording her every move, and that somewhere in the house Gunther watched her.

Probably with the woman, whoever she was.

Ileana shivered, despite the heat of the water in the tub, and decided to tease, giving them their money's worth. She sank beneath the bubbles, slowly, out of view.

They would be glued to the closed-circuit picture, she knew.

Would she soap herself, stroke herself, fondle herself? Would she remain horizontal in the tub? Or would she stand to soap or rinse herself?

Would she assume some even more provocative posture?

"Come in, my dear. This is Inge," said Gunther. "And Inge, this is Ileana."

Ileana stood there in the doorway, feeling delectable in her coral print, coral earrings and matching coral shoes and purse. Gunther had had lunch with the other woman. Ileana had had hers alone on her terrace. And now, the summons.

Ileana's first reaction to the woman on the couch was quivering fear. She tried to suppress it. She politely shook the hand of the languid terrifying creature.

An older woman. Ageless. A beauty. No, the word was too delicate. The hand was cool and dry and the look mocked. "Inge," she introduced herself.

Ileana blushed.

Inge turned to Gunther. "She is exactly as you described her. Sweet. Full of promise."

Ileana experienced a distinct sexual throb, then an echo, then another full throb. She was aghast. Her face showed it.

"Are you all right? You keep changing color," Inge said.

"Inge and I are old friends," Gunther said.

Inge chuckled. The sound thrilled Ileana. She had another distinct vaginal shiver and realized that she was moist. With fear and desire.

"Gunther says you have been good to him," Inge said gleefully. "I can't wait to find out."

Ileana looked down.

Gunther flushed. "Do you remember what you promised?"

"Of course she does," Inge grinned. "Look at her. I am tempted. I confess I am. Temptation. I never resist it."

Ileana surrendered. "What do you wish?"

"Where do we wish? That seems to be the question first," said Inge, who was having a marvelous time.

"How about my room?" said Ileana. "Such a big bed."

Gunther said, "There will be perfect."

"Gunther?" said Ileana.

"Yes?"

"The bath I took. May we see it?"

Gunther was embarrassed. Inge said, "I was right, she is delicious. Go ahead, Gunther, rig it."

Gunther turned the TV set and VCR on and popped in the cassette lying on top of it. Ileana sat primly on the bed. Inge reclined beside her. Gently she stroked the back of Ileana's neck. Ileana trembled. Inge smiled. She reached up to turn Ileana's face to hers. Gently, Inge kissed her. It was soft and Ileana responded.

Gunther sat on the bed.

They watched Ileana bathe herself on the television for five full minutes. When Ileana stood in the tub and commenced stroking herself, her face tilted up toward the light and her eyes closed in rapture, the image clear, the sound and color perfect, Inge murmured and moved closer to Ileana. She reached around the girl, her right hand lightly stroking Ileana's neck, her left hand unbuttoning Ileana's coral dress. Ileana sat motionless. Inge slipped the dress down over Ileana's shoulders. She pulled Ileana to her and the two kissed passionately once again, Inge's knee between Ileana's, her knee and skirt thrusting against Ileana's pubis.

Gunther said, "Jesus."

Inge said, "Shhh." Her left hand reached around and unhooked Ileana's bra. Ileana raised her arms and Inge lifted the bra off her. She handed it to Gunther, who took it.

The two women lay side by side, facing each other, one naked, one dressed, except for shoes. They kissed. Inge stroked Ileana, who shivered, and started to come. Inge chuckled. It thrilled Ileana. Inge kissed her neck, shoulder, breast and took Ileana's nipple in her mouth, all the while stroking her. She put Ileana's hand between her own legs and moved against it, avidly. Ileana expertly searched Inge with her fingers, and Inge, too, shivered. She continued to stroke Ileana's hair, hairline, cheeks, lips, neck, shoulders, breasts, flanks, belly, bottom, light pubis, thighs, long long legs with long long strokes, her knee now pulsing in Ileana's groin, both kissing and coming violently, Inge making soft grunting noises, Ileana desperate whimpers.

Gunther said, hoarsely, "I'm sorry, I can't take this."

Ileana reached for him.

Inge turned on him and laughed. "My my. Both ready and naked." Her hand reached out and caressed his penis.

Gunther was transfixed.

Inge said, "You back off, now, she's mine, you wait."

Gunther did as instructed.

Inge moved up over Ileana. They kissed, and now, for the first time, Inge reached between Ileana's legs and stroked her with her fingers. Ileana went wild and thrashed on the bed. She passionately kissed Inge. Inge's lips moved slowly down her body. Ileana reached out with both hands and stroked Inge between her legs. Inge shifted her hips even closer where Ileana could more easily reach her.

Inge's mouth moved down past Ileana's belly. Inge moaned, quivered and fiercely came. She continued to kiss Ileana, the insides of her thighs, her vaginal lips. Ileana thrashed wildly on the bed, both women coming together.

Gunther kneeled at the foot of the bed and thought he would lose his mind or worse, he might even ejaculate, with frustration, not desire. Inge turned her head and snapped at him. Insanely, he could not focus on the words. "What?"

Inge laughed. "You may kiss her. Nothing else."

Gunther moved forward, alongside Ileana. Ileana reached for him. Desperately, he kissed her. Inge had moved around behind Ileana's head and was bending over the girl, licking between her legs again, and Ileana was responding fiercely, her head thrust sideways, her tongue and teeth now kissing Gunther.

Gunther caressed Ileana's breasts. He licked her breasts. He was close!

"Back away!" Inge commanded.

Gunther sat back.

Inge straddled Ileana. Ileana reached up for Inge, pulling Inge down toward her, each with her mouth probing the other. Both women shivered, throbbed, whimpered. Seconds passed, minutes, it seemed to go on forever.

"You, now," said Inge.

Gunther moved over between Ileana's legs as Ileana rhythmically moved her pubis up against Inge's mouth. Inge relaxed slightly, taking her mouth from Ileana. There it was. He could penetrate her.

"No!" said Ileana, beneath Inge, before he could.

Inge was glaring at him.

Gunther was bewildered.

Ileana cried out, "Her! Always do your own first." Inge laughed at the look on Gunther's face. "She's the one who's important," said Ileana.

Gunther hesitated. Then he scrambled around behind Inge, behind Ileana's head. Ileana had buried her face in Inge again. Inge was quivering, hunched forward away from him, over Ileana. There it was—he could enter her! He moved up toward her.

Ileana's hands reached back for Gunther. He slid forward. Ileana took him in her hands, guiding him into Inge. Inge groaned in a fierce, hoarse whisper. Gunther thrust and she responded, backing hard against him, thrusting toward him. He shoved harder. She responded still more, bucking wildly, coming insanely. Her back glistened, the slight down at the base of her spine had a sheen. Gunther seized her hips and slammed into her. Again and again, he thrust into Inge, and Inge came, over and over.

Inge pleaded, "Gunther! Please? My God! My Gunther! Please? Please!"

Her contractions on him were unbearably sweet.

Ileana released him.

Gunther exploded.

The telephone rang. It jolted Gunther awake. Sleepily, he picked up the phone, noting as he did so that it was shortly after seven P.M. according to the clock on the bedside table.

Gunther said into the phone, "Hmm?"

"Grigor."

"Where are you?"

"Vienna. They have phoned from Bad Ischl. That is a small town west of here—

"Why? There are problems?"

"Yes. Yes, sir."

"Summarize what has happened."

Grigor cleared his throat. "The American took the file from your Jew friend at breakfast at the Hotel Sacher."

"Yes, you told me yesterday. So?"

"He returned to his own hotel and had an argument with the woman."

"And? Come, come. Where is this going?"

"All the time, they were under surveillance. She walked out and took a plane to Athens. He drove to Bad Ischl. It was perfect. They were sure they had him. Then, as they moved, there was an incident."

"What kind?"

"A fight. The police stopped him." Grigor hesitated.

"And?" Gunther snapped. "What happened?"

"He did not have the file."

Gunther took a deep breath. "I see. The woman took it to Athens."

"That is what we must assume," said Grigor. "Our young men are angry. But without the file?"

"You were right to stop them. Where is he?"

"At the airport. Olympic Airlines."

Gunther said, "I do not wish to do anything there. Set it up in Athens."

Chapter 56

IT WAS MORNING on the Acropolis, full sun, clear sky, cool, crisp. The pale light was dazzling.

Sarah arrived by limousine with a driver and two silent Israelis. Sarah stayed in the air-conditioned car. She looked out the window, around the square, up at the Acropolis. She consulted her guidebook, looked at the Parthenon, back at the book. She opened the door of the limo.

One of the guards held it open. Sarah got out and put her sunglasses on. The sunlight was glaring.

She climbed up toward the Parthenon.

The two guards walked behind her, flanking her, one to the right, one to the left. There were very few people about, none of them interesting.

Sarah wandered through the Parthenon.

She saw no one anywhere, nothing. She was surrounded by silence and the brightest of light. She checked her guidebook, looked up at the capital of the column to her right, looked down at the base and clutched.

I was seated, my back against the column.

She looked dizzy, lightheaded from the heat and sun. "My heart fluttered," she said.

"You do have the most beautiful upper lip," I said.

"You told me that the day we met," she said.

"Have I ever told you I like to kiss it?"

She shook her head.

I stood. We came together and kissed. She closed her eyes, held me. Shima had explained at least part of it; all was forgiven. The guards watched stonily. I glanced at them, all about, saw nothing. I looked at her.

"Hello," I said.

Arms still around me, head against my cheek, she murmured, "You deliberately drove me away like that, and I, like a fool, believed it. Shima laughed."

"What did he say?" I said.

"He opened the back of my case first thing."

"And you knew what had happened."

"No. I don't know what the papers are," she said. "I hate it when they keep me in the dark, but I have no need to know what they are and I suppose I could be questioned." She smiled. "I believed you about Grossbart."

"I really didn't like him."

"But you are not anti-Semiten. I was so relieved." She shook her head.

I led her outside, past the columns, to the top of the stairs. It was eerie in the light and silence. I felt spacey and disconnected. Even Sarah, leaning against me, touching me, her warmth and scent a part of me, seemed detached, her voice distant. We sat, viewed the spectacular view. The guards vanished behind us into the columns.

She said, "Promise you'll never do it again? No, you can't. It was your assignment."

"Were you very angry?"

"Incensed," she said.

"I lke that. Shima and spices and angry smoke."

"I was all right when I got off the airplane."

"Even before the explanation?" I said.

She put her arms around me again, kissed my cheek, kissed the corner of my mouth, kissed my mouth again and noticed the book I was holding, Plato's *Republic*. She looked at me quizzically. "I don't believe it."

"It's the perfect place to read it. This is where it happened."

She reached for me and we kissed again. The guards both appeared. Down below, the driver stood by the car.

She had closed her eyes.

I dropped into the kiss, warmed to it, lost myself, kissing her, fiercely, hard.

The Acropolis was naked old marble, stark against the sky in the sunshine.

Chapter 57

GRIGOR CHECKED THEM IN. He signed the credit card slip. Diego scanned the lobby and was silent.

The reception clerk and porter joined them. On their way to the elevators, Grigor detoured to pick up a package from the concierge. The reception clerk and porter took them up to the suite. The reception clerk tried German, then English, then French. Grigor smiled. Diego played the same game and purported not to understand them. Roman was always silent.

They entered the suite. Grigor dropped his package on one of the bed. Neither Diego nor Roman said a word. They checked the windows, closets and bathroom.

Grigor swept the suite carefully for any sign of a listening device. He took his time, the greater part of an hour. He did it in two passes, the first time visually, the second with an electronic detector from his carry-all. He spent a long time on the telephone. You could never be quite certain.

He went to the door and said, "You stay here."

"For what?" Diego smiled his nervous smile.

Grigor said, "In the package, you will find weapons." He went out and closed the door behind him.

Roman was at the door. Diego said, "Where are you going?"

"Out."

"He said to wait."

"That's why I'm going."

Diego looked at the door. The buzzer sounded again. Either Roman or Grigor would have a key. Diego worked the slide on the Sig-Sauer 9 mm, held it muzzle up and moved silently to the left of the door. *"Oui?"*

"Moi." The muffled voice was Ileana.

Diego unlatched the sliding bolt. *"Entrez."*

Ileana entered and closed the door behind her. She smiled at the automatic.

"Where is he?"

"Who?"

"The old man." Diego flashed his quick nervous smile.

"Here. In his apartment," she said.

"How do you know?" he said.

"I know he's here, I flew in with them and I've been to the apartment."

"Them?"

"Gunther and Werner. I am to bring you there."

"What of Grigor?" Diego said.

"He is there now." She looked about. "Where is Roman?"

"Out."

"I see." Ileana smiled and shook her head. "Shall we wait for him?"

"No!" Diego said. "You know, I've always wondered and never asked. Have you been to bed with Roman?"

Grigor said, "The American who shot you will be there tonight with the woman who carried the file for him and the head of Mossad operations."

Diego looked around the apartment. "And you want me to kill them."

Gunther said, "All of them."

Diego rose. He paced the room. The others watched him. He said, "You have this from Roman."

Ileana said, "What?"

Grigor said, "They have approached him. That's where they want to meet him."

Ileana was stunned.

Diego continued pacing. "The restaurant where you took me the first time. The Israeli would never go there alone. There will be others. At least a dozen. But the roofs, there are all those lovely roofs, and the buildings, the other buildings. Yes. I like the challenge. I will need men, six as a minimum."

"There are three," said Werner. "They are all here. And you, Ileana, Roman."

Diego sat on the couch again. The others looked at him. Diego shook his head. "No. It is too uncertain."

Gunther said, "This one is very important to me. The file they took will embarrass me. I do not know what other things they know. I do not wish them to find out anything more. I do not wish to worry about them."

"No," said Diego.

Ileana stirred. "Roman will be there. He can lead the group. And I will do it with him."

They looked from her to Diego to Gunther again.

Diego said, "Tell her about Roman."

Ileana said sharply, "Herr Waffen, what about him?"

Gunther gestured at Werner. Werner searched in his briefcase and came up with a bank statement. He handed it to Ileana. She scanned it in silence.

Diego said, "Roman's bank accounts."

Grigor said, "You will notice the deposits that match your own. Each of our payments."

Ileana studied the statement. "And the rest? There is too much here. Who paid him?"

Grigor cleared his throat.

"Mossad operations."

Ileana laughed. She said, "You can't be serious." She saw that they were. She said to Diego, "How long have you known?"

He said, "A week."

She said, "Why haven't you killed him?"

No one answered.

Gunther said, "Because of you."

Diego said, "What would you do if we asked you to kill him? You may have to. I think you could. If you wished."

Gunther nodded. "I agree. You are a very strong woman. And the only one of us Roman would not suspect. He will be on his guard with the rest of us."

"Is there any other evidence? Corroboration?" Ileana's voice was strident.

Werner reached into his briefcase. He came up with a printout from the French telephone company. He gave it to her. "From the post office phone in Lyon when you were there. To the Israeli embassy in London first. Then a hotel in Boston. The Mossad head of operations we mentioned before was registered at the hotel in Boston."

Ileana was ashen. "To warn them about Paris? But he couldn't! He didn't! They didn't know!"

Diego said, "He couldn't because he didn't know. None of you knew when we left Lyon precisely where we were going." She looked at Werner.

Silence.

Gunther said to Ileana, "I am sorry."

Ileana stood. She walked to the door. Grigor opened it. They both went out. Grigor closed the door behind him.

Gunther looked at the door. He said, "You need not kill the American tonight. There are things I would ask him."

"Shall we take him?" said Diego.

"If you can. Grigor can ask what I wish to know. Then I will give him to you as a present."

Chapter 58

GREEK MUSIC was being played on classical string instruments by three old men in peasant dress and a thin, wild-haired woman with the clear singing voice and flutelike pipe woodwind. The restaurant was crowded. Business was booming.

Busy cooks manned the semiopen kitchen. The salad and dessert buffet was manned by one short and one tall Levantine. The view of the city lights was impeded by the haze rolling in. There were twenty-two tables in all. I noted the huge potted plants, the flowers and the vine-covered arbor. The checkroom girl seemed innocent. As for the bartenders, maître d's, captains, waiters and busboys, who could tell? They were all Balkan.

Shima's hard-faced men in business suits occupied the table next to us. Two more flanked the rickety elevator doors. Another guarded the door to the back stairs. There were shadowy faces at at least two of the overlooking windows in the building immediately adjacent. On the rooftop of the next building, there were two men on the parapet. It was first-class security, platoon-sized, but open.

Across the table, Shima watched me count. He looked cynical, holding his unlit cigar in his mouth. Sarah was happy, sitting close to me, listening.

Shima chewed on his cigar and said, "There are more than you see."

"Now this is what I call dangling," I said.

Shima said, "If you have a chance to pick the battlefield, you pick it and prepare it, as best you can. And they cannot protect the informant here, it is too big and too out in the open."

I said, "I see you really trust him."

Shima shrugged.

Two waiters with slightly soiled white coats and the sad faces of two millenia of doomed and mournful tragic choruses replenished our doughy rolls and heavy sweet white wine. Shima looked around at the salad and dessert bar, and gestured to the waiters beside us with three fingers, "Hors d'oeuvres first, then the salads."

"Yes, sir," said the waiters.

"Whatever you want, just bring them."

The waiters adjourned to the salad and dessert bar where the two salad chefs heaped hors d'oeuvres on three enormous china plates. The restaurant throbbed with energy and chatter and the harsh hysteria of laughing Greeks.

Shima said, "If we lose him—" But the waiters were returning with our salads. One of them presented Sarah with her plate, and the other presented a selection of salad dressings in eight china boats on a huge tray.

We waited while Sarah selected.

Shima was watchful. I smiled up at the waiters. Shima tensed. "He is here, behind you. His sister is with him."

There was a flicker beyond Shima. I took a deep breath and continued, "Well, what do you know? There's a fly in my soup. Excuse, salad, not soup."

Sarah said, "What in hell are you talking about?"

I had risen. I put my napkin on the table. My napkin clunked as I did so. Underneath there was something metal.

Shima stiffened. This was it. Now.

Sarah, bewildered, looked at me.

I was holding my salad plate up in the air. I signaled one of the waiters and shouted, "Hey!!" I waved to the waiter and said to Shima under my breath, "I'm going to throw my salad in your face, and you start to go for me, only don't, instead you drop to the floor, and Sarah, when he drops, you drop, too, whoops, here it comes, let's do it—now—"

I screamed at Shima, "You son of a bitch!! You bring me here and feed me shit!!" and threw my salad, plate and all, in Shima's face.

Lettuce and dressing dripped. There was stunned silence everywhere.

I glowered at Shima. In the background I caught a glimpse of the two salad chefs, one of them reaching for something down below. Sarah shriveled, had I lost my mind?

With a growl, Shima reached for me—and dropped to the floor. Sarah dutifully fell, too.

The two salad chefs, now holding Uzis, hesitated a moment too long.

I had grabbed my .45 Gold Cup from under my napkin. I stepped wide and dropped to one knee, holding the automatic in both hands and leaving the salad chefs with no clear shot.

They fired anyhow, barely missing Shima, the slugs chewing into the table. People screamed. Shima scrambled away, dragging Sarah. She cowered. Shima's guards reacted too slowly to help.

I whirled. The Balkan brother and sister were still seated four tables away.

I spun away from them. Instantly, both Uzis swung toward me. Each fired a short burst, one wild to my left, the other high. There were more screams somewhere. I fired—smashing the tall Levantine in the chest. He dropped his weapon and fell. There were screams everywhere. Everyone hugged the floor. The short salad chef, now kneeling, fired another short burst at me, again to the left but closer—and swung his next burst back toward Shima. I fired twice more, hitting the short salad chef in the shoulder with the first shot and in the chest with the second. Done.

The man sat down slowly, his Uzi wavering in a wobbly ellipse up into the air. As he sank to the floor, Shima's men finally fired, the slugs slamming him over onto his side and jolting him repeatedly, four hits, five hits, six hits—and then sudden quiet.

A beat of silence. Sarah and Shima started to rise.

Crouching behind the table, I shouted, "Not yet!!" They dropped back down.

The Balkan pair were still seated.

Shima's men were fanning out, looking up, and then, from the rooftop to the right, two more attackers crouching in the shadows fired at Shima with shortened Kalishnikovs.

There were screams and pandemonium. Shima's guards fired back.

The attackers fired wildly, the slugs chewing crockery and tablecloths.

I fired once. It was low, a carom off the parapet. The attacker at whom I had fired swung his gun muzzle at me.

I fired again. The shot was higher. It hit the man in the face, driving him back against the bulkhead and into the path of his comrade, who was spraying slugs into the restaurant all around Shima.

Patrons screamed. Shima's guards fired.

The remaining attacker was driven back but managed to loose one final burst before he was hit three times in the neck and head.

I held my fire, watching as the man crumpled. I lowered my notched sights and turned.

The Balkan brother and sister were no longer at their table.

Shima dashed for the doorway to the back stairs. I went after him. There were others following. Down one flight, around the corner, down the second flight. Around the corner. Footsteps clattered below. Shima shouted as he dashed down the third flight, taking the stairs three at a time. Around the corner, shouting, down the fourth flight, skidding to a halt. I halted beside him. The others pounded down the stairs toward us.

The Balkan brother and sister stood by the door to the street looking up at us. The man's face was twitching. The woman hugged his arm. She was lovely. With his free hand, the man gestured toward her, introducing her. "This is my sister—"

She shot him. She shot Shima. She fled into the street.

I charged after her. I was the first person out the door. She was in the back seat of a Mercedes, the door open. She beckoned to me. "Come!"

I never saw the blow that struck me.

My head exploded. Rough hands dragged me forward onto the floor of the Mercedes. I felt a stabbing pain in my upper thigh. A needle.

She had killed her own brother.

Was Shima dead?

Who was she?

God help me.

Chapter 59

I KNEW WHERE I WAS, part of the time. In a wheelchair, happy and giggly. Most of the time I was sleepy. When I came awake, they would stick me. I figured that out and pretended to sleep, and sure enough, they left me alone. I laughed at that.

Next time up, I was curious. I was in a car. I was in a chair again, bundled against the chill of dawn. Elefsis. I recognized the name. A small airfield west of Athens used by the military. When the plane took off, I came wide awake in a full-press panic, clutching the seats—and then of course they stuck me again.

I felt the jolt as we landed and panicked again. They carried me down the ramp, then wheeled me across the tarmac. Through the terminal. I heard Arabic. Some of the people were wearing the robes but most were dressed Western-style. I heard French and more Arabic. The terminal was a strange mix of sleek modern and jerry-built primitive, ultraclean gleaming and closet filthy. Uniforms. Small ordnance. Russian. Official photographers in civilian clothes snapped pictures at apparent random. Not mine. My caretakers shooed them away brusquely. Video cameras were everywhere, slow-scanning relentlessly.

Outside, I squinted in the sunlight. A burly man in a brown suit I had seen somewhere previously fingered open one of my eyelids.

I smiled at him happily. They put me in a car and did not stick me. They did not have to. I was sleepy.

They were keeping the dosage as light as they could.

Someone wanted to talk to me. They would not kill me until they had done so. And I knew where I was. Damascus. Somehow that pleased me.

The city was spectacular, a hazy hot plain stretching for miles away from the blue mountains. No one went there anymore. They should have. I was lucky.

At dawn, the muezzin greeted the day.

Somehow, I was in a car again. People stirred in the shanties, on the rooftops, gazing past minarets at office buildings.

First, there were uniforms. Then there were none. It was flat and rocky and dusty.

I was alone in a tiny room.

Book V

Chapter 60

IT WAS WHITE AND SPOTLESS.

The fluorescent lights were painful. There were no windows. There was some air coming through a tiny vent. There may have been a fan somewhere. I felt dreamy. There was a single tiny wooden chair and no other furniture. The floor was clean and I lay on it. They entered the room and stuck me.

When I awoke, I remembered. I wandered the room. Eight steps by ten steps, heel to toe. I felt dizzy. I liked the room, I told myself.

Since childhood, I had had a recurring dream of a clean white room, a bed, one sheet and a window looking over a meadow. There were trees and mountains beyond the meadow. This room, I told myself, was exactly my dream, except of course that there was no bed, sheet, window, trees, mountains or meadow. There were no sounds and no people. Hours of nothing. I would enjoy the peace. When this was over, I would spend some slow time in the mountains. Or by the ocean, with Hugo.

I slept. Peacefully.

The noise from the door startled me.

I jumped to my feet and wobbled. Three soldiers entered and stood at attention. Through the door came a beautifully cut Savile Row suit on an extraordinarily handsome dark-haired man. Familiar suit, familiar man.

I groped. I couldn't place him.

"Hello, there!" I said cheerfully and reached my hand for his. My hand shook. We both looked at it. "Collins," I said. "Don't I know you?"

The room spun and I sat on the bed. The horse-faced Slav in the brown suit had appeared in the doorway.

"You have committed three murders," he said, unsmiling.

Smiley! That was who he was. Ben Hassan. Bassam. Smiley.

He went on, "You are an agent of the Israelis."

"They were only trying to help me." I smiled at him.

"You will answer some questions," Ben Hassan said.

"Sure," I said. I wanted brown suit to like me. Brown suit was poking my eyelids now. I sat there, smiling passively. One of the soldiers held me.

But brown suit stuck me again. I lay down. Clang! The door was shutting.

My, I was sleepy.

Time passed. Hours.

They brought food but I was not hungry. A piece of bread. One bite of foil-wrapped cheese. There was water in a bottle with a cork in it. I drank a sip. The bottle was empty. Presently it was full again. Another bottle probably. I drank that, too. I was thirsty.

It was dawn. The cries were muezzin. They came for me. I was shivering.

"Hi," I said, smiling at Horse Face. "Do you have a name?"

"Grigor," he said, "Him, you know."

I squinted at the man behind him. It was hard to focus but I did. I giggled and said, "I shot him in the belly!"

Diego tried to get at me but Grigor would not let him touch me. There were things Grigor wanted to ask me. He started the questions slowly. Why had I been in Athens?

I told him. Because Sarah was there.

Did I love her?

Absolutely.

Where was she now?

With Hugo, I hoped.

And where was that?

I shook my head. I didn't know. We were going there in the morning but the night before, they snatched me. I found myself weepy and trembling.

Had Sarah taken the file to Athens?

Yes.

Did I know what was in it?

I told him I had skimmed the file in Vienna on the way back to the hotel in my taxi. It established the deposits in bank accounts, the transfers to certain other accounts and the control by the Syrian government of all but three of the transferee accounts. For the support of the camps, here, I said.

Oh, did I know where we were?

No, but I assumed the Bekaa Valley.

Did the file establish the source of the deposits.

No, I said, and giggled. It was a tempest in a teapot, not proof, not satisfactory.

To whom?

To the Israelis.

And?

The Central Intelligence Agency, or so Shima had told me.

Diego said, "And the three other accounts?"

I said, "You and the brother and sister. The brother gave them the numbers. He's dead. I saw her shoot him. She must be quite a lady—"

Diego said to Grigor, "That's it, you'll get no more from him."

Grigor waved Diego back and said, "And who did you think was the source of the funds?"

"The banker man?"

"Who? What's his name?"

I was fuzzy. I tried to remember. "I do not think Shima told me the name."

"But he gave the name to CIA."

"Oh, yes, and they knew the man. They already knew him."

"What else did you know about him?"

"The murders."

"Tell me about the murders."

I did. I told him about the murders and the reasons for the murders, and about each of the bank transfers. I smiled at Diego. "Tell me. Did you know the purpose? That it was all about money?"

Diego glared at me.

I was thirsty. I reached for the bottle of water.

Grigor said, "What do you mean by that? All about money?"

I told him about my analysis of the banker's grand strategy.

"And you told that to the Israelis?" he said.

"Yup."

"And they told it to the CIA?"

"Yup," I said. "The CIA was unhappy."

"Why were they unhappy?" Grigor said. "About what? Specifically?"

"Control of the currency markets," I said.

"And what do you know about trading currency?"

It was that question that saved me.

What did I know about trading currency?

I told him my money management theories. I told him my pyramiding theories. I told him the rationale of my system, its mathematical underpinnings and the way it had always worked for me. I told him about the $11,600,000 I had made for the Israelis. I went on and on. I told him about every single trade I made. The reasons, the tactics and strategy.

Diego was going crazy with boredom.

Grigor was recording everything. From time to time, he asked questions. He sent for more water without my asking him when he saw I was thirsty.

Once I asked him, "You don't really know what I am talking about, do you?"

He said, "I work for a man who will."

"The banker man, whose name I don't know?"

"Proceed, I do not wish to answer that."

"Fucking genius, ain't he?" I laughed.

"And what is it you admire so?"

"The whole plan, the grand strategy, the control of the economy." I beamed. I hoped the man would hear me.

"The ten million dollars you made—"

"Eleven million, six hundred thousand. More."

Grigor said, "Tell me the rest of the story."

Outside the cell they were arguing. I heard Diego shout, "You promised him to me!"

Grigor said, "I must telephone."

Diego said, "He promised him to me!"

I dozed. I was sleepy.

Presently, they returned. I sat up. "Hi! What else do you want to know?"

"I'm not sure," Grigor said. "What else do you want to tell me?"

"How I made my stake," I said. "My first ten mil. Did I tell you that I gave them that, too?"

"The Israelis? Yes, I knew. Tell me how you made the first ten million."

I would love to, I said, and I did. In detail. And enjoyed it all.

Grigor was fascinated.

Chapter 61

THEY DROVE ME BACK TO THE CITY.

Slowly, in the back of a limousine. Grigor, Diego, three armed guards and a driver. I felt weak. Dizzy. Thirsty. Happy.

Someone wanted to meet me.

We approached a hotel.

We parked in front of the entrance. The doorman ostentatiously paid no attention. I peered up at the hotel above us. What now? Everyone except the driver got out. One of the guards held my door open.

I got out of the limo unsteadily. Grigor helped me.

Everyone was looking in another direction.

They walked me through the lobby carefully, one in back, one on each side. Hotel personnel looked the other way. Something of the kind must have happened before. Clearly, they all knew just what to do: see nothing, hear nothing, speak nothing. I walked on unsteadily, Grigor and Diego trailing us, my three guards around me.

There were additional security men in the lobby; I spotted at least five. They were well dressed and in civvies. Maybe they were going to throw me out of the country. That would be a good laugh. Maybe they were going to throw me out a window. That would not be a laugh at all. What was the word? Defenestration? Maybe they were going to drop me down the elevator shaft.

We came out of the elevator three abreast, Grigor and Diego behind us.

There were four more security men in the corridor up here. The large one with the stone face produced a key. I waited for him to unlock the doors.

Stoneface unlocked the door and stepped back. I should enter.

I gestured. Stoneface should enter first.

Stoneface pushed the door open. Grigor took me by the arm and pushed me in. He and Diego moved up close behind me. I stepped forward. If I moved swiftly enough, could I shut the door on the rest of them?

I felt the adrenalin rush. I gathered myself to slam the door shut with my shoulder—and froze.

They were voices and the sound of crockery in the living room. Suddenly, I was starving.

The guards closed the door behind me. There was no need to

slam it on them. That was the end of that great idea. I moved unsteadily into the living room, Grigor and Diego with me.

Ben Hassan and another man were seated, having coffee. Ben Hassan stood to greet me. The other man was older. He did not. I stood in the doorway between the foyer and the living room. They had muscle deployed against the walls, two by the door to the connecting suite and one over by the windows. Ben Hassan gestured for me to sit. "Would you like breakfast? Coffee?"

I indicated Diego. "I should eat with him?"

Ben Hassan said, "Eat while you can."

"That sounds ominous," I said. I sat in a chair. I looked at the old man. I knew who he was, I said, "I am honored to meet you. Sir."

He looked at Grigor. "You told him?"

Grigor said, "He is guessing."

I said. "Who else would want to meet me?" I finished the coffee and poured another cup. My hand was still shaking.

The old man said, "Speak to me of money."

I heaved myself to my feet and walked to the windows. I studied them and the tiny balcony and city view beyond. I said, "I don't have any, any more. I gave it to the Israelis."

He said, "I have listened to the tapes of what you said. I will listen to them again. Several times. I think they are worth preserving. I am impressed with your system and trading skills. But that is not what I wish to ask you about. Tell me what you told the Israelis."

I could hear the German accent now. I missed Sarah. What would she make of it? I said, "About you? Your grand strategy?"

"That is correct. Tell me."

"I told them I think you seek to control the market prices of currencies."

He laughed. "But that is not possible. The central banks—"

I said, "You know what they are thinking about."

"True, but not the Japanese, and they have the most money."

I was thirsty. I sat and had more coffee.

He watched. "Go ahead, tell me."

"I think you control lots of banks who play. You control the funds the banks control. A vast pool of funds, probably."

"And?"

"You determine the currencies in which they place those funds. You probably control, if I read you right, the brokers who make the markets for those currencies. And yes, the Japanese have more money. But I think you trade for the Japanese. You control the markets in which they trade in most of the key hours of every day. I think you are a genius." I smiled at him happily.

He shook his head. "Amazing. What a fantasy. And you told this to the Israelis. And the CIA."

"No, but I think they did."

"To Santry at the CIA."

"I do not know that," I said. "But I have heard the name Santry." Diego interrupted. "Look, we have heard all this—"

The old man snapped at him. "And you are not interested, but I am!" The old man gestured and Grigor approached him. The two of them whispered to each other.

I said to Ben Hassan, "How is she?"

He said, "Who?"

"Sarah."

Ben Hassan looked at Diego.

Diego grinned, "The married girlfriend."

"We have her," Ben Hassan said.

"No!" I shouted. "You are making that up." I was seething. I had more coffee. I was running out of time. "Oh," I said to the old German.

He and Grigor looked at me.

I said, "Do you know what I would do, if I were you?"

He said, "No, why don't you tell me?"

"Run the dollar," I said. "Our financial system is rotten, the banks, insurance companies, pension funds, we can't print money fast enough, the only way out is inflation, running the currency down into nothing, you start it, and you could, it would snowball! I could see the Deutschemark at parity! Thing is, you gotta tell me when!"

He looked at me steadily. "I am afraid that will not be possible."

"No? Why not? It's what I've always dreamed about, a bet-the-ranch opportunity. I need the money! I'm down to nothing!" My voice was rising.

"The dead do not need money."

I shouted, "What? A sure thing and you won't let me in?"

He said to Diego, "Take him."

Ben Hassan smirked. "And then you can take his woman."

I heard a noise, an inarticulate grunt, a growl in my throat, an internal scream I strangled. It increased in pitch to a howl. "No!!"

Diego was smirking.

"I am sorry," said Ben Hassan, "I really am—"

"Nooooo!!" I howled. I threw myself from my seat, and—as they sat there, stunned, and then made a dash after me—I crashed through the glass windows, shattering them, bulled my way out onto the terrace outside, planted my hands on the rail and vaulted over.

Chapter 62

I WAS LUCKY.

The glass windows had been single hung and exploded outward away from me. My clothes had taken the brunt of it. I had shallow scratches on the heels of my hands and a nick in my right earlobe. As I kicked in the windows to the suite below, I heard them struggling up above and curses as if someone had cut himself. Someone shouted, "There's a terrace on the floor below!" I thought it was Diego.

By then I was through the windows.

I flashed through the suite on the floor below. It was empty, I darted out the door and down the corridor to the service stairwell. I pounded down nine flights. There were two doors at the bottom of the stairwell. One of them was marked *"Sortie."* It opened with a push bar into the alley at the rear of the hotel. There were taxis

at the mouth of the alley, the end of the rank around the corner
from the entrance. I jumped into the last taxi. *"Libre?"* I said.
"Allez! Vite!"

No response. The driver stared at me.

I produced my money.

We were approaching the outskirts of the city.

I had not told the driver where we were going. I had pointed
and handed him dollars. That had been fine. He had been happy
enough to take them.

Now we were proceeding slowly. There was traffic. We stopped
at a traffic light. The start-and-stop driving was awkward. I thought
there were two cars following us. I kept looking over my shoulder.
I was making the driver uneasy.

The light changed. We moved ahead. I learned forward. I
pointed, move over. The driver protested. I shouted in French,
"Maintenant!" The driver, with reluctance, pulled over. Horns
behind them blared angrily. The tails both drove past us. Their
drivers glared at mine.

I leaned forward and barked orders in French again, *"À droit!"*
The driver protested. I hammered at the driver's shoulder. The
driver started moving. We turned. I looked behind us. We had
lost the tails. I ordered the driver to turn right again. He did. This
street was wider but potholed. It was dirty and there was almost
no tarmac. We bumped along through piles of garbage. The driver
protested—he was protesting everything now—and we continued
to bump along. I decided to stop here. *"Arrêtez!"* I ordered. The
driver shook his head.

I leaned forward and shouted, *"Arrêtez!* Stop the car!!"

I reached forward and seized his head. I slammed it hard to the
left against the window frame. The car lurched up onto the curb
and then off it. I shoved him forward, hard, over the wheel. The
car slowed as his foot came up. He fought to control it with his
left hand, pushing back out at me in protest with his right hand,
a very feeble effort. I slashed him hard in the neck with the heel
of my right hand. I pushed him out of the way and wrestled the
car up over the curb. The taxi skidded sideways and halted.

The driver reached for me. I grabbed his shirt and dragged him out of the car. I slammed him against the building and smashed both hands against his ears. I turned.

I jumped in behind the wheel and took off in the taxi, careening around the corner. There they were. Both Mercedes. They had narrowed the gap.

I turned right into a pitch-dark alley, accelerating into a skidding turn, and stood on the brakes.

A tank blocked the street. On it was a searchlight.

It blinded me. I twisted the wheel left, gave it gas and the taxi jumped up and over the curb. I braked, twisted the wheel right and reversed. The taxi bounced back down into the street. I turned left, smashed up over the curb, back down into the street.

I heard shouts and a 105 mm cannon exploded! Wham! Whack! The shell caromed off the building to my right, smacking off a spray of clay. I skidded left around the corner into the path of the two Mercedes. They headed right at me. I accelerated, threatening to drive between them. They drew closer together. I swerved right, ran up on the sidewalk, sideswiped one of the Mercedes, banged off the building and got past them. Again, I skidded left around the corner.

There were lights up ahead. This street was wider. I braked, turned the wheel left, threw the taxi into a rear skid right and accelerated left around the next corner. There were too many lights up ahead. I braked and twisted the wheel right, throwing the rear into a sliding skid left, and accelerated into the cross street, my best slick racing turn—and again had to stand on the brakes, skidding left sideways into a doorway.

The street was blocked from wall to wall by three tanks. Behind them were trucks with searchlights.

I had to get out of there! Quick!

I dashed into the building. Wham! Whack! Behind me, the taxi exploded.

I ran and ran.

I made it.

Chapter 63

THE *Mirabelle* was a sleek fifty-footer with a French-designed hull built in Hamburg in 1962 to the chintzy specifications of a Düsseldorf manufacturer of plastic cups, and subsequently rebuilt for progressively less affluent and less satisfied owners in Marseilles in 1968, Trieste in 1977 and Piraeus in 1985.

The ship was overpowered and would have been fast if the engines had been minimally maintained. They had not been. The ship had a captain, a mate and a crew of two, none of whom had passports that would withstand scrutiny, and was available for charter out of Latakia or any other Syrian anchorage or north Lebanese port, by the day, the week or the month, for sportfishing or errands.

It was proceeding south along the Lebanese coast at flank speed with a very nervous captain at the helm. Ali Baraak was forty and bisexual. He purported to be Lebanese. He spoke guttural Arabic, French and English with a Greek accent. Only once did he register a question about my elaborate Arab dress. I had stolen it. Along with the money in my pocket.

Ali Baraak's repeated glances at me had an unmistakable meaning: I was sufficiently good-looking so that Ali Baraak was responding to me physically. I had not bathed for several days and did not feel physically appealing today. Ali Baraak was all I needed. I had to be very careful not to give him a chance to hit on me. Fortunately I had recognized the problem in our very first moment. Dressed in my rich, graceful Arab robes, and speaking peculiar clipped French with my imitation Arab accent, I had chartered the *Mirabelle* for half cash in advance at dawn that day for an agreed twelve hours of fishing, which we would not do, as I knew and Ali Baraak suspected. Once outside the Latakia harbor, we had headed south. We had continued on the same course ever since without a sign of interest in fishing.

Ali Baraak had correctly concluded that I, standing in the broad open stern cockpit behind and below him, was rich, armed, dangerous, on the run, political and obviously not Syrian. He had also concluded, incorrectly, that I was either insane or on drugs and, partially correctly, that the purpose of the trip was illegal and that I was planning to meet someone.

Ali Baraak studied the shoreline off to our left. Seagoing traffic was as usual sparse. I could practically see the spinning of his sluggish mental wheels. Did he dare head in closer to the shore? That was dangerous. There were shallows. Furthermore, Israel lay just ahead and Israeli patrol craft were vigilant and unforgiving. Perhaps, if the ship were seized and released, that would be a cheap way out, assuming I could be persuaded to pay the rest of what I owed, which was a very big assumption. I seemed crazy but I would pay if left alone. Ali Baraak was a good judge of who would pay, and he was right, I would pay him. On the other hand, I was crazy, and how would I react if the Israeli navy approached, waving guns? It might be difficult. It might well be costly. It could be fatal, although that was less important. The captain looked behind him down at me and started to speak. "Monsieur—?"

I interrupted, "No, thank you. Hold course and speed."

The captain murmured and shook his head. It was time to do something, or at least to try something. What were his options? Put the wheel over hard? What would I do if he did that? He glanced down at me again and reacted.

I had produced a Walther .25 popgun from my Arab robes. It was not much of a weapon but it was all I could buy at any price and I had had a hell of time getting it. I had loaded the gun for a demonstration and then had to threaten to use it. I held it close against my body, visible to him, but not to the others, "I'm sorry. Assemble the crew. Please."

The captain picked up the microphone. Should he—?

I read his mind. "I do not need either you or them. I will be fine if you all go over the side. So don't say a word. Just call them."

Ali Baraak did, over the microphone.

The mate and two crewmen slowly appeared. They were perfect casting, unappealing and untrustworthy, but they were also unarmed and silent. They appraised the situation, me and the gun.

I stood with my back against the stern rail. I shouted orders in

French. They lay face down in the cockpit where I could watch both them and the captain up at the wheel at the same time.

Captain Ali Baraak shouted down, "I need them!"

"No, you don't. What for?" I asked.

"That is Israel." He pointed straight ahead.

"Good."

Ali Baraak protested. "We can't go! Look! Patrol craft! Two of them! We are heading straight for them!"

It was true. They were there.

"Hold your course," I told him.

The two patrol craft split, one to starboard, one to port, obviously going to flank us and approach for inspection. Ali Baraak tried once more, desperately, "You must take off the robes, pretend to be Jew! You are English, you can be anyone. If they think you are Syrian man, they may kill you!"

I said nothing.

The *Mirabelle* maintained course. As the two cutters came abreast, I shouted at the captain and the *Mirabelle* slowed. A loudspeaker hailed us from the cutter to port, first in Arabic, then in Hebrew.

I stood on a deck chair. I lifted my Beretta and pointed it straight up. I emptied all eight shots into the sky. A stunned moment later, the Israeli cutters closed. They boarded us, bristling with weapons.

Chapter 64

SHIMA WAS ALIVE, sort of.

He was in intensive care in a small hospital somewhere on the outskirts of Tel Aviv. I never knew precisely where it was. They took me to see him in a limousine with the rear and side windows blackened and a curtain over the divider behind the driver. On the way, they told me what had happened. Shima had somehow twisted sideways when we stopped on the restaurant stairs and she fired. The bullet had perforated his heart and collapsed a lung. He had had a pulmonary collapse in the ambulance to the airport and a cardiac arrest on the plane going home. He was going to make it, they assured me. Probably. Without brain damage. Probably.

Visitors were strictly limited and I was the last person they wanted him to see, the central figure in a failed operation. They said I could have ten minutes with him. I timed it. They gave me seven.

He smiled when he saw me. They had told him I had escaped and he knew I was coming to see him. We shook hands and he clasped both of his around mine. "Was it bad?" he said.

I said, "They gave me something. By injection."

"That's all they did?"

"I was lucky. They wanted to keep me talking and I did. Oh, and I did meet him."

His eyes gleamed. "What did he say?"

"Not much. He was interested in what I had to say. I was the one did the talking."

"What's he like?"

"Old. Shrewd. Cold. German. How are you?"

He made a face. "She made the same mistake you did. In East Berlin."

"A .32?"

"A Beretta. A woman's gun." He tried to smile. "But she did more damage than you did. Michael, it was a good plan. It could have worked. I'm sorry it didn't. But it could have been worse. We didn't lose a single man."

"No," I said, "just one woman."

He looked at me. "What are you talking about?"

"What happened? Where do they have her?"

"Sarah?"

Hope glimmered.

"What did they tell you?" he said, "That they had her? They were lying. She's fine."

I could feel the tears. I suppressed them.

"She went back. She's with your son. Hey." The feeble man in the bed reached for me, hugged me. I could not speak. I sat on the bed. He smiled. "What now?"

"I don't know, sir," I said. "No more plan?"

"No. Not for the moment. Too many sedatives. Soft in the head. Give me time. Can you sit still for a month?"

"Will he?"

"No. I doubt it."

"Then what are my options?"

He said, "With Sarah and the boy or without them?" He reached for a glass on the table beside the bed. I filled it with water from the pitcher and gave it to him. He had trouble swallowing. He went on, "If I were you, I would not go near them. If he finds you, he'll go for you and they'll be safe. If he finds them, he will wait for you, I think. You are more vulnerable when you're with them and you're his primary target."

"You'd prefer that I wait."

"Until I have a plan."

"We have differing objectives. You've got your banker. I have me and mine."

"Which makes you suspicious," he said. "Where will you go now? Geneva? Canada? South Africa? Australia?"

"I don't know. I haven't thought about it."

They opened the door behind me and beckoned. I stood.

Shima smiled once more. "Do you want your money back?"

"You've given me my money's worth."

"Good luck, Michael."

"Thank you, sir. I remember what you told me in New York. No matter how good your plan may be, whenever you start one of these things, you never know what is going to happen."

Chapter 65

I FLEW from Israel to Geneva.

There are easy-out and easy-in towns. Geneva is both easy-out and easy-in, and I was in no mood for complicated.

Easy-outs are towns where you can get to a major airport in a hurry. Geneva Cointrin qualifies. Easy-ins are more unusual. Those are the towns where I am most comfortable, where I can arrive without a reservation or baggage, not even a toothbrush, and feel at home. Geneva is a standout among the easy-ins. No one tries to hustle you. Everyone wants to help you. It is safe, it is clean. It even has good eating.

And my money was there.

I needed a few days to sit and think with a little less sense of danger.

I took a taxi to the center of town. Rush hour had not yet started. I sat on a bench beside the river. I hadn't been a solo since Shima had entered the game. I wanted someone with whom I could talk it through. Instead, I was isolated.

Hugo and Sarah were in danger because of me. If I had been killed, they would both have been safe by now. Was Shima right and should I stay away? Or should I go to them? If I could find them?

I dozed.

"M'sieu?"

It was a policeman. I assured him I was all right. I checked my watch, shocked. It was nearly noon. I stood, embarrassed. I would go to a hotel. It was a better place for sleeping.

I walked across the street and checked in.

Geneva had two four-star restaurants right next to each other, Le Gentilhomme and Le Chat Botté. I slept till dusk and made a reservation at Puss in Boots.

It was nearly deserted in the early evening. The maître d' gave me a corner table. I ordered a Tanqueray on the rocks. Presently, an elderly American couple came in. He kissed her cheek as the waiter held her chair. I was jealous of the husband. I ordered a second Tanqueray, a Caesar salad, steak tartare and a half bottle of Dole.

My second gin arrived promptly. The maître d', assisted by two waiters, wheeled up two serving tables, one with the bowl and utensils and the other covered with ingredients. He mixed the Caesar salad in front of me. "You love Caesar. Have one," the husband said to the wife. The two of them had nice faces.

"It does look wonderful," she said. She peered at me as they served me mine. She was still a beauty. They murmured to each other. She looked at me. Was mine good? The man looked sheepish.

I said, "It is delicious."

He said to me, "What are you going to do about your son and Sarah?"

"I'm sorry, I shouldn't have done that," the man said.

"No, you shouldn't," she said. "Beano so loves to be dramatic."

"Look," he said, "you have never heard of us, but we are fans of yours."

"Supporters," she said.

"We know about and admire what you have done, and the funny thing to us is, you have no idea how much you have accomplished. By the way, I am Oliver Nelson Brooke. And this is my wife, Marjorie."

"Beano came to Geneva to see you, Mr. Collins," she said. "I'm just a friendly face along to make you less suspicious."

I said nothing.

He smiled at me. "We heard about your arrival in Israel. That was certainly dramatic, I must say. Why don't I do the talking here. It is safe, although you would not know that it is. I had it swept right after you called."

"Called?"

"For your dinner reservation."

"You bugged my call."

"Not me," he said. "I wouldn't do a thing like that. Someone else did it."

He talked.

I was fascinated. I had always suspected that there were inner circles like his, but no one who belonged to one had ever admitted it. Brooke went pretty far. He gave me the names and numbers of the players. Of course, I had heard a lot about Price Santry of the CIA, who had testified before Congress. I was surprised to learn that Santry knew of me.

Brooke paused.

"What do you want from me?" I asked.

"Not yet. I still have more to say."

"You say I have accomplished something?"

"You have made us face the dimensions of the problem."

I said carefully, "Which problem?"

He gave me the smallest of smiles. "We had Paul Volcker in. Paul says that the man could run the mark up a good 25 percent. Maybe even to parity. Parity with the dollar, if you can believe it. One to one. If he did, we could not afford to import a thing. It would cut our standard of living to the bone. No one would buy our Treasury debt if the dollar was declining day by day."

Mrs. Brooke said, "The government would stop running."

Brooke said, "Unless we forced interest rates through the roof again and then we could sell our Treasury bonds but it would be 1982 all over again, businesses would collapse under the interest burden, all sorts of people would be thrown out of work, we'd have us a revolution. Lovely, huh?"

"If it happened. But it doesn't have much to do with me," I said.

"Oh, yes it does." He grinned. "I want you to understand how much I know about your attitude and problems."

He told me. He knew about Hugo. They both said sympathetic words. He shocked me by mentioning East Berlin. "Bad luck and the wrong caliber," he said. I looked for disapproval and did not find it in their faces. Strange.

He knew about the money I had provided the Mossad. He knew about Vienna. Athens. The kidnapping. My escape from Damascus.

"How?" I said. "CIA?"

"Shima," said Brooke.

I was staggered.

"Who do you think sent me?" he said.

"Santry," I said. "That's what I assumed."

He chuckled. "Santry thinks he sent me."

"We've known Shima for years," Mrs. Brooke said. "We were shocked to hear of his injury."

"Wish he could be here and functioning," said Brooke. "Believe me, I do miss him."

They gave me my choice of places after dinner. They were staying at the Richemonde. I picked the front outdoor terrace. I sat in the shadows in the corner. I had espresso. They had citrons Perrier.

It felt a little like a dream. I had new godparents wanting to watch over me. Two mouthfuls of mashed potatoes from Boston. Legitimate Harvard and true parked cars. Concern and sincerity. Did I trust them? It was so bizarre. Brooke said, "Let us talk about him. You've met him."

I said, "The German banker?"

"Yes, of course," he said.

She said, "A man who finances terrorists. Including the one who hurt your boy."

"He was in Damascus, too."

Brooke said slowly, "I know. I don't suppose the man said anything we could use as proof against him?"

I shook my head. "I did most of the talking. But he was there."

" 'There' meaning in the camps, perhaps? If you could place him in the camps, that would sure be something!"

"No," I said. " 'There' meaning Damascus."

"Oh."

"What you want is proof of his plans for the currency move."

"Rape," Brooke said. "It would be a rape not a move. Understand, we do not need judicial proof. Just enough to convince certain people for sure. Facts. Details. Admissions."

I said, "You can only get that sort of thing from a confidante."

"Perhaps." Brooke was grim.

"And when we've established whatever it is," I said, "what then?"

"Take him out." It was Mrs. Brooke.

Her husband looked at her. "My goodness."

She said to me, "I admire what you did in East Berlin. I never thought the day would come when I would feel that way about a thing like that but I do. I admire the attempt and the courage."

I said, "Look. What do you want from me?"

Brooke said, "I don't know. Some sort of plan, I suppose. Shima will be out of it for months. No one else seems to be active."

I got up and paced the terrace. They watched. And it started to come together in my head. What they all wanted, what I had to have. A long shot, but it was possible. "Do you know where Hugo is?" I said.

"No," Brooke said. "But I can ask. They can bring a phone in to Shima. And I have a Citation here at the airport. Take it if you want, wherever you want."

"Okay," I said, "I know what to do."

"You do?" he said.

I said, "Can I have the plane in the morning?"

They picked me up at six A.M. and saw me off at the airport. The Citation took off with me at 6:30 A.M.

Brooke told me he had made the arrangements I wished. The supplies would all be waiting. His last words, over the noise of the engines, were, "I don't suppose you want to change your mind."

"No," I said. "Please, just Mossad. No one else."

"No CIA?" he said. "Seems wrong not to use our own."

I shook my head. "Too many interrelationships, too far away, too many chances for one wrong leak. You can arrange it with the Israelis?"

"I already have. And I told them your words, 'loose cover.' "

"Very loose," I said. "If Diego spots them, and he may, he's trained, it's all over."

"Good luck. My goodness, I almost said 'son.' Marge?"

"He's a lucky boy, your son. And she's a lucky woman. Tell her that for me, please. Someday I hope to meet them."

"Thank you," I said. "That's an especially nice thing to say to me. I will try very hard to arrange it."

They watched the sky as the plane took off. We circled. I looked down and saw them.

They were waving.

CHAPTER 66

"GET RID OF HER," said Inge. "She's an addiction."

Gunther smiled, he was feeling that good about things. The three of them had spent the weekend at Inge's family home on the shore near Bremen. It had been as fiercely sexual as the week before and had focused on the huge rear bedroom. It was the first time Inge had permitted him to visit there since their very first springtime. Gunther adored the view and smell of the sea and the architecture, which had once been considered degenerate. It was stark white modern.

Their relationship was definitely on again. Inge was full of plans. She was speaking of entertaining. They would share their apartments and houses. Gunther was not normally a sociable man but he was looking forward to the coming season. His success was a certainty. The enigmatic Inge would be his once again—their reconciliation unexplained but spiced by the salacious gossip Inge could not help stimulating—and Gunther would be making money for everyone, or at least, everyone who would listen. He would put them all in Deutschemarks before the first of the American incidents.

Yes, the Americans had been warned and yes, the wild man, Collins, was still on the loose, but Gunther had all he needed and was ready to go. No one, not even Santry, could stop him now. Even if he could prove something. And he never could.

The profits would be quick and impressive. He would leverage the profits with options. He would then trigger the full terrorist plan, the American disruptions. Those who held dollars would panic. Those who had listened to him would be effortlessly rich beyond reason. They would owe their affluence to him. Gunther would be as popular as a friendless man could be. He would not discuss it with Inge, but he would continue to feel the distinction. It would be poignant vindication of his road through life, his misanthropy and cynicism.

The girl sex toy had made such a difference! She had helped him to discover his sexual self, to exorcise all that old humiliation and to regain Inge. His Inge was his again. Indeed, what the two of them now had in the bed was all the passion and ecstasy Gunther could imagine. And he had the girl as well, a relationship his wife shared and sanctioned! No one else whom Gunther had ever known had had such an exotic arrangement, except perhaps for his grandfather; Gunther had not known that side of him at all. Gunther was judging by his grandfather's reputation. And his grandmother had not been in Inge's league. And Inge would never give him up again. She was too devoted to her own gratification. Realizing this, Gunther had decided that it would be best if they and the girl cooled it for a while. He had explained this to Ileana, pleased with his use of the modern phrase. Ileana had been amused. She had packed the prior evening and made the nighttime long and memorable. Gunther had sent her with the driver to the airport at false dawn so that he and Inge could breakfast on the terrace alone.

Inge looked physically radiant in the pale light. He wished he could say as much for her mood. Gunther enjoyed the croissants, coffee and view. He was happy, looking forward to the day. The grand plan was rapidly developing. Not all banks played currencies. But he controlled many of the banks that did. Even now, at that very moment, if you added up all the funds he managed and could place in whatever currency he wished, he had more money in the currency markets than anyone anywhere else in the world. And he would triple his capital with his dollar play! Thereafter, all currencies would be worth whatever he said they were worth. He could, in effect, control the world economy. He could be, if he wished to be, the richest man in history! If wealth was the measure of victory, he would soon win World War II after all. It would be the great purpose and triumph of Gunther's life. After fifty years

of waiting! It was a shame there was no one to discuss it with. All
the old ones were gone now. He could never discuss it with Inge.
She could not tolerate that much success in a mate; she would
turn shrike and try to destroy him.

Gunther had Werner to talk to, for what that was worth. But
Werner was only a servant. Grigor, the Russian, would never understand and it would be a mistake to explain too much to him.
Ileana probably did know most of it, possibly more than was prudent, but she could never understand either the magnitude or his
pride in the accomplishment, and presenting the culmination of
his life's work to a Romanian, let's face it, a slut, albeit a sweet
one, was something Gunther would find demeaning. What a shame
that he had had no sons. He had had hopes for the Austrian bastard
or whatever he was. What a shame the boy had no interest, but
what can you expect from a peasant? Gunther had told Ileana to
return to the boy in Damascus or the camps, wherever he was.
Sleep with him, tell him all, goad him. They would soon locate the
American again. Now that would be satisfaction.

After breakfast he would take Inge back to bed again. Gunther
was a man close to, yes, contentment.

Across the table, Inge seemed sullen. Probably because he was
smiling. She had never been pleasant in the morning and black
coffee was all she took for breakfast nowadays. Whatever it did for
her figure, it did little for her disposition. "Did you hear what I
said?" she said.

He chuckled. "Yes, *liebchen.*"

"She's dangerous."

"Yes. But I am not the addictive type. It will not be a problem."

"No? Men are such fools."

"Oh dear," said Gunther lightly. "I fear that includes me. Does
it?"

"Yes."

"Have I been insensitive about something once again?"

"Yes. You are a *scheisskopf,*" she said.

"That is not a term of endearment."

"No."

"My love," Gunther said, "do not worry. I assure you again. I
can take her, or I can leave her alone."

Inge shook her head. "And who is worried about your addiction?"

Chapter 67

SPETSAI WAS a flat seven-hour run from the dock outside Athens. We arrived late in the afternoon and cruised offshore in the glassy Aegean, searching till we spotted the place: green hills and a sheltered bay, a tiny beach, sparkling sand, deep blue water, a narrow cove flanked by a rocky point on the north, a cliff on the south, another cove beyond it. The house faced the dock and beach and nestled at the base of wooded hills. They dropped me on the dock, with the boxes. Electronics, ammunition and weapons.

No Hugo. No Sarah. Silence.

I loaded a Taurus 9 mm and an extra clip and walked slowly up the dock toward the house. I paused at the end of the dock on the shore.

"Papa!" Hugo exploded out of the woods, stumbling toward me on the leg and cane. I ran toward him. He jumped like he did as a child, wrapping his arms and legs—leg—around me. I could barely hold the gun. He was babbling. He could not wait to show me the house. And he could swim!

Sarah came out of the woods.

"That is one happy kid," I said. "Thank you."

She said, "Welcome to our island, darling."

Redolent. What a pungent word. Redolent with scented resin, the woods were moist in the chill of the Aegean dawn. The sky was high, wispy cirrus streaked with pink, the new sun yellow with the day's first heat. The sea rapidly shifted from gray to blue. Spetsai was fine sand, algae, rock and scrub, sheltered cove, steep

cliffs and craggy peaks, dense groves of tall trees and thick vege-
tation.

It was going to be far too hot to do anything later in the day.
Hugo and I had gone out early to plant our electronic security
system. We wore identical khaki T-shirts, jeans, socks and sneaks.
We lugged a brown canvas laundry sack and a case with the gun
and equipment. Hugo was moving well on his cane. I was hardly
aware of his limp. He seemed to enjoy himself most of the time.
He was not, however, talking very much. He kept looking at Sarah
and me. My son was being observant.

I finished tapping the code. I crouched to plant the seventh
mini-bugging device near the moss at the base of an elderly spruce.
I covered it with a layer of damp earth. I swept the top with a
crust of pebbles, needles and rotting leaves. Hugo watched me.
He would do the next one.

I examined my tracks. They were light. With my toe, I smoothed
them out. Hugo did the same with his. There were nine of the
tiny sentries. I checked the sack. There were two left, one for the
dock and one for the point. We had taken our time and been
careful. It ought to work, but, like any security system, it was only
reasonably secure against anyone who knew security systems.

Next, we did the point. The logical access route was obvious: a
sandy slot, a narrow channel between the rocks, concealed from
the house. Hugo dug the hole with the small spade. I tapped the
code in and gave the device to him. He planted it perfectly. He
put brush, shells and tiny sea stones over the stand. He looked up
for approval. I reached for him. We hugged, held, then turned and
went out to the tip of the point.

It was high and overlooked everything, the woods, the cottage
and the dock.

Sarah was swimming. I had given her the boundaries, where
she could go. She had protested—she liked to wander, it was gor-
geous—but I was having none of that. I could not afford to take
any risks with what we were expecting. We watched her swimming. She did move in the water beautifully. A woman who liked
dawn swimming might like living in a house on a beach.

Hugo said quietly, "She has taught me the swimming."

I said, "Yeah, you swim fine, do you like it enough? I mean to swim on vacations and such?"

"Yes!" He smiled. I said nothing. Regardless of what he said, he did not like removing the prosthesis every time he went in and it was hard with only one leg kicking. A good kid. He was trying.

"I have to ask you something," I said.

"*Oui*, Papa?"

"Do you think you could kill someone?"

"Papa?"

I waited.

He said, "I have never shot a gun."

I opened the gun case and took out the Heckler & Koch 310, seventeen pounds of a sniper's dream. I assembled the tripod and laid out the clips and the cartridges. He picked up a cartridge. "So big," he said.

"It's called stopping power," I told him. "You will have to hit him with the first shot and we want to be sure you stop him."

"Ah," he said. "That is the lesson of East Berlin."

I sat back on my heels. "The Marquis told you?"

"And Maman."

I said, "The man I shot there is the man who blew up your restaurant."

"I know."

"And he is the man who is coming."

"Papa? I don't know—that is, I cannot be sure—that I can kill someone."

"You never know till you try." I smiled.

Hugo tried to smile. "Papa, I am not joking."

"I know you're not. And if you can't, you can't. But here is the situation. There will be at least two and possibly three of them. They will come at night to surprise us if they can. I will be the primary target. Sarah also, but second. They will not consider you a danger."

"Because of the leg." He picked up the infrared scope. "What is this for, the nighttime?"

"Yes."

"Let us start the training."

We did, that very morning.

Sarah cooked and sunned herself. At noon, she went swimming again. Hugo joined her.

I placed the last of the bugs near the end of the dock and lay face down to do it, with my arm around the second piling. I leaned over the side. There it was, the Greek equivalent of a two-by-four, bracing the piling. I scrambled back to a sitting position. I reached into the bag for the plastic. Sarah and Hugo were watching.

"Is that an explosive?" Sarah asked.

"It's a fixative," I told her. "Waterproof and quick-setting. How's the water? Cold?" I kneaded the plastic.

"It's great. Almost uncomfortably warm. Why don't you come in?"

"I will." I reached over, clutching the planking at the edge of the dock, and tamped in the plastic. It would hold. I scrambled back for the sentry, tapping the buttons and setting the code.

They swam again. Their voices carried over the water. "Sarah?" Hugo said.

"Yes?"

"I see you watching it. You do not look away. Is it ugly?"

I held my breath.

Sarah said, "No. It makes my heart stop when I see it. But it is not ugly. It has healed. All it is, is a strange shape, an elbow, a heel, short finger."

He said, "If you were a girl, and you liked me, would it bother you?"

"No, Hugo. Never."

"You are sure?"

"It will not matter to anyone who matters."

I think she kissed him then. I could not look.

He said, "That is what Papa says, too. It will not matter to one who matters."

They swam closer. I held on to the edge of the dock. I reached over the side and oh so carefully fitted the sentry into the plastic. It was wrong. Too close to the two-by-four. The sensors were blocked in that direction. There was a piling between the sentry and the point, too. I moved everything, the plastic and the device, both, a mite farther out toward the end of the dock, to increase the angle of exposure toward shore, and to pick up some of the approach from the sea. One if by land, two if by sea. We were in big trouble if they came by sea. That would be overkill, a platoon-sized operation. I hoped he would keep it closer to one-on-one. I had delivered a one-on-one challenge. I worked everything farther out toward the end of the dock. My right arm holding the dock ached. The plastic would hold the sentry where I had it. I was done.

I scrambled up on the dock and sat there for a moment, resting my back against the piling.

They were swimming again, Hugo kicking hard as they swam, making some progress, splashing. Sarah rolled onto her side and looked at me. "Well?"

I grunted, "Coming." I started to rise. I was suddenly motionless.

She frowned. Hugo stopped swimming. I was looking about. "What is it?" she asked.

Hugo said nothing.

"I don't know."

"What do you think? A man?" she said.

"A man would have tripped the sensors." I gestured at the cottage. "I turned it on. It's the light over the porch door."

"The yellow bug light?"

"Yes," I said. "That's the outside warning. Shh."

"Sorry." She was trying but her voice was tense. "What's the problem?"

"Land, sea or air?" I said.

"Can't you say it in English?" she said.

"If they come by land, we should be okay. Unless they come in force."

"Force?" she said.

"Truckloads, boatloads, helicopters, parachutes."

"And in that event?"

I sat there with my back against the piling.

Hugo was dog-paddling.

Eventually, she said, "You don't want to come in? Swim?"

"Separation anxiety," I said.

"I don't understand."

"My weapons are up in the cottage."

"Oh. Well, then, of course you must go to your weapons."

I scrambled to my feet and went up the dock to the cottage. Behind me, I could feel them watching.

I came out of the cottage carrying a large metal lockbox. I paused, sniffing the air. There was nothing.

I put the box on the porch table. One by one, I took the weapons out and lay them down, side by side. I commenced cleaning them. It would take most of the afternoon. They were in perfect condition as Brooke had arranged, in individual heavy plastic envelopes. I would field-strip, clean and oil them anyhow.

Sarah stood there, drying herself with a towel. Hugo came up the path behind her, limping. She paused with the towel. "You're not making too much sense," she said.

"No?"

"There's this guy you left in Damascus and you're sitting here waiting for him to show up as if you made a date for cocktails. Do you really expect him to find you here?"

I continued cleaning the weapons one by one. "Sooner or later. No problem."

"Will you teach me guns?" she asked.

"Didn't the Mossad?" I said, stalling.

"I asked," she said. "They said no."

"No training in weapons?"

"None at all."

"All right," I said. "I'll teach you handguns."

I finished wiping the gun oil from the four-inch Smith & Wesson .38, thumbed the release, shook the cylinder open and put the open weapon into her hand.

She looked at it. "Thank you."

"Hugo?"

"Papa?"

I took the huge Colt .357 magnum, thumbed the release, shook the cylinder open and put the open weapon in his hand.

"Énorme, Papa."

"The first thing you do when someone hands you a gun is open it. Make sure it's empty. Look down the barrel and the cylinder holes. Go ahead. Is it clear? See daylight?" They did. I showed them how to close a gun, how to hold it. "Point it at the ground and squeeze the trigger, slow, so you don't know when it'll fire. It's empty. It'll click."

They squeezed slowly. Their pins clicked.

"Very good. That was single action. The pull on the trigger moved the hammer back until it released and then you got the click. Okay? There's also double action. Reach up with your thumb and pull the hammer back till it locks." They did. "Okay. It'll fire easier now, so just squeeze smoothly so you don't know when it's going to shoot—"

Click! She was startled.

"Hugo?"

Click! I corrected his grip. Two hands. He squeezed his trigger again. Click!

"See that rag, the red piece of flannel?" I pointed to a rag down by the dock. "Point your thumb. That's your target. Keep both of your eyes open. Is your finger on the trigger?"

"Yes," Sarah said.

"Take it off. Keep your finger outside the trigger guard. That's the best possible safety. No finger on the trigger. Okay? Now aim. See the notch in the rear, line up the little sight in front and line them up with the target. Okay? Now put your finger on the trigger. Now the gun wants to shoot. Squeeze, don't pull the trigger, so you can't tell when it's going to shoot. Hold it on the target, so after you fire, you're still lined up, notch, front sight, target—"

Click!

"It moved down," she said. "After it clicked."

"Hugo?"

"*À droit. Un petit peu à droit.*"

"Try again. Hold on target," I said. "Dry-fire. Without the bullet. Hammer back with your thumb. Hold on target. Take a breath. Let half of it out. Hold on target. Now, slowly squeeze."

Hugo was calm, focused. He smoothly dry-fired. Sarah was unsure of herself. Very serious, biting her lip, she cocked the hammer, took a deep breath, let half of it out, aimed, squeezed and it clicked! She was pleased. "Now what?"

"Take your finger off the trigger," I warned her.

"Sorry," She took her finger off the trigger. "Fine. What now?"

"We try it with bullets," I said. "You first." I took her gun and loaded it. I handed it back to her, being careful to keep it pointed away from us, at the dock. Hugo watched us.

She said, slowly doing it, "Just cock it with my thumb, finger on, aim, breathe in, let half out, slowly squeeze? That's all there is?"

"Hold it a minute," I said. "Take your finger off the trigger." She did. "You should have earplugs and we don't. The noise will startle you and it will kick, jerk, up and to the right. Don't compensate. Just hold on target. Okay?"

She put her trigger finger on the trigger, aimed, took the breath, let half of it out, tensed.

I said, "Relax if you can. Squeeze it—"

She fired. The noise was deafening. The kick nearly tore her arm off. The rag was untouched. I grinned. I couldn't help it. Her jaw was set. Hugo watched us.

"Finger off the trigger, please?" I said. "As you squeezed, you moved the sight to the right and down. Squeeze slowly, try not to do it. You missed the rag by two inches. Which isn't bad. Hugo, did you get this?"

He nodded, looking at her.

I said, "The next shot is the worst. You'll flinch. Everyone does. It's the noise. You can't help it. So relax, enjoy it—" She was aiming again. I went on, "Hold it steady, squeeze it and don't mind if you miss—"

She fired. The noise was deafening, the kick huge.

The rag was untouched.

She was angry. She turned toward me, dangling the gun, her finger on the trigger. Her eyes flashed. I did not like the look. She was teasing, but with a gun you don't take chances. Hugo was watching us. She said, "Relax. Enjoy it. Try not to flinch."

"Don't joke," I said, "and don't point that gun at me. Or at anyone, unless you're prepared to shoot. A gun is a gun. It wants to be shot. Anytime you point a gun, you shoot. Don't hesitate, don't talk and never let anyone talk to you. Shoot. Shoot and keep shooting. A person who talks or lets someone else talk isn't sure of what he wants to do. Maybe you can distract him, while he's figuring out what to do, I like you with that foolish look on your face." I took the gun from her hand.

She glared at me. She walked into the cottage.

It was a lesson.

Hugo was frowning. I took his magnum and loaded it. The first heat bugs of the day chirped. I handed him the gun. "Okay?"

Hugo did not like it.

Hugo hit the rag six times out of six. He was terrific. The cannon he was holding kicked all over the place.

Hugo held target and ignored it.

It was booby-trapping time.

We planted the first two heavy steel snares. We put one in the approach in the woods near the house and the other in the copse up on the overlooking slope. We camouflaged them with care and took a long time doing it. When we were satisfied, I went back for the other two snares and left him there.

It was our first concession to the leg. It was hard on him walking in the woods. The poor kid was tired.

Sarah was nowhere in sight. I had told her to stay by the cottage and not to cross the tree line. She could get lost. They could pick her off. I wouldn't know what had happened.

Anyone you couldn't trust was enemy.

I ran back inside. I grabbed the Taurus 9 mm, slipped the clip in, took the other two clips I had loaded and ran outside again. I waved to Hugo, pointed to him, then down. Hugo dropped to the ground. I ran for the woods.

It was damp underfoot. I worked my way quietly forward up toward the high ground, where it would be drier. A wanderer might go there. Twice I saw track, crushed moss, needles disturbed. Someone had been there. I approached the top of the bluff with the greatest of care. She had been there all right. I knew. I would find her. I would have to—

I did.

She was in the tiny clearing at the top of the bluff, enjoying the view of the sea and the tiny islands in the distance. Lying on her side, languorous, she was rubbing pine needles with her thumb and fingers and smelling the resin. I watched. She sensed me. "Hi."

"Hi." I crouched down beside her. "Would you please tell me what you're doing here?"

"Pretty. Isn't it?" She looked out over the water.

"What you see is."

"I'm happy."

"You won't be if they get you. You wander off alone like this, they can pick you off and I won't even know it."

It did not reach her. Her smile was mischief. "You're so serious," she said.

"You're right, I am, and it is. Can't you feel it?"

She said, "No, I can't feel it. Frankly, I doubt they'll find us. If I kissed you now, would you like it?"

"A lot. But later would be better. The kid is waiting and he's worried."

She scrambled to her feet. "I forgot!"

"Don't worry about it."

Hugo nearly wept, he was so relieved to see her.

It became uncomfortably hot by mid-afternoon. Sarah went back to the cottage. Hugo and I went into the woods again. We spent a long time together debating the right places for the other two booby-traps, and it was dark before we decided, so we left the traps there, unplanted, and rejoined Sarah in the cottage. She had cooked. We had an early dinner. It was my night for the dishes. Hugo and Sarah played video chess.

Afterward, Hugo and I went out to the point. It was a bright night, cloudless. There were reflections from the water. Hugo practiced sighting with the H&K infrared scope. He fired twenty-five rounds at one hundred yards. It took the greater part of an hour. I watched through the night glasses. Six shots of the twenty-five hit a two-foot by three-foot target.

"Not good, Papa."

"Not good enough."

"It is very different in the night."

"Every night we will have the practice."

"Yes, Papa."
"We will try it in the daytime next."

Lights out, bedtime, Sarah and I kept our promise.

Chapter 68

GUNTHER SAID FAREWELL to Ileana in the manner in which one does that sort of thing. They did it thoroughly and took their own sweet time, enjoying what they were doing.

She had met him at four o'clock in the afternoon in the apartments in Athens. They had dinner and she spent the night. They did everything he could remember them ever doing before. He had even brought down from Zurich his grandfather's rare *Secret Garden* edition, and they did that again. He had faked coming every single time. About two o'clock in the morning, Gunther, feeling satisfied, had remarked that it felt like a review session.

Ileana laughed. "Tell me honestly, do you miss her?"

"Inge? When I'm here with you?"

"Yes. Do you? Tell the truth."

"Well, she does add something," Gunther said. Ileana guffawed. It was one of the funniest things she had ever heard in her entire life. She shook with laughter until Gunther laughed, too.

"You love her, don't you?" she said, and kissed him fiercely. "You do. And she loves you, to the extent she can. She is my fairwell present to you." Gunther's face worked. "Dear Gunther, you're surprised I knew. I know you. I can tell what's happening. She told you to get rid of me, didn't she?"

"Yes."

"*Wunderbar*," Ileana said. "Then I want it to be. I leave you a perfect situation."

Actually, Gunther's "yes" was incomplete. Inge had embellished her first instruction. "Throw her back into the pit," she had said. "Send her into action."

"I don't want to see her hurt," Gunther had foolishly said.

Inge had withdrawn into herself for three full days. Gunther had waited patiently at first, and then with mounting anxiety, but they had had their extraordinarily physical reconciliation. After which, Inge had insisted on knowing, "Do you need her now?"

And Gunther had said, "How could I need her or anyone? I am beyond exhaustion." Inge had then said such an extraordinary thing: "Go kiss her good-bye for me, too. And think of me while you are doing it. I'll be jealous of each of you. I am a very passionate woman."

Gunther told Ileana what Inge said when the awoke in the morning.

"Kiss me for her?"

"That's what she said."

"But not what she meant." Ileana grinned and said, "The things she likes are better three in the bed. I want one for the two of us. It is our farewell session." She drew Gunther after her into the bathroom. "Do you always take a cold shower first thing every morning?"

Gunther acknowledged that he did.

Ileana giggled. "Then I will fix it so that you will think of me in your cold shower every morning."

She soaped him and rinsed him. She wrapped herself around him and kissed him and moved against him till the first stirrings. She knelt and took him in her mouth. Her hands stroked him. He became fully erect. Still partially asleep, he heard himself murmuring, and found himself moving rhythmically into her mouth. Her hands kneaded his buttocks. He groaned and felt the violence build. He was hard, he was strong, he kept thrusting. Harder and harder, thrusting. Her left hand cupped his scrotum. Each time he withdrew his penis from her mouth, her left hand grasped him, stroking, prolonging the erectile stimulation. All the way in, all the way out, she was there for him, on him, exciting him, maddening him. Her right hand on his buttocks kneaded him, goaded him, forced him toward her, hard. He was close. She put two fingers of her right hand into his anus and worked them up toward his prostate. Her left hand cupped, stroked, harder, harder, taking him up, her fingers in him probed, hurting. He went wild, bucking, thrusting and came. And came and came. It was close to pain. It was the wildest ejaculation he had ever had. He staggered against the wall. She stayed with him. Would it never end? She eased, let him down. Little quivers. He felt like collapsing. He closed his eyes. She slithered up the length of him, hugging him, holding him, supporting him. The cold water was numbing.

They had breakfast outdoors on the terrace with the view. It was early summer and very hot, even this early in the morning. Ileana made and brought Gunther the espresso he loved.

He drank it slowly and looked at her. She was so young, such a child and so delicate. He felt a strange surge of affection and sudden tears rising. Ileana put her hand over his. "Oh, Gunther."

Gunther shook his head and tried to speak.

She said, "Dear Gunther, you needn't feel badly for me. For me it was a good thing. In a way it isn't ending. I love you now and I always will. You have always been so good to me."

"Because I gave you money?" Gunther croaked. He coughed to clear his throat and said, "I have shifted Roman's funds to your account and I have made a new deposit on my own. Another one million Deutschemarks." She gasped her thanks. "Not for anything specific you have done, but it's what I felt like doing. If Diego asks, tell him nothing. Does he ever ask if I give you things?"

"No," Ileana said. "He does not believe in asking."

Gunther heard himself say, "You need not do this mission."

She sat there for a moment. He blushed. She smiled. "Oh, Gunther. You're worried about my safety."

He made a face, demurring.

"I have to do what I am good at doing," she said.

He said, "Your choice."

She smiled. "It is not the money. That's not what I meant. When I said that you have been good to me. You have given me much more than that. You have permitted me to share your life for a while."

"My life and my wife." Gunther tried to smile.

"And that, too, has been something. Dear Gunther."

"I like it when you call me 'dear.' It is something I would never have permitted when we met."

"Thank you for saying that. And I will always be there for you."

"That's what I meant. I will remember you."

"That's not what I meant," Ileana said. "Some day when things are not going well, you will want to call me. And you can."

He swallowed. He said, "I doubt that I will."

"You never know what will happen."

"I suppose. And thank you for offering."

Ileana sat in his lap and kissed him. He held her for while, kissing her.

She insisted he remain on the terrace. "You love the coffee and the view. You will hear the car down below, but don't peek." Gunther remained on the terrace with the coffee and the view.

Ileana dressed, packed and left the house. He did hear the limousine down below. It had a loose tappet which needed repairing. Gunther stood and looked over the parapet. The chauffeur was helping her into the car. As she got in, she looked up and saw him and smiled.

Gunther waved to her.

Chapter 69

THE NEXT DAY WAS EVEN HOTTER.

The heat beat down fiercely through the trees. The needles and leaves underfoot were warm. The humidity was rising. Hugo and I went up the slope after breakfast. We rigged the third of the four steel snares. We took our time with the branch-and-layered-moss-and-leaf shield, tinkering, pushing, smoothing, rearranging. Finally, it was done. We moved down the slope to the fourth snare. We hunkered down and went to work on it.

Sarah appeared. "Hi," she said. "Unfinished business. I never apologized for the gun thing. I am sorry. And embarrassed."

"All right," I said. "We accept the apology. Let it go. These things happen."

Hugo had rifle practice. He did well. He hit the paper twenty-three times out of twenty-five. "Day is easier," he said.

"No. You are rested. You are also getting better."

"Papa? Should we not do the holes in the ground?"

"The foxholes?" I said.

"The Hugo holes."

"It's too hot."

"No, Papa. Let's do it."

We dug the Hugo holes and the slit trench off the first one. It took hours. We broke twice to swim. Sarah met us on the dock with a picnic.

At half past three, I sent Hugo up for a shower and a nap. He was wiped out, exhausted. He protested, nevertheless. I insisted.

The summer sunset was sudden. One moment it was still light, the east in shadow and the west gold, the red ball above the horizon. The darkness was overpowering. The sea was glass, a black diamond on which the first stars glittered.

Sarah was waiting on the porch, with two iced Tanquerays on the rocks. The kid was still asleep.

The porch creaked beneath us. There were no insects despite the heat. We finished our drinks in silence, steeping in the light change, side by side in the crude wood chairs. The sky gave us mood colors, mellow with a purple tinge, blue sadness for what might have been, red, danger expected.

"Dinner," she said. She looked up.

It was Hugo in the doorway. He rubbed his eyes.

"Now that is one tired kid," I said.

"Man," she said.

He staggered to the table with us.

He ate very little.

Have a heart, Michael. "Why don't we let it go for tonight."

"No."

"You're dead. We'll do it tomorrow."

"No."

"Be sensible, kid."

He grinned at that. "That is impossible, Papa. I am your son. *Tel père, tel fils*, and how you say, all that."

"Okay, kid. Let's do it."

He insisted on going out of the cottage through the trap in the floor and the crawl space. He insisted on crawling along the rocks and scrub at the edge of the beach, and through the sand, scrub and rock channel out onto the point, working himself by inches the entire way on his knee and elbows.

Meanwhile, I put up the paper target in the usual place. Using the fat magic marker, I drew two ovals, the top one head-sized, the larger one below for the torso. I put a vertical cross marking the sternum in the upper part of the torso. Then I joined Hugo out in the first hole.

He was yawning as he loaded the rifle. I watched. He sighted sleepily. I watched the target through the night glasses.

BLAM!

I smiled. It was a perfect bull's-eye. I said, "Way to go, Hugo."

"What is that?"

"It is an expression. It means you did well."

He grunted. BLAM!

His second shot was two inches low. His next four shots were all within an eight-inch circle. His seventh shot tore a flapping hole in the middle of the target.

I replaced the torn target with another one. I walked around behind the house to the edge of the woods. I put a target there as well.

I returned to Hugo.

"Look, kid," I said and squatted. He was wide-awake. "You'll have time for two shots. You're good enough to hit him with the first shot. If you do, you shift targets. Over there is where he'll put the backup man."

"Papa?" I could feel the question coming. "Papa, how many are coming?"

"There's no way to tell, Hugo. One, for sure. That's definite. There's a woman he likes to work with. A backup man? Maybe. Three. Any more? I don't think so." Hugo gulped. I smiled. "You'll be fine, kid."

"What if I miss with the first shot, Papa?"

"You'll shoot at the same man again."

"And if I miss again?"

"You'll make him nervous. What the hell."

Hugo laughed. It was a little hysterical.

We practiced on a count of five. Click! One. Lift the gun and tripod, two. Swing the muzzle to the right, three. Set the tripod down, four. Sight and fire again. Five. The Heckler & Koch was heavy. It was a difficult maneuver for Hugo.

He practiced over and over.

I said, "Shall we let it go till tomorrow?"

"No. Ten more pairs. Okay?"

He did well with the first target. He put seven shots in the torso, one in the head and missed the target on the other two. He hit the second target dead center twice. One shot hit the torso. When he was finished, he rolled over and said, "What do you think, Papa?"

I hugged him. "I love you, Hugo."

Hugo went to bed at midnight.

I sat on the porch with Sarah until nearly one A.M.. I was sure Hugo's mother would not approve, but my son was in danger, and the guns might help. At least, they could give him a sense of what he could do, and make him feel potent, somehow.

It was silent in the darkness. The woods were piney, soft and still. Faint dew glistened on lichen. The sea was flat, with small ripples.

Chapter 70

LATE THE NEXT DAY, there was no wind. The sea was glass, more green than blue. At sunset, Sarah went for a swim. Hugo joined her, looking grim. It had not gone well for him that morning, up in the hole with the rifle.

I stayed near the house in the lengthening shadows. I moved slowly when I moved at all. I kept thinking telephoto.

I looked at the woods. I saw nothing. I listened to the sound of Sarah swimming. I crossed to another window. I watched her swim. I crossed to another window. I looked through the curtains. There was nothing there. I started to turn away and stopped.

On the box, a red light glowed. A moment later, a second red light glowed.

I stepped away from the windows.

Sarah climbed out of the water up on the dock.

She shivered. She took her towel from the piling. She toweled off. She looked over the towel at the trees. She saw nothing. She shivered and toweled again.

I was standing inside the doorway of the cottage.

Come on, baby. Come to me. Come now, before he changes his mind. Come now, before he drops you to see what I will do. Please come to me. Please come now. I don't dare signal.

Sarah walked up the dock toward the cottage.

Inside it, I loaded the Walther P-38 for Hugo's crawl. Next I loaded the shotgun.

Sarah watched. She held the towel.

"Who?" she said.

"There are at least two," I said. "And that's as close as you've ever come to getting shot."

"Are you sure?"

"Yes."

She put the towel on the table.

I went to wake Hugo. He was sitting up on the edge of the bed. He saw the Walther in my hand. "Now?"

I handed him the gun. Hugo's eyes had widened. He slipped his belt out of two loops, put the end through the holster, then through the loops and buckled his belt. We rejoined Sarah in the big room. I went to the tape recorder on the bookshelves. I turned it on and fiddled. The woman's voice was clear. It said, *Hdoud.*

She frowned.

"What do you think?" I said.

"Syrian. It means 'quiet.' Play it again."

I played it back once more. She sat there, thinking. I switched it off.

"It isn't right," she said. "There's something about it. I don't know. Are you certain she's an Arab?"

"Why?"

"The accent is Bucharest."

"The girlfriend comes from Bucharest."

"Then it fits. It isn't foolish," she said and studied me. "What is it?"

Smile. Don't rattle the troops. I tried. "She wasn't speaking to him, I'm afraid. The lady was giving orders."

Hugo shivered. "How many of them do you think there are, Papa?"

I turned to the strongbox. I took a long, slender two-edged knife and a black scabbard. I lashed the scabbard to my right calf, under my pants leg. I turned to Hugo. "I figure four."

"*Merde alors,*" he said. "Papa, I would like to start now."

"Not yet," I said. "Eat. Have some yogurt."

"I cannot."

"Have some yogurt, Hugo."

Outside, the darkness was heavy and moist. Crickets chirped. Ugly princes in the shape of bullfrogs honked their stuff-strutting mating calls. It was evening in the summertime.

Inside, Sarah covered her head. She lit the candles and said the prayer of lights. I said the prayers for the wine and bread. Those were all we remembered. Hugo was fascinated. We took sips of the wine and broke the bread. Then we ate the dinner. Hugo could not eat. I insisted he have more yogurt. Sarah and I ate a little.

"Papa?"

"You want to go now?"

He nodded.

"Okay, kid. Do it."

He hugged me, then kissed Sarah. He opened the trap and disappeared under the floor. His hand reached up and closed the trapdoor.

I cleared the dishes by candlelight. I stayed close to the walls, away from the windows. Sarah boiled the water for the coffee. She washed and I dried the dishes. They were not going to attack for a while. Later, when they thought we had gone to sleep, they would rush the house. We finished the dishes and I opened the little carton of yogurt, ate a spoonful, then another spoonful.

"For the protein?" she said.

"It's one of the things I do. For energy. It's probably stupid."

She ate three spoonfuls. I took my muglet and circled the room. I turned a light on here and a light there. I was careful around the windows.

"What about Hugo?" she said. "Aren't you worried?"

"Don't."

"Sorry. It's hard on you."

"Yes," I said, "but all is quiet. That's what we want. No news is good news."

In the woods, Diego watched the cottage through his infrared scope, his teeth gleaming in his nervous smile. Ileana lay beside him on the ground. They had identical Russian automatic rifles.

Together, they had picked the other two. One from the West Bank, one from Beirut. Both young and both fearless, they would do as they were told. They had been ordered to move down the slope and flank the house. Both should be in position now. Diego had selected the locations. The Palestinian on the edge of the woods south of the house had the best view of the porch, the little beach, the dock, the water in the cove. The Beiruti was backup, in the woods behind the north of the house, covering the north and west approaches.

The plan was simple. Diego would join the Palestinian. Ileana would join the boy from Beirut. The Palestinian and the Beiruti would approach the house. Each would throw a stun grenade, then an explosive grenade. The decisions when, where, how and who would rush the house would then be made by Diego.

"Turn that light out beside you," I said.

She did. I switched off another light. I handed her the little Colt Cobra. She tucked it into the oilskin at her waist. I switched off the bedroom light. That left two lights in the large room. I left them alone. Sarah was puzzled.

I said, "Are you confused? That's the point. So is he."

"They."

I continued, "Lights out should mean time for bed. Right? Lights out there, lights on here in the bedroom, right? The other way around, they have to think. It's time for the swimsuit."

"Couldn't we wait?" she said.

"No, dearest, we don't wait. We keep on moving all the time. We switch out a light, do anything, they have to figure what we've done, and why, and what we'll do next. If we keep doing something all the time, they won't have time to figure it out."

She was changing into her swimsuit. She tucked the oilskin inside the waist.

"I do like your body," I said.

"You're repeating yourself."

"World without end," I said. I reached for the last light switch. "When I turn it off, you count two, laugh out loud and run out of here. Stop at the dock. Wait for me there. Awkward. In the light. Exposed. I'll come out on the porch, look at you. The moment I step out, don't wait, just go. Run out on the dock and jump in. Go. Got it?"

I picked up the shotgun with my other hand. She swallowed. "Say something. Good luck. Break a leg."

"You make your own luck in this sort of thing. Do the best you can."

"God, I hate that phrase."

"Go now, and I love you."

I turned off the light. Sarah counted two, forced a loud, strange laugh. I made a face. Then Sarah ran out of the house.

Chapter 71

SARAH RAN DOWN ONTO THE DOCK, turned and nearly skidded to a stop.

I stood inside the cottage with the shotgun in my hand. The yellow light outside the door left me in the shadows.

Sarah shouted, "Come on in! Bring Hugo!" She raced to the end of the dock and dived off it into the water.

The instant she dived, I came outside. I moved to the left, out of the yellow light, and disappeared into the porch shadows. It was a dangerous moment. I figured that Diego was on my right at the edge of the woods. It never occurred to me that he might send someone else. The man there had a clear shot at me as I came outside. If he dropped me, that would have left Hugo asleep and Sarah defenseless in the water. I gambled that he would not be ready. I had argued the point with Hugo. Now it had worked. They no longer had a clear shot at me. The man behind me in the woods could see flashes of me but he would not dare shoot at me without clearing it with Diego.

Sarah bobbed and shouted again, "Come on in!"

I shouted, "It looks too cold!"

"Wear your clothes!"

"Okay, okay."

"Come on in, Michael."

I clunked the shotgun butt down on the porch and leaned the gun, muzzle up, against the house, then ran for the water and dived in, headfirst, north of the dock, on the opposite side from Diego. I splashed and swam noisily toward her. The backup man, behind the house, never had a shot at me. The corner of the house

blocked his view. When I thought he might see me, I dived underwater and did not come up until the end of the dock. Out there,
I was a dot on the sea.

I turned and hollered, "Hugo!"

Diego watched through the infrared scope.

He was pleased. He smiled his nervous smile, gesturing at
Ileana. Time to move out. Together, they started down the slope
to the house.

Sarah called to me, "Out here! It's perfect!"

She ducked again like a porpoise, remaining near the end of the
dock. I swam toward her. She laughed and said loudly, "Where is
that kid?"

Voices carry on the water. I said, "Asleep. Shall I get him?"

She said, "Let it go."

I shouted again, "Hugo?"

Diego paused in the brush at the corner of the house.

He looked through the scope. The two tiny heads in the water
were partially obscured by the end of the dock. It was a long shot.
It was possible. He would sidle down next to the porch, pick up
the shotgun and get a better first shot from beside the dock. His
first shot would be crucial.

Diego silently moved down alongside the porch. There were
reassuring splashing noises out on the water.

Sarah laughed.

I reached for her head and playfully ducked her. She spluttered,
then came up laughing and swam for the dock.

Diego took the shotgun from the porch.

He grinned nervously and checked the load. He held it in his
left hand. He moved farther alongside the porch and sighted on
the woman and the American through the scope on the automatic
rifle.

In the water, I caught Sarah before she reached the dock. I ducked her.

Annoyed, she grabbed for me. I fought her. She struggled. We went under. We came up and Sarah spluttered, "What—"

BLAM! We heard Hugo fire. We both dived.

Silence. Black water. Bubbles.

Blam! We heard the second shot from underwater. Blam again! Another shot. We counted, one second, two seconds, three. More silence. There were no signal shots. We surfaced briefly at the end of the dock. Took deep breaths. Went down again. Separated underwater at the end of the dock.

What had happened to Hugo?

Hugo's first shot had been high. It slammed the Palestinian in the mouth. It took off most of his head.

Hugo saw it through his scope. He froze. Then lifted the gun and tripod, two. Swung the muzzle to the right, three. Set the tripod down, four. Sighted and fired again. Five. But where was the other Arab? There! BLAM! The man winced. Hugo had grazed an ear! The man was stunned! Hugo fired again! BLAM! But the man had ducked.

Hugo dropped below the edge of the hole, ejecting the clip. He dropped the rifle and backed toward the trench. He turned and squirmed into it, moving ahead as fast as he could, taking the clip with him. Behind him, someone fired an automatic weapon. Then a second burst of shots. At the end of the trench, he scrambled up, clawed his way over to the second hole and dropped into it. He pulled over him the camouflage brush as he heard the third burst of automatic weapon shots.

Pause. The world exploded. The explosion was the loudest he had ever heard, louder even than the blast that had taken his leg. It knocked him flat and semiconscious.

There was something he was supposed to do. Hugo could not remember what it was.

I heard the automatic weapon bursts. I had surfaced beside the dock. I had barely gone under again when the stun grenade went off.

The impact underwater nearly knocked me cold, as far away as I was. They had thrown it at Hugo. He was lost.

Oh, my God!

Sarah heard the automatic weapon fire while she was underwater. She was on the surface when the blast went off. The thunderclap was deafening. She froze. Then she went under again.

She realized that the man in the woods should have shot her. She had stayed up on the surface too long. He had had a clear view of where she was. Unless he were dead.

If Hugo had scored with his first shot.

What were the other shots? What had happened?

Diego saw the Heckler & Koch muzzle flash on the point. He dropped off the porch and disappeared into the rocks.

The second and third shots blasted into the woods to his left. He heard the Beiruti curse and move off into the brush.

The two in the water had disappeared. The Palestinian had not returned the fire. He must be dead. Ileana should be moving down toward the Beiruti in the brush.

No. The Beiruti was moving toward the point. Diego fired a covering automatic rifle burst. Then another. Then another. He saw the Beiruti throw the stun grenade and duck.

Diego ducked, too.

The boy from Beirut had been well trained. As soon as the stun grenade exploded, he charged. He spotted the first hole immediately and emptied a full clip into it. He reloaded, fired a second burst and dropped into the hole, through the camouflage cover.

He saw the rifle with the clip missing, and the trench, and fired another burst into the trench. He reloaded again. He charted up the trench firing burst after burst as he rounded each corner.

He came to the blind end. Cursing, he climbed out of the trench. The quarry had gone farther out on the point. The Beiruti moved forward. He was careful.

Hugo lay there in a stupor. He heard the clip being fired into his first hole. He knew what was happening. A reload. Then the second burst. Hugo pictured the man dropping into the hole. He must have found the rifle. Would he notice the clip was missing?

Hugo giggled. He held the clip in his hand. The man must have spotted the trench by now. There! Another burst of shots. The man would crawl up the trench, firing more shots. Hugo listened. There were four more bursts. Hugo smiled. The man would have found the blind end now.

He heard the curse. Now the man would come for him.

Hugo lay there. There was something else. But what? He could not remember what it was.

He giggled, shell-shocked, waiting.

I was trapped. I hugged the dock. Diego was on the shore, huddled in the rocks. There was someone coming down toward him through the woods. Out on the point, to my right, I heard the shots.

They were cleanup shots.

Behind me, in the direction of the south cove, I heard nothing. Sarah would be close to it now. Should I join her if I could?

I should, could, would.

Out on the point, there were more cleanup shots.

The boy from Beirut darted forward. A short zig, and his foot caught. He pitched forward into a camouflage cover, whipping his rifle down and into play.

BLAM! A single shot.

Hugo knew the man was close.

There was something he was supposed to do. If only he could remember—what? Numbers: 3, 5, 7. That was it. The odd numbers in the middle. But what did they mean, 3-5-7? The magnum! Hugo snatched at the plastic bag, took the .357 magnum in both hands, raised it, heard the footstep, saw the foot and fired, BLAM!

The camouflage cover of the foxhole collapsed onto him, a heavy weight. Blood. He had shot this one in the mouth, too! He giggled. He never even heard them speak.

Hugo lifted the .357 magnum over his head and fired two more shots.

It was Hugo! He had done it! I knew the gun! The .357, it had to be him! Two dead! Dammo! Two sweet kills!

I hugged against the dock and watched.

Rounding the promontory at the north end of the south cove, Sarah found herself tearful. She had recognized the shots. Hugo was alive! Thank God!

And now it was up to Michael.

Diego watched.

Out on the point, there was nothing. The Beiruti must be dead, too. Ileana was approaching, behind him, from up above. The sea was quiet. Could the targets have swum to the point? No. They could not have made it underwater that far and there had not been a single surface ripple. They must have gone the other way. South. To the next cove.

Diego lurched to his feet and rushed off.

I saw him go. Sarah's problem was my luck.

Hold still. There was another one up there in the woods behind the house. Would he wait and cover the dock and the point? Or would he act as Diego's backup man, and circle south, on the slope up above him?

Time to move. I would swim underwater.

Chapter 72

DIEGO CUT THROUGH THE WOODS to the south cove. He moved out toward the promontory, keeping low, hugging the base of the cliff. There! Out on the water, one head bobbed, went under. Black water, then another small splash. The water stilled. There was silence.

Then more splashes.

Diego edged back into the darkness. He looked over the flat, unbroken surface of the water beyond. There was no sign of the other one. One at a time, then. The head was moving past him toward the tiny beach in the center of the cove. Diego circled to his right in the brush.

The swimmer sputtered into shallow water, found footing and lurched forward. The black water was disturbed only by the stumbling swimmer rising up. With a gun in each hand, Diego came forward. The woman waded toward the shore. She stumbled, dropped to a knee, stood up weakly, froze.

Diego smiled. " *'Allo, bébé.*"

She looked at him, swayed.

He gestured with the automatic rifle at the water. "Where is he?" The woman coughed. "He disappeared. He got shot." She moved forward, coughing water.

Diego had not budged.

I moved silently through the shadows in the woods. Sea water dripped from my jeans. I clutched the Taurus with both hands.

Sarah backed up.

Diego had the shotgun in one hand, the automatic rifle in the other. Lazily, he lifted the shotgun muzzle. Sarah fumbled for the little Colt Cobra in the oilskin at her waist. Diego laughed.

I charged him, crashing through the brush.

He wheeled toward me and fired. The shot chewed into the bushes on my left. I fired the Taurus twice. Simultaneously, Sarah fired six times, emptying the Colt Cobra at him. One shot—we could not tell whose—creased his shoulder. It spun him around. He scrambled for cover. I fired twice more, missing. It was too far. He made it to the bushes. The shotgun was useless at that range. He flung it into the water.

It splashed. Sarah ducked.

I could not see him. I had no shot.

Diego had the rifle on semi. He fired twice at me, again near misses.

I fired again. Blind. But closer. He retreated up into the woods.

I fired again, near where I thought he was. I scooted uphill into the woods after him, reloading.

The other one was out there somewhere.

Sarah submerged in the water.

Ileana lost the man again. Her scope panned the water, waiting for the woman to reemerge. She hesitated. The man was the danger. If she fired, she would have to kill him or the man would know where she was.

There was the woman! Panicky, the woman churned below the surface of the water.

Ileana shrank backward into the trees. Her infrared scope scanned for the man—and picked up Diego instead. Ileana swung her scope further to the right. She caught another glimpse—of the man, she thought—but again lost him in the darkness.

Diego charged past her, below her, through the brush. He did not see her. She could not call to him. Her scope panned the brush, back, forth. She shriveled deeper into the shadows. Diego had stopped but she could hear him breathing. She wondered if the man could hear Diego. She sensed something and swung her scope to the right, panning over the shadows. She panned left, past where Diego was, farther—yes! She fired!

But the man was not there. He was behind her. He fired at her, once, twice, three times, pinning her down.

Diego fired bursts from his automatic rifle blindly in the direction of the shots. He whirled and zigzagged up the slope.

I was motionless. I waited.

She retreated. I now knew where she was. Silently, I moved toward her. I forced my eyes open wide, scanning slowly from left to right and back, sensing differences in the quality of the darkness—and there she was. Perfect. I even knew the place. Now if only—I edged forward.

There was a faint sound.

I waited.

She moved sideways, one step, another—her leg tripped the snare! It whipped her leg up into the air! She screamed and lost the grip on her rifle. She thrashed in the air, frantic, upside down. Helpless.

I picked up her rifle.

She thrashed some more. Her mouth opened, she started to scream. I crashed the rifle stock into her head. She flopped unconscious.

I took the two-edged knife from my leg scabbard, cut wire from the snare and tightly bound her wrists. I slashed cloth from her pants leg and gagged her with the cloth and wire. Bound, gagged, unconscious, dangling upside down by one leg in the snare, yes, I could leave her there.

I put the knife back in the scabbard. I ejected my Taurus clip, reloaded it and slipped it back into the Taurus. I worked the slide, bringing a cartridge into the chamber. I ejected the clip, loaded one more cartridge and smacked it in again. I moved off into the dark.

Chapter 73

DIEGO MOVED BACKWARD AND SIDEWAYS, crablike, up the slope. He was higher, and the man was coming to him. The high ground was an advantage.

Near the top, Diego slowed and looked around in the darkness. One shot, that was all it would take. One good shot. It was familiar ground. He had been here before. The small copse. Diego smiled tightly. His backpack was there, where he had left it, with more ammunition, his pistol and his hatchet. He took them out of the backpack in the darkness.

He lay on his belly and looked down the hill through the scope.

He saw nothing. But he would wait. He knew the man was coming after him. He checked the woods without the scope. He found that, without it, he could see quite well.

He looked down at the cove. It was dark. The water was black. There was no sign of the woman—*hola!* There was something at the edge of the water. He looked down at it through the scope.

Collins would charge, of course, if he shot her.

And there she was. Crouched in the brush.

He braced the rifle on the rock, sighted, the crosshairs on her chest. The crosshairs jiggled. *Mierda.* He was tired. He switched the rifle to semi and sighted again, slowly squeezing the trigger— sensed something behind him, fired, rolled and slashed up with the rifle butt.

The butt struck my hand holding the Taurus. I dropped on him. I reached for this throat. He dropped the rifle. He grasped for the hatchet. We rolled over. He swung the hatchet. The edge slashed my back. I pounded his head against the rock. He swung the hatchet. I pounded his head against the rock, again, over and over. His mouth went slack. His eyes rolled.

He was unconscious.

My hand was numb, still holding the Taurus.

I dragged him by the feet through the brush. I found the snare. I shoved his foot through the wire. It triggered, whipping him upside down and up. I took the free wire and cut a loop.

I left Diego trussed with wire, gagged, upside down, out cold and dangling by his leg in the darkness.

"Hugo?"

"*Ici*, Papa." The voice was the faint voice of a child. Far away. Shaky. Muffled.

"It's me and Sarah. We are both okay. Are you all right?"

We heard a choked noise. "*Ici*, Papa."

We rushed the second hole. On top of the collapsed camouflage was the nearly headless corpse. Sarah screamed, "Oh, my God!"

I hauled it away.

Hugo was drenched with blood. I dropped on him. "*Bonne soi-rée*, Papa?"

"Are you all right, kid?"

"I am fine. It is all his blood. Papa, you are getting it on you. Papa? What's the matter, Papa?"

"It's all right, kid." I held him.

In the middle of the night, I stirred.
Sarah stood by the window.
"Hmm?" I said.
"Shh." She was listening. Her face showed strain. The dock was silent. The sea was flat. Wind sighed gently in the trees. There were noises up the hill in the brush.

The control box pinged softly. Red lights glowed. Sarah whirled and looked at me wide-eyes. "I thought—"

"Shh," I said. "Don't worry. I know what it is."

"Michael, they could have gotten loose—"

"It's the bureaucracy cleaning up," I said. I reached for her in the dark. "Come back to bed."

She did and I held her close. In a while the pings ceased, the lights glowed green and we slept—while the Mossad cut Diego and the woman down and took them off.

Chapter 74

WE TOOK A HOUSE in Montauk. It was in the dunes and isolated. I had it thoroughly cleaned by a service twice, and then I had it painted. White.

Sarah and Arnold were going well. They kept having meetings with the lawyers and the surrogate. She kept insisting she wanted nothing; Arnold kept insisting on being generous. The lawyers and the surrogate kept insisting on redoing the papers.

Also, she had obtained a Ford Foundation grant. She did it in part to have something to do, in part to prove she needed nothing from Arnold and in part to keep her in one place for two years. The foundation was more than supportive; they kept increasing the scope of the project. She had proposed a standardized course for teaching the ten most commonly spoken languages of the world to children in grammar schools. She had expected them to cut it back to four languages. Instead, they decided to try the program in full. They were going to put it into two schools in the second year and they asked her to supervise it.

Hugo came to stay with us for six weeks, starting on the first of August. Surprisingly, the long stay was encouraged by his mother and the Marquis.

"He is impossible. He was turned into you," she wailed.

"In what way?"

"He does exactly what he wants," she said, "and whenever we tell him something else, he just sits there and smiles at us."

"He is an adolescent boy."

"It is terrifying with the girls. It's the article in the papers. Hasn't he sent it to you?" she said.

"No," I said. "In fact, he hasn't mentioned it. You said you were going to take care of that. You told me that the Marquis could. Remember? When you got the calls from the reporters?"

"He did," she said. "*Le Monde* never published a single word. *Paris Soir* killed it."

"But?"

"*Le Canard Enchaînée*. That rag!"

"Hugo never said a word. Could you send it to me, please?"

"*Mais oui.* They got it from your Israeli friends. 'Unnamed sources in Israeli intelligence who were involved in the Spetsai cleanup.' What does that mean, 'cleanup'? Picking up the bodies? My husband said it was deliberate. The Mossad wanted the story. A French boy who is a hero. A cowboy who is Jewish."

I was relieved. "Then it is not hostile? Not pro-Arab?"

"*Mais, non.* On the contrary. Even I was moved. Of course, I could not recognize my son. And then the telephone calls started. Girls he does not know, has not met. You cannot believe how aggressive they are!"

"I remember you," I said.

"I was older!"

"Not much. Anyhow, I am sure he can handle it."

"The ones at school are the worst," she said. "They make up

stories about him. And then the parents call. The Marquis and I have discussed it."

"And?" I did not dare hope.

"It would be good to get him out of Paris for a while."

"How about a month?" I said.

"How about more, six weeks? So long as he is back by the start of his school. He can come on the first of August."

The first week was bliss. We talked a lot. There was no sign of the trauma we had feared. Killing two men and lying there covered with blood had apparently been a rite of passage. He never mentioned the article.

Sarah and he played computer chess. I taught him to drive my Lexus. It was illegal at his age, but what the hell. I drove a car at age fourteen. I wanted the pleasure of teaching him myself. I think the French drive like shit, and I did not want him to learn in Paris.

On the first day of the second week, we took him to Gosman's, to teach him to eat lobster properly. Genevieve was our waitress.

I have always hated the name, Genevieve. It is a perfectly proper name for a car. For a woman, it is ridiculous. Introducing her takes five minutes. No one is sure how many syllables it has, let alone how to pronounce it.

This one, unfortunately, was pretty and had verve. She was a student at Choate-Rosemary Hall in Connecticut. She was living on the island with three other girls and supporting herself as a waitress. Fully supporting herself, she told us firmly.

Hugo was impressed.

The three girls had a house, she said.

Did they have a telephone number, Hugo asked, and I dropped my fork. Sarah put her hand on my arm. Hugo gave the girl a pen and a piece of paper.

Sarah laughed at me.

"He's only fourteen!" I said.

"You are prurient."

"You know what?" I said. "His mother was right. I am going to send him back to Paris."

"Yes," she said. "And what about the Lexus."

"Oh, my God."

"You taught him to drive," she said.

"He has no license," I said. "He won't dare ask."

He did ask.

Genevieve worked, fortunately, six lunches and six dinners. Otherwise, I might not have seen him at all. I even had trouble with the ground rules.

"One," I said. "If you are ever stopped, ever, by anyone, or if there is ever an accident of any kind, whether or not it is your fault, you are grounded. Get it? Permanently."

"*Oui*, Papa."

"And two," I could not remember number two.

"*Oui*, Papa?"

"I want you home for breakfast."

"Oh."

"What's the matter? Don't you think that's fair?"

"Papa, breakfast is the only meal she and I can take together."

Labor Day weekend, Mr. and Mrs. Brooke docked their "overnighter" in Sag Harbor. They rang us up. We met at Hobson's for dinner.

Everyone was impressed with everyone else. Mrs. Brooke was positively shy with both Hugo and Sarah. They could not have been more gracious. "I like it here," said Mrs. Brooke.

"Our kind of place," said Brooke.

"You haven't tasted the food, dear."

"No matter, the martini is excellent," he said.

"And you do like the prices."

"My treat," I said.

"Nottattall," Brooke said. "We phoned you."

"No one picks up checks on him," Mrs. Brooke said. "He's an old man and crotchety and easily insulted."

"Thank you, sir," Hugo said. And that was that. I said thanks and so did Sarah.

"And besides," said Brooke, "this is both a thank-you and a celebratory dinner. How's it going with Ford?"

"My grant?" said Sarah. "You've heard?"

"We are on their mailing list," said Mrs. Brooke. "And I do love the concept. How many languages do you speak, young man?"

"Only French, ma'am," Hugo said.

Sarah said, "He speaks English obviously, and he is one of my guinea pigs in Russian, Japanese, German and Spanish."

"Modest," said Brooke. "I like that. Have you ever shot trap or skeet, son?"

"No, sir."

"I understand you're an excellent shot."

My boy was being tested. I started to intervene. Sarah put her hand on mine.

"One does what one has to," Hugo said.

They both loved it.

"Would you like to come visit?" said Mrs. Brook. "We have a small boat in Marblehead. We could teach you to sail."

Hugo said, "Thank you, Ma'am. I would like that."

Over the pecan pie with vanilla ice cream, Brooke said, "I don't think I've actually said it, but thanks."

"Thank you, sir."

"Have you heard?" said Brooke. "The man died. Gunther Waffen. The banker. On the road outside Hamburg. Went over a cliff. Burned to a crisp. With his driver. Man worked for him for many years. You met him. Once. In East Berlin."

"Ah," I said. "The ex-Stasi man."

"Werner something."

I said, "How odd."

"That's what Beano said," said Mrs. Brooke.

"We've put together this enormous file on what the Mossad has sent along that they got from their two prisoners. You can't believe some of the stuff! Shima gave it to the German government. Austria. France."

I said, "How long after that did the man die?"

"Three days."

Mrs. Brooke said, "The bodies were burned beyond recognition from the crash, and after the service they were cremated."

"A clever, dangerous man," said Brooke. "The central banks took charge of the whole thing. His banks, whatever stock they could find, his interests in the currency brokers. You'd think the damn dollar would strengthen after that, removal of the threat and all, but it tanked."

"Did you bet that it would?" said Mrs. Brooke.

"Only a little bit," Sarah said.

Hugo said, "While I am here, Papa is staying out of the markets."

"Good idea," said Brooke. "Dangerous stuff. Gambling. Currency. All of that. Don't pretend to understand it."

"What about the camps?" I said.

"No more German funding anymore. And the proof they're for hire has hurt them, especially with the Arabs. Set them back a couple of years."

I said, "Then some good did come of it all."

"More than you think," Brooke said. "If they ever try their stunts over here, we'll look through them to whoever controls them. I hope."

"Let's hope it never happens."

In the parking lot, as we separated, Brooke said, "You should read the evaluation."

"Of what?"

"What you did. And the risk you took. And the role of the Mossad in the whole thing." Brooke grinned at me. " 'Unprofessional but stunning.' That's what they said. That's what your government thinks of you. That's what they said about me, too. 'Unprofessional but stunning.' "

Hugo asked as we were driving home, "Have the two of you agreed on a name?"

I forgot to mention it. Sarah was pregnant. Two months. Probably Spetsai, she thought. The Big Night. After. We were all certain it would be a boy. She had not yet had the amniocentesis. "No," she said.

"Oh," Hugo said.

"Whatever she wants," I said.

"How nice," said Sarah, "but it's not up to me. It's open for discussion."

"Hm," I said.

"What do you think?"

"I haven't thought about it."

"Do."

"Shima," I said.

"You are joking, of course," she said.

"Oh, Papa, that's a terrible name," Hugo said.

I said nothing.

"You mean it," she said to me. "Damn it."

"Do you hate it?" I asked. Hugo looked from me to her and back. "Sleep on it," I said. "If you still say no, we'll forget it."

"Fine."

"I admire the man," I said, "and I like him, and I figure that we owe him."

"Yes," she said.

"What does that mean?" I said.

"I'll think about it."

Chapter 75

SARAH TOOK THE SEVEN A.M. Hampton Jitney to New York. I ran her over to the bus stop in the rented Avis. I couldn't let the unlicensed kid drive a rental. He had dropped us off the night before and taken the Lexus to meet the girl after work.

The Lexus had become his. Sort of.

He was not home for breakfast.

"About the name," I said when I dropped Sarah off at the bus. "How about Sam?"

"How about it?" she said.

"I don't know, that's why I asked," I said.

She kissed me. Enigmatic.

Hugo came back after breakfast.

We had coffee on the terrace. We watched the surf off Montauk.

"Have you settled the name thing?" Hugo asked.

"I don't know. She hasn't told me," I said.

"Oh," he said and grinned.

"Don't you grin at me," I said.

"Oh," he said. "I am sorry, Papa." He laughed. "I can't help it."

"What's in a name, anyway?" I said.

"Exactly, Papa," Hugo said. "And anyway, he'll be crazy, of course, like the rest of us."

"Where do you get this crazy stuff? I'm perfectly normal, and so are you."

"*Oui*, Papa."

"You've been talking to your mother."

He grinned.

"You want to go see the whales today?"

He hesitated. Polite kid.

"You have plans?" I said.

"Genevieve is off today."

"That's all right. Bring her."

"She has made a picnic."

"Bring it on the boat," I said. "Oh. That isn't what you had in mind?"

"No, Papa." He hesitated once again. "Her cousin has a place on the North Fork. They are away through the weekend. A private beach with no one. You can see for miles if someone comes."

"Sounds beautiful. You can go swimming."

"*Oui*, Papa."

"I'd love it. Can Sarah and I come?"

"Papa?"

"I'm sorry, I'm teasing. I shouldn't, I know."

He was so relieved. "You never tease. You are very good about that. Can we see the whales tomorrow, Papa? The whole day? Right after breakfast? I promise to be home by then."

"Tomorrow's fine. Let's do it."

Hugo went into the house to shower and wash up. His showers sometimes took an hour and a half. I nursed my black coffee and watched the waves. I could watch waves forever, I told myself.

He would be going back to France in two more weeks. I would miss him terribly. More than ever. It would get worse. They grow up. You feel deserted when they go. And they all do.

Sam would be born in late March. That would help. I could play father again for another while. Meanwhile, I was listening to the grass grow. It was healthy to listen to nature, I told myself. Good for the soul, I told myself.

For the first time in my life, I was happy, I knew.

But I was restless for something. A risk to manage? Maybe that was it. Or maybe Shima had been right when he said that what I really wanted was to bet it all.

Maybe that's what I was missing.